EDGE OF
MIDNIGHT

SHANNON McKENNA

EDGE OF MIDNIGHT

BRAVA

KENSINGTON PUBLISHING CORP.

http://www.kensingtonbooks.com

BRAVA BOOKS are published by

Kensington Publishing Corp.
850 Third Avenue
New York, NY 10022

All Kensington titles, imprints and distributed lines are available at special quantity discounts for bulk purchases for sales promotions, premiums, fund-raising, educational or institutional use.

Special book excerpts or customized printings can also be created to fit specific needs. For details, write or phone the office of the Kensington Special Sales Manager: Kensington Publishing Corp., 850 Third Avenue, New York, NY 10022. Attn. Special Sales Department. Phone: 1-800-221-2647.

ISBN-13: 978-0-7582-1185-9
ISBN-10: 0-7582-1185-6

First Kensington Trade Paperback Printing: August 2007
10 9 8 7 6 5 4 3 2 1

Printed in the United States of America

EDGE OF MIDNIGHT

Prologue

*G*ordon watched his videotaped TV soap as he performed his usual calming post-job ritual of cleaning his guns, although he had not used them for today's hit. Images of blood-soaked bodies from the multiple murder-suicide he'd staged that day appeared whenever he closed his eyes. Stupid soaps worked best for soothing his jagged nerves.

Occupational stress. It was a bitch, but he was coping.

Tonight's evening news had buzzed with the shocking story of the famous Seattle cardiologist who had snapped under the strain of his job, murdered his beautiful wife and two young sons, and then ended his own life. Dreadful. Tragic. Almost jerked tears into Gordon's own eyes.

Though the bank transfer of the second half of the kill fee would dry them very fast, he reflected. All in all, it had been a satisfying day.

An actress tearfully confessed her secret pregnancy, and Gordon grabbed the remote to fast-forward through the local news piece that began to play. That was how he saw her. By pure, random chance.

A hot-cold rush of shock went through him. He had seen that perfect face only once. Magnified through the scope of a sniper rifle.

He would never forget those big, dreamy eyes. His heart thudded.

The program was a tedious feel-good piece about the revitalization project in historic downtown Endicott Falls. A perky commentator was interviewing his lost girl about her new bookstore café. Gordon picked up the phone, dialed. His fingers vibrated with excitement.

The man who answered the phone did not waste words. "Yes?"

"I found the girl," Gordon said. "From the Midnight Project fuck-up."

There was a startled pause. "You're sure it's her?" his sometime employer asked. "After fifteen years? She was just a teenager."

Gordon didn't bother to answer the insulting question. "Want to find out what she knows before I take her out?" His eyes explored the lush curves of his lost girl's body. "I'll interrogate her. No extra charge."

The other man grunted. "Forget indulging yourself. It's been years. Just end it. Get a police file started first. Some dirty letters, a dead pet, and when you finally do kill her, nobody'll be surprised."

Hah. Like he needed to be told how to do his job. Gordon hung up, rewound, and studied her face. Just look at her. Fresh as a daisy—or so she seemed. He knew the truth. She was sly. Selfish. Look what she'd done to him; disappearing on him, eluding him for fifteen years, putting a massive dent in his professional reputation. Anger rose inside him like a boil, ugly and inflamed. He reveled in its hot, burning itch. Gave himself up to it. Just look at that bad, bad girl. She'd been laughing at him, all that time. Thinking she'd made a fool of him. Thinking she'd won.

Self-satisfied bitch. She was about to discover how wrong she was.

He freeze-framed, and placed his finger against her throat on the screen. Traced the laughing curve of her scornful pink mouth, imagining its hot moisture. Electricity from the TV screen buzzed against his finger.

This was going to be fun.

Chapter
1

He had this dream so often, it gave him déjà vu. His twin, Kevin, sat on the rock behind the house, looking as he had right before he died, twenty-one, sunburned, cutoffs, flip-flops. Dirt-blond hair he'd cropped himself with kitchen shears. A dimple carved deep into his face, like there was some big secret joke that Sean eternally failed to get.

"You're supposed to be dead," Sean snarled. "Would it be asking too much for you to just cut out this shit and leave me alone? Go into the light, or wherever the fuck it is you need to go. Move on, already!"

I just want to help, Kev said mildly. *You could use some help. You're going down the drain, buddy. Swish, glug, bye-bye.*

"You can't help me!" Sean bellowed. "You are *dead!* And this bullshit is torture! It does not help me! It will *never* help me!"

Kev was unperturbed by his rudeness. *Stop being a spaz.* His ghost voice took on that irritating tone he'd always used when dealing with his more volatile twin. *You've got to do something about Liv's car. She's—*

"Forget about Liv! Stop torturing me! Leave me alone!"

Alone . . . alone . . . alone . . . The echo accompanied him into waking consciousness, where there was never any way to brace himself for it.

He had to sort it all out over again. Like it had just happened.

Yeah, it was another fucking day. Yeah, Kev was still dead. And yeah, Kev was going to keep on being dead. Forever.

It would be so much easier to accept this if his twin would quit it with the spectral visits. But try explaining that to Kev. Stubborn jerk.

Light pried between his gummy eyelids. He ventured a slit-eyed peek. Unfamilar room. A clock on the bedside table read 12:47. Data crunched in his aching brain. Reality settled down, heavy and cold.

Another failure. His annual effort to erase August the eighteenth off the calendar hadn't worked yet. Pinheaded optimist that he was, though, he just kept right on trying. The clock clicked over to 12:48. Eleven hours and twelve minutes of this goddamn day to get through.

He started to roll over, stopping as his leg encountered a silky thigh. The angle of that thigh to that ass wasn't anatomically possible.

He struggled to focus his eyes. Oh. Yeah. There was more than one pair of female legs in the bed. The stripes of light slanting through the blinds made it tough to sort out the tangle of slender limbs.

Two girls lay crosswise to each other. A blonde and a brunette. Nice butt cheeks, all four of them. Round and smooth as duck eggs. The brunette lay with her face hidden by a heavy fall of dark hair. The blonde's head was under the pillow, curly wisps poking out.

He stroked the butt cheeks closest to him and scanned the room for evidence that he had engaged in protected sex. One, two, three . . . huh, a fourth condom wrapper, on the bedside table. It would seem he had done his sacred manly duty by the sleeping cuties. That was good.

And it was starting to come back to him, in disconnected chunks. Stacey. The blonde was Stacey. The brunette was Kendra.

He extricated himself carefully from the bed. He didn't want the babes to wake up on him, no matter how round and rosy their collective butt cheeks were. He wasn't up to being sweet and charming today.

He stared at them, trying to reconstruct the impulse that had drawn him to them last night. Probably the brunette. With those kissable dimples in the small of her back, he could almost imagine she was Liv.

Not that he'd ever seen Liv's naked ass. He'd just worshipped her from afar, like the lofty virgin goddess that she was. Although he'd worshipped her pretty thoroughly with his fingers once.

His dick jumped up like a puppy whenever he thought of that warm summer night when he'd cornered her in the historical collection room, and put his hand up her skirt. He remembered her pussy, tender and snug around his fingers. The way her soft thighs squeezed his hand. The choked, helpless sounds she made when she came.

The smell of old books made him hard to this day.

That sashay down memory lane had rendered him stone hard, hangover and all. He massaged his turgid cock. Eyed the brunette's peachy ass. Half tempted to suit up with latex, close his eyes, and . . .

Christ, no. He shook away the bad idea, and froze, motionless, as a punishing bolt of pain reverberated through his head like one of those big Chinese gongs. *Ouch.* Fifteen years, and still hung up on that chick.

It would be funny, if it weren't so fucking pathetic.

Sean massaged his throbbing forehead and let the Liv tape play through his head; he'd done her a favor, dropping her before doing anything unforgivably stupid—like marrying her, the equivalent of lying down and offering to be her personal throw rug. He would have tied himself in knots trying to be a good boy, and ultimately failed. Torture, agony, humiliation, blah blah blah. He knew the drill so well, he bored himself.

But he still saw the look in her eyes when he told her to get lost. He saw it every night, at four AM and whatever girl's bed he woke in. Always with that same sucking hole in his gut as he pondered the most spectacular fuck-up of his life. The one that defined him as a person.

He eyed the brunette's tantalizing ass, and sighed. He must have screwed hundreds of girls in his effort to get that chick out of his system. Hadn't worked so far, but hey. He was nothing if not persistent.

He felt betrayed by his own body. The amount of tequila he'd drunk last night should have guaranteed a longer blackout.

Maybe he should bash himself over the head with a bigger pharmaceutical nightstick. Hard drugs weren't his scene, though. The desperation that clung to the people who dealt and used them was a big, flesh-crawling downer. He didn't even like alcohol that much. It made him fuck up in embarrassing ways. Not that waking up behind bars or in the emergency room really mortified him all that much, but it upset the hell out of his brothers. Upright, respectable family men that they now were. Pillars of the community. Legally wed to their fine and lovely lady wives. Soon to spawn big families too.

Connor and Erin were well on their way. Only four months to D-Day. A baby, whoa. Uncle Sean. So cheerful and normal. As if his brothers hadn't grown up in the same gonzo parallel universe that he had. Crazy Eamon's wild boys.

Even worse was this new family phenomenon he now faced; a pack of concerned sisters-in-law ganging up on him, trying to get him to open up and *share*. Suffering Christ, save him. They were great women, and it was sweet of them to care, but no fucking way, thank you.

His jeans were draped on a leather couch, beneath assorted lingerie. Another condom wrapper fluttered to the ground as he pulled on his jeans. He grunted, unimpressed, and rooted through his pockets.

Typical. He'd blown his emergency cab fare buying drinks for those girls, from the looks of them. So he was stranded, on foot, who the fuck knew where. Partying was such a freaking chore sometimes.

A trip to the john revealed two more condom wrappers. So he'd engaged in sink and/or shower sex. He stared at the scraps of foil as he pissed, trying to remember the aquatic adventures. He felt soiled.

Not that he had moral problems with an anonymous three-way. On the contrary. Girls were yummy. Bring 'em on. He was just lower than dirt depressed today. And it was just going to get worse from here.

The face that stared back from the bathroom mirror was both familiar and strange. The face of his dead identical twin, as Kev might have been. They hadn't looked as much alike as some twins did, but his own mug was still Sean's best point of reference. The superficial details were the same. Hard-muscled body, give or take a few scars. Wavy dirt-blond hair, which had gotten shaggy lately. A mirror image of Kev's one-sided dimple in his own lean, stubbly cheek.

The grim face that stared back at him had no dimple today. Eye sockets smudged with purplish shadows, which made his light green irises look weirdly pale. The hollows under his cheekbones looked like they'd been chopped out with a hatchet. He looked grayish in the harsh light. Zombie pale. Something to scare the kiddies into good behavior.

Looking into a mirror on August eighteenth forced him to reflect on how much his face resembled Kev's—and how much it no longer did.

He was harder, sharper, after fifteen years of hard living. Had a fan of squinty crinkles around his eyes. Grooves bracketing his mouth.

Years would go by, and the resemblance would continue to fade, until Sean was a gnarled, toothless, yammering old coot who'd lived many times the span of Kev's short life. A yawning gulf of years.

He yanked open the medicine cabinet and scanned the contents. Excedrin. He shook out four, tossed them in, crunched, gulped.

He leaned over, pressing his throbbing forehead against the cool porcelain sink, and let out a long, hissing string of vicious profanity.

This sucked ass. Utterly. Shouldn't time have healed him? Wasn't it a natural process, like continental drift? He tried so hard to dodge it, but this goddamn feeling circled him like a vulture, waiting for its chance to pick out his eyes and feed on his flesh. Sometimes he just wanted to lie down flat on his back and let that old vulture have its way.

And so it began. The sucking sound of Sean going down the drain.

He had to get the fuck out of here. Slinking away without coffee and pleasantries was rude, but better to leave before the charming sex machine of last night mutated before their eyes into a grunting zombie.

A cautious sniff at his pits practically knocked him out. A shower was too risky, though. So was coffee, he concluded with regret, gazing at the gleaming coffee technology on display in the kitchen. The bean grinder would wake up the cuties, and there he'd be, up shit creek. Forced to smile, chat, flirt, give them his phone number. God save him.

He stumbled out into a bland residential neighborhood. No money, no wallet. He never went out on the eve of August eighteenth with credit cards, or anything with his address printed on it. Just cash and condoms. Flashing lights, blasting music, sex, dancing, liquor, anything that blotted out higher cognitive function.

Fighting worked fine, too, if anybody was ass-for-brains stupid enough to get in his face. He loved a good fight.

He had no clue which direction to go, so he picked a vaguely downhill slope. Uphill would make his heart beat faster, and every *lub-dub* smacked at his brain tissues like the blow of a splitting mall.

Downhill. Down the drain, like Kev's dream scolding. The partying, the fucking, the fighting, on days like this he saw it for what it was: a cheap trick to distract him from the sinkhole under his solar plexus.

His whole life, one big goddamn flinch.

The sinkhole was getting bigger, ground shifting, threatening to pitch him in. He might never find his way back up if he fell. Dad hadn't. Neither had Kev. They'd fallen like rocks. All the way to the bottom.

Thunk. The muted thump of a car door had him spinning around and sinking down into guard before he knew he'd moved.

The tension sagged when he saw his brothers getting out of Seth Mackey's Avalanche. Seth got out. Then Miles, from the passenger side.

Sean's stomach sank. It was an ambush. He was so screwed.

The guys flicked each other glances that made him feel about six years old. *Sean's having one of his freak-outs. Quick, get the trank gun.*

The one person in the world who had known him better than Con and Davy knew him had died fifteen years ago, to the day. He'd have calculated it to the second, if he could, but time of death had been impossible to determine. Kev's body had been charred beyond recognition, after taking that swan dive into Hagen's Canyon. He'd plowed through the guardrail, fallen for a few timeless seconds, then a rending crash, a hot *whump* as the pickup exploded—and that was it.

The blunt, chopped-off finality of it still baffled him.

There had been no skid marks leading up to the ragged hole in the guardrail. He'd searched and searched. Kev hadn't tried to brake.

Sean saw Kev's falling pickup reflected in Davy and Connor's eyes too. He looked away fast. Couldn't bear it, couldn't share it. He had no comfort to offer, and he was too raw to accept any from them.

He just wanted to hide, alone. In a culvert somewhere.

It was easier to look Seth and Miles in the face than his brothers. He directed his glare there. "Who invited you guys to this freak show?"

Miles shrugged, his face worried. Seth's mouth twisted into a humorless smile. "I had a brother once. I don't need an invitation."

Ouch. True enough. Seth's younger brother had died too. Very badly, and only a couple of years ago. His loss was fresher than Sean's.

Great. Another thing to feel like shit about. Thanks, guys.

Sean's gaze slid away, leaving him with no place at all to rest it except for Seth's black Chevy. "How'd you guys find me? X-Ray Specs?"

"We monitored you this time," Con said. "From a safe distance. Bailing you out of jail for a drunk and disorderly is embarrassing."

"So don't bother, next time," Sean suggested. "Leave me to rot." He fished his cell out of his pocket. A transmitter inside sucked off the phone's battery. Usually, it gave him the warm fuzzies that his family cared enough to plant spyware on him. Aw, how cute, and all that.

Connor, Davy, and Seth had all had freaky wild adventures that had convinced them that beacons were a great idea for the whole family.

Most of the time, he agreed. Maybe if Kev had carried one on his person, Sean might have found him in time to stop him from—

No. Don't go there, he told himself. Just don't.

Impotent fury welled up inside him. He hurled the thing over a chain-link fence. It exploded against asphalt with a tinkling smash.

"That was stupid and wasteful," was Davy's dour observation.

Sean kept on walking. His brothers, Miles, and Seth kept pace behind him. Like dogs hanging onto a bone. The only way to get rid of them would be to beat them into unconsciousness, but each of the three older men was more or less a match for him. Even Miles wasn't half bad these days, with all the training he'd been putting in at the dojo. The four of them together . . . nah. Pain sucked. He'd pass.

"He was our brother too," Davy said quietly.

Sean sucked in a sharp breath. "I had no intention of inflicting my tantrum on anyone. Still don't. I love you guys, but kindly fuck off."

There was a brief pause. "Nope," Connor said simply.

"Don't bother asking again," Davy said.

There was a brief pause. "Uh, ditto," Seth added belatedly.

Sean sagged down onto a low stone wall that bordered a flower bed, and rested his hot face against his hands. "Where am I?"

"Auburn," Davy replied. "We followed you around last night."

"I'll get the truck," Seth said. "You guys keep an eye on him."

Sean grunted his disgust. Like they expected him to start twitching and frothing.

"Whose house did you just come out of?" Connor asked.

He shrugged. "Couple of girls," he mumbled. "A blonde, a brunette. Nice bodies. Met them at the Hole, I think."

"You filthy slut." Davy's voice had a superior note, which bugged the shit out of Sean.

"Don't judge me," he growled. "You've got the love of your life in your bed every night. So do Connor and Seth. So fuck you all, OK? The rest of us assholes have to get through the night somehow."

"Poor lovelorn baby," Davy said. Miles made a choked, snorting sound. Connor covered his mouth and looked away. The Avalanche pulled up. Davy and Connor seized his elbows.

Sean wrenched out of their grip and got to his feet unassisted. "May I ask what is the point of busting my balls today?"

"You may ask, if you like, but we don't need a point," Davy replied. "We bust your balls out of sheer habit. Mouthy little punk."

Hardly little. He was as tall as either of his brothers, and bulkier than Connor, but he didn't have the energy to argue. He heaved himself into the back of the Avalanche. Connor got in on one side, Miles on the other, squishing him into immobility. Seth put the vehicle in gear.

"You free to take on some work?" he asked. "You don't look busy."

Sean stifled a groan. He sometimes did freelance bodyguarding for SafeGuard, Inc., the security company that Seth and Davy had recently founded. Usually they called him when they had explosives to deal with.

Today, the idea bored him into a state approaching rigor mortis.

"What, a bodyguarding gig nobody else wants? I'm not in the mood to ego-fluff some executive asshole, or carry shopping bags for some fat cat's trophy wife. Take me off your list. Permanently."

"It's not a bodyguarding gig," Connor said. "And it's not for Safe-Guard. It's for me. I'm working on a weird case. Real flesh-creeper. The Cave called me in to consult. Thought you might be interested."

And Connor's consulting gigs for various law enforcement agencies were always fascinating, in a gruesome sort of way.

He caved almost instantly. "What's so creepy about it?"

"We've got a predator who likes math and science geeks."

"Huh." Sean blinked. "Wow. Weird."

"Yeah. Six cases in four months. College age, males and females both. They turn up dead, ostensibly an OD outside dance clubs, but nobody remembers seeing them inside. All gifted in math, computers, engineering. All with the same unexplained cerebral damage. None of them have family. Someone's picking them out real carefully."

Sean considered it. "Evidence of sexual violence?"

"In the girls there's evidence of recent sexual activity, but this prick's careful not to leave any DNA. He doesn't like to fuck the boys, evidently. I've already got Miles on it. I could use your help, too."

Sean had his private misgivings about "the Cave," the covert FBI task force that his brother used to belong to. Mostly because they'd practically gotten Connor slaughtered, on more than one occasion.

"What makes you think I could help?" he growled.

"Don't be an asshole," Con said. "You're useful, when you're not bouncing off the walls. And you could, ah, use a distraction."

"Ah," Sean said slowly. "So this is, like, a mercy fuck."

"Shut up," Connor snapped. "You're bugging me."

"It's mutual," Sean said. "Don't project your own twisted coping mechanisms onto me, Con. The Superman cape drags on the ground when I wear it. I'll find my own distractions. A hot three-way with a couple cute babes is more my speed. Shallow butterfly that I am."

"I've known you since you were born," Connor said wearily. "Don't even try." He passed a brutally scarred hand over his face, a souvenir of one of those near-death experiences. Sean got an unwelcome flash of just how bad his brother felt. He blocked it. Didn't want to know.

He shook himself. "I appreciate the thought, but I'm not hurting for money. I've got my own projects to keep me busy. Consulting for law enforcement agencies feels too much like real work to me."

"It *is* real work, you lazy slob," Connor lectured him. "You come into focus when you've got real work. That's what you should be doing, not this frivolous bullshit . . . what's your latest craze again? Consulting for goddamn fight films? Give me a fucking break."

Sean had gotten very sick of this deep-rooted disagreement long ago. "It's lucrative frivolous bullshit," he growled. "I'm busy, I'm off the streets, I'm not in trouble with the law, and I'm not hitting you guys up for money. What the fuck more do you want from me?"

"Not from you. *For* you." Davy swiveled his head, fixed his brother with a laser beam gaze. "This isn't about money. It's about you concentrating on something other than your own miserable self."

Sean flung his head back against the seat and sealed the light out with his hand. Here was the blood price he had to pay for a ride home.

Experience had taught him that to put up a fight at this point in the lecture was useless. They'd just keep at him with their meat mallets until he was quivering, bloody pulp. Not that they had far to go.

Best to keep them talking til he got a chance to cut and run.

"You're going down the drain, and we're sick of sitting around with our thumbs up our asses, watching it happen," Davy went on.

Going down the drain. Goose bumps prickled up Sean's back.

"Funny you should say that," he said. "It gives me the shivers. Kev said the exact same words to me last night."

Connor sucked in a sharp breath. "I *hate* it when you do that."

His tone jolted Sean out of his reverie. "Huh? What have I done?"

"Talked about Kev as if he were alive," Davy said heavily. "Please, please don't do that. It makes us really nervous."

There was a long, unhappy silence. Sean took a deep breath.

"Listen, guys. I know Kev is dead." He kept his voice steely calm. "I'm not hearing little voices. I don't think anybody's out to get me. I have no intentions of driving off a cliff. Everybody relax. OK?"

"So you had one of those dreams last night?" Connor demanded.

Sean winced. He'd confessed the Kev dreams to Connor some years back, and he'd regretted it bitterly. Connor had gotten freaked out, had dragged Davy into it, yada yada. Very bad scene.

But the dreams had been driving him bugfuck. Always Kev, insisting he wasn't crazy, that he hadn't really killed himself. That Liv was still in danger. And that Sean was a no-balls, dick-brained chump if he fell for this lame ass cover-up. *Study my sketchbook*, he exhorted. *The proof is right there. Open your eyes. Dumb ass.*

But they had studied that sketchbook, goddamnit. They'd picked it apart, analyzed it from every direction. They'd come up with fuck-all.

Because there was nothing to come up with. Kev had been sick, like Dad. The bad guys, the cover-up, the danger for Liv—all paranoid delusions. That was the painful conclusion that Con and Davy had finally come to. The note in Kev's sketchbook looked way too much like Dad's mad ravings during his last years. Sean didn't remember Dad's paranoia as clearly as his older brothers did, but he did remember it.

Still, it had taken him longer to accept their verdict. Maybe he never really had accepted it. His brothers worried that he was as nutso paranoid as his twin. Maybe he was. Who knew? Didn't matter.

He couldn't make the dreams stop. He couldn't make himself believe something by sheer brute force. It was impossible to swallow, that his twin had offed himself, never asking for help. At least not til he sent Liv running with the sketchbook. And by then, it had been too late.

"I have dreams about Kev, now and then," he said quietly. "It's no big deal anymore. I'm used to them. Don't worry about it."

The five of them maintained a heavy silence for the time it took to get to Sean's condo. Images rolled around behind his closed eyes; writhing bodies, flashing lights, naked girls passed out in bed. Con's predator, lurking like a troll under a bridge, eating geeks for breakfast.

And then the real kicker. The one he never got away from.

Liv staring at him, gray eyes huge with shock and hurt. Fifteen years ago today. The day that all the truly bad shit came down.

She'd come to the lock-up, rattled from her encounter with Kev. Tearful, because her folks were trying to bully her onto a plane for Boston. He'd been chilling in the drunk tank while Bart and Amelia Endicott tried to figure out how to keep him away from their daughter.

They needn't have bothered. Fate had done their work for them.

The policeman hadn't let her take Kev's sketchbook in, but she'd torn Kev's note out and stuck it in her bra. It was written in one of Dad's codes. He could read those codes as easily as he read English.

Midnight Project is trying to kill me. They saw Liv. Will kill her if they find her. Make her leave town today or she's meat. Do the hard thing. Proof on the tapes in EFPV. HC behind count birds B63.

He'd believed every goddamn word, at least the ones he'd understood. Why shouldn't he have? Christ, he'd grown up in Eamon McCloud's household. The man had believed enemies were stalking him every minute of his life. Up to the bitter end. Sean had never known a time that they weren't on alert for Dad's baddies. And besides, Kev had never led him wrong. Kev had never lied in his life. Kev was brilliant, brave, steady as a rock. Sean's anchor.

Do the hard thing. It was a catchphrase of their father's. A man did what had to be done, even if it hurt. Liv was in danger. She had to leave. If he told her this, she would resist, argue, and if she got killed, it would be his fault. For being soft. For not doing the hard thing.

So he'd done it. It was as simple as pulling the trigger of a gun.

He stuck the note in his pocket. Made his eyes go flat and cold.

"Baby? You know what? It's not going to work out between us," he said. "Just leave, OK? Go to Boston. I don't want to see you anymore."

She'd been bewildered. He'd repeated himself, stone cold. Yep, she heard him right. Nope, he didn't want her anymore. Bye.

She floundered, confused. "But—I thought you wanted—"

"To nail you? Yeah. I had three hundred bucks riding on it. I like to keep things casual, though. You're way too intense. You'll have to get some college boy to pop your cherry, 'cause it ain't me, babe."

She stared at him, slack-jawed. "Three hundred . . . ?"

"The construction crew. We had a pool going. I've been giving them a blow by blow. So to speak." He laughed, a short, ugly sound. "But things are going too fucking slow. I'm bored with it."

"B-b-bored?" she whispered.

He leaned forward, eyes boring into hers. "I. Do. Not. Love. You. Get it? I do not want a spoiled princess, cramping my style. Daddy and Mommy want to send you back East? Good. Get lost. Go."

He waited. She was frozen solid. He took a deep breath, gathered his energy, flung the words at her like a grenade. *"Fuck, Liv. Go!"*

It had worked. She'd gone. She'd left for Boston, that very night.

He'd paid the price ever since. He knew just how those surgeons felt. The poor bastards you read about in magazines, the ones who fucked up and cut out the wrong eye, or lung, or kidney. *Oops.*

Seth pulled up at the curb outside Sean's condo, pulled out his cell phone, and dangled it in front of Sean's face. "Here."

Seth waved it away. "Forget it. I don't want—"

"Take it," Seth snarled. "Or else I'll hit you with it."

Sean sighed, shoved it into his pocket.

"Short string gets to babysit this bozo til midnight." Davy held out his huge fist. Four pieces of string dangled from it.

"Aw, shit," Sean protested. "I don't need—"

"Shut up," Davy said harshly. He pulled out a string—long. Con grabbed his. Long. Seth and Miles drew.

Miles grunted in resignation. He had the short string.

"Congratulations. You got your work cut out for you," Seth said.

"This is humiliating," Sean complained.

"Tough. If you don't like it, stop doing this to us every year."

Sean shut his eyes. The weight of his eyelids made his eyeballs throb. Red bloomed like a bloodstain in his head. Black bloomed from the center and took its place. Red again. Then black. The drumbeat of his stubborn heart. And behind it, Kev's pickup. Endlessly falling.

Miles shoved open the door and slid out. Sean followed him.

"Hey. Erin had a sonogram yesterday," Connor said abruptly.

"Oh, yeah?" he inquired politely. "Everything's fine, I trust?"

"Yeah, everything's great. It's a boy," Con said.

"Ah. Uh . . . good. Congratulations." He felt like he should say something more profound, but his mind was as blank as the white sky.

"We're going to name him Kevin," Con added.

Something squeezed like a vise around his larynx, horribly tight.

Con laid his hand on Sean's shoulder. "It helps, you know?" his brother said, his voice intense. "Trying to make a difference. And if it all comes together and you get there in time to save somebody, oh, man. It's the best damn thing in the world. It makes up for so much."

"Yeah? And then? What happens after? When the thrill is gone?"

Connor hesitated. "You get out there and do it again."

Sean nodded. "Right," he muttered. "It never lasts, does it?"

"No," Connor admitted. "But then again. What does?"

Sean contemplated that. "Sounds pointless and exhausting."

His brother did not contradict him. He just turned away, his face stony. Sean let the door swing shut. The Chevy sped away.

Chapter 2

Sean and Miles stared at each other. Miles's mouth was settled into a flat, stubborn line. "Don't even start," he said. "It's useless."

Sean groaned inwardly. Not that he didn't love the guy to pieces. Miles was a great kid. A good friend. Crazy useful when it came to the gearhead techie computer details that bored Sean out of his skull. In the last couple years since he'd taken on the role of McCloud mascot, he'd proved his worth many times over. But Sean wasn't up to being anybody's mentor, love counselor, cheerleader, or fashion guru today.

"Buddy? You know I love you, right? But I don't want company," he said wearily. "So get lost. Disappear. See ya."

"Nope." Miles's face was implacable.

Sean realized that clenching his teeth so hard was making his head throb harder. He made an effort to relax his jaw. "OK. Let me phrase this differently," he said. "Disappear, or I'll rearrange your face."

Miles looked unimpressed. "If I leave you alone and you get into trouble tonight, Davy, Con, and Seth will rip my head off and plant it on a stake. There's only one of you. There's three of them. Forget it."

Sean started up the stairs to his condo. Each step was a hammer blow to his skull. "I won't get in trouble. I don't have the energy."

"I'm not going to get in your face, either." Miles followed him up the stairs. "Just pretend I don't exist. I'm used to it. Look at my track record with the women. I'm, like, the Invisible Man."

Sean shot Miles a critical glance as he unlocked his door. "Do not say stuff like that if you want to get lucky with women," he lectured, out of habit. "Don't even think it. It's the kiss of death."

"Yeah." Miles rolled his eyes. "By the way. I need a favor."

Sean slapped the door open. "It's not a good day to ask favors."

"You owe me," Miles reminded, following him in. "Big-time."

Sean spun around, planted his feet, and gave Miles a death look that knocked him back two paces. "What the fuck do you want, Miles?"

Miles gulped. "I want you to drive me up to Endicott Falls."

Sean started to laugh at the irony of it. He breathed the shaking feeling down before it made him hurl all over his own kitchen. "Dream on, buddy. I hate that town, especially today, and it hates me worse."

"I taught your Thursday kickboxing classes for the entire past month when you were in L.A.," Miles reminded him. "I spent three days fixing your computer when that virus crashed it. Free of charge."

"Aw, shut up. What do you want with that backward hole, anyhow?" A thought struck him. He shot Miles a darkly suspicious look. "Isn't Cindy up there, doing band camp? Don't tell me you're still—"

"Absolutely not. I am totally over Cindy." Miles's tone was stony. "She's up there, but I avoid her like the frigging plague."

Sean was unconvinced. Miles had been pining for Cindy Riggs, Connor's wife Erin's seductive little sister, since before the McClouds had met him. He'd finally gotten a clue, after a spectacularly public episode last summer at Connor's wedding, but it had not made him happier. On the contrary. He'd been in a funk ever since.

"I'm sound and light technician for the Howling Furballs at the Rock Bottom Roadhouse tonight," Miles told him. "And tomorrow, I start assistant teaching karate at the Endicott Falls School of Martial Arts."

Sean was startled. "No shit. You've got, what, a brown belt now?"

"Nope. Passed the test for my first dan black belt last month. Got an honorable mention for my kata, too." The pride in Miles's voice was palpable. "Davy gave my name to a guy who runs a dojo in Endicott Falls. They need someone to help with the class while the regular teacher recuperates from knee surgery, so . . . it's no big deal."

"It's a very big deal," Sean said. "It's great. Good for you."

"Plus, my folks just bought a car. They're giving me their old Ford. This is the last time I'll have to blackmail you into giving me a ride."

"That's reason enough in itself to drive you up," Sean said sourly. "Don't tell me. Let me guess. Early nineties sedan, right?"

Miles looked wary. "So? What of it?"

"Beige, right? I'll bet you my left nut it's vomit-tinted beige."

Miles jerked his shoulders in a defensive shrug. "So what if it is?"

"Fogeymobile," Sean said. "The Invisible Car, for the Invisible Man. You gotta drive something with testosterone, my friend."

"It runs," Miles grumbled. "It's free. I know you think of motor vehicles as fashion accessories, but it's sexier than taking the bus."

"Barely," Sean muttered. "I thought you were working on Con's nerd killer project."

"I will be. Cyber stuff. I'll work from up there."

Sean grunted, and yanked a couple beers out of the fridge. He handed one to Miles, chug-a-lugging half of his own. "God, I feel like shit." The red light blinked insistently on his message machine. He stabbed the button to see what the outside world wanted from him.

The first two calls were work-related; one about an invoice he'd sent for a consulting job he'd done a few weeks before, another from an independent film director in L.A. who was shooting a movie about GIs in Iraq. Sean punched the fast forward button over both of them. He'd deal with them later, when his brain was back online.

The next message rooted him in place, bottle poised at his lips.

"Yo, Carey Stratton here. Tried your cell. Fucker was turned off. I was doing a trawl for your long lost lover-doll. Computer coughed up some new data. Olivia Endicott has had a misadventure, pal. Somebody burned down her bookstore. Oh, and she's moved. She's in Endicott Falls, Washington, now. That's pretty close to you, huh? This might be your chance. Go for it, buddy. The skulking from afar shit is not good for your health, even if it does pay my rent. I sent you an e-mail with the links. No charge for this service. Take it easy, OK? Later, dude."

Sean was rooted to the floor. Mind blank, mouth slack.

"Sean?" Miles's voice was cautious. "You're spilling your beer."

Sean jerked, startled, and righted the bottle. He couldn't breathe. He tried to swallow. His throat was choky dry, like desert sand.

Liv. Back in Endicott Falls. The last news he'd gotten from the private investigator had placed her in Cincinnati, Ohio, working as a research librarian. The latest photos Carey Stratton had sent him had been taken there last December. Black and whites, long range lens. Liv, coming out of her apartment. Liv, petting a dog, smiling. Liv getting her mail, hair swirling around her head like a halo, patterned gypsy skirt billowing in the wind. Her socialite bitch mother Amelia Endicott had loathed those long, swishy, hippie-mama skirts.

So Liv was still a rebel. Thank God for that.

The most recent photos, plus his all-time favorites, were kept in a folder on the shelf over his computer. Conveniently near to hand.

They were dog-eared and battered around the edges.

He slipped in the puddle of beer as he bolted for the computer room, downloaded Carey's message, clicked the links. Read them all. Read them again. It was true. Arson, for Christ's sake. His hands shook.

"So she's the one, huh?"

Miles's quiet voice from the doorway made him jump. He'd forgotten the kid was there. "What? She's what one?"

"The one you keep that huge computer file on," Miles said. "The reason you never stay with any one girl for more than four days."

"What the hell do you know about my file?" he barked. "I never gave you permission to mess around in my private files!"

Miles dropped his long body into the other computer chair and gave Sean his long-suffering puppy dog look. "Remember those three days I spent trying to recuperate your data when your system crashed?"

"Oh." Sean covered his face with his shaking hand. "Fuck me."

Miles cleared his throat. "It's, uh, real hard to keep secrets from your computer doctor." His tone was apologetic. "Sorry."

Sean stared into the screen. His face felt hot. Nobody was supposed to know about his hobby of keeping tabs on Liv Endicott. It was just a small, private insanity that did not bear close inspection. By anyone. Not his brothers, certainly. Not himself.

"You never said anything about it," he muttered.

Miles shrugged. "Figured I had no right to point fingers. It was funny, though. Didn't know you had it in you. To be obsessed, I mean."

Sean winced. "I am not obsessed. And it's no weirder than that vid clip of Cindy blowing a kiss that you used for your screen saver," he said through clenched teeth. "Now *that's* obsession for you, dude."

"I trashed that screen saver," Miles said, his voice lofty. "Now I have a flock of migrating birds. It's very relaxing."

Sean whistled. "Wow, sounds like a real dick-tingler. Relaxation, is not what you need, buddy. You need—"

"To get my bone kissed, yeah. You've told me that already, like, a thousand times," Miles said impatiently. "So who is she, anyway?"

Sean buried his hot, throbbing face in his hands. "Hometown girl," he said dully. "A direct descendant of our city's illustrious founder, Augustus Endicott. His great-great-granddaughter, I think. You know that bronze statue of the pioneers in front of the library? The tall guy in the front who looks like he's got a rifle shoved up his ass?"

"Oh, man," Miles said, whistling. "Them? So she's, like the heir to that huge construction company? Yowsa. Bart Endicott practically owns this town. And what he doesn't own, he built."

"Tell me about it." Sean's voice was bleak.

Miles studied him, slouched in the chair, his dark eyes heavy lidded and thoughtful. "Huh. So she's the reason you do it, then?"

Sean gave him a wary look. "Do what?"

Miles's eyebrow lifted. "Fuck everything that has a pulse."

Sean was stung. "I do not fuck everything that has a pulse," he said haughtily. "I have my standards. I limit myself to endoskeletal organisms. I always go for vertebrates. And I don't do reptiles. Ever."

"Aw, shut up," Miles grumbled. "Man slut. It's not fair."

Sean gave him an appraising glance. Miles had changed since he'd started hanging with the McClouds. The results of two years of relentless martial arts training, dating from the historic battle of the Alley Cat Club, to save Cindy from her pusbag pimp of a then-boyfriend.

Miles got pulped that night, but he'd developed a burning yen to learn to fight, just like the McClouds. Which was a tall order, but they'd made big progress. He had a black belt, for God's sake. They'd finally gotten him to stand up straight, and his lanky frame and sunken chest had filled out nicely with all the weightlifting Davy made him do. He ate real food now, not just Doritos and Coke, so he no longer looked like an undernourished vampire. Sean's tireless lecturing about grooming was beginning to bear fruit, too. Miles wasn't a sharp dresser yet, by any means, but his T-shirt was clean, and his black hair was pulled back into a shiny ponytail, no longer lank, greasy wings framing a pallid face. He'd ditched the weird round glasses, and his big hooked nose looked better without them. He'd taken antibiotics for his zits, praise God. The resultant scarring gave his face a tough, weathered look.

Add in the big puppy dog eyes and the bulging biceps, and voilà. Not too fucking bad. If he would just lighten up, maybe even smile occasionally, he would look like a guy who could get laid with minimal effort on his part. About time, too. The guy was a volcano about to explode.

"Are these karate classes you're teaching mixed?" Sean asked.

Miles snorted. "I'm working with little kids. Ages four to twelve."

Sean shrugged. "There's always hot and hungry single moms."

"This might come as a shock to you, but some people actually do things for reasons which are not specifically aimed at obtaining sex."

Sean widened his eyes. "Really? It worries me to hear a healthy twenty-five-year-old male say stuff like that. Either you're ill, you're pathologically screwed in the head, you're a closet gay, or you're lying."

"I'm not—"

"Gay, yes. I know damn well you're not," Sean finished. "You've been obsessed with Cindy since I met you. You don't look sick, either. That leaves screwed up, or lying. Take your pick. I'd buy either one."

Miles's mouth hardened. "I am totally over her. And I do not want to hear her name spoken for the rest of my natural life. Get it?"

Sean winced, pained. He'd overdone it again. He was used to kicking around his rawhide brothers. Sometimes their little buddy Miles was too soft for hard-core McCloud style teasing. "Fair enough. Sorry."

"So, what's the deal? Are you giving me a ride?" Miles gave him a crafty look. "You do want to check out this girl's bookstore, don't you?"

Sean let out a grim snort. Opportunistic, guilt-tripping little bastard. He turned back to the computer and read the articles again.

He wouldn't, of course. He wasn't that stupid, that masochistic.

But something inside him was buzzing, wide-eyed, totally zinged from hearing Liv's name spoken aloud. He hadn't felt that kind of buzz since he didn't even remember. Maybe not since . . .

Since he'd seen her last? Oh, please. Give him a fucking break.

He'd do a thorough and exhaustive inventory of every single high point in his life before he'd admit to that. Talk about pathetic.

Still. Who *was* she, now?

Not that this burning itch of curiosity would be mutual. On the contrary. Liv hated his guts. She thought he was the embodiment of all evil in the known universe. Rightly so. And getting disdained, spurned, scorned, or otherwise dissed by Liv Endicott, well . . . damn.

That would suck like a vacuum cleaner.

Chapter
3

It was the bouquet of white irises that got to her the most. The sneering, in-your-face rudeness of it. As if the guy had spit on her.

Liv clenched her fists and tried to breathe. Her belly muscles were so rigid, she had to deliberately unknot them to let her lungs expand. That coffee she'd drunk some time ago churned in her belly, threatening to rush back up the way it came. She might be better off without it, but barfing made her cry, and the firebug who had torched her bookstore might be watching through a pair of binoculars.

Giggling evilly to himself. Licking his slavering chops. Watching her out of his cold, beady little reptile eyes, like a Tyrannosaurus rex.

She scanned the buildings around her, their outlines blurred by the haze of smoke. He could be watching from one of those windows. She shivered. She would not let him see her snivel like a hurt little girl.

T-Rex had left the bouquet on top of the kerosene, right out front. No attempt to hide what he'd done. He'd even attached a letter. *For Olivia, with love, from You Know Who*, was printed on the front. Same font he'd used for his previous e-mails. The ones she'd tried to ignore.

Evidently, T-Rex didn't respond well to being ignored.

Well, hell. She was paying attention now. He'd gotten the big re-action he was looking for. The police were completely disgusted with her for contaminating the crime scene. She hadn't thought about practical details like fingerprints, etc., when she'd ripped the flowers apart and stomped them into the ground, shrieking at the top of her lungs. She'd put on quite a floor show. Her parents had been mortified.

Ah, well. Nobody was perfect.

She forced out a breath. Her mind kept churning out platitudes about the virtues of non-attachment. All things must pass, blah, blah. The stuff she'd so recently stocked her Self-Help, Spirituality and New Age sections with. Big sellers, all that woo woo stuff. It made her want to smack someone. Who cared about the illusory na-ture of reality when you were staring at the ruins of your lifelong dream?

She wasn't evolved enough not to feel like total crap about it.

And she was so angry. She wanted to hurt the guy who did this. Hurt him bad. Make it last. Make him sorry his parents had ever met.

This, from a woman who caught spiders and put them in the yard because she couldn't bear to kill them. Even the big, freaky, hairy ones.

God, it hurt. She'd invested so much of herself into this place. Everything she had, and a whole lot more besides. She'd never cared so much. Ever, in her life. About anything.

Except for one notable occasion, her inner commentator piped up.

Oh no. Uh-uh. No way was she going to let herself think about Sean McCloud. One charred disaster at a time, thank you very much.

She scuffed through the ashes, mind churning. Who *was* this guy? What did he have against her? She had no natural enemies. She was Miss Compromise. Sweetness and light. What you reap is what you sow, wasn't that how it worked? Wasn't there a goddamn *rule?*

That New Age fluff she'd been ordering had done a number on her brain. Or maybe she'd done something horrible in a past life. She'd left a swathe of destruction in her wake. The Countess Drac-ula, or some such. She'd just get her inner evil countess to hunt this guy down and serve his balls up to him on a plate. Here ya go, buddy. Open wide.

If he didn't get her first. She shivered, despite the August sun, and the heat waves that rose, shimmering, from the smoking coals.

She dashed the tears away with grimy hands and blinked madly, staring at the mess. All those months of work, reduced to nothing.

It had felt so good, bringing her dream bookstore into reality. Like she'd finally come home. Books & Brew was her baby. Her idea, her investment, her risk. Her own miserable, incinerated failure.

Be grateful it happened at night. The fire didn't spread. The staff was home. No one got hurt, she reminded herself, for the zillionth time.

A hand clapped down on her shoulder. She jumped. "Don't worry," came a familiar voice. "It's no big deal. It's all insured, right?"

It was Blair Madden, the VP of Endicott Construction Enterprises, and her father's right-hand man. Blair had never possessed much of what you might call tact, but this was a bit raw, even for him.

Liv turned. "Excuse me? No big deal? Don't *worry* about it?"

"All I meant is that it's replaceable." Blair took his hand off her bare, dirty shoulder and wiped it discreetly on his perfectly creased tan pants. "It's not like it was a cultural landmark. Keep it in perspective."

"Livvy? Good God! You're *still* here?"

Liv winced at the razor tone of her mother's voice. Amelia Endicott climbed out of the Mercedes idling on the curb and minced toward them, careful not to smudge her sandals. "You shouldn't be out in the open!" she scolded.

"I'll come when I'm ready, Mother," Liv said.

The older woman's hackles rose, visibly. "I see," she said. "As always. You have to do things your own way. You must suit yourself."

"Yeah, right," Liv muttered. "As always."

It took energy, opposing her mother. The woman had run her childhood like a dictator, picking her clothes, her schools, her friends.

Except for that one very memorable summer.

Yeah, right. Mother had cast the Sean debacle up to her for years as an example of what happened when Liv didn't listen to her. For once, she'd actually had a point. It stuck in Liv's craw even now.

She'd finally forced her parents to accept that she was an adult who made her own decisions. Enter T-Rex, with a can of kerosene, and suddenly her parents felt justified in bundling her into a suffocating gift box again. Tying her up with a big silken bow. Olivia Endicott, groomed to be a credit to the family name, if she would only: 1) lose that pesky fifteen pounds, 2) wear the right shoes, 3) dress like a lady, 4) marry Blair Madden, and 5) work for Endicott Construction Enterprises.

Blair chose this inopportune moment to throw his arm around her shoulder. She jerked away before she could control the reflex.

Blair folded his arms over his chest, affronted. "I'm just trying to help," he said stiffly. "You're being childish, you know. And bitchy."

I'm under a wee bit of stress, in case you haven't noticed. She bit the sarcastic words back. "I'm sorry, Blair," she said. "I just can't stand being touched right now."

Her mother's eyes flicked down over Liv's body, mouth tightening. "I can't believe you are out in public dressed like that."

Liv looked down at her baggy pants, the shrunken tank top. She'd rushed to the fire right after she got the call, not bothering to change out of her jammies. She hadn't had a belly flat enough for that look when she was twenty, let alone thirty-two. No bra, either. Woo hah, she could throw 'em over her shoulder like a continental soldier. And as for her pants, well . . . best not to focus on her big butt at all.

But the scolding made her chin go up. "I'm decent," she said. "The important bits are covered. Nobody'll faint from seeing my jammies."

Certainly not Blair, she refrained from adding. He'd been badgering her for years in a half-joking-but-not-really way about giving into the inevitable, and marrying him. Sometimes, when she was lonely, she was a tiny bit tempted. Blair was smart, nice, hardworking. Her parents would have frothing fits of joy. And it would be company.

But there was no heat between them. Absolutely none.

Of course, her criteria of "heat" was based almost exclusively on her memories of Sean McCloud. Maybe she'd just imagined all that wild intensity, that giddy excitement. She'd been not quite eighteen, after all.

She swallowed, her throat raspy from smoke and suppressed tears. Maybe a marriage without heat would be more stable. After all, all she had to do was look around to see the damage heat could do.

"You're making a spectacle of yourself," Amelia said. "I'll see you at home, when you condescend to come." She flounced back to her car.

"I'll take you home," Blair said. "You're aware that you have to be accompanied everywhere now, right? You should pack your things."

The look on his face abruptly reminded her of why she kept saying no to Blair's proposals. Pompous bossiness was so unsexy.

"Pack?" she asked. "Why am I packing? Where am I going?"

"You can't stay at your place, Liv," he lectured. "It's too remote, up on the hill, and you don't even have an alarm. You'll be staying at Endicott House, where we can keep an eye on you. Bart's contacting a security firm to provide you with full-time bodyguards."

"Bodyguards?" Her smoke-roughened voice broke on the word.

"Of course." His chest puffed out. "I'm going to tell Bart and the police where we're going. Stay where I can see you, for God's sake."

She stared bleakly after Blair. Bodyguards? Full time?

Now her parents could monitor her night and day. Make sure she was constantly living up to the Endicott standard. She might as well just embalm herself right now, and save everyone else the trouble.

"Hey, Liv," a low male voice said from behind her.

Oh, God. She knew that voice. She couldn't turn. Her muscles wouldn't move. It was like that time she'd gone rock climbing. She had looked down in the middle of a steep bit and frozen solid, fingers numb. Her bones, all rubbery and flexible. Her insides, vast and empty.

He didn't speak again. Maybe stress had driven her to auditory hallucinations. And there was only one way to find out, so *move.*

She commanded her muscles to obey, and turned.

Oh boy. It really was Sean. Her insides tightened. She felt faint.

Holy crap, just look at him. He occupied so much space. The air around him seemed charged. He was so tall. So incredibly . . . big.

Had he really been that big fifteen years ago?

Certainly she herself hadn't been. The thought stung like a spider bite. To think that with her bookstore trashed, her dreams in ruins and T-Rex to stress about, she was still uptight about her oversized bum.

And her tank top did nothing to control the jiggle and sway of her boobs, which were likewise bigger now, if somewhat, well . . . lower. Plus, the poochy side pockets on her pants had been designed by the devil himself to make her hips look even wider than they really were.

She tried to speak, but her voice was rough and hoarse from all the smoke. She coughed, and tried again. "Hi," she squeaked.

She didn't want him to see her like this. Wounded, bereft. It was too much like the last time he'd seen her. Except that then, the smoking ruin had been her heart. And he was the arsonist who had torched it.

They stared at each other. She felt empty-headed, exposed.

She'd pictured running into him after she'd decided to come back to Endicott Falls. Many times. But in her fantasies, she'd been thinner. Boobs hoisted high in a power bra. Romantic, swishy white skirt and poet's blouse, showing a faint, tasteful hint of sexy cleavage. *Eat your heart out, you brain-dead chump* being the subtle nonverbal message.

She'd be bustling around in her crowded bookstore, looking trim, taut and fabulous. Hair swept up in a tousled twist. Skilfully understated makeup. Elegant gold earrings. Busy, happy, fulfilled Liv!

"Sean who?" she'd say. Then her eyes would widen, recognition dawning as she looked past the beer paunch, or whatever other defects he'd developed that had rendered him harmless. "Oh! I'm terribly sorry, I just didn't recognize you!" she'd say, oh so sweetly. "How *are* you?"

This was not the current scenario. Her eyes kept dropping, darting up, trying to reconcile this man with the Sean of her girlhood memories. He'd been dimpled, laughing, gorgeous. A sinuous young panther on the prowl. The embodiment of dangerous male sexuality.

That succulent golden boy had become a grim, inscrutable man.

Faded jeans and a green T-shirt showed off a long, powerful body that seemed thicker, denser than she remembered. His face seemed carved out of something hard. Longish hair blew loose and shaggy around his face in the hot gusts of air. Sun glinted off the bronze ends. A diamond stud flashed bright rainbow fire in his ear.

His eyes were keen, shadowed. No twinkle. No dimple. No flash of white teeth. He looked tempered, and tough. Harmless, her ass.

He looked about as harmless as a long, sharp knife.

She had to tear her eyes away and look at her feet before her lungs would unlock and suck in a shuddering gasp of badly needed air.

Wow. He had a flair for the dramatic entrance. Deliberate or not, it was effective, how he'd framed himself in a fire-blackened brick arch of the turn-of-the-century brewery she'd converted into her bookstore.

Backlit by sun slanting through the arch, wreathed with billows of smoke, he was like a rock idol taking the stage. Accepting the adulation of his screaming fans as his right and due. He smiled at her, and she crossed her arms over tingling breasts. No, not like a rock star.

More like a fallen archangel, guarding the gates of hell.

"What are you doing here?" she blurted. "I thought you'd left. Everyone said—" She stopped, realizing how much her words revealed.

Bleak amusement flashed in his eyes. "My brothers and I keep Dad's old place up behind the Bluffs for occasional weekends, but we all live in the Seattle area now." He hesitated. "So don't worry."

"Oh, I'm not worried." Embarrassment sharpened her voice. "So did you just come to gawk? Quite a spectacle, isn't it?"

He looked around. "Yes, it is."

"Must be a real satisfaction to you." She regretted the words instantly. Everything that came out of her put her at a disadvantage.

His eyes flickered. "Not in the least," he said quietly. "I never wished you anything but the best."

Her vertebrae stacked, clickity-click. That snotty bastard. After all the horrible things he'd said to her, he dared to get up on his high horse and make her feel in the wrong. "Isn't that sweet," she snapped. "I'm so touched, but that doesn't explain what the hell you're doing here."

He crossed his arms over his chest, and it took all her willpower not to stare at his ropy, powerful forearms. His long, graceful hands. The bulge of his biceps, distending his T-shirt sleeve. "I heard about the fire," he said simply. "I wanted to make sure you were OK."

She swallowed back an unreasonable quivering in her thoat.

"This place . . ." She gestured around with her hand. "This used to be my brand new, fabulous, beautiful bookstore. Did you know that?"

"Yeah," he said, his face somber. "I did know that."

"Some reptilian asshole burned it down," she said. "On purpose."

He nodded. "That sucks. You've got no idea who—?"

"None." She struggled with the quiver in her throat. "I assume it's T-Rex, though. The weirdo who's been sending me the e-mails."

His eyes sharpened. "Who's T-Rex? What e-mails?"

"I've been getting e-mails for the past few weeks," she explained wearily. "I call him T-Rex, just to call him something. Declarations of love, comments on what I'm wearing. He's been watching me. Up close."

"You told the police about the e-mails?" he asked.

"Of course," she said. "What could they do? There was nothing particularly threatening in them. Just, you know, slime."

"Did he leave a note today?" he demanded.

She choked off the laughter before it could become hysterical. "Oh, yes. Today he told me how I would twist and burn in the fire of his passion, and then . . . how did he put it? That soon we would be as one. That our union would be explosive. All written in this sticky, psuedo-poetic prose that makes my flesh crawl."

Sean made a sound in his throat, like a wild animal's growl. It made her hairs prickle up. "That sick fuck needs to be disemboweled."

She gaped at him, then forced her mouth to close. "Ah. Thank you, Sean, for putting that lovely image in my head."

"Sorry," he murmured. "You haven't been in town very long?"

"A few months. Ever since I bought the Old Brewery. I just opened the store about six weeks ago." Her voice quivered again. "It was going well. It was a great location. I had the college crowd, the writing workshops at the Arts Center, and they've been spiffing up the historic downtown for the tourists, too. It would have paid off. I'm sure of it."

"So am I," he said. "I'm sure it still will."

He was just humoring her, but it was all rushing out, dignity be damned. "I always wanted to do this. Always, since I was a little girl." Her voice was almost defiant. "Bookstores are my favorite places. They're like wonderland. Endless goodies. A candy shop for the mind."

"It's good to know what you want to do," he said. "You're lucky."

"Lucky?" A bitter laugh hurt her. She looked around herself. "Excuse me? You call this lucky?"

"You'll get past this," he said. "It would take more than a can of kerosene to keep you down, Liv. This is just a blip on your screen."

She felt her spine straighten, her chin go up, her lungs fill. His words gave her a jolt of energy and pride. She didn't dare examine the feeling too closely. She might kill it, and she needed all the help she could get. "I did a lot of renovating myself," she hurried on. "I've studied woodworking. I can handle big power tools. You name it, I can use it."

"Wow." His eyes widened, impressed.

"Yeah, my folks about had kittens. And there was the café. Picking out fixtures, bar equipment. Ordering books. I was in hog heaven. I'm so deep in debt, it's not even funny, but I didn't care. I just didn't give a shit."

"Good for you," he said gently.

"I painted the murals in the childrens' corner myself, did you know that? Of course you don't. What a silly question. Why would you?"

She was barely making sense, at this point, but Sean was taking it in stride, his face calm and attentive. She rubbed furiously at her eyes. "They turned out pretty well, if I do say so myself," she said, voice wobbling. "Scenes from fairy tales. I'm no Leonardo Da Vinci, but those murals weren't half bad. They really weren't."

"I'm sure they were beautiful. I'm sorry I never got to see them."

Oh, God. His words were so exactly what she had needed to hear.

Her parents had seemed hardly surprised by the disaster. What did she expect, when she went against their well meant advice? They'd been tapping their feet, waiting for her to fail from the beginning.

One crumb of genuine sympathy, and she fell right to pieces.

She covered her face with one hand and fished with the other one in her pocket for tissues. All that was left were wet, soggy wads. Bleah.

She would stay like this forever. A cautionary tale for unwary entrepreneurs. Birds could come to roost on her. She didn't care.

Sean's warm hand came to rest tentatively on her shoulder. Awareness sparkled through her nerves at the gentle contact, and the sobbing eased down. Startled into hiding, no doubt. She peeked over her hand. "I don't suppose you've got a tissue? I'm leaking."

"I'm sorry." His voice was full of regret. "I'm not the kind of guy who carries packs of tissue around."

"Don't worry about it," she mumbled. She couldn't use her too short, too tight shirt to blot her face without flashing her bare tits to Sean McCloud and the rest of the Endicott Falls business district, but hey, why not offer the gawkers a final act of public indecency to round off the day's array of entertainments? It was just that kind of a day.

She blinked to bring her vision into focus, and sucked in a bubbly gasp of shock. Holy crap. Sean McCloud was pulling his shirt off. Right out here, in front of God and everyone. Talk about public indecency.

"What the hell do you think you're doing?" she hissed.

He stopped partway through the act, the tight microfiber shirt jerked up high enough to show off his thick, broad, muscle-bound chest.

Oh, man. Amazing. The tight brown oblongs of his nipples adorned hard, cut pecs. His fuzz of bronze hair thickened into a treasure trail over his washboard belly, vanishing into jeans that hung low on lean hips. Hard muscles moved beneath the gold skin of his abdomen. A jagged scar gleamed silvery, on his side. She wrenched her gaze away.

"It's clean," he said earnestly. "Just out of the dryer. And I took a shower and smeared perfumed goop over myself," he checked his watch, "just three hours ago. Use it for a handkerchief. Go ahead. Please."

Oh, yeah. Like he didn't know just how stunning his body was. Dazzling her to distract her from her sobfest. The humiliating thing was, it was working. "I'm not using your damn shirt for anything."

"I spent all that time in an air-conditioned car, so I've barely sweated." He whipped the shirt off, and presented it to her. "It's not worthy of your Divine Highness's royal snot, but it's all I've got to offer."

No. She would not laugh, and let him score points at her expense.

"Go on," he urged. "Just honk right into it. Never let it be said that I'm not willing to sacrifice my shirt for a lady's convenience."

He stuck it in her hand. Her fingers closed around it, leaving a greasy black splotch. The shirt was soft and incredibly warm. A spicy, woodsy smell rose from it. Smothered giggles made her nose run even more copiously. "You're making it worse!" She thrust the shirt against his chest. "Put this thing back on before you get me in trouble."

He took his own sweet time pulling it back on. Sure enough, he had a black handprint on the front of the T-shirt, as if she'd grabbed his pec and given it a tight squeeze. He looked at it. His smile made her toes curl.

"You'd do anything to make me stop crying, right?" she accused.

"Nope. Tears don't bother me," he said. "It's just that once I get a laugh, I have to follow up and try to get another one. I just can't help myself. It's, like, an obsessive-compulsive thing with me."

"I don't want to hear about your obsessions or compulsions, thank you. That's way too much information for me." She sniffed violently, mopped her face with her hand. "Sorry about your shirt."

He petted the black mark tenderly with his hand. "I'm not," he said. "I'm never washing this thing again. I think I'll frame it."

Her breath stopped. She stared over the edge of her hand. His eyes looked straight into her mind, sifting through thoughts, memories, fantasies. Drawing his own inscrutable conclusions. His lips curved, as if what he'd seen had given him license to take any liberties he liked.

"The thought of you using power tools is really arousing," he said.

"I—I cannot believe you just said that to me," she floundered.

"So put me in my place," he said. "You're Her Divine Highness, the Crown Princess of Endicott Falls. Who dares to mess with you?"

Who, indeed. She realized, after it was too late to stop, that she was licking her lips. "You never stay in any place that you're put."

He shrugged. "True enough. I can just see you, in my mind's eye, looking sleek and powerful. Using a table saw. Dominating the hell out of it. Muscles flexing. Sweat dripping. Sawdust flying. Metal screaming."

"Oh, you are so full of shit," she said. "Just stop it, right now."

"Scold me. Show me who's boss." His eyes glinted. "I go for that."

She covered her face again. "You can stop jerking me around any time now," she forced out, between helpless, hysterical giggles.

"Not yet. I drop to my knees and offer you a cold beer. You tilt the bottle back. A drop slides down, trembles on your collarbone, keeps on sliding. That's when I fall on my face . . . and beg for mercy."

She remembered that coaxing charm, that could get her to agree to anything he wanted. But in the end, he hadn't wanted it. Or her.

She stepped back. She couldn't slide into this honey-baited trap.

"So," she said brightly. "How are your brothers these days?"

Sean's eyes went blank as he switched gears from full-out seduction to bland pleasantries. His mouth twitched. "Uh, great," he said. "Davy and Con are blissfully married. Con's about to have a kid."

"That's fabulous. What about Kev? Is he blissfully married, too?"

His face hardened. A cold flash in his eyes sent a chill through her. "No," he said. "You never heard about Kev?"

Her stomach dropped. "Heard? What should I have heard?"

Sean's throat worked. "Kev's dead. Ran his truck off a cliff." He paused, eyes boring into hers. "You mean you never heard about that?"

She tried to speak several times before her vocal cords would respond. "No," she whispered. "I left that same night. They put me on a plane for Boston. No one ever said anything to me about it."

"Of course they didn't," he said. "Why would you ask?"

That hurt. It implied that she didn't care, which was unfair.

But his eyes were haunted with old pain. How petty, to get huffy about semantics in the face of his loss. "I'm sorry. Kev was special."

Sean silently inclined his head, accepting her words.

She gulped before asking the next question. "So, um, was it . . ."

"Suicide?" Sean jerked his chin. "So they say. Who knows?"

"And that stuff he told me? About the guys trying to kill him?"

Sean paused. "We never found any evidence that it was true."

She took a moment to process that. "So it was . . . he was . . ."

"Yeah. Paranoid delusions. Persecution complex. Like our dad. That was the official conclusion, anyhow."

The bitterness in his voice prompted her to ask. "And your own conclusion?"

"My own conclusion doesn't count for shit. I keep it to myself."

She could think of nothing to say. Or rather, she could think of many things, none of which were appropriate. Like grabbing him by the throat, yelling that he shouldn't have gone through that without her.

Stupid *bastard*. Her throat tightened, like a fist.

"What the hell?" Blair was loping towards her, his face alarmed. "Liv! Are you OK? You look like you've been crying. Did he—"

"My eyes were watering," she said hastily. "From the smoke."

Blair handed her a handkerchief. When she came up for air, Sean and Blair were having a curiously hostile staring match.

"I'm surprised you have the nerve to show your face," Blair said.

Sean's eyebrows lifted. "I wanted to make sure Liv was OK."

"Liv's fine," Blair said stiffly. "We've got her covered."

"I'll leave you in his capable hands, then," Sean said to Liv. "Take it easy, princess." He nodded politely at her, turned, and walked away.

Like a scene out of an old western. Broad-shouldered guy strides off into the sunset. Liv felt perversely abandoned as she stared at his retreating back.

Chapter
4

One foot in front of the other. Play it cool. Don't look back.

Or he'd mash that lying piece-of-shit Madden's nose into pulp. And then drag Liv off to a cave. He narrowly missed walking into a telephone pole. His mind was blank, hands shaking, stomach wonky.

Madden's sticky, possessive vibe made him want to cave that arrogant prick's head in with a rock. The shit-eating insect didn't deserve to breathe the same air as Liv Endicott. Not that he himself did, either, but whatever. Fuck Blair Madden anyhow.

Wow. He thought he'd let that old anger go. After all, Blair's amateur attempts to mess with him back in the old days had paled in significance compared to the real problems Sean had faced. That was the thing about the hammer blow of tragedy. It put the small stuff into perspective. And Madden was small. Like, scuttling cockroach small.

Keep it together. Impulse control. Actions have consequences.

The endless stern lectures from his father and brothers had clubbed into his head looped in his brain in a chaotic babble of mental noise.

Hey, he was trying. He'd controlled his impulses. Except for the impulse to come on to Liv. There were limits to a guy's self-control.

One lofty look from those big gray eyes turned him into a grunting caveman.

Maybe it was the sexpot cavewoman look that did it to him; the wild hair, the soot-smudged face, the notable absence of underwear.

The effect could only be improved by ripping the clothes off, pinning her down on a fur rug, and having at her like a wild beast.

God, she was fine. What a woman. *Girl* was too frivolous a word. The world was full of girls. His address book was full of their phone numbers. *Girl* was a category, a concept. A consumable.

The word *woman* had a different feel to it. It filled his mouth. Round, soft, mysterious. Unique, singular. Liv, grown up, filled out.

He had lots of photos, but Liv tended to wear big sweaters and long skirts in the winter and loose, baggy sundresses in the summer. A body like that had to be seen to be believed. She'd developed full, swaying tits. And that ass, those hourglass curves from waist to hip, Jesus. He'd thought she was perfect fifteen years ago, but nature had decided to go all out. Fudge sauce, whipped cream, nuts and sprinkles.

Those scanty clothes showed every tremor and sway. No wonder half the town was lined up to watch. He was an equal opportunity ravening wolf-pig when it came to female yumminess. He appreciated all colors, sizes and shapes, though he particularly went for lush curves.

But Liv was a different category of female beauty altogether.

It wasn't just the way she looked, though she was drop dead beautiful. It was something intrinsic to her. Something so regal and proud. Dignified. Elegant to her bones. She took no shit off anyone. He felt like a dog on the furniture, unworthy to lick those tiny, arched feet, but slavering for it all the same. Bouncing like a puppy, tongue hanging out. He'd do anything to make her smile. Or better yet, get one of those smothered, giggling snorts. Scoring one of those was like winning the lottery. He'd gotten a few today. He was still jittery with triumph.

So his sweet talk still made her cheeks blush pink and her brights go on, *ping*. Raspberries, crowning those jouncing ta-tas. What a rush, to get the princess all hot and flustered using nothing but words.

That knife cut both ways, though. No coat, box or bag to camouflage his raging boner. He'd had the same problem the first time he saw her. He'd been working construction, and the crew had stopped dead when the boss's daughter walked by. Gauzy skirt, tits bouncing under her prim blouse, cloud of dark curly hair, downcast eyes. Luminous, rose-tinted skin. No makeup. No need for it.

The whole package screamed "virgin." Delicious, innocent, succulent virgin. Unaware of her power over men. She hadn't even noticed the crew wiping the strings of drool off their chins. She just wafted along. On another plane. La la la.

He'd been naked to the waist, wearing boots, ragged jeans and a hard hat. Dripping with sweat, rank as a goat. No way in hell to hide his woody, not that it mattered. She didn't notice him.

Her sandals had made tiny, dainty prints in the cement dust.

It had started out as a game, just getting that floating uptown angel to notice his raggedy-ass self. It swelled quickly into something hotter, wilder. He wanted to make her want him. He wanted to spirit her off into the woods. Lay her down on a bed of pine needles and rock lilies, peel off her panties and lash away at her delicious, candy-sweet girl body with his tongue until she was begging him to deflower her.

And he would oblige. Oh, yeah. He'd been dying for it.

That plan had backfired when he fell madly in love with her.

Kev had been pissed with him for going after a girl like Liv. *She's not the fuckbuddy type*, he'd lectured. *She's gonna get hurt.*

She won't, he'd assured his worried twin. Hurting Liv was the last thing he'd ever do. He worshipped her. He was saving up for a diamond.

Thinking about Kev made this morning's dream flash through his mind again. *You've got to do something about Liv's car*, Kev had said.

Strange. He didn't even know what kind of car she drove.

What a jolt, when she'd asked about Kev. For a split second, it was like Kev had never died at all. None of the bad stuff had happened.

Kev had gotten his doctorate, become a famous scientist, published papers, won prizes, patented amazing inventions, fallen in love, gotten married, had kids. The whole sequence of Kev's hypothetical life played through his head in a blinding flash, *whoosh*.

And man, it hurt when reality came crashing back to displace it.

The sinkhole in his gut widened into a crater. He had to haul ass. Bursting into tears in downtown Endicott Falls was his idea of hell.

He'd always sucked at hiding his feelings. Macho stoicism was Davy's specialty. Kev's, too, in a lighter way. Davy's stoicism had a steely weight to it, like Dad's. Kev's had been more like a zen monk's calm. Like a reflecting lake. So mellow.

Christ, he missed Kev so bad. His throat felt like a burning coal.

He clenched his jaw, loping toward where his truck was parked. He was history. Miles was a grown-up. He could fend for himself.

You've got to do something about Liv's car.

He wished he hadn't interrupted Kev in the dream before he'd finished that sentence. Something was eluding him. Tickling his mind.

Our union will be explosive.

He wished he could look at T-Rex's letter. The e-mails, too.

Stay away. The cops were all over it. Her folks had mountains of money. If anybody ever had her ass covered, it was Princess Liv.

The something's-not-right feeling was swelling, bigger and badder. Fire ants in his head. Itching and twitching. What had T-Rex said? Burning in the fire of his passion? *Our union will be explosive.*

He'd stared at the twisted wreckage at the bottom of Hagen's Canyon for hours, before they'd climbed down and hauled him away.

Our union will be explosive. Repeated in his head, pounding like a jackhammer. His brother's body had been charred black. Carbonized.

"Hey! How'd it go?"

Sean jerked as if he'd been stung by a bee, but it was just Miles, coming out of the computer store, his eyes big with curiosity. "Did you see that girl? What did she say? Was she surprised to see you?"

Sean couldn't speak for the pressure building inside him. He doubled over, pressed his hand against the sucking crater in his torso.

"Jeez. Are you OK?" Miles grabbed his shoulder. "Are you sick?"

He was going to hurl his coffee and sweet roll, right into the potted geraniums in front of Endicott Falls Fine Antiques and Collectibles. Oh, man, what a way to repair his social image.

Our union will be explosive.

He peered back through the haze of smoke. His eye fastened onto Liv's graceful form. Blair Madden marched beside her, chest flung out.

Liv's car. Burning. Explosive.

They split to walk around the battered pickup. That wasn't a trophy vehicle a pompous dick like Madden would drive. Must be Liv's.

Click. It fell into place. His panic released, like a coiled spring.

He took off towards that pickup like he had rocket launchers under his feet. He barely recognized that howling voice as his own. Time warped, like in combat. People flinched away as he pounded by. Madden goggled at him behind the windshield. Liv's eyes were huge.

"Get away from that car!" he bellowed. "Get *back!*"

Liv froze, one foot already inside

Madden locked his door, lunged across the seat, grabbed Liv's wrist to yank her in, the cretin. *Fuck.* Sean shattered the driver's side window with a flying kick. He unlocked the door, wrenched Madden out.

The guy grunted as he hit the hot asphalt. Liv backed away 'til she hit the glass display window of Trinket Trove Gift Emporium.

"Get away!" he yelled, waving his arms at her and everyone else he could see. "Back! Farther! *Now*, goddamnit!"

Everyone obeyed. Nobody wanted to be near the howling psycho.

The keys were in the ignition. He popped the hood. Any movement could trip the bomb, but he had to take that risk upon himself. Nobody was going to believe him. He knew that from bitter experience.

He wasn't even sure he believed it himself, but hell. He had no choice but to trust an impulse strong enough to make him practically blow chunks all over the spit-shined Endicott Falls shopping district.

He scanned the Toyota's engine for bomb designs he was familiar with, but there were infinite variations, endless new strategies, and he'd never tinkered with the guts of an aging Toyota. He wouldn't recognize a wire out of place if it bit him in the ass. He stared at it, stomach churning. He dropped to the ground, shimmied under the pickup on his back. Switched on the penlight on his keychain. Peered around.

A thrill of confirmation jolted his nerves. A wire wrapped around the drive train. Old classic. Easy to spot if you were looking for it, but why look? He poked around delicately. There it was. A wad of plastic explosives, molded between the gas tank and the truck body. If Madden had driven a few inches, the turning driveshaft would've pulled the trip, and ka-boom. He let out a jerky sigh. Tension drained out of him.

The smell of sunbaked asphalt tickled his nose. Scratches on his back began to sting. He stared at the destruction clinging to the belly of the truck, like a malignant growth. So close.

He wiggled out from under the Toyota. It took some eye-rubbing to recognize Officer Tom Roarke. The man had put on weight in fifteen years, but the hostility in his face was immutable.

Sean hardly blamed him. Punching an officer of the law in the face and restraining him with his own cuffs was a very undesirable course of action. Even in his wilder days, Sean had known that.

And all for nothing, in the end. He'd been too late to save Kev.

"Mr. McCloud, would you like to explain to me what you're doing vandalizing Ms. Endicott's car?" Roarke's voice was as harsh as gravel.

"Verifying the presence of unexploded ordnance," Sean replied.

Roarke's face went blank. "Huh?"

Sean sat up. "Take a look," he offered. "There's plastic explosives around the gas tank. A wire around the driveshaft. Could be a decoy, though. Somebody could be watching with a remote detonater."

"You're kidding." Roarke's face went an odd, purplish shade.

"I wish I were. I suggest you evacuate this block right now."

Roarke yanked his walkie talkie out of his belt. Sean turned, and found Liv standing in the street, way too close to her car. Miles, too, was wandering closer than he should, goggle-eyed and slack-jawed.

"Detonator?" she echoed faintly. "You mean . . . a bomb? In my pickup? But I drove it this morning. I parked it here at five A.M. It's been right out here in public, all morning. How on earth—"

"Get the fuck away from the car, Liv. You, too, Miles. *Move!*" Weird, to hear his father's drill sergeant voice coming out of his own mouth. It had no discernible effect on Liv, though. She didn't bat an eye. Sean spun her around, and shoved.

"Get your hands off her." It was Madden, his voice shaky and high. His face was wet with sweat. He grabbed Sean's arm.

Sean just towed the guy along with them. "Let's have this pissing contest out of blast range," he growled.

"I'd like to know how you knew about that bomb, McCloud."

Sean's gut clenched. A lot of people were going to be unpleasantly curious about that. *I had a funny feeling* didn't get you far when people were casting around for a scapegoat, and he made a kick-ass scapegoat.

He braced himself. "I had a hunch."

"I see," Madden's voice heavy with scorn. "A hunch. How convenient and timely. You're so obviously an expert, I'm surprised you're not defusing this so-called bomb all by yourself, on the spot."

"I probably could, but I won't." Sean kept his voice even. "Not without equipment, and backup. I'd do it off the cuff if somebody's life depended on it, but given the choice, I'd rather call the EOD techs."

Patrol cars began to pull up. People were trickling out of nearby buildings, scurrying away. Miles was hunched over his phone, ratting him out to his brothers. Then he saw Roarke and two other officers, marching towards him with grim purpose in their synchronized step, and an unmistakable look in their eyes. Oh, great. This rocked.

So he was ending up behind bars today, after all.

August the fucking eighteenth. It never failed.

"Will it hurt?"

Dr. Osterman threw a reassuring arm around the shoulders of the girl he was steering into his private examining room. He flipped on the lights, enabled the video cameras. "Not at all. X-Cog 10 will just enhance your neural activity, and the electrical stimulation will augment blood circulation to selected portions of your brain," he lied smoothly.

Caitlin's eyes widened, intrigued. "Cool."

Osterman gave her a smile brimming with charm. "Basically, we're trying to use more of your already remarkable brain potential."

Caitlin gave him a world-weary smile. "There are lots of drugs that help you use more of your brain," she said. "I've tried a bunch already."

He chuckled. "No doubt, but my approach is more systematic. I hope to develop ways to treat learning problems, enhance academic performance, and ultimately, contribute to human evolution."

"Wow," she whispered, her eyes big.

Osterman experienced a flash of doubt as to whether this was worth the risk. Caitlin's test results were only borderline. Off the charts compared to a normal teenager, and extremely talented artistically, but she was more or less mediocre by his own standards. On the plus side, her family profile was perfect. She was a product of the foster system. Behavioral problems, drug problems, no nosy parents to ask awkward questions when she disappeared. And he'd been waiting so long for a suitable test subject. Helix Group needed results, if he was to keep getting this lavish funding. Demonstrable, profitable results.

Osterman tilted her face up, noting the lovely bone structure. She had big, startled brown eyes. Her lips were shiny with flavored lip gloss.

"You're special, Caitlin," he said gently. "This project is important. I can't trust the others the way I trust you. Do you understand?"

She blinked in the bright light. "Uh, OK."

He stroked her cheek with his thumb. "You're lovely," he said.

Her eyes widened, startled. Osterman drew his hand slowly away. "I'm sorry, Cait," he whispered. "I shouldn't have said that to you."

Caitlin's eyes glittered with tears. "It's OK. I, uh, don't mind."

Ah. Working with girls was so gratifying. It was difficult to find extremely gifted girls who fit his exacting social profile, but the ease of management canceled out that disadvantage. Just tell them they were beautiful and special, and the deal was done. It didn't matter how smart they were. Girls were so vulnerable, so desperate for love and validation.

And he had discovered, by laborious trial and error, that his precious secret baby, the X-Cog neural interface, was easiest to establish and maintain with highly intelligent female subjects.

She batted her eyes at him. "You've got a good body," she coyly said. "For an older guy." The invitation in her fluttering glance was clear.

Osterman considered it, briefly. These girls were destined for use and discard, so he never had to worry about repercussions. Being married to his work, he preferred to keep his sex life extremely simple.

But all that bucking and heaving took on a tedious sameness after a while. And coming in contact with bodily fluids was unsanitary.

He preferred passions of the mind, when all was said and done.

He stroked her cheek. "Work first, play after. Into the throne."

She clambered into the chair. Osterman snapped the padded wrist restraints on quickly. "Hey!" She struggled. "What is this? You didn't say anything about tying me down!"

"Standard procedure," Osterman soothed, snapping on the ankle restraints. He adjusted the rubber head clamp so that he could position the X-Cog helmet on her head. "Relax. You're doing fine."

Her lips really were beautiful, he thought, with a pang of regret. She was babbling anxious questions that he no longer bothered to answer. He was miles above her now, preparing for the grand event.

Cait might have grown into a beautiful woman, given other circumstances, he mused. But she was so damaged. One might go so far as to say he was giving her life a meaning it would never otherwise have had. Progress ground ever forward, for the good of humanity in general. And for Christopher Osterman, MD, PhD, in particular. He slid the needle into her arm, taped it, started the IV drip. He put his own master crown on. Now all he had to do was watch, and hope.

"Fucking pervert," said a low, grating voice behind him.

Osterman jumped, spun around. He let out an explosive breath when he saw Gordon, his pet assassin, clean-up man and factotum.

Well, "pet" wasn't quite accurate. Keeping Gordon on staff was like holding a tiger by the tail. One kept a tight grip. The corollary being that Gordon's grip on Osterman's own tail was correspondingly tight.

Osterman found the resulting forced intimacy quite unpleasant.

"Do not sneak up on me like that," he scolded.

"You didn't answer your phone. I figured you were playing doctor with one of your girlies back here in the pervert playroom," Gordon said.

Osterman exhaled, and let that insulting comment pass. "Did you take care of that item of business you mentioned in your last call?"

"Ah." Gordon chewed his lip. "There's been a new development."

Osterman waited, hands clenched. "And that is?"

"Kevin McCloud's brother made contact with the girl."

Osterman stared. "What do you mean, contact? You were supposed to kill her. How can he make contact with a corpse?"

"I hadn't concluded the job," Gordon said. "He talked to her today, at her bookstore. The one that I burned to the ground last night."

"Burned?" Osterman gaped at him. "Have you gone crazy?"

"You told me to work up a stalker scenario, didn't you?" Gordon's voice was faintly sullen. "I took you at your word, Chris."

"I was thinking dirty letters, slaughtered cats, that sort of thing!"

"I can't go from dirty letters and dead cats to homicide," Gordon protested. "You need natural buildup. The violence has to escalate in a way that makes sense. Trust me. I know my abnormal psych."

"I don't doubt it," Osterman muttered.

"Watch the snotty remarks. As I was saying, McCloud talked to her. Then he pulled her out of her car before my bomb could go off."

"Bomb?" Osterman's voice rose in pitch. "What bomb?"

"Chunk of Semtex I've had lying around. Don't worry, I wasn't showing off. Any fool with access to the Internet could build it. I rigged the final touches this morning, while everyone was looking at the fire."

Osterman's heart thudded. "This was supposed to be a discreet hit! A bomb in a shopping district? I thought you were a profes-sional!"

Gordon looked hurt. "Think outside the box, Chris. My stalker craves attention. It fills the void inside him. The bigger the gesture, the more he imagines that it will impress the object of his deranged love."

"Your pseudo-psych bullshit is not a justification for—"

"I enter my character's personality structure, and follow its direc-tives," Gordon lectured, enjoying himself. "That way, each crime has its own coherence. Which keeps me, your buddy Gordon, from leaving a signature. In fact, the lack of a signature is my signature."

"You've explained your criminal philosophy to me before. It won't keep the cops from investigating the shit out of this!" Osterman fumed. "I don't want to spend the rest of my life in prison!"

"Oh, prison wouldn't be so bad. With that pretty face of yours, I'm sure you'd be very popular."

Osterman forced himself to breathe. "Are you showing a desire to stop the downward spiral of violence? Is this a cry for *help*, Gordon?"

"Fuck, no." Gordon's toothy grin was cheerfully manic. "Nothing will stop my downward spiral. I live for this shit."

"The Helix Group will not help us, if the police find your tail."

Gordon's shrug was casual. "You do your job, and I'll do mine. Back to McCloud. As I said during the Midnight Project fuck-up—"

"Do not say the name," Osterman ground the words out.

Gordon rolled his eyes. "I told you we should take out Sean Mc-Cloud in a preemptive strike—"

"I didn't want the body count to get higher," Osterman snarled.

"You always get squeamish at the wrong moment," Gordon com-plained. "That girl passed the info on, and went into hiding."

"Then why haven't they come for us? We haven't heard anything in fifteen years," Osterman argued. "He might have been passing by. A burning bookstore attracts attention. Or did that not occur to you?"

"Yeah. Right. Coincidence." Gordon hawked, and spat on the floor tiles. "McCloud is on to us. He guessed my bomb. He knows, Chris. The question is, do we kill him now, before trouble has time to begin?"

Osterman stared at that hateful glob of yellow mucus, and contemplated ways of killing Gordon. He did not like cleaning up his own messes, but things were getting seriously out of hand.

On the other hand. The prospect of training someone new was daunting.

"I should question the girl before I put her down," Gordon mused. He glanced over at Caitlin. "Speaking of which. Want me to dump this one for you? She looks like a shredder to me."

Oh, God, he'd forgotten all about Caitlin. He turned, and knew instantly, as Gordon had, that the attempted interface had failed.

She was twitching, straining against the restraints. Broken blood vessels marred the whites of her eyes. Her mouth was wide, as if she were screaming, though she made no sound. Hallucinations, no doubt. X-Cog had paralyzed her motor functions, but the side effects had fried the rest. Or maybe the electrical stimulation had been too aggressive. He made a note to dial it down for the next subject.

He averted his gaze. That silent scream effect was grotesque.

"Nice titties," Gordon crooned, fondling them.

"Stop that," Osterman snapped. "Let's get back to McCloud. And the girl. Just kill them, for God's sake, and get it over with."

"So let's talk fee adjustment. And take off your pervert crown."

Osterman lifted off his master crown, and carefully smoothed back his thick, glossy dark hair. "I'm paying you a fortune already."

"McCloud is high-risk. Ex-special forces. One brother who's an ex-fed, another who's a private investigator. Those men are going to be unhappy. It may be necessary for me to relocate. That takes capital."

Osterman was tantalized by the fantasy of Gordon disappearing from his life forever. "How much do you want?"

Gordon named a sum. Osterman stared at the man, appalled.

"You're welcome to call someone else," he taunted. "Feel free. I'd be happy to wash my hands of this. Because you're bugging me, Chris."

"Too much," he said testily, already making the calculations in his head, liquidating assets, transferring this, converting that.

"Your slush fund should cover it. And the big boys at Helix won't have to worry their pretty little heads, right? We'll keep it between us. He jerked his chin at Caitlin. "Want me to load her up?"

"Yes. I'm sick of looking at her. I'll mix up a dose of heroin and fentanyl. Inject her right before you dump her. Don't let her asphyxiate in the trunk of your car. It looks suspicious to the forensics techs."

"Might take her a while to finish dying," Gordon warned. "You want to risk her ending up in the emergency room?"

"Doesn't matter." Osterman adjusted the knobs. "She'll have so much cerebral damage, she won't be able to tell them her own name."

Gordon whistled softly. "Now *that's* cold."

The silence behind him made him suspicious as he loaded the syringe. He turned, to see Gordon peeking under Caitlin's shirt.

"Why do you do that?" he snapped. "It's disgusting."

"Why does a man do anything? Why does a dog lick his balls? Because he can, Chris. Because he can."

Osterman shuddered with distaste. "You are such an animal."

"So throw me a chunk of meat." He moved his hand down to caress her crotch, and snatched it away with a hiss of distaste. "Yuck. She's wet herself. I'll back the van up to the cargo door. You got any more body bags? I don't want her leaking in my trunk."

"I'm almost out. It's really hard to get those in bulk," he said.

"Yeah, ain't life difficult? Is that one of your annoying passive aggressive ways of asking me to get some more of them for you?"

The door swung shut on their wrangling, leaving the vidcams to record the subject's response to X-Cog NG-4. Wrists straining, heels drumming. Face locked in the rictus of an endless, silent scream.

Chapter
5

Crash. *Bam.* Kitchen cupboard doors bounced shut, and swung open again. Sean watched in horrified fascination as his older brother stormed around the dim kitchen of their father's old house.

"I don't know why you're so pissed with me," he said plaintively. "I haven't done anything wrong." He paused for a moment. "Yet."

Davy made a snarling noise. There was a squeak, and he was staring at a detached drawer, its handle torn half off. Rubber bands, nails and other detritus rattled onto the kitchen floor. He flung it away.

"Hah," he muttered. "If I weren't so pissed, that would be funny."

The sun was long since hidden behind Endicott Bluff. They hadn't bothered to light up the kerosene lamps yet. In fact, considering Davy's current mood, perhaps the kerosene lamps were best left unlit.

Shadows were swallowing the room. The west window was a light show, ranging from fire-edged pink to mauve to deep, cobalt blue. A star hung in it. OK, a planet—Venus, if he recalled Dad's astronomy lectures correctly.

But Davy wasn't enjoying the sunset. He assaulted the cupboard, and another handle came loose. "Fuck," he muttered. "Goddamn flimsy rotten piece of *shit*." He hurled it against the opposite wall.

Crash, the handle hit a picture. Sean winced as glass shattered.

This was unnerving. Davy usually maintained near-pathological control over his emotions, with the notable exception of his passion for Margot, his new wife. On a normal day, it took the emotional equivalent of a catastrophic earthquake to make him lose his temper.

Davy rummaged through the cupboards. "I know there's a bottle of Scotch around here. Unless you drank it and didn't replace it."

"Nope. I wouldn't drink that stuff if you held a gun to my head. Would you calm the fuck down? You're making me tense."

"I'm making *you* tense?" Davy spun and kicked the swinging door. *Smash*, and one side dangled forlornly from its bent, twisted hinge. "I'm the one who bailed your ass out, and I am making you tense?"

"You did not technically bail me out," Sean pointed out. "I was not technically under arrest! I didn't—"

"Nah, just hanging out in the interrogation room for fun, chatting on the technical aspects of car bomb construction with local officers of the law. All of whom think you're a delinquent. Many of whom, like Roarke, have personal reasons to hate your guts—"

"That's not my fault!" Sean protested.

"You've been using that excuse ever since you learned to talk!"

"Well, sometimes it's valid. And you did not bail me out," Sean said obstinately. "No money changed hands. And you guys are my alibi for last night, so there's no reason to get all—"

"Oh, yeah? How lucky is that? How does it look, that you're so fucking unstable that your brothers have to follow you around to make sure you don't hurt yourself when you go out drinking and whoring?"

"Whoa! Harsh words! Those girls were not whores! They just like to party! They were very sweet, cute, ah—sexually emancipated—"

"Aw, shut up," Davy snarled. "Imagine the scene if we hadn't followed you. Can you tell us where you were the morning of August the eighteenth, Mr. McCloud? Uh, well, Officer, I was having a drunken clusterfuck with some chicks that I met at the Hole, but I don't remember their names. They had nice butt cheeks. Gave great head."

"I do, too, remember their names!" Sean pondered for a moment. "Their first names, anyhow," he amended.

Davy snorted like a maddened stallion and kicked the wall.

"It's not like you guys have to follow me around all the time," Sean argued. "I'm usually a good, solid citizen. It's only on August—"

"The eighteenth, yeah. Think about it, if you remember how that's done. Is it in your best interests for anybody to remember that today is the anniversary of your twin brother's truck bursting into flames?"

Sean sat without breathing. "Maybe not," he conceded.

Davy slammed both fists onto the countertop. The jars rattled nervously on the shelves. "Where the *fuck* is my whiskey?"

Sean got up with a frustrated sigh. He spotted the bottle, in plain sight on top of the propane refrigerator, and handed it to his brother.

Davy yanked out the stopper and sloshed a shot into the glass. He drained it, and fell into the chair. It creaked under his weight.

A heavy silence fell between them. Davy was a master at heavy silences. Sean was not, as a rule. He liked movement, dynamism, noise. But he felt tired enough to stare blankly into the dark today.

He chose his words carefully when he finally broke the silence.

"You've already ripped my head off about my past stupid stunts," he said. "I don't feel like getting lectured for them all over again."

"Oh, no." Davy poured another shot. "No, you did plenty of brand new stupid stuff. The last time you got within a hundred yards of Liv Endicott, you landed in jail. Did that fun fact flash through your head?"

"If I'd stayed away, Liv and Madden would be fine particles in the stratosphere, and there would be a crater where the Trinket Trove Gift Emporium used to be." Sean pointed out. "Be glad that didn't happen."

"That's not the fucking point," Davy muttered.

"Then what is the point? For Christ's sake, enlighten me."

"The point is, you're doing it again. Putting yourself in the worst possible place at the worst possible time! Throwing yourself in front of a locomotive because you're bored, or someone dares you, or you want to impress some girl. Or you feel like shit and can't handle your feelings. You never apply logic. And I'm getting déjà vu. I've said this all before."

"Many times," Sean confirmed, his voice heavy with resignation. "Lecture 967. Impulse Control. Part C: Actions Have Consequences."

"And you know what burns my ass the most?"

Sean cringed. "Uh . . . shoot, Davy, I'm not sure if I do."

"This is all about your dick!" Davy yelled. "You can't keep your pants zipped to save your life, so you end up in custody, surrounded by people who would love to see you burn in hell. Every fucking time."

"What was I supposed to do? Slink away like a whipped dog?" Sean flung his hands up, helpless. "The thing with the police, I don't know why the fuck that keeps happening to me. I swear to God, I don't go looking for them."

Davy snorted. "Right. No clue. Like when you lost your scholarship and got thrown out of school. Why? For boffing the Dean's trophy wife. No thought for consequences. No thought for your future. Your brain just kicks back and lets your glands run the show."

Sean fidgeted on his chair. "She came on to me," he mumbled.

"Yeah, don't they always. I bet she had to tie you down."

Sean tried to recollect the details. "Now that you mention it, she was pretty adventurous that way. She had a closet full of fun toys—"

"Zip it, you smart-ass punk. I'm not in the mood for your crap."

"When are you ever? I don't blame the woman. Hot, sexy thing, married to a physics nerd with dandruff in his eyebrows. I was just a squeeze-toy for her. And she was so good at squeezing my—"

"Shut your flapping face before I put my fist through it."

Sean leaned his face in his hands. It was dumb, to goad Davy when he was all cranked up like this, but once he got on a roll, he couldn't help himself. He was just wired that way. He got up and peered into the fridge, hoping he'd left a beer from a previous visit.

Oh, joy and rapture. He had. He twisted that sucker open and wandered over to the west window to drink it, leaving Davy to stew by himself at the table. Sunset had faded, mauve shading to smoky gray beneath the rectangle of cobalt. Beyond the meadow rippling in front of the house, the pine and fir forest looked dense and impenetrable.

It reminded him of when he was a kid, bedding down at night. Shivering at the dangers Dad said lurked out there. There was a real monster on the loose tonight. Thinking about Liv. His neck prickled, like a ghost had touched him.

Maybe one had.

Kev had helped him today. For some reason, that thought made him feel less alone. He knew better than to share it with Davy, though.

"I want to see the e-mails that stalker sent to Liv," he said.

Davy laid his head on the table, and bonked his forehead heavily against the rough slabs of wood. "See? This is how it always begins."

"He used the word 'explosive' in his note. That was what made me think of a bomb. I want to see the other letters. I want to feel their vibe."

"You're not a cop," Davy said. "You're not her bodyguard. Or her boyfriend. Wanting to bone her does not give you the right to stick your nose or any other protruding body part into that family's problems."

Sean took the final swallow, and tossed the bottle, sinking it into the trash basket. "You and Con got all over my ass this morning for being so self-serving and frivolous. I get interested in the welfare of somebody else, and you jump all over my ass again. I can't please you guys. I might as well not try. Have you got a set of beacons on you?"

Davy's face hardened with suspicion. "Why?"

"She needs to be tracked. She needs twenty-four hour coverage, with a four man team, until they nail this guy. Her people are idiots."

"So knock on the door of Endicott House," Davy said. "Lay out your proposal. See how warmly they welcome your suggestions."

Sean paced the kitchen. "Do you have the beacons?" he repeated.

"They'd have the cops on you the instant they laid eyes on you."

Sean shrugged. "Who says they have to lay eyes on me?"

"I'm having a stress flashback." Davy bonked his head on the table. "My brother has decided to break into the house of the richest guy in the county and seduce his sexpot daughter, under his nose."

"I'm not going to seduce her," Sean said crabbily. "I'd go through the front door and talk to her right in front of her mother if I could, but those people think I'm festering sewage sludge."

"No. They think you're dangerous, mentally unhinged festering sewage sludge," Davy corrected. "If they catch you, your ass is grass."

"If you didn't have a set of beacons, you would have said so by now. So stop yapping at me and hand them over."

Davy got up, kicked his chair out of the way and grabbed a bag that sat next to the kitchen table. He yanked out a ziplock bag full of sheets of cardboard, each with radio transmitter beacons attached to it.

He flung them onto the table. "Here. Knock yourself out."

"Thanks," Sean said.

"Don't thank me til we find out if you end up in prison." He plucked out a strip of foil packets and tossed them on top of the beacons. "Take those."

Sean stared down at the condoms. "Hey. You've got the wrong idea. I don't plan on fucking her. I just want to—"

"Plan? Of course not. You never plan. You lack the part of the human brain that governs planning."

"I resent that remark," Sean said. "I just don't want Liv to get offed by this prick just because her parents have the brains of slugs."

"Take them." Davy's voice grated. "I'm not asking you to be responsible, because that would be a contradiction in terms. I'm just asking you to face reality. I know you, Sean. If you sneak into that girl's bedroom, you'll end up fucking her. It's a mathematical certainty."

Sean stared at him, dismayed. "Chill, Davy. You're scaring me."

Davy's grim expression did not change. "Put them in your pocket."

Sean folded the condoms up and tucked them into his jeans. "Anything to calm you down," he said. "See? It's done. Better now?"

Davy turned around, and stood in the dark, fists clenched.

Sean stared at his brother's back, barely visible in the dimness. "This feels strange," he said quietly. "Usually I'm the one freaking out, and you and Con are the ones talking me down. What's up?"

Davy's eyes glinted in the shadows of the room. "Did it ever occur to you that this day on the calendar really rots for me and Con, too?"

Sean held his breath, and willed his knotted guts to relax. "It's crossed my mind," he said. "I'm sorry. I'm not much help with that."

Davy's laugh was dry. "Sure you are. It's one mother of a distraction, chasing around after you, trying to keep you from getting killed or maimed or imprisoned, or whatever. Who has time to mope?"

"That's one way of looking at it," Sean said dubiously. "Do you have low blood sugar, or what? You should eat. I'd cook you something, but you've trashed the kitchen all to shit. Grab yourself a burger on the way home. Is Margot waiting dinner for you?"

"Nah." Davy's voice was hollow. "I'll just, uh, crash here tonight."

Sean froze, playing and replaying his brother's comment in his head. "You mean you're voluntarily sleeping more than a millimeter away from Margot's voluptuous body? What is up with that?"

Davy's shoulders lifted, and dropped.

"What's going on?" Sean demanded. "You asshole. She's the best thing that ever happened to you. Don't tell me you're fucking this up. Did you fight? Did she throw you out? What did you do?"

"Nothing," Davy said testily. "And no, she didn't. And it's none of your business. We both just need some, ah, breathing room."

Now he was alarmed. Davy usually had to be pried away from his bride Margot's side with the use of a crowbar and a pair of oversized bolt cutters. When the McClouds fell in love, they fell hard.

"Breathing room is a piss-poor idea," Sean said. "Awful things happen when women have too much breathing room."

"What the hell do you know about it?" Davy demanded. "You've never been married, you snot-nosed punk."

Sean didn't bother responding to that. "So is she pissed at you?"

Davy threw up his hands. "Sure, she's pissed at me."

"Why? If you don't tell me, I'll just call Margot and ask her."

"Oh, Jesus. No. Please don't do that," Davy said fervently.

"So out with it. Go on. Spit it out."

Davy struggled, helplessly. "I just . . . well, we're not . . . she's just angry at me because I can't, um . . ." His voice trailed off, miserably.

Sean squinted at his brother, perplexed. "Can't what?"

Davy dropped into the chair again, evidently unable to speak.

Sean gazed at him with dawning horror. "Holy shit. Are you talking about sex? You can't have sex? With Margot the walking wet dream? What the fuck is wrong with you? Are you seriously ill?"

"No," Davy spat out the word. "It's just that . . . she's, ah, late."

Sean gazed at his older brother's slumped form, unable to make out his expression in the dimness. "Late?" he echoed. "Late for what?"

"Use the tiny brain God gave you and figure it out," Davy snarled.

Sean cogitated for a second, and sucked in a sharp breath. "Oh! Oh, shit! You mean, like, *that* kind of late?"

Davy's sigh was jerky and labored. "Yeah. She can't be sure yet. Her cycle isn't regular. But she's never been this late before."

"Oh, man, that's too much information for me. I'm not sure I can handle the intimate details of my sister-in-law's reproductive cycle—"

"Grow up and deal with it, jerk-off," Davy snarled. "You asked."

"True, true," Sean soothed. "Sorry. So can't she just, you know, do a test, or something? Put you out of your misery?"

"Not yet." Davy's voice was clipped. "There's some complicated reason why you have to wait a certain number of days before a test is valid. She explained it to me. I don't remember the details."

"Oh." Sean pondered this news. "Uh, well? So? Shouldn't I be crossing my fingers? Isn't this a good thing? A cousin for Kevvie. Cool. They can tumble around on the rug like a couple of puppies."

Davy shook his head. "Yeah," he whispered. "Sure, it's a good thing. It's a great thing. Fantastic. Yeah. But I can't—I can't—"

"You can't have sex with your wife because you think she may or may not be pregnant? That's pretty medieval."

"Yeah, that's what Margot thinks." Davy stared down at his fists, clenched before him on the table as if he were trying to hang onto something invisible.

"It's not going to be like it was with Mom," Sean said cautiously. "Living out here with Dad was like living in another century. Margot'll have third millennium medical care, from a major medical center—"

"I know that." Davy's voice was taut. "I fucking know that."

Davy's eyes were shut, but Sean knew what his brother saw. Their mother, bleeding to death from an ectopic pregnancy, while the truck tires spun out in three feet of snow. His father, trying to stanch the blood. Ten-year-old Davy had been driving, or trying to.

Sean, Kev, and Connor had stayed behind in the snow shrouded house. He'd been four. Old enough to know that something terrible was happening. It was one of his earliest memories. Maybe not the earliest, because he remembered Mom, like a glow in the back of his mind. Or rather, he remembered remembering her. He shook the poignant feeling away. "Statistics are on your side. Women these days—"

"I know the statistics," Davy said. "I've informed myself, Margot's informed me. I've been lectured, scolded, screamed at."

"Ah. I see," Sean murmured.

"When she told me . . . Christ." He rubbed his eyes. "She thought I'd be happy. Hell, I thought I'd be happy. But I almost lost my lunch."

"Whoa," Sean murmured. "Drag."

"Yeah, tell me about it. Ever since then it's like I can't breathe." He swallowed, audibly. "I close my eyes, and I see blood."

Sean whistled. "Ouch. I can see as how that might put a crimp in a guy's boner."

"This is not a joke," Davy growled.

"Do I look like I'm laughing?" Sean touched his brother's shoulder. It was rigid as steel cable, vibrating with a charge that was approaching lethal. The guy had to chill, before he hurt himself.

Or worse, wrecked something irreplaceable.

It had been such a relief, to see his tight-assed brother finally loosen up and get happy. He was so in love with Margot, he was goofy with it. He was having fun for the first time in his more or less grim life.

No way in hell was he going to let Davy fuck that up.

He folded his arms over his chest, considering his options.

"I don't know why it threw me." Davy sounded lost. "Considering how much we get it on, it's amazing it hasn't happened sooner."

"Got it on, that is," Sean corrected. "Past tense. That's all over for you, buddy. Kiss your dick goodbye. You're never having sex again."

Davy glared at his brother, slit-eyed. "Do not fuck with me, Sean."

"Oh, I won't," he assured his brother. "Neither will Margot. Nobody will, being as how Mr. Big-n-Friendly's gone south, leaving your bride to shrivel alone, sexually unfulfilled. What a waste. Poor Margot."

"Keep your trash mouth away from Margot, punk."

"What an asshole, letting that sexy lady sleep alone," Sean mused. "But she'll land on her feet. Just looking at Margot makes a guy want to procreate. Being as how you're giving her all this breathing room, it shouldn't take her long to find someone capable of—nngh!"

Bam, he was clamped to the wall, Davy's forearm pressing his trachea. Good. He struggled to breathe. It worked. He'd goaded the grizzly out of its cave. Now all he had to do was not get killed.

"You know what your problem is?" Davy spat. "You never know when to shut up. You're going to learn. So shut . . . the fuck . . . *up*."

Sean gave him a big, unrepentant grin. "Make me, meathead," he wheezed. "Let's take it outside. I don't want to trash the kitchen any more than you already have."

Davy jerked his hand away. Sean's feet hit the floor.

He massaged his throat as he followed Davy out, and barely got into guard before Davy's boot swooshed past his face, displacing air.

Woo-hah. *Yes.* Savage joy jolted through him. A no-rules fight with somebody as dangerous as he was, damn. Better than sex.

Maybe. He'd withhold judgment on that, since he'd never done the wild thing with the princess. Davy came at him like a Mack truck. His mind retreated while he ducked, punched, parried. Davy was a berserker, face contracted into a furious grimace. He didn't seem to feel the blows Sean landed. He drove Davy backwards with a series of flying kicks, and his brother stumbled into the irrigation ditch their father had dug decades ago to feed the garden, and that split second while Davy fought for balance left him wide open for a kick to the groin.

Sean pulled it, not wanting to rupture his brother's balls.

Davy hooked his legs and jerked him to the ground. "What the fuck was that?" Davy snarled. "You arrogant little shit! You choke on another one of your kicks, and I'll cave in your skull."

"And maim the golden gonads?" Sean dug an elbow into Davy's ribs. "Castrate the great Inseminator? I couldn't do that to Margot."

Davy snarled like a wild animal, and they were at it again, grappling and flailing. Davy wrenched him into a hammerlock, gaining ascendancy by dint of sheer muscle mass. Sean had plenty of muscle, but Davy had him beat by twenty pounds. Goddamn buffalo.

Sean struggled for breath, face shoved into the dusty grass. "I mean, the woman was born to breed." He gasped as Davy yanked his arms higher. "Look up the word fertile in the dictionary, and you'll find her picture. Just look at her, for Christ's sake. She's a walking advertisement for the joys of procreation. Those pillowy tits, those wide hips. Yum. Make way for the next generation."

Yank. Oh, *fuck*, that hurt. "I told you to shut up," Davy said.

"Can't," Sean said, spitting out grass and dirt. "It's not in my nature. Hey, what if she's pregnant with twins? Doesn't it run in the family?"

Yank. Agony. He tried not to shriek.

"Bite your tongue, jerkwad," Davy growled. "Monozygotic twins are a random freak of nature. No hereditary component whatsoever."

"Huh," Sean grunted, coughing. "So you can have the other kind of twins. That would keep you too busy to pitch stupid-ass fits like this."

Davy's body started to vibrate, racked by silent, helpless shudders. Sean held his breath, and slowly relaxed. The worst was over.

Davy's grip slackened. Sean wrenched his arms free, and with a heave and a grunt, shoved Davy's weight off of himself.

Davy rolled over onto his back, covering his face with his hand. Sean discreetly turned his back and waited. God forbid that he inhibit his super-macho idiot brother from working out his bad ju-ju.

When Davy finally sat up, he still wouldn't look Sean in the face. He just sat there, breathing hard, big shoulders slumped. "Gotta hand it to him," he muttered. "Can you believe the sheer balls of the guy?"

Sean was baffled. "What guy? Who are you talking about?"

"Dad." Davy's voice was barely audible. "Delivering all of Mom's babies, up here, in the middle of nowhere. All alone. Shitty roads. No phone. Twins, too." He shuddered. "Just imagine. Sweet holy Jesus."

Sean made a noncommittal sound as he brushed dirt and grass off his filthy shirt. "Given the choice, I'd rather not imagine it at all."

Davy mopped sweat off his forehead and stared at the dark mass of mountains, his face stark. "I'd rather have every bone in my body broken one by one than take on that kind of responsibility."

Sean got up, stretching and rolling his neck around, searching for the sore spots to rub. "Remember two things. One, Dad was nuts. He thought he was protecting Mom from the evil establishment. Two, he was an arrogant prick. He thought he could handle anything."

"He was wrong," Davy said bleakly.

"Yeah, he was. But you aren't nuts. You aren't an arrogant prick, either. At least, not all the time. And furthermore, Margot can look out for herself. You think the whole world is on your shoulders. It's not. OK?"

Davy nodded, struggling up onto his feet. "Yeah," he muttered.

Sean reached over and touched Davy's shoulder. His brother was hot as a coal, soaked with sweat, and still shaking, but that deadly lethal, thrumming electric charge was gone. "So?" Sean demanded.

Davy shot him a wary glance. "So what?"

"So can you breathe now?"

Davy's head jerked, in a curt nod.

"Good." Sean gave his brother a hard shove that made him stumble. "Then go home and fuck your wife. Dickless pussy."

Davy's leg swept Sean's feet out from under him, dumping him on his ass. "We'll see how well you deal when your turn comes."

He turned back before climbing into his truck, and gave Sean a steely, squint-eyed look. "If you get in trouble tonight, I'm going to rip off one of your arms and beat the shit out of you with it," he warned.

Sean grinned. "I love you too, man," he replied. "Drive carefully."

He watched his brother's taillights winding down the switchbacks that led up to the house. *We'll see how well you deal when your turn comes.* The thought gave him a tug, around the center of his chest.

Right. Like he was ever going to found a dynasty. With who? A dance club fuckbunny? Someone like Stacey or Kendra?

Besides, Davy and Con were always on his case about his short attention span. The way they talked, he'd be liable to forget his own kid in a basket on the top of the car and drive off onto the expressway. He ought to do his hypothetical kids a favor. Give fatherhood a wide miss.

His two brothers had the preservation of the species well under control. He should probably just go to the doctor and snippity snip himself right out of the gene pool. Make it a non-issue, forever.

For some reason, the idea depressed the living shit out of him.

Chapter
6

From: **witchywomanBware: hi is anybody out there**
Miles checked the message he'd sent out, in the dialog box in
the chat room. No bites yet. He turned to his other computers. He
was futzing around in several chat rooms, using different characters
and e-mail idents. Nobody interesting had come by, but it was early
yet.

He still marveled that he could dick around in cyberspace and actually get paid for it. He was racking up the billable hours as a cyberconsultant in Con's Geek Eater investigation, pimping his various
fantasy personas in chat rooms where nerds and geeks hung out.

Mina, aka witchywomanBware, was his most succesful lure so far.
She got lots of attention. He was hoping for a hit from Mindmeld
tonight. He'd been the only one who'd wheedled Mina into a private u2u room and asked about her childhood, under the guise of
wanting to know her better. Miles had spoon fed him Mina's hard
luck story in a self-deprecating tone that he was proud of; junkie
mom, deadbeat dad, raised by grandma, but Gran was dead, sniff
sniff . . . going to college because of Gran's inheritance . . . etc, etc.
He might actually turn out to be good at this social engineering
stuff. And Mindmeld, who had confessed that his name was Jared,
seemed to have a hidden agenda.

Miles could smell it. Like a fart in a car.

He turned away from the monitors, with their soothing blue glow. It was oddly depressing, being in his basement lair again. The Mc-Cloud brothers had kicked his ass until he rented a place in Seattle, just a room over someone's garage, but it was good to be independent. Still, it made no sense to rent another room in Endicott Falls for two months while his folks' basement stood empty. He didn't have money to burn.

The problem was, the place reminded him way too much of his longtime crush on she-who-must-not-be-named. He'd spent years in this hole, listening to tapes of her playing her sax. Watching video montages of her. Wanking off to wishful, erotic scenarios where Cindy had an epiphany from God, and started seeing him as something other than a convenient adjunct brain. An external hard drive she could program to do her coursework while she went out partying with other guys. And he shouldn't even go there. God knows, enough guys had already been there before him. A path had been blazed, by God.

A flash on the screen. A response to his query. He shot across the room on the rattling swivel chair. Excellent. Mindmeld himself.

R U still there witchywomanBware

He dove for the keyboard, typed. **Yes hi how R U**

Good tnx did U like my abstract

Jared had sent Mina an abstract he'd written on using roex filters to represent the magnitude response of auditory filters. Miles intuited that it was either a love offering or a sort of test, so he'd ripped the sucker apart. He grabbed his notes, and began to type. **Yes but I have problems wt roex filters—fits 2 notched-noise masking data R unstable unless filter is reduced 2 a physically unrealizable form & there's no time domain version of roex (p,w,t,) 2 support . . .**

His hands clattered away. His reasoning was that if Jared was a garden variety boy dweeb trolling for sex and validation, he would be scared away by a girl who showed him up, and Miles wouldn't waste any more time on him. But if Jared was the Geek Eater, he would lick his slobbering lips and make another move. And Miles might start earning the money Connor was paying him. He wanted some results.

It was embarrassing, but he felt a constant need to prove himself to those McCloud guys. They were so good at every freaking thing they did. Hanging out with them was a sure recipe for a bitching inferiority complex. He gritted his teeth and coped, partly because he wanted to learn the crazy stuff they knew. Mostly because he really liked them.

Still. Every one of those guys, Seth included, was a super-solvent, successful sex god and ninja maniac. Fucking unreal. It would give him a lot of satisfaction to make a contribution to Con's investigation. Helping nail the Geek Eater would be a coup. A big self-esteem fluffer.

"Hi, Miles."

The soft voice from behind him made him levitate about five inches out of his chair. He spun around, heart pounding. Geek Eater, Jared, Mina, McClouds, utterly wiped out of his mind in an instant.

"Fuck," he gasped out. "Cindy? What are you doing here?"

Cindy stood there, smiling uncertainly, backlit by the light that spilled down the stairs from the kitchen, front lit by the eerie blue glow of the computers. She was wearing a lace-up red thing that clearly demonstrated that the wearer had no need for a bra.

"Your mom told me you were down here," she said. "Erin told me about the car bomb, and the cops, and Sean, all that stuff. Totally wild."

"Yeah." His voice was thick. He coughed. "It was, uh, intense."

Cindy rolled her eyes. "Those McCloud guys can't do the simplest thing without it turning into a life or death drama."

Miles let out a noncommittal grunt.

Cindy perched her taut ass on the edge of his worktable. Faded jeans showed off her smooth, tanned belly. A silver ring gleamed in her navel. If she turned around, the waistband would be just low enough to show off the Celtic knotwork tattoo. It pointed at the crack of those pert buttocks. As if any more attention needed to be drawn to them. He shifted in his chair. Crossed his legs, to hide his inevitable reaction.

"You lost the specs," she commented. "Are you using contacts?"

"Nah. Got laser surgery a few months ago."

"Oh. Wow." Cindy twisted her hands together, at a loss. She looked different. Her face was spattered with freckles, hair yanked into a ponytail. Her eyes looked shadowed. Too much partying, probably. No makeup. She was ten times cuter without all that crap on her face.

"So?" she said brightly, throwing up her hands. "What's up? What are you doing up here? I thought you were sick of this town."

"I thought you already knew everything worth knowing."

"Oh, come on, Miles," she said softly. "Don't."

He shrugged, with bad grace. "I'm teaching a karate class at the dojo up near the Arts Center," he said.

"Oh!" Her eyes widened, impressed. "That's cool!"

"And I'm doing some sound gigs. Got one tonight for the Howling Furballs, up at the Rock Bottom," he went on grimly.

"Yeah? I know those guys. Maybe I'll come. And oh. The Rumors have a gig next week, and our sound guy just bagged. Could you—"

"No," he said curtly. "I don't want to do sound for the Rumors."

He'd done free sound for years for the Vicious Rumors, the band in which Cindy played sax. Just to stare at her, to be near her. Chump.

Cindy wrapped her arms across her belly, a thing she did when she was tense. "OK. Uh . . . maybe I'd better not see if I can make it to the Furballs's gig tonight, then."

She waited for him to tell her to please, please come. He sat like a lump, and let her wait. Let her see how it felt. He'd waited for years.

"OK," she said. "I have a good imagination. I'll just pretend that we're having a polite conversation, being as how we've been friends for years. Let's see. You would start with, hey, Cin, great to see you, how's life? Oh, yeah, Miles. Same old same old. Band camp is crazy, plus I'm working at the Coffee Shack in my free time, so if you get the urge for a Mexican Iced Mocha, come on down, and I'll frappé one up for free. For sure, Cin, you bet I'll be there for that iced mocha, with bells on. Great, Miles, I'll be waiting for ya. Other than that, just gigs with the Rumors, pick-up bands, weddings. And I'm getting my own place, in September."

"Yeah?" He broke his own vow of silence. "Who's the lucky guy?"

Cindy touched her tongue to her upper lip, a trick that drove him crazy with lust. "Um . . . there's no guy. I'm not seeing anybody."

"Wow, sounds like a state of emergency," he muttered sourly.

"It's a group house. With Melissa and Trish. In Greenwood."

"And your mom can manage her mortgage plus your rent?"

Cindy looked hurt. "Nobody's going to pay my rent. What do you think I'm doing, busting my ass with three million jobs? Jeez, Miles."

"I just figured you'd hook up with some guy with a Maserati and a baggie full of coke, and be his happy little concubine," Miles said.

Splotches of color bloomed on Cindy's face. "Ouch," she whispered. "That was really cold and nasty."

That was Miles Davenport. Cold as an iceberg. Nasty as a pile of fresh dogshit. He sat there, glaring, and didn't take it back.

"You're still mad about what happened at Erin's wedding?" Cindy's voice was tight. "It's been a whole year! Forgive me already!"

"I'm not mad," Miles lied. "I'm just not particularly interested. And if you don't mind, I'm working down here, not just dicking around."

She brushed angry tears out of her eyes with the backs of her hands, and turned to go. "Fine," she muttered. "Fuck you, too, Miles."

He felt like shit for making her cry. "Cin," he called out. "Stop."

She stopped at the door. "What?" Her voice was small and hurt.

"What do you want?" he asked wearily. "Do you need to pass an exam? Do you need somebody to help you move? What the hell is it?"

She sniffed. "I don't want any favors. I just miss shooting the shit. Watching *Battlestar Galactica* with you. Can't we just be friends again?"

Miles swallowed. Yeah, sure, she missed being adored by her panting, drooling personal slave. Of course she missed it. So did he.

But he couldn't afford to adore Cindy. It tore him to pieces.

"I'll burn you some copies of my DVDs. I'm too busy to lie around watching the tube, Cin. I have a life." He rummaged through the disc tower. *"Battlestar Galactica?* You want *Firefly,* too? I have the movie."

Cindy's face contracted. "That's not the point. You stupid dork."

Miles threw up his hands. "Then I don't know how to help you." She was so fucking pretty, her eyelashes glittering with tears.

She blinked at the screen. "Who are you chatting with?"

"Oh, that." He turned to look, and grimaced in dismay.

guess ur busy, bye 4 now, Jared had written.

"Oh, shit," he moaned. "I lost him. Damn!"

"Lost who?" Cindy's wet eyes brightened with curiosity.

"It's a work thing. For Connor. I'm not supposed to talk about it."

"Aw, shut up." Cindy peered at the monitor. "The gain and asymmetry of a parallel compressive gammachirp filter is comparable to . . . jeez, Miles, what does Con have to do with this techno stuff?"

"Nothing. There's this predator who's killing science geeks," he admitted. "I'm creating characters with profiles similar to his victims. Then I put them out there in cyberspace, and hope he'll hit on me."

"Brr." She squinted as she read the screen. "WitchywomanBware? You mean, you're a girl? Oh, Miles. That's, like, kinky."

His face got hot. "It's just the way I work. This guy Jared really likes Mina. I was hoping he'd make a move, but he's wandered off."

"Sorry." Cindy shot him a sidewise glance, and read. "Chatter personal profile: Mina. Where'd you come up with that?"

"Dracula. We're hunting a vampire. Not the sexy TV kind. The kind who sucks out your blood and kicks your corpse out of its way."

Cindy shuddered. "Creepy. That is so negative."

"Dealing with serial murderers will do that to you," Miles said loftily. "Get out of my dungeon, if I'm too creepy for you."

Cindy leaned closer to read the box headed *Physical Description.* "Height, five feet, four inches," she murmured. "110—115 pounds. Eyes, dark brown. Hair, long, dark. Bra cup size?" Miles had duly filled in *B-cup*. Under *Distinguishing Characteristics*, he'd typed, *pierced navel*."

"Hmm," she murmured. "So, um . . . basically, you told this guy that you were me."

Miles's rolling chair shot back and hit the table behind him with a crash. Cindy jumped back, eyes big. "That's the thing about you that bugs the shit out of me, Cin," he snarled. "You think it's all about you. It's not, OK? So take your perky tattooed ass and get it out of my face."

Cindy squeaked, and fled.

Miles dropped his head onto the keyboard and swore, the most vicious, horrible epithets he could come up with.

It didn't help worth dick.

"Change your name? Run away? You're out of your mind! You're giving in already? Where is your backbone? Where is your pride?"

Her mother's ringing tone made Liv's head throb. Reasoning with Amelia Endicott was difficult under the best of circumstances, and these were far from the best. "Pride isn't the issue," she said. "I just—"

"An Endicott does not hide and cower and skulk! You should be proud! Grateful for the sacrifices your family has made so that you could have all these privileges! Go look at the statue of Augustus Endicott in front of the library, and reflect upon all that he did for you!"

Yeah, giving T-Rex a perfect opportunity to blow her head off with a sniper rifle, at his leisure. Liv squeezed her reddened eyes shut to block out her mother's outraged countenance. Right now, cowering and skulking sounded very good to her. Very calm and restful.

"Sure I'm proud of being an Endicott, Mother," she said wearily. "But this guy is trying to kill me. I don't want to be dead. That's all."

"Stop being overdramatic," Amelia Endicott snapped. "Are you insinuating that I don't care about your safety? I've tried your whole life to help you make all the right choices, and have you ever listened?"

Liv forced herself to exhale, and slowly inhaled again. "This is not my fault." The words fell one at a time from her lips, like little rocks.

"Saying 'it's not my fault' will get you nowhere. Just look at yourself!" Her mother gestured at the mirror on the dining room wall.

Liv looked, and wished she hadn't. She was wild-haired, hollow-eyed, white-lipped, grimy. A chimney sweep from a Dickens novel, but for her out-of-control bosom. Just one more of the many things that offended Amelia Endicott. She'd tried for years to convince her daughter to get those indecorously bouncy boobs surgically reduced. Ouch. Not.

Her father gave her an uneasy look. "Honey, maybe you should ease off," he murmured, in a wheedling tone. "It's been quite a day."

"All I want is what's best for her." Amelia's voice quivered on the edge of tears. "It's all I've ever wanted."

"I know that." Liv fought off the weariness that rolled over her like a tank whenever she argued with her mother. "The police-woman told me that changing my name and starting over is an option to consider when you're dealing with a dangerous—"

"Not an option," Amelia said crisply. "Not for you. Other familes prominent in politics or business make high security part of their lifestyle. They simply adjust their attitude and expectations!"

Liv sighed. "But I—"

"Your father and I are willing to invest in round-the-clock protection so that you can live your normal life as an Endicott!"

Liv tried again. "But I don't—"

"I don't want to hear that negative attitude," her mother warned. "You'll have to give up this whim of running a bookstore, of course. Far too much exposure. The same goes with library work. I can't fathom why you ever wanted to do anything so dusty and fusty in the first place, but never mind. Let it go, and move on, honey!"

"But I'm not fit for anything else," Liv protested. "All my training and education is in literature and library science."

"You can do what I've been trying to persuade you to do since you were in college," her mother announced triumphantly. "You can go into the advertising department of ECE! Any location you like, darling. Seattle, Olympia, San Francisco, Portland, Spokane. Location is virtual these days. You could work from home, with this new video conferencing technology. You're so creative and imaginative, Livvy. You were wasted as a librarian, or a shopkeeper, for God's sake. In fact, this whole thing might just end up being a blessing in disguise."

Hah. Liv gritted her teeth. "I wouldn't be any good at—"

"Nonsense. You'd be brilliant. And the best thing about it is that anywhere you worked, you'd be guarded by ECE corporate security! Imagine what a load off our minds, honey! Knowing that every day, you're as safe as if you're locked in a bank vault!"

Liv winced. "I'd go bonkers if I worked for ECE."

"Stop doubting yourself, Livvy! We've always believed in you!"

Believed in who? Whoever this person was that Amelia Endicott so ardently believed in was light years away from the daughter she actually had. But there was no point in trying to make her understand.

"We'll find a high security condo, wherever you decide to settle," her mother went on. "You'll have to give up all that hiking and running, but you can work out indoors. There's always grocery delivery . . ."

Her mother's babble faded into a faraway hum in Liv's ears, as if she were alone beneath a glass bell. She thought of her mother's collection of antique dolls in the parlor of her Seattle town house. Each stood alone, stiffly poised, a perfect ceramic smile on each painted face.

Pretty. Content with their lot. Happy to please. Compliant.

It was so painful, disappointing her mother for the umpteenth time. Forever rowing against such a powerful current wore her out, but this current was pulling her towards a deadly waterfall.

She thought of the life in store for her. No more wandering on hiking trails, staring at the mountains. No more walking on fogbound beaches, watching the surf wash away the tracks of the seagulls. No more cuddling at night in her armchair in the ramshackle house in the pines, reading fantasy and sci-fi and romance novels. No more morning jogs, watching the sunrise. No more poring over book catalogs as she decided what to stock. No more ripping opening boxes of shiny books, leafing through crisp pages, making notes of what to read later. No more reading to starry-eyed little kids at Story Hour.

Nope. She'd be a lonesome rat in a cage in an antiseptic condo. Running on a treadmill in a basement room. Crammed into hose, heels, and a power suit. Ferried back and forth in a car service to a job that bored her silly. Locked in a bank vault. She shuddered with inner cold.

". . . have the courtesy to concentrate on what I'm saying, Livvy! Didn't you hear me at all?"

"Sorry," she murmured. "I'm kind of wiped out."

"Concentrate," her mother snapped. "Your father and I have decided that you and Blair should announce your engagement."

That snapped her right to attention. She stared at them wildly. "What engagement? What on earth are you talking about?"

"I hate to rush you, Liv." Blair's voice was earnest. "I know you want to wait until you're sure, and I respect that. But we don't have to get married right away. It's just theater." He grabbed her hand and dropped a gallant kiss on the back of it. "For now," he added coyly.

"You have to move fast, now that McCloud is showing his hand," her mother said. "We'll work out the details later."

She blinked "What hand? What does Sean have to do with this?"

Blair and her mother exchanged glances. "You mean the possibility hasn't even crossed your mind?" Her mother's voice was pitying. "That we've identified your stalker? Liv. Honey. Wake up."

Liv was so startled, she let out a burst of laughter, which turned quickly into a phlegmy coughing fit. "You think that Sean is the stalker?" she gasped out finally. "But that's totally ridiculous!"

Blair's face hardened into that pompous, judgmental mask that had always stopped her short whenever she'd been in danger of sliding down the slippery slope into being his fiancée. "There are precedents," he said stiffly. "His father was severely mentally ill. He's trained in the use of explosives. He's worked as a mercenary. His twin committed suicide. He's unstable. I went to school with him, Liv. I know what he's capable of. He set off a bomb in the teachers' bathroom in the sixth grade. He had no concept of civilized behavior. He was constantly fighting, constantly mouthing off. The teachers were desperate."

"Uh, Blair? Small detail. He was twelve." She couldn't keep the irony out of her voice, even though she knew she would pay for it.

Right on cue, her mother let out a distressed huffing sound. "Here we go again. Defending him again, just like old times. You never learn."

"Reality check, people," Liv announced, looking around at each of them in turn. "Sean McCloud saved my life today. Yours, too, Blair."

Her father leaned over, groaning, and clutched his chest. Amelia leaped to his side in an instant, making anxious, solicitous sounds.

Liv had seen the melodrama before, so she turned back to Blair. "I cannot believe that Sean would ever do that to me."

"Of course not," Blair said. "You think the best of people. That's very well and good, in normal life, but this is not normal life. Sean McCloud is strange. His family is strange. What's happening to you is strange. Don't you feel how the strangeness matches up, like a puzzle?"

Nope. Sure didn't. She shook her head. "I don't get your reasoning, Blair. Why did he stop us from getting into the car?"

"Because he wanted to impress you. He wanted the glory of saving you. He wanted you to be grateful to him. He staged the whole thing to make you feel vulnerable. Don't you see? It's so obvious."

There was no point in telling the truth to Blair when he had that look on his face. Sean McCloud did not have to throw himself in front of a bomb to impress her. All he had to do was crook his finger and smile.

Barely that. He could just be his own charismatic self. Watch the women drop like flies. Herself being the first to hit the pavement.

Whoever T-Rex was, he had an rotting dead spot inside him. In her recent crash course on arsonists, assassins, serial killers and rapists, she'd learned that they were usually loners, failures. Men with no interpersonal skills, no talent at relating with women.

Sean McCloud had no problems relating to women. He had to beat them away from himself to breathe. As for his interpersonal skills, well. The man was capable of talking her into multiple orgasms on the phone. Weird though he might be, there was nothing dead about him.

And since none of these reflections could be profitably shared with the present company, she changed the subject. "Why didn't anybody tell me about Kev McCloud committing suicide?" she asked.

Blair and her parents exchanged uneasy glances.

"It didn't seem relevant, dear," her mother said.

Liv stared at her. "He was my friend," she said quietly.

"Friend, my foot," Amelia said tartly. "He was deranged, and probably dangerous. It's tragic that he didn't get the help he needed in time, and I'm very sorry for his family, but you were my first concern, honey, not him. You needed to make a clean break, and telling you hard-luck stories about those unfortunate McCloud boys would have just made things more difficult and confusing for you."

Liv twined her fingers together. Her hands were cold and clammy, white beneath the grime. Her eyes stung with tears. Maybe her mother was right, but that didn't make it easier to swallow.

The last time she'd seen Kev McCloud, he'd been sweat-soaked, wild-eyed, raving about people who were trying to kill him. She'd had no idea at the time that he was mentally ill. He'd scared her out of her wits when he scribbled down that coded note, shoved his sketchbook into her hand, and told her to take it to Sean and run, or they'd kill her, too.

She'd run, all right. He'd been pretty damned convincing.

Poor Kevin. He'd been so sweet. Funny and brilliant. Sean had been immensely proud of his brother's genius, his accomplishments.

It broke her heart. And speaking of heartbreak, that had been the same day as that horrible five minute conversation with Sean at the jail. The five minutes that had ended her innocence and split her life in half.

She stared down at her hands, realizing how badly she stank of smoke. She got up, knees wobbling. "I'm going to take a shower."

"Excellent idea," Amelia said. "You just relax. We'll take care of all the details. Shall I have Pamela bring you up a sandwich?"

Her stomach clenched unpleasantly at the thought of food.

"Nothing," she said. "Thanks. 'Night."

She hauled herself up the stairs, and made her way to the bedroom. She stumbled, but her exhaustion had a jittery, excited edge.

Because Sean had flirted with her? Please. He flirted with every woman he saw. He was programmed that way. It was nothing personal.

Even so, thinking about Sean was so much more fizzy and fun than thinking about the tar pit of her family life, or the ruins of her bookstore. Or T-Rex, out in the dark somewhere, thinking about her.

She shuddered. T-Rex's attention felt like a foul lake of toxic waste, lapping up against her consciousness. The only thing that helped was the foolish fancy that Sean McCloud was thinking about her, too.

That evened out the score. Just enough so that she could breathe.

It was just a mind game, of course. Sean didn't care about her, she knew that. But who cared? If the trick worked, she would use it.

She stumbled in the dark room, tripping over her suitcase, but hesitated before flipping on the bedside light. She had no desire to announce to any malevolent presence outside that someone was in the bedroom. She flipped on the light in the internal connecting bathroom and left the door a few inches open. A fine sliver of light was enough.

She perched on the bed, and doubled over, pressing her face against those ugly, baggy pajama pants. How pathetically lame, that she hadn't grown out of this lingering obsession. After thousands of dollars' worth of head shrinkage, she and her therapist had concluded that she badly needed to transgress against her family's control. Well and good. She still needed to transgress, evidently.

What better way to distract herself from all this crap than to drag out her fantasy man, with his gorgeous body, his warm lips, his clever hands? Watch Liv forget the past, her pride, her own goddamn name.

It was ironic. Their affair had lasted one month. They'd never even had sex. He'd just worked her into a hot, sweaty fever on the phone, telling her how it would be when they finally did the deed. What he would do with his hands, his tongue. And all the rest of his manly stuff.

Her on her bed, beet red and speechless with longing. Him, slouched in the phone booth, slipping in quarter after quarter so he could keep on stroking her, touching her. Torturing her with words.

In the hindsight of sexual experience, she knew how improbable his promises were. They'd done nothing but spoil her for the real thing.

She'd been almost eighteen that summer. She hadn't known anyone her own age in town, after being shuffled from one elite private school to another. She was shy, withdrawn. The only constant in her life were books. They had been her refuge—until she met Sean.

It started with that summer school course. She'd gotten a C+ in chemistry her senior year, trashing her perfect four point average. Her mother's response had been to bully the school into letting Liv retake a summer school equivalent with the hopes of adjusting her grade.

It was a waste of time, since she was already accepted into the college she wanted, and had no further interest in chemistry. But no. That C+ was a moral failing, to be corrected by wholesome discipline.

Her mother never imagined what kind of trouble was going to saunter into Schaeffer Auditorium. So much for wholesome discipline.

The lecture hall had been nearly empty. Most of the students were swimming at the Falls. Liv had been there, though, dutifully scribbling notes. It was surprisingly interesting. The grad student lecturing was great. Kev McCloud was his name, a tall, skinny guy with blond hair that stuck out all over his head. When he talked about chemistry, his eyes lit up like green flashlights. That enthusiasm was contagious.

Then the door to the hall creaked open. She turned to look, and bye bye, carbon structures. That was the last note she ever took.

The guy in the doorway looked as out of place as a wild panther. Luxurious blond hair. Sleeves ripped off a denim work shirt, showing off thick, ropy arms, broad shoulders. The lecturer, who she learned later was his twin, said "Don't come to my class late, you furry little punk."

Shocked murmurs and giggles swept the room. The pantherlike

apparition was unfazed. "Lighten up, you tight-assed geek," he replied.

The guy lecturing rolled his eyes and launched back into his lecture. The panther turned, scanned the hall. His eyes lit on her.

She looked down, face hot, heart tripping, as he paced to the back of the auditorium. He found her aisle and began slithering towards her between rows of seats. She was hiding in the back behind her hair, the hall was nearly empty, and he was coming to sit with her. She'd entered a parallel universe. The sky had fallen. Time ran backwards. Pigs flew.

"Is this chair free?" His voice had been so low and soft.

This one, plus ninety others exactly like it is what she should have said, to spare herself a decade and a half of obsession and regret. But she hadn't.

She'd jerked her head yes. Sealed her own fate.

His body lowered itself with sinuous, catlike grace into the chair. His shoulders were so broad, he exceeded the space alotted to him.

His bare arm touched her own. Oh. He was so . . . so *hot*.

His arm was thick with sinewy muscles, glinting with sun-bleached hair. She was frantically conscious of that scorching contact between his arm and hers. It was connected to every nerve in her body.

He smelled like herbal shampoo. His hands, resting on jeans-clad thighs, were long and battered, covered with scratches, ink stains.

Things like this never happened to her. She let her hair fall across her face and vibrated with emotion, studying whatever she could without turning her head. The holes in his jeans, the split tops of his boots, mended with silver duct tape. The class ended. People rustled and murmured. It made no sense that such a gorgeous guy should single her out. There had to be a punch line. She braced herself for it.

Then he brushed her hair to one side and looked behind it.

She made a squeaking sound that only a dog could hear. Every strand of her hair transformed into an exquisitely receptive sensory organ. Hot-cool ripples of excitement chased themselves over her skin.

He looked into her face, his eyes full of intense curiosity. She was immobile, open-mouthed. Vibrating. Seconds passed.

"Wow," he whispered.

And that was all it took. She was his. Heart and soul. Lost.

Liv dashed the tears out of her eyes and heaved herself up off the bed. She tossed her smoky, nasty clothes into a pile and plucked her cream silk robe out of her suitcase with the tips of her fingers, hoping not to smudge it. Which reminded her of the greasy handprint on Sean's T-shirt.

Of course. True to form. Everything referred right back to Sean, in an endless, obsessive feedback loop. Seeing him had brought back so vividly the way he'd made her feel that summer. Strong and connected, so aware of the grace around her. Certain that all her dreams could come true, because Sean's very existence was proof of that.

How unbelievably innocent she'd been. How stupid.

The closest she'd come to that feeling, post-Sean, was when she finally decided to open her bookstore. Well, hell. So much for that. Maybe it was just a mirage. An ephemeral cocktail of endorphins.

She stared at her pale, pinched face, the hell-hag snarl of hair. She must have looked like such horrific crap when he'd seen her today.

And it *did . . . not . . . matter*. Goddamnit. Let it go. Forever. Let a hot shower wash it away.

Done, purified, she wrapped a towel around herself, opened the door—and would have screamed, if her lungs had been capable of sucking in air.

Sean McCloud was sitting on her bed.

Chapter
7

Sean winced as the bathroom door slammed shut in his face. Ouch. On the plus side, it had been a fabulous stroke of luck to catch her in the shower, giving him the perfect opportunity to dust her stuff with beacons. Tonight he was a firm adherent to the classic McCloud school of thought; plant bugs first, apologize later.

He'd been trying to figure out how to spare her the adrenaline rush when she came out of the bathroom, to say nothing of the embarrassment should she prove to be buck naked. Unfortunately, he hadn't come up with any bright ideas in time. His brains were fried.

The door burst open, and Liv marched out, no longer wrapped in a towel. Her skimpy silk robe was swathed around her so tight, it showed every detail of her taut nipples. Christ, she was pretty. He loved that uppity, chin-in-the-air posture.

"You practically gave me a heart attack." Her voice was chilly with royal hauteur. "Are you nuts? What are you doing? Did you sneak in?"

He snorted. "Can you see your mother inviting me in?"

"Don't answer a question with a question. It's snotty and annoying. What are your intentions, Sean? Should I scream for help?"

"Please don't." His smile faltered. "I didn't know your number. Your parents would have me wrapped in chains and sunk into a lake if they saw me, so sneaking was my only option. Sorry I scared you."

"How did you get in?" She flounced past him, dug through her suitcase for her comb. "I thought there were policemen outside. I thought they had alarms all over the place. For all the good it's done me, I might as well be in my own place."

He shrugged. "The cops didn't see me. I slithered alongside the hedge, climbed the maple, crawled onto the oak that grows up next to the roof. Then I came in through the attic gable window, which was not alarmed, for your information. Through the crawl space, down through the trapdoor into the laundry room . . . and here I am. Piece of cake."

"What enterprise." She wrenched the comb through her hair.

"I wanted to see how safe you were in the bosom of your family."

He couldn't stop staring, though he could tell it made her uncomfortable. She pulled her robe tight, evidently unaware of how the sheer silk showcased her awesome body. Her white throat bobbed.

"So?" she demanded. "What did you conclude? How safe am I?"

"Not at all," he said flatly. "If T-Rex is a tenth as good as me, he could be sitting right where I am now. I'm betting he is. Somebody should tell your folks this. That somebody probably should not be me."

"Yes, they're prejudiced," she admitted. "But if you hadn't stopped us from getting into the car, I'd be dead right now."

"There is that," Sean agreed. "Did that earn me some points?"

"With who?" She laughed nervously. "With my mother?"

"I don't give a shit about your mother. I'm only interested in you."

She fended him off with sarcasm. "I'm so honored," she said. "But you were way, way down there into the negative numbers, point-wise."

His mouth twisted in a humorless smile. "Am I up to zero yet?"

She dragged the comb through another tangled lock. "I don't know," she said. "I don't know why you're here, what you want, why you care. What does zero mean? A blank slate? Like nothing ever happened between us? I'm sorry, but I just can't pretend that."

He shook his head slowly. "I wouldn't want you to."

They stared at each other until Liv's eyes dropped. She dug the comb into another thick snarl, her fingers trembling.

So she wasn't immune. Angry, but not indifferent. Triumph leaped inside him, like flames. He wrenched his gaze away from her face. The wad of condoms was stiff in his jeans pocket, digging into his thigh. T-Rex. He had come here to talk to her about T-Rex.

"So you have no clue who this guy is?" he asked. "Most stalkers are known to their victims."

"Yes, I know that," she said shakily. "But I have no idea."

"No jealous ex-boyfriends?"

She shook her head again. "Not a one."

"I don't see how an ex-boyfriend of yours could be anything but jealous, princess."

The statement hung in the air. She lifted her chin. "Are you jealous, Sean?"

He clenched down on the hot flare of excitement. "What, you mean, I count as an ex-boyfriend? I rate the list? I'm honored."

Her gaze was penetrating "Don't wiggle out of the question."

He took a deep breath, and threw it out there. "Is this a sneaky way of asking if it was me who burned your store and rigged a bomb in your car? Is that what those idiots have been telling you?"

She opened her mouth, but nothing came out.

"My brothers can vouch for me, if there's any doubt," he told her. "But even if I were so jealous I was sick with it, I would never hurt you, Liv. Not you, nor any other innocent person. Never. Is that clear?"

She stared into his eyes, and nodded. "That's clear," she said.

"You believe me?" He could hardly believe it.

"I believe you."

He let out a jerky sigh as something inside him finally relaxed.

"I still want to know how you knew about the bomb," she said.

Sean stared down at the pink hooked rug. "It'll sound strange."

"Try me."

It took a while to puzzle out the best way to describe something so intangible. "I have . . . feelings. When I'm in a combat situation, I get warnings. Prickles on my neck, tingling in my balls. I was trained to act on it without thinking. It only works if you trust it blindly."

Her clear white brow furrowed. "You mean, like, intuition?"

"You could call it that," he said. "Maybe it comes from growing up with my dad, I imagine. You know about his illness, right?"

"Yes, I heard that he was—"

"A nutcase? Yeah. He saw danger everywhere. Every place was a potential minefield. Anything, a pen, a jar of nails, a carton of milk, could be a bomb in disguise. It was stressful, living with the guy."

"Oh. Uh, wow," she murmured. "I see how that might—"

"Skew your perspective, yeah," he finished, matter-of-factly. "My brothers and I didn't have any other point of reference. Dad's bad guys were behind every tree." He paused, reflecting. "It's not that far from reality, now that I think about it. Look at T-Rex. You never know."

She was shaken. "I'm so sorry."

"I'm not trying to make you feel bad for me," he said impatiently. "I'm just showing you my train of reasoning. The letter was part of it. You said T-Rex wanted to make you burn. He used the word 'explosive.' That made me think about Kev's truck exploding, which reminded me of a dream I had. Kev was in it, and he was worried about your car."

She was oddly gratified by that. "My car? Kev? Really?"

"Yeah. So I saw you and Madden walking towards your car, and it all came together. The note, the explosion, the dream." He lifted his hands. "There it is. My convoluted mental processes laid bare."

Her thoughtful eyes stayed on him, making him twitch. "This is the part where you tell me I'm a lunatic, right?"

"I don't think you're a lunatic," she said. "Or if you are, I'm lucky that you are. I'd be blown to bits if you weren't. So thank you."

"You don't have to thank me. I didn't have any choice."

She looked perplexed. "What's that supposed to mean?"

He shrugged. "It means what it means. I'm not playing word games. It's not something I did voluntarily, so thanks are meaningless."

Liv wrapped her arms across her tits. He got real busy trying not to think about how soft and lush and hot she must be under there, all perfumed from her various girl goops. He forced his mind back on track.

"I was wondering if you'd let me look at T-Rex's e-mails," he said.

Her eyes narrowed. "Why?"

The question stymied him for a moment, but there was no reason not to tell her the naked truth. "Because I'm interested. Because I don't want you to get hurt. Because I'm so curious, it's fucking killing me."

"Ah. Well. If you put it that way," she murmured.

She pulled out a laptop out of her suitcase, sat down and tippety tapped on it. The light from the screen lit up her face, serenely lovely in concentration. She gave him a quick smile, and laid the opened computer on his knees. "I opened the folder. There are nine of them."

The dates ranged the past three weeks. He clicked and read them in sequence. They were just as she had described. Pseudo-poetic slime. Clingy declarations of obsessive love, minute observations of her physical charms, comments on her clothing and activities. The last three had suggestions that grew more sexually explicit with each succeeding letter. His jaw tightened as he read them. Scumbag asshole.

He nodded, snapped her laptop closed, and handed it back to her.

"So? What do you think?" she asked, setting it aside.

"My first impression is self-conscious, artificial," he said. "Like he's following a template."

"The fire and the bomb weren't artificial," she said.

"No, they sure weren't," he agreed. "Thanks for letting me look."

"You barely looked." Her tone was faintly accusatory. "It took you, what, two minutes?"

"I have a photographic memory," he told her. "I'll be reading those e-mails all night long." His gaze swept the dim room and came to rest on the chemistry textbook on the bedside table. He leafed through it. "Wow, here's a blast from the past. I thought you hated this thing."

"I did hate it. I only liked it when your brother was explaining it."

Sean nodded. "Yeah, Kev was a genius at making that stuff inter-esting. He got his undergrad degree in two years. Could have done it in less, if he hadn't had to work nights. He was already working on his thesis when he . . ." He stopped, swallowed. "Ah, shit. Never mind."

"You were pretty brilliant at it yourself," she said, to break the poignant silence. "You didn't even need the textbook."

His short laugh hurt his burning throat. "Son of a bitch cost eighty bucks. Why buy it when you can read the one at the library?"

"You never took notes at the lectures, either, but you always re-membered everything," she said. "It made me so jealous."

He flipped the textbook shut. "Dad taught us to remember what we heard. For him, taking notes was a sign of mental sloppiness."

"Wow," she murmured. "That's rigorous."

"Rigorous. Yeah. Good word to describe Eamon McCloud. The trick is to make your selections as the data comes in. You organize the important stuff. The rest you toss into the garbage." He paused. "I throw away the garbage. But I remember all the important stuff perfectly."

Her eyes grew wary at his tone. "Oh yeah? And what stuff is that?" She picked up the comb and dug it into another hank of her hair.

He flinched when she yanked it through. "For Christ's sake, would you stop that? Give me that comb." He plucked it out of her hands and held it out of reach when she tried to grab it back.

She lunged for it. "Sean, this is not funny—"

"Sit," he ordered. "On the bed." A brief wrestling match ensued which he promptly won, and soon she was seated on the bed, clamped in the vee of his thighs. He grabbed a lock of her hair and started in on it. "Where were we? Oh, yeah. We were talking about what's important enough to remember, and what's insignificant enough to forget."

The position was intimate. Her silk-clad hips were so smooth, so hot where they touched the inside of his thighs. His body thrummed.

"Sean," she whispered. "I'm not comfortable with this."

"Your hair will be," he assured her. "Just relax, and let me be your lady-in-waiting for a few minutes. It's no big deal."

She was silent as he worked slowly up the length of the lock of hair, smoothing out every little tangle until it combed smooth and easy down the entire length. He laid that lock over her shoulder and chose another one, taking it patient and slow, like he had all the time in the world. Drawing it out, as long as he possibly could.

"So, ah, what do you think is important enough to remember?" she inquired, in a brisk, let's-move-on type of voice.

He draped a smooth, perfect lock of hair over her shoulder, and chose another one to lavish his attention on.

"You," he said.

Oh dear. This was like one of her private middle-of-the-night fantasies. Sean, materializing in her bedroom and telling her she was important to him. She could not fall for this lethally dangerous hooey.

"Oh, get out," she quavered. "Let go of me. This is a bad idea."

He grabbed her around the waist as she tried to get up. "I remember every detail," he said. "From the moment I first saw you. What you wore, how your hair was dressed, the smell of your shampoo. Everything. 3-D, full sensory overload. I can't shake it."

She twisted and gave him a quelling glance. "Shut up, Sean. That is just so much calculated bullshit, and I'm not falling for it."

"The first day, at the construction site, you wore a white blouse," he said softly. "Your skirt was blue. Your hair hung down to your ass."

"Construction site?" She frowned. "I met you at Schaeffer Auditorium. At your brother's class."

"I'd seen you before," he told her. Every slow stroke of the comb through her damp hair was a caress. "All the guys on the crew were talking about the big boss's gorgeous daughter, back from prep school. Then one day you came to the site with your dad. You didn't even notice us poor bastards staring after you. Tongues dangling to our knees."

She racked her brains, trying to remember. "I don't believe you."

"It's true," he said. "You wafted past, looking off into the distance. There goes the porcelain princess. You can look, but you can't touch."

"I am not made out of porcelain," she whispered.

"I know that. I know exactly how warm and soft you are." He tossed the comb onto the bed, and ran his fingers through her hair, fanning it out over her shoulders. "I'll tell you a guilty secret," he murmured. "I wasn't auditing Kev's class to learn organic chemistry. I knew that material by the time I was twelve. I came for you, Liv."

Sean McCloud in full-out seduction mode was deadly dangerous. She groped around for something to deflect, distract. "Is it true that you bombed the teacher's bathroom when you were in sixth grade?"

He froze, and started to vibrate with laughter. "Wow. Of all the ghosts from my past, that's the one I least expected. Who told you that? Was it that asswipe Blair Madden? He always was a fucking snitch."

"Just answer the question, please," she said primly.

"Aw, hell. It was just a couple of molecules of gunpowder packed into a milkshake straw, duct taped shut with a fuse attached. I wouldn't dignify that by calling it a bomb. I did wire the door to that stall shut, so no one would use it, and when Harris headed in to take his afternoon dump, I sneaked in and lit the fuse. I wanted to teach him a lesson. I didn't want to blow his ass off."

She twisted around to see his face. "Why did you do it?"

He shrugged. "I was angry at him. Kev aced all the math tests. Harris accused him of cheating. As if Kev needed to cheat on seventh grade math. He was already studying theoretical physics. On his own."

"I see," she murmured.

"Harris got Kev suspended. That pissed me off."

His hands were busy in her hair, stroking slowly down its length. She turned, caught him pressing a lock of hair to his lips. He dropped it, lifted his hands, his face mock-guilty. "Oops," he whispered. "Sorry."

She looked away, stifling a giggle. This was nuts. She'd almost died today, and this man was making her act like a silly girl.

It was so easy to laugh with him. It was one of the most seductive things about him, and practically everything was seductive about him.

She'd been so shy back then. Not only with boys. With everyone. But once she got over her initial slack-jawed stupor at how gorgeous he was, Sean had been just pure, goofy fun to be with. He made her feel smart and witty. Never made her feel like she'd run up against a blank wall of incomprehension. Never made her feel like what she said was being picked apart and twisted to serve someone else's hidden agenda. He just listened to her, thought about what she'd said, and responded.

It was effortless, it was wonderful. It was magic.

And it still was. Damn him to hell, it still was. *Those who do not remember the past are condemned to repeat it.* Or at least to repeat that saying.

She steeled herself. "Has it occurred to you how weird this is? Sweet-talking me, after what you said to me the last time we met?"

His stroking hands stopped, and his body went very still. "No, actually," he said warily. "I was just enjoying being close to you."

"So that conversation is one of those insignificant things you decided not to remember?" She was horrified to feel her throat start to quiver.

He didn't answer. She felt the heat of his face, pressing hard against her shoulder. "I remember it," he said. "I'm sorry."

"Sorry?" She shoved his knees apart to free herself, and kept her back to him while she adjusted her robe, and her face. "You must have a split personality. There's the sweet, cuddly Sean, and there's the cruel, horrible Sean. Is it fun to wind women up and then watch them flap around when you dump them? Do you secretly hate women?"

"No." His mouth was a hard, unhappy line. "I don't. Not at all. I especially don't hate you. I'm sorry I did that. I had my reasons."

For some reason, this infuriated her all the more. "What an odd thing to say. Shove somebody off a building, then run downstairs, stand over their broken body, and say, "Sorry, but I had my reasons."

"Liv, I—"

"I know your reasons. Having a clingy chick like me glomming onto you bored you. So why are you here? I'm the same damn person, just older and stodgier. If I bored you then, I promise, I'll bore you now."

"You never bored me," he said.

"So had you found someone more exciting than me? Someone more sexually skilled? And that was your way of getting rid of—"

"No," he said. "Christ, no. Can we please just start again?"

"No, Sean. We can't." She spun on her heels and headed towards the door, but as she grabbed the knob, he seized her from behind, sliding his arm around her waist and pulling her back against his body.

"No. Wait," he pleaded. "Just a second, Liv. Please."

She gathered her breath to scream. He clapped his hand over her mouth. She bit, squirming. "Shh," he crooned. "You have a right to be mad. Bite me, kick me, just don't force me to cope with your mother."

She betrayed herself with the muffled snort of laughter. He carefully lifted his hand away. "If you don't want to deal with my mother, don't break into her house," she said. "You're suspiciously good at it. Is burglary the career path you finally settled on?"

"No. Believe it or not, breaking into houses is not something I do on a regular basis. I only broke into this house because you were in it."

He sank to his knees. She backed away, suspicious of the wicked gleam in his eye. "What the hell are you doing now, for God's sake?"

"Begging for mercy. Trying to come across less threatening. I'm too tall. Do I make you nervous?" He lurched towards her on his knees.

"Certainly." She backed up until she hit the wall. "And kneeling does not make you look harmless. It makes you look ridiculous."

He grinned. "Cool. I get all kinds of mileage out of ridiculous."

"Not with me you won't," she warned. "The clown game will not work with me. I am so not charmed, you get me? Not. Charmed."

He lurched across the room towards her on his knees. "Being scolded by a tough, unrelenting bitch goddess in a silk robe is just about the most fun I've had in fifteen years."

"Stop it! I cannot believe we are having this conversation. I should be screaming about the armed intruder in my bedroom."

He blinked at her innocently. "How do you know I'm armed?"

"Oh, just a wild guess? You look like the type."

"I do? Aw, shoot. And I thought my disguise as a normal person was working. Usually I don't pack. It makes me tense. But I was already tense today, what with bombs and whatnot, so I brought my trusty SP 101 Ruger." He pulled up his jeans, showed her the revolver in the ankle holster. "I've got a knife on the other leg. And my hands and feet could be considered lethal weapons, if you wanted to be picky about it."

"Oh, give me a break," she muttered. "Lethal weapons, my butt."

"I have a legal permit to carry concealed," he assured her.

"Are you showing me all your macho hardware to impress me?"

He chuckled softly. "I don't know. Would it work? What would impress you the most? Tell me. I'll try to deliver."

"Seeing you act like a grown-up, for once in your life," she snapped. "Though actually, that wouldn't just impress me. It would astonish me."

His smile faded. He gazed at her, and rose to his feet. "What's the grown-up thing to do?" he asked. "That's a toughie, for a maturity challenged clown like me. The most grown-up thing would have been to stay away from you in the first place. I've already fucked that up. Next best would be to crawl back out of the rathole I came in. Slink back to the gutter with my tail between my legs. Is that what you want?"

Liv opened her mouth to say yes. The word would not form. She coughed, and tried again. "Don't guilt trip me," she said. "It's not fair."

"Hold your breath. I'm going to act like a grown-up for the first and probably only time in my life. Don't blink, or you'll miss it."

"Would you just stop being ridiculous—"

"That's what I'm trying to do." His voice rang. "I need your help, though. Say it simple and clear, in a language that even a cement-head like me can understand. Say, get the fuck out of my bedroom, Sean, and stay away for the rest of my natural life."

She swallowed, over a lump in her throat. "And you'll go?"

"And I'll go."

Seconds ticked by. He stared, waiting. She couldn't speak, couldn't move. Seconds turned to minutes.

"You're not saying it, princess," he prompted finally.

Goddamn him. Her hot face quivered. She put her hands over her face before it could crumble. Sean watched her cry, unembarrassed.

She couldn't stand it. She spun around, put her back to him.

"I'm getting more confused every second," he said softly. "It's dangerous to confuse me, baby. Ask anyone."

She shook her head. "Just shut up. You sadistic bastard."

"That's a good start, but it's not what I told you to say. Say it. Toss me out, if you're going to, because the suspense is killing me."

"Fuck you, Sean McCloud." The words burst out with breathless violence.

"Sure, baby." He sounded as if he were smiling. "In a heartbeat."

"Don't." She forced the words out through the knot in her throat. "Don't jerk me around. Stop torturing me."

"I didn't mean to." He sounded puzzled. "I just wanted to talk. See T-Rex's emails. Make you smile, since you had such a shitty day. I didn't mean to make you cry." She shivered, as his hand came to rest on her shoulder. "If you don't want me to leave, what do you want?"

"Why even bother asking?" The words burst out with a bitterness she hadn't known she felt. "I can't get what I want. You taught me that."

"I did?" He parted her damp hair, and pressed his hot lips against the back of her neck. "I'm sorry I did that. But you know what, Liv?"

"What?" she whispered.

He kissed it again. "Sometimes you can get what you want."

She shivered, almost whimpering at the soft, hot caress of his mouth, the light pressure of his teeth against her sensitive nape.

"No. I can't," she replied, voice quivering. "The price is too high."

"Sometimes the price is worth it." The edge of his teeth dragged over her skin, then his lips, in a devastatingly gentle kiss.

"I'm crazy to let you touch me," she whispered.

"Yes," he agreed. "Crazy wild. I love the way your hair grows down to a swirly cowlick, right here at your nape. With that sexy beauty mark right beneath it, at four o'clock. So fucking beautiful, it just kills me."

She shook with a shaky mix of laughter and tears. "Get real."

"I am real. I remember every last one of them." He circled his fingertips tenderly over the silk covering her shoulders. "Go on. Test me. I'll draw you a map of the beauty marks on your shoulders and back. I memorized them, like the constellations. Then we can compare."

"Yeah, right," she muttered. "I know your slimy dog tricks."

His lips moved over her shoulders, his breath a delicious caress. "I went nuts for the one on your left foot. About an inch above your big toe. I always wanted to just fall to your feet and smooch away at it until you were giggling like crazy. Then I'd work my way up. Slowly."

Liv opened her eyes. The door to the bathroom hung wide open. Drops of condensation rolled down the full length mirror on it, making a surreal, striped field in which their dark forms were half reflected.

Sean's eyes burned into hers. Her face looked almost frightened, eyes dilated. Her cheeks flushed hot, moist red. The sash of her robe had slipped loose, as if mischievous fairy fingers were teasing it open.

She didn't move to stop them.

Chapter
8

The sash fell open and slithered over her hips, landing on her feet with a whisper of silk. Her robe was open, less than an inch, revealing a shadowy strip of her body between long panels of pale, gleaming fabric.

Close it, goddamnit, the little scolding voice in her head said. *Yank that sucker closed, tie the sash tight, and say what has to be said to make this guy disappear. He's more trouble than he's worth. Way more.*

The yammering voice faded into a meaningless blur of white noise in the back of her head. In the forefront, the image of the two of them in the mirror grew ever clearer as drips coursed their way inexorably downward, each one washing its own stripe through the steamy surface.

The robe gaped a little more now, though neither of them had moved. He could see her body. Her taut nipples pressed against the delicate silk. The valley between them, the heavy undercurve of each one, the swell of her belly, the dip of her navel was all clearly visible. The tuft of dark hair that covered her mound.

And she was letting him look. As if he had a right. As if she wanted him to. As if she'd been waiting for years, offering for years. Aching for him to look at her, to touch her. To take her.

The silence, the darkness, wove a spell around them both, thickening until it was palpable. It was a deep, throbbing hum, blotting out thoughts, fears, doubts and leaving only feelings. Wild, unruly feelings that were gathering a huge momentum, swelling into a power she could not hope to control. Her eyes were locked with his in the mirror, and the slow-growing realization became a certainty.

The impossible, the unthinkable, was about to happen. She was actually going to do this. He was going to seduce her, and she was going to let him. His hand drifted around, touched her face. Cupped her cheek. She blushed even hotter beneath his hand. Turned her face to him, leaning into his touch, like a cat being petted.

She terrified herself. She hadn't thought herself capable of such depths of self-destructive stupidity, but she wanted this, desperately.

Why not? Why the hell not?

The decision abruptly made itself, without her help. *Yes.* She would live this fantasy, in full. No stupid romantic expectations.

Just hot sex. After all this drama, she was entitled to that much.

He traced the edge of her ear, swirling in tenderly to circle the inner whorl, sending shudders of pleasure through her startled nerves.

He smoothed a clinging lock of hair away. She licked her lips, her breath coming sharply. He touched her lips, his hand moving with majestic slowness in the breathless silence, the way a tangle of clasped hands moves over a ouija board, searching for mysteries and magic.

He trailed his fingertip over her chin and below, moving with delicate precision over her throat. He paused over her racing pulse, dipped into the hollow of her collarbone. His touch was reverent; so soft, she could barely feel it—and yet, she could feel nothing else. As if his fingertip left an incandescent thread of glowing light in its wake. He continued his relentless journey downward, pausing over her heart. It thudded against her ribs. Her breath was ragged. He was walking a fine line through a minefield of anger and doubt, with such sure steps. He didn't try to open her robe, he didn't grope or grab. He just stayed the course. Sure that she would open for him.

Like a flower blooming open to the sun.

His hand ventured lower, circling around her navel. He dragged in a sharp breath, and his hand dipped lower still, hesitating for an agonizing moment before it brushed across the very ends of her pubic hair. The faint, teasing contact jolted excitement through her body.

His hand stopped moving. And he waited, muscles trembling, his erection pressed against her bottom. Waiting for a signal.

She moaned, her thighs unlocking with a shudder of surrender.

He let out a low, triumphant sound, like a growl that raised the hairs on the back of her neck. His finger traced the damp slit of her vulva and delicately parted her, sliding into her slippery hot center.

The sensation was unbearably intense. Her knees buckled, her muscles gave. Sean caught her across the waist, pulling her back against himself to steady her. "I've got you. Let go. I'll hold you."

Her wiggling and heaving had opened her robe, and he could see it all, her heavy breasts, her plump belly, her rounded hips. His teeth sank into her neck, the growling sound vibrated against her neck. God, he was good, and she was so excited. So hot and soft, swollen and throbbing. The tiny muscles of her groin clenched around his hand, fluttering in frantic excitement, and her thighs clenched and released, and he was swirling his fingers around her clitoris, fluttering, pressing, and she tipped forward right into that terrible, wonderful moment of no return. A breathless free fall through space, and then . . . oh God.

It went on and on, the cresting wave that broke and pulsed like sea foam surging and frothing over gleaming sand. Pleasure that throbbed through every limb, to her fingers and toes. Leaving her drenched, gasping, dangling in his arms like a puppet with cut strings.

When her eyes finally fluttered open, she hardly recognized herself in the mirror. Her flushed face, heavy-lidded eyes. Sean's golden, muscular forearm clamped across her middle, her hair draped across it, breasts spilling over it. His hand still clamped between her thighs.

She usually had to try so hard to guide her lovers down the long, twisty path toward making her come, but it was an arduous journey with no guarantees, and normal men didn't have that kind of patience.

No biggie. She'd gotten over it. Sex was about cuddling and company, not about orgasms. She had better luck when she flew solo anyway. Accompanied by her vibrator and her Sean fantasies, of course.

This was a whole new universe of dazzling sensations. Emotions.

"Can you stand up?" he asked, still nuzzling her neck.

His erection prodded her back. His arm clamped across her ribs so hard, she couldn't expand her lungs, just make choked, shallow gasps. She locked her knees. There was a desperate urgency in his shaking grip.

"My God." He pulled his fingers out of her and held them up to his face. He licked them greedily. "You taste amazing. I'm starving for it."

"Good." She twisted around, and grabbed the buckle of his belt. She had to do this quick, before she lost her nerve. "So let's eat, then."

He stood there, oddly passive and uncertain, while she struggled with his belt. When she got it open, he seized her arms, stopping her. "Wait. Before we do this we need to, uh, clear some things up. I wanted to tell you why I said what I said in the jail. I can explain—"

"No," she cut him off. "Don't. Please. I don't want to know."

She gave his belt buckle such a hard, angry wrench, he stumbled towards her with a low exclamation. "But it's important."

"No, it's not. I'm not interested," she said. "I don't care. Don't spoil this for me, please. Give me this much. Let me play out my fantasy."

He scowled. "This is not a fantasy, Liv."

"It is for me," she told him. "And that's all you are. I don't want to hear any bullshit. I don't want to be lied to or made a fool of, by anyone, ever again, you hear me? I've got real problems, Sean. My life is screwed. My business is wrecked. There's a guy out there who wants to kill me. What was going on in your mind fifteen years ago is no longer relevant or even interesting to me."

"But it's not what you think," he protested. "I didn't—"

"I don't want to know why you thought it necessary to hurt me like that. I cannot imagine anything that could justify it. I won't give you a chance to do that to me again. All I want is . . ." She trailed off.

"For me to fuck you," he finished flatly. "No more than that."

She actually laughed, the words were so incongruous. "What do you mean, more? What more could there possibly be?" She jerked her gaping robe shut. "Don't get huffy. If it offends your delicate sensibilities to be used, just put your hard-on back into your pants and get out."

She was horribly reminded of his metamorphosis in the jail. The warmth in his eyes had gone out like a candle, leaving blank chips of green reflecting glass. It unnerved her to see his face like that.

She locked her knees and concentrated on not wobbling.

"OK," he said, after a tense pause. "I've made my decision."

"Oh, have you?" She knotted her sash with a jerk. "And?"

"I'll stay and service you," he said. "I can't leave here in this condition. My dick feels like a steel spike. I'd probably injure myself."

She couldn't breathe at all, now. He was so scary, with that remote expression on his face. Sexual energy pulsed off him in waves.

He whipped his shirt off over his head, flung it to the floor. Crouched down and unbuckled his ankle holster, the knife strapped to his other calf. He pried off his shoes, his movements swift and practical.

The seduction that had imbued every word and gesture was gone. He was just getting down to business. Her belly fluttered with doubt.

He shoved his jeans down, stepped out of them, kicked them away. He did not wear underwear. He stood before her, his legs in a wide, aggressive stance, his erection jutting out before him.

His thin smile had no warmth to it. "Want to take a closer look? Check my teeth, measure my cock? See if I'm up to standard?"

Hah. As if she needed to. His sarcasm deserved a sharp reply, but she couldn't come up with one. She was too busy staring.

Don't gape. Don't give him the satisfaction, her little voice nagged, but it was useless. She was speechless.

He was amazing. Big and broad, jutting out of the springy bronze tangle of hair at his groin. His thighs were hard with muscle, rough with hair. A thick knotwork of veins throbbed along the base of his shaft, the huge, flared glans was flushed an angry red. A gleaming drop wept from the slit. He covered it with his fist, rubbing it over himself with a rough hand. She'd never been with anyone that big. Nowhere near.

"So? What's the verdict?" he asked. "Do I make the cut?"

"Oh, would you just shut up and do your job," she said shakily.

"Fine. We don't have anything to talk about, so let's get right to it." He advanced on her, and she backed away instinctively, sitting down abruptly on the bed when she hit it with the back of her knees.

Sean loomed over her. His scent was heat and salt and sweat, the dark musk of maleness, the spicy hint of some soap or cologne. She let out a tiny squeak as he grabbed her hands, and wrapped them around his penis, sliding them roughly up and down his length.

"Here," he said. "Get acquainted."

Oh, whoa. He was so hot and stiff, his skin so soft. He pulsed beneath her cool, trembling hands. She felt his heartbeat in her fingers.

More gleaming liquid dripped from him onto her hands, and he pressed himself against her cupped palm. "Squeeze it," he said. "Hard."

"I'm—I'm not very—"

"Get your hand wet with your lube, too. Rub it over me until I'm all slippery. I want those lily white princess hands to rub royal pussy juice all over my cock. Mmm. Luxurious."

"Would you quit it with the princess cracks?" She touched her fingertips to the hot, throbbing moisture of her vulva.

"No." He sank to his knees and pushed her thighs apart. "That's not going to do the job. Do it like this."

She gasped as he thrust two fingers slowly, deeply inside her, and wiggled, whimpering, as he curved them into a gentle hook, pressing upward and circling a soft, throbbing spot inside her that grew and flushed, wider and wider, until it encompassed everything. It resolved into deep sobbing jets of pleasure, like a fountain inside her.

She sagged over his hot damp shoulder, panting. His hair was silky and fragrant against her face. She sucked in gasps of his scent.

"Ah," he murmured. "That was amazing. So hot. You squirted girl jism right into my hand. God, I fucking *love* that."

"I did?" She lifted her head, bewildered.

He pulled his dripping hand out of her, grinning triumphantly, and stroked himself with it until he looked like he'd been oiled. "Magic juice. Makes me hard enough to drive nails. Hold me, Liv. Squeeze me."

He dragged her hands up and down his shaft until the slow, pulsing rhythm milked another shining drop of fluid out of him. His penis bobbed in her face. He cupped the back of her head in his hand and tugged, very gently, a wordless question in his eyes.

She let out a nervous little giggle. "You can't expect me to . . . oh, dream on! That thing wouldn't fit in my mouth."

"I don't care," he said. "Kiss it. Taste me. Seal our bargain."

He stroked the hair on the back of her head, his eyes fixed on hers. She could feel the power of his will, working on her like the huge, inexorable force of a magnet. She gripped him tighter, so that the bulb shone, taut and swollen and hot. Desperately eager for her touch.

He swayed obediently closer, his breath harsh and audible.

She pressed her lips to the end of his penis. Flicked her tongue over the small slit. Licked up the drops of moisture. He shuddered, groaned. *Yes.* He was salty and good. His body made magic juice, too.

Emboldened, she assaulted him with her tongue. His hands tightened in her hair as she twirled her tongue around the ridge of his glans, flicking at the tender part beneath it, stroking the taut, delicate skin, savoring the metallic taste of his flesh, hot and swollen.

He gripped her hair and tugged her head away from him. "Back off," he said, breathless. "I've got a job to do. You can suck on me later, when I'm exhausted. I'll fit better then, anyhow."

"But I'll be exhausted, too," she complained.

"That's your problem, not mine." He pushed her down onto her back. "Right now, it's your turn again."

"My turn for what?" She braced her hands on his hot, hard chest. She could feel the rough puckers and ridges of a scar beneath her hand.

"To touch yourself. I want to watch you come again. I love that."

She felt desperately exposed as he pressed her knees wide open and stared at her. "Show me how you do it," he urged.

She swallowed, biting her lips. "But I don't do it like this."

"No? Then how do you do it, baby?"

She realized that she had never told this to anyone in her life.

"With my legs closed, tight," she admitted. "Squeezing really hard. I don't know if I can do it any other—"

"What if I help?" He seized her hand, guided down between her legs. "Put your hand in your pussy, and I'll play with your clit at the same time. We'll get you where you need to go."

Her fingers slid into the silken, slick opening of her sex, and she fell back onto the bed, staring up at the shadows on the ceiling. He pushed her legs wide, and put his mouth to her.

Her legs flailed, slipping on the satin comforter. His hair tickled her thighs, her groin, his beard stubble rasped her skin, the hot vortex of his lips fastened over her clitoris. He sucked, stroked, swirled. So much intense sensation, her brain couldn't process it all. She fell to pieces, delicious explosions that went on and on, and he watched it happen, hot-eyed and pleased with himself. His gaze made her feel so vulnerable. The hot quivering began to shake her face, her chest.

Sean didn't seem turned off by her weeping. On the contrary, when she opened her eyes and dashed away the blur, she found him straddling her, his penis hot and hard against her belly. Waiting.

"I'm sorry," she whispered. "I can't seem to stop."

"It's OK," he said. "Lots of girls cry when they come."

That infuriated her. She tried to shove him off, but he leaned forward, pinning her to the bed. "What the hell is wrong with you?"

"Lots of girls, huh? Have you had so many that you can run your own personal statistical analyses?"

"Why should that bother you? I'm just a convenient piece of meat for you, right? What difference does it make how many girls I've had?"

She shoved at his hard chest. "It bugs me to be lumped into a category. There's the umbrella group, Girls Sean Has Screwed, and there's subsets, like Group F-12b, Girls Who Cry When They

Come. Just slot me in, file me with the rest of the teeming masses. Get off me!"

"I thought you wanted to keep this emotionally uninvolved."

"I guess I suck at that," she said. "Surprise, surprise. Get *off*."

Sean rolled off, and she struggled into a sitting position, pulling her robe around herself. "Time out," she said. "This isn't working. It's making me feel worse, not better. I can't afford to feel any worse."

"Not working?" He looked incredulous. "You came like crazy."

"It's more complicated than that." She jumped off the bed, belted the robe. "I'm sorry to leave you high and dry, but I—"

"Oh, you won't, babe. Forget it. I'm not going anywhere." He spun her around and pushed her up against the wall. "Not now."

She stared into his eyes. The peonies on the wallpaper pulsed in her peripheral vision like a fever dream. Her pulse pounded. She was terrified, aroused, furious. He jerked the robe open, cupped her breast, fingers tracing shivering circles around the under-curve. He bent down, took her nipple in his mouth, his tongue a hot rasp of need.

He cupped her face, smoothing away her sweat-dampened hair. "I would never hurt you. You know that, don't you?"

She thought of all those nights spent sobbing until dawn. All those years of useless therapy. "I cannot believe you have the nerve to say that to me," she hissed. "You have no clue, do you? You *idiot*—"

He cut off her words with a frantic kiss, but the aggression melted down into ravenous sweetness, and the kiss went wild, tongues seeking, limbs twining. They wanted to punish each other, devour each other.

He pulled his mouth away. "Too late to blow me off," he said. "We passed that point of no return, oh, maybe three orgasms ago?"

"Don't muscle me around, you ape!"

"Or what? You'll call Mommy and Daddy, or Blair the Ass-wipe Madden to save you? I'd like to see you explain why you're stark naked and cherry red and slippery with lube all the way to your knees."

"Goddamn you, Sean—"

"How about if I just slide down here—" he did so, dragging wet, hungry kisses down over her breasts, her belly, "to my knees and lick some more of that sweet pussy juice off of the royal clit."

Liv struggled, but he held her hips and pressed his face against her mound, his long tongue squirming its way into the divide of her sex, fluttering skillfully. "Stop," she begged. "I can't take any more."

He lifted his face away. "And when you've had enough orgasms, you'll already be in the perfect position to kick me in the face."

She wrenched out of his grip, and pitched off balance with her own frantic momentum. Sean lunged to steady her. They careened against the dresser, and caught the cord of the lamp. It clattered to the floor along with them. They landed on her soft, fuzzy pink hooked rug.

She was pinned beneath his big, hot weight. He was so steely hard, heavy and huge, vibrating with emotion. "Aw, shit. You OK?" he asked breathlessly. "Did you hurt yourself?"

She shoved at his chest. "You weigh a ton, and you're squishing me into jelly, and you're a rude, horrible jerk, but other than that, no."

He lifted himself off her rib cage, still keeping her trapped beneath him, and grabbed a pillow that had tumbled off the bed in the tussle. He tucked it behind her head, and scooped her hair, spreading it out over the pillow. Kissed her face, her forehead, her cheeks, her throat.

"I didn't want to hurt you," he whispered. "Really. Ever."

Then why did you do it? The question echoed between them.

He groped for his jeans and plucked a condom out of the pocket. He ripped it open with his teeth and rolled it on himself with careless expertise. She felt like a virgin sacrifice, splayed out wide on a silk draped altar. Offered up to a sensual, merciless demigod.

She couldn't breathe, she was trembling so hard. He pressed against her, and she gasped at the electric shock of contact. He swirled himself around, caressing her folds. She squirmed towards him, biting her lip to muffle the eager, sobbing sounds she made.

He pressed deeper, staring into her eyes as he bore down. Oh. Whoa. Yikes. He was huge inside her. Her nails dug deep into his arms.

Rap, rap, rap. "Livvy? Honey?" It was her mother's sharp voice. "We heard noises. Is everything all right?" *Rap, rap, rap.* "Livvy?"

Sean went motionless. His body began to vibrate with laughter.

He pressed his face against her throat. "Yeah, Livvy." His tiny, taunting whisper tickled her ear. "Are you all right?"

She shook with laughter. It was the ultimate moment of no return. And she had to get herself under control, or the choice would be taken out of her hands. In the worst possible way.

"Livvy?" *Rap, rap.* Her mother's voice rose in pitch.

She tried to coordinate her trembling vocal cords. "Ah, no, Mother, I'm fine," she called. "Sorry, I didn't hear you. I was moving my suitcase, and I knocked over a lamp. Sorry I scared you. Good night."

"I heard you talking to someone," her mother said suspiciously.

"Yes. I was, ah, talking to Alison on my cell phone."

"Ah. Can I come in? I want to talk."

Liv's fingernails dug into Sean's shoulders. "Um . . . I'm indecent, Mother. I was about to step into the shower. Can it wait?"

Her mother made an irritated noise. "Oh, I suppose. Set your clock for five AM. We're interviewing bodyguards tomorrow. Sleep well."

"OK," she said. "You, too."

Her footsteps receded. Liv's eyes were shut tight. Her teeth almost chattered. Sean's lips teased her mouth open, touched the tip of his tongue to hers. Her hands skittered over his chest, feeling every dip and curve, the coarse rasp of hair, his nipples. The air felt heavy against her skin. She felt his heartbeat pulsing in the glow between her legs.

"Thank God," he whispered. "Your waffling was driving me nuts."

Her eyes popped open. "I was not waffling!"

"No?" Sean's voice was a challenging whisper. "First I finger fuck you, then you lick my cock like a lollipop, then you sob in my arms, then I suck on your clit, then you tell me to fuck off and leave. Good thing we're on the ground with my cock inside you. I was getting dizzy."

She dragged in a sharp breath as he penetrated deeper. "I can't believe you can be a smart-ass at a time like this. Oh. My. God."

"Am I hurting you?" He went still, his body vibrating.

"Duh," she muttered. "You're enormous. It's so typical. Like everything else, that would have to be ridiculous, too."

His chest jerked with a burst of muffled laughter. "I don't think anybody's ever called my cock ridiculous before. He doesn't mind, though. Not while he's finally squeezing into that tight, juicy pink flower of a pussy after years of dreaming about it. Can I give you more?"

She nodded. He was sliding more easily now, oiled by her own body's writhing eagerness. His weight shifted. *Click*, and she felt the pressure of light against her eyelids. "Open your eyes," he said.

She did. The pink silk lamp lying on the floor cast a rosy pool of light. Sean grabbed a pillow off the bed and tucked it behind her.

She stared down, mesmerized. His thick, gleaming phallus slowly disappeared into her body. He arched over her, his sex-dampened pubic hair grinding against the darker thatch between her spread thighs. He was lodged so deep, rocking, swiveling. His eyes glittered.

She shut her eyes against their piercing intensity.

He cupped her head, his hands tightening in her hair. "I want you to see my cock going into you. I want you to remember every detail."

She pulled against his hand, swatted his chest. "Let go of my hair. I don't go for the grunting caveman act. Cut it out."

"Oh, yeah," he muttered. "Scold me while I fuck you. Put me in my place. I love that. Can't get enough of it."

She wound her fingers into the hair on his chest, and yanked it.

He sucked in a breath. *"Fuck."* He pinned her hands to the pillow on either side of her head. "Goddamn, princess. That was dirt mean."

She stared into his eyes. "You started it," she said. "You deserved it. Provoking me on purpose. You arrogant bully."

They stared at each other, panting. Afraid of the wild energy, the momentum of desire. Each challenging the other. Unable to back down.

Liv hooked her ankles around his and pressed against him. Clenching around that solid club of his flesh embedded deep inside her.

He let go of her hands and gathered her up beneath him, slamming into her body. Her breasts jiggled with each jarring thrust. She strained beneath him, arching, jerking to meet every frenzied lunge with one of her own. It was amazing. It hurt, and she didn't care. She incited him, demanded more, with teeth and nails and gasping cries.

At some point they were on their sides, then on Sean's back with her on top, then he rolled her back beneath him. The position didn't matter. Nothing could break that wild rhythm, or slow the hard, slapping blows of flesh against flesh. The pink carpet worked its way across the floor beneath their grappling bodies. They clutched each other. A shock wave of pleasure teased, beckoned . . . and hit.

She spun, soared through the spangled darkness. Settled slowly, conscious only of shimmering delight that rippled endlessly, spreading from the center of her soul. Extending out into a starry black forever.

Chapter
9

Holy *fuck*.
Earthquakes jolted from the epicenter of his groin and racked his body. He came, and came, and came. An endless, wrenching explosion.

Some instinct of self-preservation had prompted him to clap his hand over her mouth. Damn good thing, too. She was a screamer.

She was still whimpering and moaning, wiggling deliciously. Everything about her was so soft, so lush, so strong.

That orgasm had detonated from some place so deep, it blew him apart. He should be in a state of bliss. Relaxed, goofy, floating.

He wasn't. He felt awful. He was thinking now, and it wasn't pretty. He'd rather be lost, in the slick pounding magic of mindless fucking. Nothing happening in his head but instinct, impulse.

Too bad. The thoughts came, like hammer blows. Liv didn't want him to throw himself at her feet and offer to serve her for all eternity. She didn't want confessions or justifications or excuses. She wanted a well-hung stud to lick her until she was juicy and hot, and put it to her deep and hard. His dream scenario. White hot, guilt-free sex with no strings. Every man's secret fantasy, whether he admitted it or not.

So why did he feel like ten different kinds of shit?

He pressed his face against her cool, fragrant hair, still damp and deliciously humid. He didn't dare look her in the face.

He felt abashed. He'd never been that rough with anyone, not even when begged to be so. It was like his body had been possessed.

He took a deep breath, raised his head. Her eyes fluttered open, heavy lidded. Unfathomable gray, ringed with indigo, lit with irregular splotches of gold. Curling black lashes. But she wasn't looking at him.

She was miles away. Light years. It made him ache.

He forced himself to lift his weight off, shoving his trembling limbs up so he was on his knees. "Who'd have thought you were a screamer?" He scooped up a handful of her damp hair. It glided through his fingers, cool and slippery as night dark satin.

She licked those red lips until they gleamed, and dug sharp little claws into his arms, rubbing the soft cushion of her mound against his pubic bone. He angled himself to oblige her, instinctively.

"Didn't even hear myself," she whispered shakily.

"I hope nobody else did, either," he said.

She glanced down at the thick, broad stalk sliding slowly out of her. "But you still didn't come."

"Sure, I did," he said. "I came with you. Didn't you feel it?"

"I thought I did," she said. "But you're still—"

"Hard," he agreed. "Very. Yeah, you inspire me, beautiful."

She wrapped her legs around him. He sucked in a deep breath and fought for control. "If you want me to fuck you again, I need a fresh condom. This one won't stay on. I must've shot a quart of come into it."

She shivered with startled laughter. "Oh, dear. Please don't use euphemisms, Sean. Tell it exactly like it is, by all means."

"Oh, I will." He slid out of her, holding the condom so that the tight cling of her body could not dislodge it. The sight was straight out of his own personal erotic fantasy world. Liv, splayed out on the floor, her soft white thighs spread. The long slit of her pussy was shockingly pink against her dark pubic hair, the puffy, gleaming lips pouting out of it a darker crimson, like some exotic flower. It was making him crazy.

"So? Shall we go at it again? Do you want more?" he demanded.

She rolled onto her side, closing her thighs and wrapping her arms around her knees. "I think more might kill me."

"Maybe," he agreed. "But damn, what a way to go."

She closed her eyes, shaking with a soft, whispery giggle.

He stared at her body, hypnotized by every angle. He wanted to draw her, to touch her, to mold her. Hold her. He loved that shadowy cleft. That hot, rich woman smell. The sweet taste, the slick texture. The amazing smoothness of her female flesh. His cock pulsed, impatient.

Keep it together. He slid the condom off, knotted it. "You got someplace I can put this?"

Liv tugged her robe around herself and shuffled on her knees over to the suitcase, rummaging until she found a plastic pharmacy bag.

She presented it to him. He dropped it in the bag with a nod of thanks, knotted the bag, dropped it in the wicker trash basket she held out to him. So polite. If you please. Thanks so much. They could be at a barbecue. She might be offering him a place to deposit his paper plate.

Like they hadn't been writhing and thrashing around on the floor, fucking desperately only minutes before.

She stared at his body, and reached out with a timid fingertip to trace the lumps of one of his scars. "Where did you get that?"

He was perversely irritated by the question. "Uh, that was an unfortunate misunderstanding with an arms dealer in Somalia."

She blinked. "My goodness. You're kidding, right?"

"Why would I kid? I wouldn't make up nasty awful stuff like that. I wish to God it hadn't happened. Hurt like hell. Nicked some internal organs, too. Real gross-out. Took for-fucking-ever to heal up properly."

"God, Sean," she said. "What on earth have you been doing?"

Something tightened up in his mind as he gazed at her. He imagining cuddling with her, gabbing for hours. Telling stories about his crazy adventures. Fifteen years was a long time to catch up on.

But her curiosity meant no more than it did from his average fuckbunny bimbo. *Where did you get those scars?* Girls always asked that, the clear subtext being *Ooh, excite me with violent stories about what a dangerous animal you are before you bang me again.*

He didn't have the stomach for it. "Never mind the scars, OK?"

She shrank back at his tone. "Excuse me for being curious," she said coolly. "I didn't mean to pry."

"I'm not offended. It's just that gunshot wounds are a big turn-off. Not what I choose to think about when I have a massive hard-on."

Her eyes dropped to his erection. He yanked on it with a rough, careless hand, squeezing until his cock head protruded, smooth and tight and purple with desperate hopefulness. Weeping out the slit.

Her face flushed, and an answering throb of blood surged through his own body. He grabbed her, and pushed her facedown against the antique four-poster, heaped with pink and white lace-trimmed pillows.

"I could do this all night, Liv. I am not speaking figuratively," he said. "Tell me what you want, and I'll give it to you. But tell me quick."

She shook her head, her hair making a soft shushing sound against the padded satin. "This is nuts," she whispered. "I don't know anything. I'm flying blind. I don't know you."

"You will," he promised her hoarsely. "You will." He slid down to his knees behind the bed, tugging her hips out so she was bent at a ninety degree angle. He flipped up the silk of her robe, baring her ass.

She squeaked in protest, flailing against his grip, but he held her fast. "No, no. Shhh," he crooned. "Let me. I've already licked it, I've already sucked it, I've already fucked it. Can't I just look at it?"

She laughed, jerkily. "You won't stop at just looking."

"Why should I? You don't want me to." He gripped her hips, so round, velvety hot, flower petal smooth, and smelling of hot woman.

"God, you're perfect," he muttered thickly.

"Oh, give me a break. My oversized butt is far from perfect."

He blinked, taken aback. She had to know how excellent her ass was. Surely she'd noticed the guys sprawled out on the ground who'd tripped over their own tongues when she walked by.

"This is the most gorgeous ass I've ever seen," he said. "Smooth white skin, and amazing curves, and those cute dimples." He ran his finger down the tender slit. "And your pussy is world class."

"I guess you would know," she said, acidly.

He carefully ignored that comment, it being a train of thought that would take them nowhere good. Distraction, diversion. He teased two fingers between her labia, and thrust them slowly inside her.

She moaned. So did he. So sexy, fever hot and slick and yielding, but snug, too. All puffy upholstery in there, super-deluxe satin slick cushions, creating tight friction. His cock throbbed with eagerness to take the plunge. Her cunt muscles clenched helplessly around him, and she clutched handfuls of the coverlet, burying her face in the cushions.

"I do know you, Liv," he said. "I know a lot about you. Secret things. Sexy things. Things you probably didn't know yourself."

"Oh, don't flatter yourself," she said breathlessly. "Oh . . . oh."

"That's the weird thing about sex," Sean said reflectively, circling her clit with his thumb. "You learn things that are so intimate. Buried so deep, they don't even have names. But hot sex like this lays it all naked. You want me to put names to all your nameless secrets?"

"I'd put names to yours, too, you know," she said, her voice jerky with excitement. "It cuts both ways."

The truth of her words blanked out his mind for a moment. He gathered his thoughts, and pushed on. "This scene, for instance. It turns you on that I sneaked in here and put it to you hard on the floor while your folks sip tea downstairs with their pinkies in the air."

She made a growling sound. "You're pissing me off, Sean."

"Yeah, I know. Meanwhile, you're coming around my hand." He dragged his teeth across her back. "You love it when I talk dirty to you. We'll find a hotel that rents by the hour. People pounding on the walls, shouting obscenities while we go at it so hard the building shakes. That would get you off, wouldn't it? Slumming with bad-ass trash like me?"

She elbowed him, hard enough to make him gasp. "Let go of me!"

"No," he said. "I'm a disobedient boy. This fancypants four-poster makes me want to spread-eagle you, tie you to the bedposts. Not tonight, though. You're too noisy. You'd shout the roof down."

"That is not my thing." Her voice quivered. "I'm not into bondage games. That stupid kink stuff strikes me as icky, so forget it, OK?"

"Yes, that would explain why your pussy squeezed my fingers so hard when I mentioned it." He licked her back. "Don't bother lying to me while I'm fucking you, princess."

"I'm serious, Sean." She twisted around, glared at him. "Don't."

"Don't worry. If it's too much, I'll soothe you with my tongue. I'll just lick those juicy pink lips for hours, until you're squirming and gasping. Exhausted from coming. I go crazy for your girl juice. I'm addicted to it. I'll lap it up until you kick me away and make me stop."

He kept his hand inside her while he groped for his jeans, caressing all those sweet spots that made her shudder and forget to fight. He tore the condom packet open with his teeth. Rolled it on.

"I want something from you," he said.

She stiffened, turning her head. "What?"

He laughed at her suspicious tone. "Nothing severely kinky. You said you make yourself come squeezing your legs together. The idea really turns me on. I want you to do that for me. I want to feel it."

"Feel it?" She twisted around, gave him a puzzled frown. "How?"

He answered by nudging the blunt head of his cock into her slick opening, pushing until it fetched up against her tight resistance.

"Like this," he whispered. "From the inside. Just squeeze."

"Oh. Ah . . ." Her voice trailed off, quivering, and her white-knuckled hands clutched thick handfuls of the coverlet. "My God."

"You're so tight. You'll have to spread your legs, to let me in. Then you can close them again. Squeeze as hard as you can. Let me feel it."

She hesitated, but slowly her thighs released. He almost blew his wad then and there, it was so exciting. This angle, this view, those peachy round ass cheeks, the agonizing, delicious shove into her gleaming pink pussy from behind. He took it easy, but soon she was shoving back against him, sucking in air with each sexy lunge. All he had to do was brace himself and hang onto his self-control until he was deep inside, hugged and squeezed with every beat of her heart.

He shut her legs again, flanking hers with his own thighs.

"Do it," he whispered. "I'm going to relax and enjoy the ride."

It was torture, staying passive as a statue, clutched in that powerful female grip. So erotic, to sneak into her secret chamber and feel how she touched herself when she was alone, squeezing and releasing, those small, strong muscles pulsing around him. She jerked and quivered as she got closer, straining desperately. His cock could feel the quick tremolo of her fingers, working her clit. He was squeezed with every pulse of her strong thighs. His body shook with excitement.

She almost dragged him along with her when she went over the top, gasping screams muffled against the crumpled coverlet. Her thighs were still closed, but he could slide and thrust more easily inside her now, oiled by another hot gush of magic, slippery-sweet girl come.

He leaned over her, savoring every gasp, every shudder and shake of her body. Finally the orgasm subsided, and she lay panting and speechless, her face cherry red, her parted lips half hidden by hair.

It had dried into big, wavy swirls. He lifted it off her face, and she made a wordless protest and hid her damp face against the coverlet.

He cupped her chin, tugged it around. "Don't hide from me." It came out like one of those caveman commands that bugged her, but she was too limp to complain. He draped himself over her, shoving the robe up so he could lick the sweat off her graceful back. A TV chattered downstairs. White noise, to screen the sounds of sex. If they were lucky.

She made a small movement, as if trying to get some more air into her lungs, and cleared her throat. "You still haven't come."

"Nope. I could have, but I was hoping for one more go at you."

Her eyes flicked back to him. "God, Sean. You are insatiable."

"Are you going to have mercy on me?" he asked. "Or are you going to send me home with blue balls as a punishment for my insolence?"

"Quit with the snide remarks. You're tempting me to do just that. One more sarcastic crack, and I'll . . . oh . . . my *God* . . ."

He dragged his cock slowly out of her, then bent down and slid his tongue hungrily up and down the length of her hot, juicy slit. Yum.

She gasped, stiffened. "What are you—God, Sean, stop that!"

"Don't punish me," he pleaded. "Cruel princess. I'll do anything you want. Just don't leave me hanging. Your divine majesty, I beg—"

"Shut up!" She wiggled away.

He grinned at her. Her eyes were glowing, and he could tell with his goof radar that she was trying not to laugh. Always a good sign.

"So?" he asked softly.

Her eyes slid away, cheeks red. "How do you want to do it?"

"You decide. From behind, on your hands and knees. Up against the wall. Ride me like a wild bull at the rodeo. Anything. Lady's choice."

"I'm too wobbly kneed to do anything acrobatic," she said shyly.

He offered her a hand. "So lie back on the bed," he suggested.

She let him tug her to her feet. "It's not too boring?"

He laughed at the worried tone in her voice. "I have never been so far from bored in my life," he told her, with total sincerity.

Liv sat down on the bed, looking uncertain.

"Sit right at the edge," he told her. "I want to stand up for this."

She nodded, scooting closer, and he pushed her down against the mountainous heap of pillows. She hesitated for a moment. He waited for her body's invitation. She closed her eyes, biting that soft red lower lip.

They both sighed as she gracefully opened her legs for him.

It started slow. Silent and fraught with meaning, like a ceremony. She was so beautiful, curvy and starry-eyed. Glowing like a pink South Sea pearl against the lacy pillows. He pushed her knees wider, staring at her dark ringlets, the vibrant colors of her sexy secret flesh. "Open your pussy lips." His voice was hoarse, his mouth dry with excitement.

She put her hands to herself, and parted her labia. A helpless sound vibrated through his body as he pressed the tip of his cock to her slippery folds, nudging inside. "Are you sore?" he asked, though it would kill him if she changed her mind. "Do I have to go easy?"

"Ah . . . yes and no," she said.

He froze. "Huh? What the fuck is that supposed to mean?"

"It means yes, I'm sore," she hissed. "And no. Don't go easy."

He took her at her word, sliding home with one deep, heavy lunge.

Ah. Yes. She took every thick inch of him, which almost never happened, and it felt so good. His whole length hugged and caressed by that snug, super-deluxe sheath, licked and squeezed and loved.

She grabbed his waist, yanked him deeper, and off he went again, like an animal in rut. No care for her pleasure, no calibrating the stroke to get at her hot spots. Just a wild, frenzied plunge and glide.

He pounded into her. The bed rattled and shook. Her soft tits jiggled with each slamming thrust. His refined sexual technique was reduced to vapor and steam. He was a fucking raw nerve.

A fist squeezed his throat, clamped his heart, but it was swelling, too big to be contained. Everything was bursting, flying apart. He saw Kev's face as he floated back. Smiling, like something was funny.

But it fucking never was.

Liv's arms were looped around his back. Soft hands petting him.

The princess, soothing her lusty love slave after he serviced her. An approving pat pat pat on his sweaty, heaving shoulders. *Excellent fucking. Good boy. Off you go, back to the stable. Ta ta. Be good.*

This could reduce him to a begging, pleading dick-for-brains who deserved no better than to get stomped to pulp beneath her feet.

He forced his throat to stop shaking. Pulled out, turned away without looking at her. He could hear her rustling around as he fished the bag out of the trash and pried it open to dispose of his condom.

"Sean? Are you, ah, OK?" Her voice was whispery soft.

He shrugged. "I'm great," he said thickly. "You're a fabulous lay, princess." He escaped into her bathroom, and splashed water into his hot, staring eyes until the inconvenient, embarrassing tears eased off.

He braced himself before going out into her bedroom. Pulled on his jeans, careful not to look at her. Strapped on the knife, the gun. Put on his shoes, his shirt, without a word or a glance. She stood silently, swathed tightly in her robe. "Sean?" Her voice had gotten even smaller.

He ignored her as he grabbed her cell phone off the dresser.

"What are you doing with that?" she asked.

"Programming my number into it," he said. "If you get the whim, just text me with a time and place. I'll be there. At the ready."

"Why are you being so cold?" she whispered.

He glanced at her, frowning. "What, wasn't the sex hot enough?"

"That's not what I . . . oh. I see. You're doing that metamorphosis thing again. You're being the cruel, horrible Sean now, right?"

He shrugged. "Whichever Sean I am, my dick will always be hard for you. Look under B for boy toy in your address function." He tossed it on the dresser, and flung open the door. To the right was the third floor stairs, the crawl space, the window, the tree. His covert entry route.

The left led to the grand staircase down to the main hall. He turned left.

Liv lunged out the door after him. "Hey! What are you doing?" she hissed. "Have you gone nuts?"

"Why not? If they killed me now, I'd die happy. And slithering on your belly is undignified. Have a nice evening, beautiful."

As luck would have it, Amelia Endicott was at the foot of the stairs, whispering with that steaming turd, Blair Madden. Gack.

Sean's tongue adhered to the roof of his mouth. He abruptly reconsidered the wisdom of his impulse to walk out the front door.

Slithering on his belly sounded real good right now.

Liv's mom turned at his deliberately clumping footsteps, and let out a shrill shriek. Her hand flew to cover her thin red mouth.

Blair jumped and put himself in front of her, puffing out his chest like a toad. "How did you get in? What have you done with Liv?"

"Nothing," Liv said softly from behind him. "I'm fine."

So the princess had taken pity on him. He allowed himself one last look over his shoulder. She was still in her sheer, sexy robe, flushed and damp and gorgeous. Like a woman who'd just had fabulous sex.

Sean did not like for Blair Madden to see her like that.

"I was testing your security," he said. "Needless to say, it's inadequate." He dug into his pocket, and pulled out a scrap of paper. "Here's a list of the best security companies in the area. Private cell phone numbers included. You could call them right now. In my name."

"Thanks for the unsolicited advice." Blair yanked the door open.

Sean stared at the other man as he sauntered down the stairs. Madden inched backwards, a muscle twitching in his face.

"The police are right outside, McCloud."

Sean turned at the gruff, loud voice. Bart Endicott stood in the door, his thick face red and mottled.

It never ceased to baffle him. How that fanged bitch and that pompous blowhard had managed between them to produce the princess would forever remain one of the great unsolved mysteries of genetics.

"Yes, I know," he said. "I saw them when I came in. But I was just leaving. Good night, everyone."

"You might as well wait where you are. We'll be pressing charges for breaking and entering." Amelia Endicott's voice dripped acid.

"No, Mother." Liv's voice was soft, but resolute. "There was no breaking or entering. I invited him in. You can call off the police."

Everyone turned horrified eyes on Liv. Sean did not envy her in that moment. She wrapped her arms around her chest and stared back.

Wow. He practically blushed. He didn't deserve that kind of support, after his raving asshole routine. That woman was pure class.

"That's hardly appropriate for an engaged woman, dear," Amelia said loudly. "I imagine you told Sean your happy news?"

Sean looked at her. His chest cavity had just been flash frozen.

She blinked. "But I—I'm not—"

"Come on, honey," Blair said. "We can't keep it a secret forever."

"We were thinking early fall," Amelia said. "Of course, this awful business might force us to reconsider the timing. Such a shame."

It took a minute for him to coordinate his vocal apparatus. "Uh, yeah." He looked into Liv's big, startled gray eyes. "I'm amazed you didn't share something so important earlier in our, ah, conversation."

"But I'm not—"

"Liv's shy about it," Amelia broke in. "But thank goodness we all have something to be happy about in these difficult days, hmm?"

"Yeah," he muttered. "Uh, great. Be happy, then. Watch your back, princess."

He was out the door. Walking blindly up the driveway towards the gate. He had to stop and explain himself to the cops that were parked outside, which was a challenge, since he couldn't concentrate clearly enough to make any sense. All he could think about was Liv.

Engaged. Jesus Christ.

Madden finally came out the door, called the cops off, waved him on out. Just to get rid of his sorry ass. Smug toad.

The big wrought-iron gate ground open for him. He took off down the road towards his truck, dazed. He'd done every last damn thing Davy had advance-scolded him for. Breaking and entering, planting spywear, ill-advised sex. The Endicotts could nail his ass to the wall, if they found the beacons. Wallet, suitcase, purse, he'd even slit open the soles of Liv's sandals. The burrs were traceable to Safe-Guard, so he'd compromised Seth and Davy as well. They didn't have much staying power, lacking an external power source. He'd risked his freedom and his brother's professional reputation for a chance of keeping track of Liv for the next day or so.

And for the wildest, most explosive sex he'd ever had.

He stumbled in the dark. Ran his hands over the stinging marks on his shoulders and ass. Fuck-me-harder marks. Wildcat woman.

He would wear them like a badge. Be sorry when they healed.

Tomorrow, they would take Liv off to someplace where neither he nor T-Rex would ever be able to find her—and the world would go flat.

Unless she called the number he'd programmed into her cell.

He stopped in his tracks on the dark road, the huge dark pine and fir trees rustling in the cool wind and thought about that.

Screwing Blair Madden's fiancée. That's what he'd just done. He made himself face it. He imagined Liv, going home after she showered off the evidence. Thinking about her secret lover while she did her wifely duty in bed. His stomach lurched. He would never survive that.

She had to be doing the guy already, if they were engaged. His imagination promptly offered up fully realized 3-D images of that worthless turd Blair, having at her. And Liv, letting him. Liking it.

Bad idea. He hung over the roadside ditch and hacked up gastric juices, fists clenched, eyes watering. Oh, that was foul. He was a flexible guy, but that level of emotional gymnastics was not in his repertoire.

Hypocrite. Like he had a right to be uptight about Liv screwing whoever she pleased. He'd worked through six condoms—or was it seven?—in a tequila haze with the fuckbunny duo from the Hole.

Though to be entirely fair and accurate, he had not been engaged to be married to someone else while boinking the bunnies.

It gave him a sad ache in his chest, to think that he'd never given any woman more than what Liv had given him tonight. It hurt when the rest was declined. He'd dished out a lot of that. He wasn't proud of it.

One of his former would-be girlfriends, Sandra, was a grad student at U of W, studying clinical psych. A chubby, fuzzy-curled blonde with intellectual horn-rimmed glasses and lovely pink-tipped tits. She'd explained the dynamic of his pathological condition to him, given him the number of a good therapist and a list of local support groups and twelve-step programs for sexual addicts.

All of this preparatory to telling him to go fuck himself.

He deserved it. Everything she said made perfect sense, but understanding it didn't help worth a damn. It was always the same; the itch that drove him out to look for sex, the approach, the seduction. It rarely took long, once he turned on the charm. He made the sex safe, hot, and prolonged for his lady friends. That much, he could guarantee.

But his liaisons rarely lasted more than a week. Usually less.

In a way, he loved them all, even the Staceys and the Kendras. He knew they deserved better. He hated to hurt their feelings. Sometimes, he reflected wistfully how great it would be if he could just decide, by brute force of will, to make some girl's unrealistic fantasies come true.

Just pick out some nice girl who made him laugh. Make some goddamn promises to her. Try like hell to keep them. Simple. Right?

What were all the guys around him doing but just exactly that?

No. Something always stopped him whenever he was tempted to try it. A presentiment of doom. Or maybe it was watching his brothers and their lady loves, wallowing in the big bubbly bathtub of true love.

It made his teeth hurt, sometimes, but damn, it looked like fun. They looked so relaxed. Like they didn't have to try and fool anybody.

He wished he could convince all those girls of how beautiful they were. How much more they deserved from the worthless, doglike men in their lives, himself included. But he couldn't argue with that sucking ache in his gut. Couldn't control it, banish it, ignore it.

It felt like grief. And Christ, he should know.

As soon as he felt that ache, and it never took long to show up, he was history. If he forced the issue, if he tried to stick around out of guilt or stubborness or loneliness or whatever, it just got worse, and worse, until it was incapacitating. And oh, that was bad. Oh, how that sucked.

It didn't matter worth a damn how much he liked the girl, how much fun the sex was, how much he wished that things were different.

He wondered why he felt compelled to endlessly repeat the whole depressing drama. He loved sex, but he hated slamming into that brick wall. Knowing even before he met the chick how it was going to end.

Not tonight. What happened in Liv's bedroom was a movie he'd never seen. A pulse-pounding cliff-hanger. He saw her naked body when he closed his eyes. He could smell her scent on his hands. It was like she had a homing beacon, and he was tuned to its frequency. He didn't even need X-Ray Specs. He could just follow his dick, like a dowser.

A strange feeling brushed over him. Ghost fingers, sending a cold, tickling shiver down his spine. He froze, listening. Slowly turned three hundred and sixty degrees, not that he could see fuck-all in this dark.

His skin crawled. His heart rate increased. On this stretch of road, he was wide open to a gunman sitting up on that bald knob of hill overlooking Endicott House. If the guy had an infrared scope, that is.

Yeah, and that was just old Crazy Eamon's hypervigilant, paranoid jive talk, forever jabbering in the back of his head. He knew it, but even so, instinct and training together were too strong to resist.

He dove over the shoulder and down the hill, sliding in the gravel scree, choking on the dust he kicked up. He hit the scrub, arms outspread to break his fall, and whack, scratch, slap, shit and *ouch*.

He was relieved when he fetched up on the washed out creek bed where he'd parked his shiny new Jeep Wrangler. Pain in the ass, having paranoid genes.

He fired up the computers and the X-Ray Specs receiver in the office as soon as he got home, and entered the beacon codes.

The map spread over the monitor screen. A cluster of icons pulsed in the location of Endicott House. His chest seized up. He had to cool it.

One, Liv was engaged to be married to a venomous snake. Two, she'd screwed him for the fun of it, because she felt like it. Three, there would be no chance to redeem the past, because she didn't give a shit. Four, she did not want his protection or his help. Five, she was leaving.

He'd just sit and watch those flashing blips move out of range.

So there it was. No reason for him to sit here, watching his own sweaty hand tremble on top of the computer mouse.

The only way she could come back and rebuild her bookstore would be if someone flattened this piece of shit. And since he was a suspect, he'd be doing himself a favor by clearing up the matter. Which gave him a face-saving justification for sticking his nose in. *Or any other protruding body part.* He choked, thinking of Davy's lecture. Sorry, bro.

He pulled up a document and started transcribing Liv's stalker e-mails from memory. Getting to work made him feel instantly more cheerful. It would be a visceral satisfaction to bring T-Rex to the door of Endicott House. Hold the scaly bastard by the scruff of the neck while he wiggled and squawked. Drop him on the colonial style porch. *Splat.*

Here, folks. A small token of my esteem.

He had to laugh at himself. The faithful hound, bringing a dead rabbit to its master. Wagging, jumping, hoping for a pat on the head.

Lovesick chump.

Chapter
10

Gordon swung the rifle scope around, unnerved. What the *fuck*? Fate had just offered him a chance to make this job's profit-to-risk ratio skyrocket in his favor. He'd let his breath slow, his mind settle into that deep stillness preparatory to squeezing the trigger, vaporizing that troublesome fuck's skull. Then McCloud stopped, throwing off Gordon's tracking. When he nailed the guy in his sights, he was looking up the hill, right at Gordon. His bright eyes were like a timber wolf's.

And then the guy dematerialized. The image in the scope bobbed and wavered. It rattled him. It was a moonless night, there was a wooded mountain slope between them, and the pisser had got wind of him. Gordon was going to be relieved when he was turned into meat.

Jarring, to have a kill snatched out from under him. All jacked up, and nowhere to blow his wad. Killus interruptus. He giggled at his own wit. A vehicle started up. Headlights sliced through the trees, jogged over the rise. Taillights rounded the curve, disappeared.

Maybe it was better. Killing him now had been a last minute decision with as many cons as pros. The rifle made a mess, and this was a main road, though lightly traveled. The cops would hear the shot, call for backup. He would have to clean up McCloud's shattered skull in record time, hoping no cars passed, hoping that what remained on the asphalt would be taken for an unlucky deer, and then find and dispose of McCloud's vehicle. Better that the impulse had been blocked.

Before McCloud walked out that gate, Gordon had been toying with the idea of executing the cops with his sniper rifle, blasting his way into Endicott House, and spraying everyone inside full of bullets. Then he'd kill Sean McCloud, hide the man's body where no one would ever find it, and let the cops speculate as to what made McCloud snap 'til they were blue in the face. That was the hallmark of a perfect job.

Tonight, that scenario had gotten even more perfect. McCloud had probably fucked Olivia, too. His DNA would be in her every orifice.

His dick swelled angrily at the thought. Nasty slut, spreading for whoever came along. The high-profile media aspect of a mass killing would make Chris squirm, but Gordon had that fucker by the balls.

The only problem with this scenario was that he wouldn't get to punish Olivia in any meaningful way for the wrong she had done him.

He put a hand on the bulge at this crotch. If he thought long enough, he would think of an excellent reason to justify kidnapping her first. But he didn't think real well when his dick was this hard.

Ever practical, he jerked his pants open.

He panted as he wanked away, picturing Olivia naked, on her hands and knees, gasping and squealing. Chris would tell him he was indulging himself. And so? What if he was? That was what life was about.

Indulging himself. Every chance he got. Until those spineless fuckers finally got the balls to hunt him down and make him stop.

The glare of three pairs of eyes made Liv feel stark naked.

"Bart? Blair?" Her mother's voice was hollow. "Would you leave us, please? I would like to have a private word with Olivia."

Blair stomped out of the room. Her father followed him, throwing a baleful glance back over his shoulder. Liv braced herself as her mother climbed the steps. She looked her daughter over, lip curling.

"My God," she said. "You had sex with him, didn't you?"

Liv opened her mouth, and closed it. Anything she said would be used against her. Silence was her only defense, and it was a poor one.

Amelia drew her hand back and slapped her, hard.

Liv's head snapped around. Tears sprang into her eyes as she touched her stinging jaw.

"You idiot," her mother hissed.

Well, hell. She couldn't dispute that, Liv reflected, with a tremor of laughter, quickly suppressed.

"You've been waiting for your chance to debase yourself with that lowlife trash and then rub my nose in it for years, haven't you? Did you plan this dirty rendezvous this afternoon? Under our noses?"

"No," Liv said simply.

"I cannot believe it." Her mother's eyes glittered with tears. "Blair is such an exceptional man. He's been waiting for you for years."

"I did not ask him to wait for me." Liv's voice was quiet.

Her mother made a dismissive gesture with her hand. "I doubt he'll want you now. I am repulsed, Livvy. This is so vulgar. So sleazy."

Liv's arms tightened across her chest. "Sorry you feel that way."

"That man was poison from the start," her mother fumed. "From the summer that you met him, that's when you became so difficult and contrary. You had a complete personality change!"

Yes, she reflected, with detached clarity. That summer, she had discovered her spine. And just in time.

"But I never expected something like this. I would never have dreamed you'd go this far. Under our very roof. With your father and myself and Blair downstairs. Brainstorming ideas to keep you safe." Amelia flung her head back and dashed tears away, careful not to smear her perfect makeup. "I cannot believe you are my daughter."

The words rang, like an iron-plated door slamming.

"Neither can I," Liv replied quietly.

Amelia's hand flashed out again, but Liv blocked it, grabbing her mother's wiry wrist. "Do not hit me again," she said. "Or I will hit back."

Amelia yanked her hand free. "You already have, Livvy," she whispered, her voice thick and froggy with tears. "You already have."

She swayed at the top of the stairs, caught herself on the newel post, clutched it for support. She descended, her back ramrod straight.

"Be ready to leave at six," she announced. "We will do our duty to you as best we can, even when you spit in our faces."

Liv drifted back down the corridor to her room. She hadn't thought it possible for her life to be more wrecked than it had been, but there were always more weak spots, more hidden tender bits. Between them, her mother and Sean had found and exploited them all.

She flung off the robe. She caught sight of her naked body in the mirror, and paused, looking at it as if she'd never seen it before.

Maybe she never had. She usually saw her body through a veil of self-criticism. Those big boobs, all over the place. That belly, not flat at all. Those hips, too broad. That butt, ay yi yi, don't even go there.

But Sean's passionate appreciation had been utterly genuine. There was no faking it. She'd felt his sincerity in every cell of her body.

She looked at her body, still pulsing with residual excitement, still jittery with the memory of all that incredible pleasure, and she liked what she saw. She looked pretty. Voluptuous, not fat. A woman that a sexy fantasy guy would scale fences, evade burglar alarms, climb trees and break laws for a chance to sneak into her room and ravish her.

She was tempted to call him right now, just to explain the whole stupid engagement fiasco to him, but she didn't dare.

Why should I care if you're engaged or not, princess? What's it to me? That was probably what he would say, and she couldn't take it.

She shivered. Tonight, that would shrivel her to nothing.

She put her hand between her legs. Her tender, inner bits were sore, muscles aching from being spread so wide open. Not even when she lost her virginity back in college had she felt so overwhelmed.

No, not even close. Her body was still charged, shaking. All she had to do was think about him, clenching her thighs, and pleasure burst through her, like a torrent of foaming water. Rippling through her thighs, right down into her toes. She caught her breath, wobbling.

Her hand slid deeper. Amazing, touching herself with Sean's electric presence behind her. His hot body arched over hers. His voice, muttering sexy words into her ear. And that huge penis wedged inside her, so deep, she could feel his heartbeat throbbing against her womb.

That set her off, and when she recovered, she was crouched on the ground. The very thought of the man brought her to her knees.

Her private fantasy world was all about Sean, but the scenarios had to be just so. Hot encounters in hotel rooms, where she reduced him to rubble with her sexual prowess—hey, it was a fantasy, right?

Then she'd take a shower, and pull her complex underwear back on with aplomb while he sprawled on the bed, licking his lips. She'd dress, briskly but sensuously buttoning, zipping, snapping herself into her clothes. A slick of red lipstick, a toss of her hair. She'd throw her purse over her shoulder. A bright, impenetrable smile, a fluttery wave of her fingers. "Have a nice day," she would say, ever so sweetly. "Bye."

In her fantasies, he begged her not to go. Demanded to know when he could see her again. She shrugged. Cruel Liv. "We'll see how I feel," she'd say, merciless. "Don't call me. I'll call you . . . if I want to."

And *snick*, the door swung shut in the face of his pleading.

There was a lot of latitude for variation in that hotel room theme, but the key element, that crucial power dynamic, was always the same.

She swallowed over a quivering in her throat. If she had that affair with him, it would be her lying on the bed, destroyed, watching him pull on his clothes. Her, begging to know when she could see him again.

How many times could she survive that? She struggled to her feet, stared at herself. Her body was marked everywhere. Almost invisible but sensitive scrapes on her face and breasts from his beard stubble, lips puffy and red from his kisses. Faint marks on her hips from where he'd held her in place while he thrust into her. Her face grew pink. But not pink enough to cover the angry red splotch on her jaw from her mother's slap.

Wow. It was her day, written all over her body. All the high points.

She wound her hair up into a roll. Back into the shower. Enough of this bullshit. Dithering over to-have-or-not-to-have sex with a dangerous guy? She had real problems, thanks very much.

Somebody was trying to kill her. A dab of perspective, please.

She thought the situation through as she soaped herself up. It was true that she'd turned rebellious the summer that she'd met Sean.

He'd started the process himself, egging her on. Then, the episode in the jail had served as an emotional vaccination. Her fear of making people angry vanished. It simply held no more terror for her. She'd experienced the worst, so why cower, why cringe? To hell with them all.

From then on, she'd suited herself. Enrolled in the classes that interested her, chose the major she wanted, hung out with the friends she liked, applied for jobs she wanted. Her mother had been hysterically frustrated by this new, inexplicably difficult Liv. She'd even cut off all the family funds in an effort to control her. But that had backfired.

Being forced to earn her own living had freed Liv completely. Maybe she ate beans and ramen, and shopped in thrift stores, but at least she could breathe. Her mother wanted to love her, but compliance was the only fuel that could make that machine function. Liv's refusal to comply was a refusal of her mother's love. Period. A tragic dead-end.

She was startled to find herself sobbing under the stream of hot water. She thought she'd given up the fantasy of maternal acceptance years ago. She must still be grieving for it. Maybe she always would.

So she was on her own. No surprise. She had been for a long time. She'd just never been on the run from a killer on her own.

Brr. It made that lonely-bird-in-a-gilded-cage scenario look almost good by comparison. Almost. She didn't have much money. Her credit cards were all maxed. Every penny she'd ever saved was sunk into Books & Brew. Her vehicle was evidence in a police investigation.

She had some jewelry she could pawn. She'd go to a resort town. Wait tables, work for tips. She'd contact the police when she got settled, ask for advice. There should be a system in place that might help her.

If she was going, it had to be soon. She stuck her head out the bedroom door. Still a low hum of activity downstairs. Not yet.

She packed and repacked her bags. Her main dilemma was her stash of unread novels. She finally tossed out a pair of jeans and a handful of underwear to make room for all of them. First things first.

Four o'clock found her, dressed and packed and vibrating with nerves, staring fixedly at the little clock on the bedside table.

She'd opted for jeans, schlumpy sandals. A plain blouse. She'd composed a careful note, apologizing and explaining as best she could.

The second hand ticked to four. Goodbye to life as she knew it.

She stuck her head out the door. It was utterly quiet.

She staggered down the corridor loaded like a donkey, lugging her purse, her laptop, her backpack, her suitcase. She made noise, but no one came bursting out to stop her.

Part of her must have been hoping someone would.

She left her bags by the back door and nicked the spare keys to her parents' Volvo sedan. She would leave it in long term airport parking and mail the keys back to them. Now to slip past the police who were parked on both sides of the property. It felt disrespectful to their efforts to protect her, but there was nothing she could do.

She silently apologized to them in her head.

Fortunately there were enough hedges and foliage to plan a sneaky route down to the riverfront garage where the Volvo was parked. She'd had plenty of practice doing that as a girl, avoiding her mother's eagle eye. No one should see her leave from there.

She disabled the back door alarm, and had a bad moment on the steps. Four AM was not a friendly time. The bushes looked like so many hunched, hungry animals lying in wait. She scurried and slunk, for a nervous, guilty eternity, as if she were doing something illicit and bad.

She finally made it, and heaved the garage door open. She started up the car, flipped off the headlights, and eased out onto the road in the moonlight. She picked up speed around the first curve, making plans as she went. A quick stop at the nearest bank to take whatever she could out of a cash machine, and then straight onto the highway—

Oh, Jesus. She screeched to a stop, just inches from the mud-spattered black Jeep parked crosswise across the road after the blind curve. Blocking both narrow lanes. Oh no, no. That was so wrong.

Terror jangled through every nerve, an awful blinding flash of exactly how brainless she'd been, how badly she'd underestimated—

The shadow sprang up. *Thunk,* an angular metal something punched through the window, scattering pebbles of shatterproof glass over her lap. *Omigodomigod that is a gun* screamed a faraway voice.

A black-gloved gorilla hand wrenched up the lock, released the door handle, plucked her out of the car and flung her onto the asphalt.

The thing squatted over her. Rough cut-outs in his black mask showed wide staring eyes. She sensed that he was smiling.

"Olivia." His voice was an oily croon. "At last we meet."

He clapped a cloth over her nose. She faded into nowhere.

The sky was heavy with bruised-looking clouds. Thunder growled, rais-ing hackles on his back. Kev sat on his usual rock, but he wasn't grinning. His hair stood practically on end. His torso was bare as always, taut with wiry muscle, but his skin was goosepimpled in the chill.

Sean pre-empted him, before he could start his usual rant.

"So? I've gotten off my dumb ass. Happy now?"

Kev's eyes were haunted, shadowy. "Not yet. Move it faster."

"Move what faster?" Sean snapped.

Kev's eyebrow twitched up. "Your dumb ass."

He lifted his arms. They were bound at the wrist with plasticuffs, so tightly that the plastic had cut deep into his flesh. Blood trickled in long rivulets down his muscular forearms, dripping off his elbows.

Sean woke with a start, knocking over his coffee. He stared around the office. It was lit only with the glow of the X-Ray Specs map grid. Cold coffee dripped onto his lap. He spun the chair back out of range. "Goddamnit, Kev," he complained. "That was a dirty trick."

He was shoving beacon paperwork out of the puddle when he saw the flash on the screen. Her icons were moving.

Then they stopped, and Sean stopped mopping coffee, muttering obscenities, feeling sorry for himself. He stopped breathing.

There was no reason for that car to stop. It was fifteen hundred meters from the driveway down to Endicott House. There were no traffic lights on that stretch of road. No crossroads. No driveways. Just an access to a long-abandoned logging track at the bottom of the valley.

The adrenaline in his system jolted up a few notches.

One of the icons detached itself, and began to move away from the others. He grabbed the phone, punched in Davy's number.

"Sean? What the fuck?" His brother's voice was grumpy, but clear. Davy always woke up sharp. A drowsy female voice murmured.

So Davy was sleeping with his wife again. Thank God for small favors. "Get your ass out of bed," he said brusquely. "I don't have a Specs monitor mounted in my truck, so you have to spot me."

"Why? What's going on? What's the—"

"The beacons I planted last night. On Liv." Impatience roughened his voice. "The group stopped on a blind curve on Chaeffer Creek Road. One of them just detached and wandered off into the river canyon."

Davy considered this. "Could there be a logical explanation for this, other than the conclusion you have obviously leaped to?"

"What? That she stopped in her limo a klom from her daddy's driveway at four in the morning, and wandered into the woods to take a piss? Get real! Is the computer booting?"

"Yeah, yeah. Calm down. Program's loading."

"You ready for the codes? Oh, fuck me. The icon's moving faster. She's in a car, on that old logging road. Maybe the guy has an offroad vehicle. Can you take the code? I've got to get off this fucking phone! I've got to move! My cell won't work until I'm on the other side of the Bluffs."

"Give it to me," Davy said tersely.

He recited the code of the icon. "I've got a handheld in my kit, but she'll be out of range by the time I get to Chaeffer Canyon."

"It's rough country," Davy said. "He could go up over Long Prairie, or turn left and head to Orem Lake. OK, I got her. Moving south, at fifteen miles an hour." He paused. "That, uh, sucks."

"Right." He flung the phone down and sprinted out the door for the Jeep. Tires spat gravel as the vehicle bounded over the driveway. "I'm hanging up. Make the calls."

"What calls?"

"Christ, Davy, do I have to tell you everything? Call her folks, call the cops, call the state troopers, call the goddamn National Guard!"

"Calm down," Davy soothed. "Do you have to show your hand already? Get to where the rest of the beacons are, see what you find. Make sure you've got a genuine situation before you blow this thing completely out of the water. I don't want to visit you in jail."

"Who cares if I go to jail?" Sean bellowed. "This is Liv's life!"

"I care," Davy said grimly. "God help me, but I do. Hang in there. She's headed south, if she's in that car. Call me when you get there."

This was a hell of a time for his combat cool to desert him. Sean usually snapped into a state of utter calm when bullets started to fly. Not worrying whether he lived or died freed up a guy's concentration to an amazing extent. But this was way different. Christ, this was Liv.

The only thing that would calm him down would be ripping the steaming guts out of this piece of of dogshit with his own hands.

The road sped beneath his wheels. He screeched to a stop at the canyon road, leaped out. Sprinted along the shoulder.

The sight hit him like a fist in the belly. A black sedan, its crumpled nose crunched against a tree at the bottom of the canyon.

He dove over the edge, slipped and slid down the gravel, struggled through the bushes. He was making guttural, animal noises, seeing Kev's charred body, flames dancing in twisted black metal, the—

No. He could not wig out yet. Not til he knew the worst.

He reached the car, peered inside.

Empty. Oh, God. No bodies, no blood. Just the contents of Liv's purse, scattered over the backseat. He started to cry, like a little kid.

He dashed tears away as he punched in Davy's number, crawling back up the hill with desperate, slip-sliding haste.

"Yeah?" Davy asked. "So?"

He scrambled over the top, leaped into his truck. "Make the calls. Someone pitched the car into the canyon. Liv's gone. Where's the icon?"

"Halfway to Orem Lake. Moving steadily at fifteen miles an hour."

He topped the rise that led down the rough logging track. "Make the calls, Davy. If this guy wastes me, you have to help them find her."

"Do not say shit like that!" Davy snarled. "You're armed, right?"

"Not really, but too bad for me. Whatever." He stepped on the gas.

Thud. Thud. Thud. Thud. "Rise and shine, babydoll."

Liv struggled slowly to the surface at the banging sound, the summoning voice. She was afraid to open her eyes. Something terrible was waiting for her. She could feel it, crouching. Waiting to leap out.

She opened her eyes, and it all rushed back, together with a crippling jolt of fear. She locked her jaw to stifle the whimpering.

Her wrists burned. They were bound with hard plastic strapping, like the ratcheted tie on a heavy duty garbage bag. There was tape over her mouth. She couldn't speak, couldn't scream, could barely breathe.

It was dark. Faint light filtered in, from a small, dirty window. From jagged cracks in the rough plank walls. The place stank of rot, mildew, and the sharp odor of fresh plastic tarp.

"Right on schedule," said a rasping voice.

She jerked her head around, staring wild-eyed at the hooded nightmare looming over her. She could smell his sharp, skunklike musk from the ground. He was holding a big, ugly hammer.

He leaned over her body, and swung the hammer against the wall above her, *bam*. She twisted to look. A nail. That could not be good.

"OK, darling. Let's get you into position." He grabbed her bound wrists, jerking her up with a force that almost dislocated her shoulders, and hauled her back against the wall, then stretched her arms up and hooked the plastic cuffs over the thick nail sunk into the two-by-four.

"Now hold real still, babydoll. Or I'll mash your fingers into jam."

Bang. She tried not to flinch as he swung the hammer one more time, bending the head of the nail up into a cruel hook.

He sat down cross-legged next to her. The position was surreally casual and friendly. He patted her leg, and peeled off his leather gloves.

"Am I too scary with the mask?" He yanked it off. "Is this better?"

Oh, no, it was not better. It was so very much not better, that he had no intention of leaving her in any condition to identify him. Her head throbbed, her stomach churned. There was a flat, metallic taste in her mouth, from whatever he had drugged her with.

She had never seen this man. He was in his mid-forties, barrel chested as a comic book villain. His shoulders and arms were swollen with muscle, his belly thick with fat. He wore an overly tight black T-shirt. His face might have been beefcake handsome when he was younger, but it had coarsened, puffy under the eyes, skin pitted, broken veins. The way he looked at her body made her curl into a ball.

"Oh, no, sweetheart." He pushed up her blouse 'til his fingers found warm, shrinking skin. He pulled out a wicked looking knife.

Liv's blood froze. His shiny lips stretched out over big teeth. "We need to talk." His tone was conversational. She stared at him, blinking.

He laughed. "Oops. I forgot all about that little detail." He grabbed the tape on her mouth and ripped it off.

Air hit her dry throat, making her cough and hack. She barely recognized the thin, high, quavering voice as her own. "Who are you?"

"I'm the one who asks the questions." He touched her face with the tip of his knife, tracing patterns on her cheekbone.

She stared, hypnotized, at the blade. It tickled. Her mind raced. What could she know that would interest him? She was a librarian, for God's sake. A would-be bookseller. What could she say that would keep her alive long enough to hope for rescue?

Yeah, right. She had organized her own doom, sneaking away

hours before anyone might sound the alarm. "What do you want? Did you send the e-mails? And burn my store? And set that bomb?"

"Of course. Who else loves you so much?" His voice had a sing-song lilt. "Don't bother screaming. There's no one around for miles."

"You were watching me?" She tried to swallow. "This morning?"

"I've been watching you for weeks," he said. "It was all so easy. You sneaky girl. You crept off all alone. Silly Olivia. I put pressure switches under all the car seats. I knew the second you got into that car. I thought of everything, you see. It's because I care so much."

His friendly tone was a bizarre contrast to the senseless things he said. "Listen up, babydoll. We have to be brisk, if we want time for the passionate physical encounter that I've been dreaming of." He giggled when she cringed away from him. "I love it when they play hard to get."

"What do you want to know?" she whispered.

He pressed the tip of the knife under her ear. She stared at his knife hand, frozen. "Where are the tapes?" he asked.

She blinked, utterly blank. "Tapes?"

The knife broke the skin. A bead of blood trickled down her neck. Hot, slow and ticklish. "It's not in your best interests to play dumb."

"I swear, I have no idea what you're talking about."

The man heaved a theatrical sigh. "Tell me what McCloud told you. Tell me about his notebook. What was in it, where it went."

"McCloud? I haven't seen Sean for fifteen years, and he didn't—"

Whack. The slap made her ears ring. "Not Sean. The other one. His brother. Don't be thick, Olivia. It makes me angry. I'm being sweet and gentle now. You wouldn't like to see me angry. Trust me on this."

"I don't know his brothers! Davy and Con are both older than him. They'd already left town when I met Sean, so I never even—"

Slap, slap, an openhand and a sharp backhand batted her head back and forth. Her eyes flooded with tears. "Not them." The fake friendliness was gone from his voice. "The other brother."

She squeezed her eyes shut. "You mean . . . Sean's twin? Kev?" she faltered. "But Kev—Kev's dead."

"Twin?" The knife lifted away. "They were twins?"

"Y-y-yes," she said, teeth chattering. "Identical."

"Hmm. Interesting. They didn't look like twins."

She was pathetically grateful to have given him something he wanted, but the reprieve was all too brief.

"Kevin McCloud told you where he hid the tapes," he said. "I had you in my rifle scope. I saw that son-of-a-bitch hand you that notebook. I never forget a face. Particularly not a pretty one."

His words blew her mind wide open and three hundred and sixty degrees around with their terrible implications. "Oh, my God," she whispered. "You're talking about fifteen years ago? Those guys chasing Kev, trying to kill him . . . it was all true?"

"You know damn well it's true," the man snarled. "We didn't know your name, or I would have taken care of you then. And that stubborn fuck Kevin never told us dick, no matter what we did to him. And we were creative. You would not believe the crazy shit we tried on that kid."

Her mind shied away in horror from the images his words invoked. "You tortured Kev?" she whispered. "Oh, my God."

He gave her a mock bow. "C'est moi. Then I saw you on TV. Remember that interview about your bookstore? You must have been feeling pretty confident, hmm? Must have thought I'd given up."

"My God," she whispered helplessly.

He plucked at the buttons of her blouse with the tip of his knife. They popped off, the shirt gaping. "Where did he hide those tapes?"

"I—I don't know anything about any tapes—"

"I'll start with your ear." The knife dug in beneath her earlobe. "I'm sorry to get you all bloody before we play, but if you insist—"

"No! Please! He stopped me outside the library," she quavered.

"What did he tell you?"

She squeezed her eyes shut, struggled to remember. "He said . . . he said someone was trying to kill him. He didn't say who."

"And the notebook he gave you? What did you do with it?"

Liv hesitated, her body vibrating with stark fear.

"I don't need to worry about fingerprints, or genetic material," he murmured, almost idly. "They'll never find your body. There's a plastic tarp to catch the mess. I'll wrap up what's left of you after I'm done. Tuck you in a nice, deep, wormy hole. It's all ready for you."

She hoped desperately that she was not killing Sean by saying this. "He told me to give it to his brother." Her voice was barely audible.

"And did you?"

She nodded, insofar as she could with a knife at her throat.

"Tell me all about this notebook, Olivia. What was in it?"

"Ah, sketches," she squeaked. "I just leafed through it. Landscapes, I think. Animals, birds, maybe."

"Anything written?"

"He wrote a note to his brother," she admitted.

"What did it say?" His voice was frighteningly gentle.

Her eyes overflowed. She hated herself for her lack of self-control. "I couldn't read it." She forced the words out. "It was in some strange code. I don't know anything about any tapes. I wish to God I did."

"Ah."

There was a long, terrible silence. She shut her eyes, and waited for him to do something horrible to her with that knife.

"You know what?" he asked, in a tone of discovery.

Her eyes opened a careful slit.

"I believe you," he said wonderingly. "I actually do. You poor unlucky little bitch. You really don't know fuck-all about any of it, do you? All of this trouble and expense and exposure. All for nothing."

Her teeth chattered. The hideous leer spreading over his face killed any hope before it could surface in her mind.

"Unfortunately for you, this state of affairs is no longer current." His face was a mask of regret. "You know way too much now. Nothing personal, babydoll. I'll try to make it up to you by making your last moments very sensual." He wrenched her blouse open. Buttons flew, pattering onto the tarp around her. The fabric gave way, fell off her in shreds. The knife bit through the cord that held the cups of her bra together.

"I love to look at naked girls. Never get tired of it," he said genially. He grabbed the waistband of her pants, started in on the buttons.

She began to scream. Grabbed the nail, closed her fingers over it until it bit into her palm. Yanked with desperate strength.

Chapter
11

There she was. He'd circled the lake, and snagged her signal on the handheld. He coasted, hoping to gain an element of stealth.

This was no deranged stalker. This had been carefully planned, by someone with time and leisure to rig an ambush, with electronic backup, skilled in demolitions, who had studied the area meticulously.

A professional. Which wrenched open doors in his mind. Doors best left shut, if he meant to maintain a passing resemblance to sanity.

Midnight Project is trying to kill me. They saw Liv. Will kill her if they find her. Make her leave town today or she's meat.

The only time Liv could have attracted the attention of a person like T-Rex was when she was hanging out with a McCloud. This was just the kind of fucked up shit that routinely happened to the men in his family. Dad had trained them for this stuff since they were born.

Orem Lake gleamed in the pink glow of dawn, its surface ruffled by the wind. It was a small, pristine lake, the ice-cold water a clear blue-green. There was only a handful of seasonal hunting and fishing cabins.

The monitor told him to bear left. He jerked up the emergency brake, and leaped out of the truck, following shallow depressions in the grass that led up into the towering forest. He passed a Jeep, its plate number obscured by spattered mud. The track dead-ended into a rock face. The cabin was almost hidden in the undergrowth. It was a ruin, siding rotten, roof almost bare of shingles. It perched on a low cliff of black granite, smeared with green, yellow and orange lichen, shrouded by vast, moss-draped trees.

No one had used this place in years, possibly decades. If not for the beacon, he would never have found her. No one would have.

If she was still alive.

He pushed the bowel-loosening wave of fear away. If T-Rex had wanted her dead quickly, he could have offed her at Chaeffer Canyon.

Doubts chewed at him. Con and Davy, bitching about how he never considered consequences. Fine and good, if it was only himself getting fucked up, but this was Liv. He wondered how far behind the cops were. If Liv's chances were better if he waited for backup.

He could doom her by racing in like a lone-ranger asshole, or he could doom her by waiting. He didn't want to spend the rest of what passed for his life seeing Liv's last moments, knowing he might have saved her if he'd been quicker, smarter. Like Kev's pickup, endlessly falling in the back of his mind. He couldn't go through it again.

He'd rather die.

Christ, how he wished he had Davy, Seth, and Con at his back. That he was packing his H&K, or the SIG. The Ruger packed a punch, but it was an emergency backup weapon, with only five shots.

But no. It was family policy not to store firearms at the Bluffs house, since it stood empty so much of the time.

Use your brain to think with, not your glands. The stern voices lecturing in his head slowed his headlong dash to a stagger.

But his goddamn brain wasn't offering up any brilliant ideas.

A wrenching scream from the direction of the cabin propelled him like a bullet from a gun. To hell with his useless brain.

His glands were the best thing he had going for him, so fuck it.

The cabin was propped on scaffolding to level it out on the slope, so the windows that weren't boarded up were too high to see through.

He scrambled up the slope towards the door. Shoved and tore his way through a jungle of thorny vines and hanging moss.

The door had a warped latch, and a rusty padlock dangling from it. Sean pushed the door. It shrieked on its hinges. So much for stealth.

Two bodies struggled on a shiny black plastic tarp in the dark, moldy room. The guy whipped around at the sound, white-rimmed, bulging blue eyes, in a thick bulldog face. He was straddling Liv. He could see her jeans-clad legs, flopping beneath the guy's bulk.

Shit. He couldn't shoot the guy with Liv right behind him. T-Rex spun around. A gun. Bullets blasted, punching into the walls, the door. Duck, tuck, and roll. Bullets whipped through his hair, his sleeve. One scored a white-hot line across his back. Filthy window glass shattered.

When he rolled up onto his feet, the guy had the gun to Liv's head. His arm held her chin back. Her wrists were bound in front of her. She was naked to the waist. Blood trickled down her torso from the side of her neck, shockingly bright against her pale skin.

"Drop the gun, or I'll blow her head off," the guy said.

Sean assessed his options in that endless nanosecond, and sent a telepathic apology to Davy and Con as his fingers loosened and let go.

He hated to make them go through it again, but they had wives, families. They would get through it. And Sean had just been marking time since Kev died, waiting for the other shoe to drop. The gun, thudding to the floor, was the sound of the shoe dropping.

"Kick it over to me," the guy instructed.

The gun made a whispering scrape as it slid across the dirty, ragged linoleum floor. He began slowly rising to his feet.

"Stay down on your knees, asshole. Hands behind your head."

"The police will be along real soon," Sean said, sinking back down. "She's transmitting a radio signal from her shoe. Want to see it?"

"Yeah, of course," the guy said. "Of course she is. Of course they are." He let out a high-pitched giggle. "Just look at this. Should I gut-shoot you, and let you bleed to death? Or sever your spinal column and leave you paralyzed? I oughta leave you alive, with the door open, for the animals. You can witness yourself becoming part of the food chain." He slid the barrel of the gun down over Liv's throat, between her breasts. "I don't even know where to begin. I want to eat her up."

Liv shrieked as he chomped into her neck and he sloppily licked the stinging wound. She clutched the nail she had wrenched out of the wall as the cold gun barrel made its way back up her half-bare body. He tucked it beneath her chin, jabbing it painfully deep.

"I've been looking forward to this for fifteen years," T-Rex said. He shoved her chin up with the gun and kissed her, his muscular tongue poking into her mouth. She tasted her own blood, and almost retched.

"As soon as I get him squared away, I'll put away the gun, baby-doll," he went on. "I'll just use the knife. Lasts longer that way."

The world narrowed down to a pinpoint of brilliant clarity.

She did not want to die slowly and horribly at the hands of this monster. A bullet in the head would at least be quick—and it might give Sean a chance. He deserved a chance. He was magnificent. Charging in to save her, against all odds, all hope or logic.

She convulsed. The gun barrel slipped up her neck, slick with blood and sweat. She jerked her bound hands, the nail protruding between her fingers, in what she hoped was the direction of his face, and sank her teeth into his wrist. The nail hit oily, slippery flesh.

He shrieked. The gun went off, deafening her.

T-Rex tried to shake her off. His skin was slimy. His blood tasted metallic and hot. His muscles and tendons strained against her teeth.

The gun went off again. She could no longer hear it. The explosion reverberated through their struggling bodies. He tried to angle the barrel to aim it at her skull. Jammed his fingers into the corners of her mouth. He was going to rip her jaw right off, but she couldn't have let go if she wanted to. She was locked on, like a maddened pit bull.

She opened her eyes. The heel of Sean's boot brushed past her face, slammed into T-Rex's hand. Her jaw loosened as the blow jarred them against the wall. The gun bounced against the wall, hit the floor.

So did she.

T-Rex swung up his massive knee. Sean barely blocked the blow to his groin, and the vicious jab to the temple. So the dude wasn't all gym-rat muscle and ego. He was scarily quick. The glow in his wild eyes suggested drug enhancement. Whatever the shit was, it worked.

The guy came at him, howling, in a blur of kicks and punches.

Blood splattered onto Sean with each new offensive, but T-Rex was feeling no pain. He herded Sean into a corner. A kick to his face knocked him off course, but he swung back, lunging for Sean's throat.

Sean blocked, grabbed, twisted. T-Rex didn't even feel the torqued tendons. Bad breath, he noted with odd detachment, as they careened toward the back of the cabin. Foul. Guy should floss. They swayed, legs splayed, trying to trip each other. Barrelling towards a warped door that led to the deck. They tore it off its rusty hinges and hit the deck with a rending crash. Panes of glass beneath them shattered, tinkled. Rotten planks shuddered and groaned, bowing at the impact.

Sean ended up on the bottom, as luck would have it.

T-Rex's face was barely recognizable as human. Sean blocked a chopping blow to the collarbone. T-Rex got his enormous hands around Sean's neck. It became a wrestling match. Sweat dripped from the guy's brow, stinging Sean's eyes. He kept his neck rigid, freeing his hand for a quick, desperate jab at T-Rex's white-rimmed eyes.

T-Rex jerked back, and Sean jabbed in a sharp uppercut that rocked the bigger man's head back on his thick neck. That broke his concentration, but Sean hadn't even rolled up to his knees before T-Rex smashed him against the sagging deck railing. Planks cracked, bowed, and gave. Nails screeched as they were torn from their long home. The deck tipped. There was nothing solid to grab. He pitched over the edge.

It was a long fall, but the cliff was not sheer, and he bounced and slid over outcroppings of granite before landing on his feet, fortunately, bending at the knees. He rolled, came to rest facedown, his nose inches from crystalline water that lapped over the multicolored pebbles.

He scrambled up. T-Rex had not fallen with him. What was left of the deck dangled at a forty-five degree angle, planks scattered on the pebbled beach. T-Rex had glommed on to a tough shrub on the cliff face, and was pulling himself up onto the rocks where the cabin was perched.

Sean looked frantically around. He was trapped in a cove, rock on all sides, thorny foliage that would take ten desperate minutes to crawl through. T-Rex would be back up there in a couple of minutes. He pried his knife out. The angle sucked, but it was worth a try. He threw.

The knife embedded itself in the back of T-Rex's ass.

The guy yelped, slid, caught himself. He reached back, and plucked the knife out of himself. "Thanks for the blade, you shiteating prick. You're going to love what I do to your girlfriend's face with it."

He stuck Sean's blade between his teeth and kept climbing.

Sawing through plastic strapping that held one's own wrists together required a cool head and steady hands, neither of which she had. T-Rex's knife was wickedly sharp, and she kept nicking herself, or maybe worse than nicking. She could be slitting her own wrists. Not that she cared. Bleeding to death was the least of her worries right now.

She knelt on the doorstep, pressing her knee to the knife handle to hold the protruding blade steady enough to saw at the cuffs. Her thighs wobbled. Her fingers were slippery with blood. The knife kept slipping to one side or the other. She shook with desperate laughter. The first time in her life that she'd actually wished she were heavier.

She found a lucky angle. The thing snapped free. She dove back into the cabin without hesitating, scrambling for the guns.

Her head rang, she saw stars, and the silence in her gun blast-deafened ears felt blank, unnatural, as if she were underwater. She scrabbled over the dirty floor. The guns, the guns. She found Sean's revolver beneath a fold of crumpled tarp. T-Rex's gun she found under a pile of yellowed newspapers. She could only deal with one, so she shoved Sean's into the back of her jeans, hoping she wouldn't shoot herself in the butt, and clutched the other gun with shaking hands.

She might not even be able to use the thing, if it came down to it. She couldn't seem to make her numb fingers contract.

"Hey there, babydoll."

T-Rex's oily croon sounded small and faraway, through the ringing in her ears. Liv brandished the gun, holding the sinking, fainting horror at bay with everything she had. Oh God. *Sean.*

T-Rex saw the wild shaking of the gun barrel. He licked heavy, shiny lips, and grinned. His face was a shining mask of blood, which made his eyes seem pale and wild, like a maddened animal.

He held a knife. It had to be Sean's. Blood dripped from its tip.

He followed her horrified gaze, and started to laugh, waving it in the air. "Yeah, I had some fun with your boyfriend, before I slit his throat. Didn't you hear him scream? Want to know what I did to him?"

"Get away from me." Her own voice sounded farther away than his. A shaking wisp. "Don't take one step closer. I'll blow your head off."

"Oh yeah? That's a Beretta PX Storm, babydoll. That's a man's gun. It'll break your little lily white fingers. It's not for a pretty fuckable doll like you. Game over."

He stepped in the cabin door. She found herself backing up. Big mistake. She could tell from the way his gloating smirk widened.

"I'm serious," she quavered. "I'll shoot you dead."

"No you won't. You're a good little girl. You won't give me any trouble. I bet you've never given anybody any trouble in your life."

"I will." She swallowed over rock in her throat. "I'm big trouble."

His big bloody hands reached for her. "You don't want me mad at you," he murmured. "You want me to love you tender. Come to papa. I'll make you forget your pretty blond boy."

Mentioning Sean was his mistake. It broke his spell, like a bubble popping. Her arms swung up. She squeezed the trigger. *Bam.* She heard the sound, as if from miles away. The recoil flung her arms up, and she almost knocked herself right between the eyes with the heavy gun.

A ragged hole appeared in the door.

T-Rex jumped. "Fuck!"

She took aim. "Wrong." She pulled the trigger. A pane of glass in the door exploded. "I don't want you to love me. Hate me. I hate you right back, you piece of shit." She took a step towards him as she shot.

He backed up as the bullet smashed into the wall behind him. His eyes looked blank, startled, as he stumbled out the door. His retreat triggered a ferocious desire in her to give chase. She staggered after him, shooting wildly, screaming out her grief and fury. He limped away, in a lopsided jog-trot. Her shots were all over the place, she had no control, no technique. She was a mindless force of nature.

She would rip that asshole into bloody pieces for hurting Sean.

A Jeep was parked in the fir trees. He sprinted for it, leaped in. The engine roared to life. Liv shot at it, shrieking with triumph as the back window exploded. The Jeep roared into reverse, bounced backwards over the rough ground, right for her. She leaped to the side, rolling head over butt into a green hollow choked with a spiky tangle of bushes. The Jeep bounded over the primitive road. Liv gave chase.

The Jeep disappeared around a curve, the sound retreating. There was an empty *click, click* under her compulsively squeezing finger.

"Clip's empty, Liv."

She spun around with a gasping shriek.

Sean. He wasn't dead. He was standing there, streaked with blood, hair caked with mud and leaves, but alive. Whole.

Icy doubt gripped her. Maybe she'd snapped under the strain, and he was just a wishful hallucination. She stared at him, eyes welling full.

"It's you," she whispered.

His eyes narrowed. "Uh, you were expecting someone else?"

She pressed her hand to her mouth, heart swelling with joy. A wishful hallucination wouldn't mouth off at a time like this. He was the real deal. Her genuine, pain-in-the-ass Sean. "I thought you were dead," she babbled. "He told me he tortured you. He told me he—"

"I thought he got you, too." He sucked in gulps of air. "Jesus. My nerves are trashed." He leaned over, panting and bracing his hands on his knees, and shot her a cautious glance. "Could you not point that gun at me, babe? I know it's empty, but I could still use a break."

She'd forgotten she was holding the thing. It slid from her fingers, thudded onto the springy mat of pine needles. She plucked his revolver out of the back of her jeans. Held it out to him.

Sean took it, and leaned down to scoop up T-Rex's gun. That was when she saw the bloody scrapes on his shoulders, his arms, his back.

"My God," she whispered. "You're hurt."

He waved his hand. "I've gotten worse playing contact sports."

"You're bleeding," she protested. "A lot. You call that nothing?"

He shrugged. "Compared to what T-Rex had in mind for us, we look ready for the debutante ball."

She doubled over, covered her face, and quietly dissolved.

"Sorry, princess," he offered gently. "Didn't mean to set you off."

"It's not your fault." She straightened up, mopped her face. "You do tend to catch me at a disadvantage."

"I think you look gorgeous. Sprinting through the woods, tits bouncing, bullets flying . . . wow. Talk about a fashion accessory."

Her whole body started to vibrate again. "Please, don't," she pleaded. "Don't make me laugh again. I warn you. I'll fall to pieces."

"But seriously." He laid his hand gently on her back. "You were hell on wheels. That was fucking amazing. The nail in the face, the bite, the gun. I worship at your shrine, babe. Who knew?"

"Hardly." His admiring tone made her redden with shame. She didn't deserve it, after the way she'd begged and trembled like a trapped gerbil. "I didn't put any holes in him."

"You sent him off at a dead run," Sean said. "Which is more than I managed to do. You rule. Remind me never to piss you off."

"Oh, I have," she quavered. "I do. You never listen."

He made a harsh, wordless sound, and grabbed her.

Their hearts pounded together, like drums. Sean's hands clutched handfuls of her hair. "I could hold you all day, but that guy's going to be back," he said. "I don't know what he wants from you, but we better—"

"I do." The words exploded out of her. "That guy killed Kev."

Sean let go, and stared into Liv's face, speechless. His world dipped and spun, changing shape with a violence that made him dizzy.

Kev. Of course.

"He tried to get me to tell him about Kev," Liv babbled. "He wants to know where the tapes are, whatever that means. He thought I'd been in hiding. It was true. Kev didn't kill himself. He was murdered. By that guy, and maybe some others. He said 'we,' like there were more."

The tapes. The proof's in the sketchbook. It's all there. Dumb ass.

He heard Kev's dream voice, saw the patient look in his eyes, as he waited for his lame-brain twin to get his shit together and figure it out. It was a paradox, how Liv's words could blow his mind into total disarray, and at the same time, be the confirmation of something he'd always known. A puzzle piece, set quietly into place.

He'd split his mind apart to deal with that paradox. The strongest, best part of himself, the part that knew Kev wasn't crazy, had been clubbed into unconsciousness and locked in a closet. The worthless garbage that was left over was what had passed for Sean McCloud.

He was paralyzed with rage. They'd murdered his brother, and fucked with his head about it. Soiled Kev's memory. Conditioned his whole life. Everything he'd done, everything he was. Every morning that he'd opened his eyes with that wrong, sucking feeling in his gut.

And then they had tried to hurt Liv. His hands fisted, white-knuckled. Liv's mouth was still moving, but he could not hear what she said. His ears roared like he'd just gone over a waterfall.

But his fury at Kev's killers was nothing compared to how angry he was with himself. For giving in. Falling for it. Fucking *idiot.*

He wiped mud off the faceplate of his watch. He had to sharpen up, if they wanted to stay alive. He'd reached the cabin less than ten minutes ago. Davy would have called the cops maybe a half hour ago.

He pulled the cell phone out of his pocket, amazed it was still in one piece. Popped the shell, pried the beacon out, tossed it. Con and Davy would be pissed, but it would resolve their immediate ethical dilemma with the cops if he removed himself from their grid.

"Are you in need of medical attention?" His brusque question cut off whatever she might have been saying. "How badly did he hurt you?"

She blinked. "Uh . . . I hadn't really thought about it yet."

He grabbed her hands. Already clotting. He lifted her hair to check the bite, the cut beneath her ear. The cut had stopped oozing, but the bite worried him. T-Rex's crocodile mouth had to be more toxic than most. "You look OK," he said. "You're not going to go into shock on me, are you? Do you feel faint? Cold? Do you have the shivers?"

She shook her head.

"Good. Then we're out of here." He scooped her into the circle of his arm and hustled her along beside him at a brisk, stumbling trot.

"Aren't we . . . shouldn't we wait for the police?"

"Nope. We are running for our lives. You got a problem with that?"

She pondered that. "Not exactly. But I would like to be consulted."

"No time for consultations." He yanked the Wrangler's door open, tossed her in. He reached into the back and grabbed the bottle of water that had been rolling around back there. "Rinse yourself off."

She took it gratefully, and poured water into her hands, splashing with it. He grabbed her right sandal and pried it off. Ripped the upper back from the sole and plucked out a flat cluster of wires and circuits.

She blinked. "Oh, my God."

"Yeah, it's a tracking device. And yeah, I put it there." He tossed the thing off into the woods. "You going to give me a hard time about it? Go on. I dare you."

She bit her lip, her eyes wary. "Um, maybe not right now."

"That's smart." He gave her back what was left of her sandal. She held the flapping, ruined thing in her hands, bewildered.

He slammed her door, and loped to the driver's side. "We're sitting ducks," he said, starting up the engine. "We can't wait around for the cops with just five 357 Magnum bullets between us and T-Rex. He's probably planning to ambush us on the road. Or pick us off from up there—" he indicated a rock above them, "—or there." He pointed at the wall of granite that bounded the lake. "I've seen enough dead bodies. I will not let this guy kill you. I have had *enough*, you hear me?"

"OK," she soothed. "I don't want him to kill me, either. It's just that . . . wouldn't we be safer on the road if we were with the police?"

"We're not taking the road." He steered around a washed out, yawning hole in the road, and picked up speed, bumping and jouncing.

She gave him a big-eyed look. "Um, excuse me?"

"Offroad. We'll cut across Long Prairie and hook up with Burnt Ridge Road, which will take us to Garnier Creek, towards Taggert. Don't worry. This vehicle can handle it. T-Rex's Jeep could, too, but hopefully he won't be expecting us to go that route."

"If you say so." Her voice was small. "So we're hiding, then?"

"Until we know who's chasing us. Kev was smart. They killed him, and got away with it. They are not to be fucked with, whoever they are."

"But the police—"

"The police didn't help the last time. I don't have any reason to think they would help me now. Get your head down." He shoved down on her head until she sprawled sideways, and dialed Davy's cell.

"What the hell?" Davy snarled, without preamble.

"We're alive. So's the fuckhead. I don't want to meet up with him again until I have a lot more firepower. I tossed the beacons."

"You did *what?* Are you nuts?"

"Tell Liv's folks she's OK," Sean said. "Watch your back. Con, too. Keep Margot and Erin close. These are the guys who killed Kev. They know all about us." He hung up, and punched up Miles's number. "It's Sean," he said. "Call me back, and enable your scrambler."

"The scrambler? Jesus, why? What's going on?"

"Do it." He hung up, stuck the phone between chin and shoulder as he guided the truck over the rough track. It rang again, in seconds.

"I need help," he told Miles. "Are you still at the Rock Bottom?"

"Yeah," Miles said. "We just loaded up the sound system. Why?"

"Is anybody listening to this conversation?" he demanded.

"Are you doing your paranoid freak-out McCloud routine on me?"

"Cut the shit. Get out of earshot. Have you got the fogeymobile?"

"Uh, yeah," Miles said. "What's it to you?"

"I want it," Sean said.

"Do my ears deceive me? You're willing to be seen in my vomit-tinted, butt-ugly piece of no-testosterone shit?"

"This is serious. I almost got killed a few minutes ago. I need to disappear."

"Oh. I get it." Miles's tone was ironic. "What better way to disappear than the magical invisible car?"

"Exactly." Sean negotiated around another gaping washout.

"Didn't Seth give you a fake ID, like he did for Davy and Con? Can't you rent a car under your false name? Why do I always have to be the schnook with no wheels?" Miles complained.

Sean gritted his teeth. "The rental places won't open for three hours, I'm covered with blood, and I've got a naked girl in my truck."

"No shit!" Miles breathed, impressed. "Naked? Really? Is it, you know, her? That girl you're so nuts about? Jeez. Why's she naked?"

Trust Miles to grasp the kernel of the situation. His own fault, mentioning a naked girl to a guy who hadn't gotten laid in ages, if ever.

"No time to explain," he snapped. "You know the Lonely Valley Motor Lodge, in Taggert? Behind the shopping center? Rent me a room. They get trucker business, so someone will be on duty. Got any cash?"

"I can get some at the all-night convenience store," Miles's voice had taken on its habitual long-suffering tone.

"Get me some. Ask for a room in back. Don't say anything to anyone. Get me disinfectant, bandages, surgical tape. And T-shirts."

"I'm on it," Miles said. "See you there."

Amazing, how the mention of a naked girl made a guy perk right up and hop to attention, any hour of the day or night.

Sean gave the truck more gas. They topped the rise out of the cleft of the valley and up onto the road that skirted the Long Prairie plateau. Dawn lit up the clouds into a fabulous range of pinks on the horizon.

Bye bye, road. "Hang on, babe." He slewed the Wrangler Rubicon around and headed it into the waving, waist-deep meadow grass.

Liv grabbed the door handle and braced herself on the dash as they jounced and tipped. Sean's face was tight with concentration. She hung on as they skirted trees, bushes, sometimes foundering in the grass, scraping over boulders that dotted the rough terrain.

Her arms felt like they were being ripped from their sockets.

Finally, they intersected a road, barely more than two long depressions in the grass. Burnt Ridge Crest. Thank God. The top of the Jeep was up, but the windows were open, blowing cool air over them.

She shivered, her chest and shoulders goosepimpling. Sean's eyes swept over her body. She crossed her arms over her bouncing bosom, and almost laughed. Embarrassed about that, after what they'd just been through. Please.

She tried to organize her thoughts. A million frantic questions jostled for space. "So you guys never found any clues? About Kev?"

The dirt road had turned to smoother gravel, and now gave way to asphalt. They were passing farms and houses and mailboxes now.

"Just the clues Kev gave you," Sean said. "Just the note."

"What did that note say?" she asked. "I've always wondered."

His face was distant. "One thing at a time. Scoot down. You're conspicuous even when you're wearing a shirt, let alone topless."

She hunched, feeling slapped, and draped her hair over herself.

They headed into an older, seedier part of town, crossed the tracks with a tooth-rattling bump and turned in the parking lot of a motel. The highway roared on the overpass above. "Look," he said. "I'm not kidnapping you. If you want to go home and paint a bull's-eye on your chest, you're free to go. I'll hate it, but I won't stop you."

Liv nodded, almost wishing he hadn't said it. After T-Rex, she wasn't in any condition to make life and death decisions. It was easier to get swept along by wild floodwaters. If the floodwaters were Sean.

"Besides, you've got your fiancé to protect you," he said.

It took her a few seconds to make the connection. "Oh, God, no! Blair is not my fiancé. That was just a lie my mother told, to get rid of you. You dashed off last night before I had a chance to make that clear!"

A door of one of the rooms swung open. A large-bellied, bearded man sauntered out, hiking up his jeans and scratching his balls.

The move was too swift to counter. Sean jerked her across the seat and onto his lap before she knew what he was doing. She grabbed his shirt to steady herself. "Don't freak," he murmured. "You need an excuse to be topless, and this is the best one I can think of." He wound his fingers in her tangled hair, and kissed her.

It's just theater, silly. Don't melt for a public act.

It was impossible to heed that stern voice. Her protective layers were torn away, leaving a naked core of shivering need. His lips were so hot, soft and urgent. She clung to him, kissed him back desperately.

Someone whacked the body of the Jeep, making her jerk. "Whoo hoo! Go for it, buddy boy! Helluva way to start yer day!"

Sean stuck his hand out the window, gave the guy a thumbs up.

He slid lower in the seat, pulling her down on top of him. Their lips parted, with a moist pop that reverberated through her body. He was burning hot, radiating emotion. He vibrated in her arms. The armored chill that had encased him ever since her revelation about Kev was gone. The kiss had melted it. The look in his eyes bordered on fear.

He hadn't shown fear when sprinting towards a bomb, or facing down a gun, or in mortal combat with a killer. But he was afraid of her.

She wanted to reassure him, but she couldn't think of words that made sense. Only kisses could convey what she wanted to tell him.

He tugged, gently, on the back of her head. A flash of insight warned her that this wordless invitation was more dangerous than the wild sex and high drama of the night before. This was the real honey-baited trap. This soft, torn-open feeling in her chest.

But it didn't matter. She leaned forward. He made a breathless sound, almost a whimper when their lips touched.

The kiss was almost reverent. They kept their eyes open, afraid the other would vanish into smoke. Sweet, perfect. A shining miracle, unfolding and blooming. They didn't want to break the spell by being too eager, so they circled around it, marvelling. Afraid to breathe.

Liv had never considered herself an expert kisser, but she finally got what kissing was all about, in a flash of bone-deep understanding. It wasn't about technique, or experience. It had nothing to do with how innately sensuous she was, or wasn't. It was about yearning, welling up from inside. She ached to touch him, to be scorched by his heat, to feel that metallic bronze sheen of beard stubble rasp over her skin.

She wanted to lavish him with all the tenderness she had.

The guy in the parking lot had been joined by a buddy. The two of them cackled and guffawed together, shouting out coarse suggestions.

She couldn't care less. They were dogs barking in the distance.

She clutched sodden handfuls of his shirt. He clutched her back. Lips and tongues fused. Asking questions, demanding answers. Begging for salvation, for redemption. It would take years of frantic kissing to sort it all out. Years of desperate loving to make up for the pain.

They needed to get started. Right now would be a very good time.

His hand clamped across hers where it gripped his thigh. He dragged it up, placing it on the bulge of his erection.

Their eyes locked. He offered her his body, silently asked for hers.

She didn't know under what terms. She no longer cared. He could do anything he wanted. Right here in the parking lot, with a hooting, jeering audience. She wanted to rip his clothes open, let the broad club of his penis fall out into her hand, hot and hard, the skin suede soft, so sensitive. She wanted to lick the thick, gnarled purple veins. To suck on him. To climb on top of him and ride. Bend over and have him fill her from behind, bracing herself against the storm of pounding violence. She needed it bad. She needed it now. She reached for his belt buckle.

"I see you've wasted no time." The low voice was faintly amused.

Sean jumped, so violently that he bumped his forehead against hers. "Shit," he hissed, rubbing her head. "Sorry, babe."

A young man stood outside the Jeep, with somber dark eyes, a memorable nose and long, shiny black hair that blew loose over his face. He gazed at her with intense curiosity. She blushed hot crimson.

Chapter
12

"Jesus, Miles." Sean struggled up from his slumped position, rubbing his forehead. "You practically gave me a heart attack."

"You told me to meet you here," Miles said. "You begged me, bullied me, guilt-tripped me. Told me it was a matter of life and death."

Sean rubbed the bump on his forehead, willed the blood in his groin to redirect itself into his brain. Just enough for minimal, baseline function. "Still is," he growled. "It's just your timing that sucks."

Miles's grin came and went swiftly. "The next time I bust my ass at five AM to do you an incredibly difficult and inconvenient favor, I'll try not to interrupt the sex." He peered in, and gave Liv a shy smile. "Hi." He shot Sean an uncertain glance. "So, uh, that's her?"

"That's her," Sean said. "She was abducted this morning. I followed a beacon in her shoe, up to Orem Lake. Got there just in time."

"I'm real glad that the trauma didn't put any dents in your libido."

Sean made an impatient growling sound. "Shut up, Miles. It's not about that. I was just creating a pretext for her to be half-naked."

"Convincing," Miles commented dryly. "Did you waste the guy?"

Sean winced. "He got away. Or we're the ones who got away. I'm not sure who racked up more points this round. Hey, Miles. Be a real man. Give the lady your shirt. Do I have to tell you everything?"

Miles looked down at his flapping, oversized gray shirt. "Oh. Uh, sure." He unbuttoned it quickly, revealing a tight black T-shirt beneath, and passed it through the window to Liv. "It stinks like smoke," he said apologetically. "I was doing sound for an acid punk band. Those degenerates were sucking on blunts all night long between sets. Sorry."

"It's fine. Thanks so much." Liv wrapped it around herself.

Miles held up a big pink plastic paddle with a key dangling from it. "You guys want to see your room?"

"God, yes," Sean said. He scanned the parking lot. Big Belly and his pal had climbed into their rigs and taken off, and the parking lot was empty and clear. He jumped out of the Wrangler and leaned into the backseat, shoving T-Rex's Beretta into his kit bag, and loading up everything that could conceivably be useful while on the run.

He and Liv followed Miles to the room at the end of the long, low building. Miles opened the door, and gestured them in with a flourish.

The room was small and stale, smelling of dust and damp and old cigarettes. He had a pang of regret that he hadn't thought of someplace nicer. He suppressed the niggling doubt, closed the hotel room door, locked it, threw the bolt. This was just a hole to huddle in, to lick their wounds. And maybe some other sweet tender bits, if he got lucky.

Miles pulled a set of car keys, and flung them to him. "Here you go. Your reasoning being that nobody on earth would ever believe Sean McCloud would drive such a pussy car?"

"Something like that," Sean said. "And you're not telling anybody. I threw my beacon away. I'm off the grid. Get it?"

Miles's eyes narrowed. "Don't ask me to lie to Con or Seth or Davy. Those bastards are mind readers."

"I'll contact them soon," Sean assured Miles.

"The trick will be thinking of something to tell my parents," Miles said glumly. "They just gave me the damn car ten hours ago."

"Say you lent it to a cute girl," Sean suggested. "It's pathetic, but credible. And literally true." He glanced at Liv. "I'm doing this for her."

Miles rolled his eyes. "Yeah, I know. The desire to get laid is the fuel that powers the universe. The Sean McCloud credo."

A crack like that usually slid right off his back, but today it stung. Sean shot Liv a nervous glance. She was carefully not looking at him, perched on the bed, her body virtually tied in a knot, her hair draped like a curtain around her face. Her mouth tight. Not good.

"Don't bust my balls," he growled. "It's been a shitty morning."

"I've been up all night myself," Miles replied. "Plus, I've got a two hour walk ahead of me, mostly uphill, to get back to Endicott Falls. You are one high-maintenance friend, you know that?"

"High maintenance equals high performance," Sean reminded him. "Think Ferrari. Think priceless racehorse. Think fighter jet."

"Yeah. Great," Miles said sourly. "I'm on foot, bozo. Don't torture me with images of super-fast modes of transport."

"Oh, cheer up," Sean snapped. "I'll make it up to you, I promise. If I get killed, you get my Wrangler. Fair enough?" His gaze flashed over Miles's shabby jeans and grayish athletic shoes. "My wardrobe, too."

Miles looked pained. "Don't say shit like that! Is it that bad?"

"It's bad. The guy who nabbed her this morning is a fucking maniac. All bullshit aside, I'm sorry to involve you, buddy. I didn't know who else to call. I'm sorry to leave you on foot, too. But you can't use my Jeep. It's red, for Christ's sake. It's too recognizable. It would be the kiss of death."

"It's OK." Miles's look of stoic calm could only have been learned by studying Davy. "I'll hitchhike. If I'm lucky, I'll get back in time to swallow a couple raw eggs, and I'll be in great shape to teach my first karate class. You're checked in until tomorrow at eleven. I took three hundred out of the machine. Bought the stuff you wanted. Here's the change." He handed Sean a crumpled wad of bills, and a shopping bag. "The car's gassed up. You want me to leave the Wrangler somewhere?"

Sean fished the keys out of his pocket and passed them over. "Dump it in the BiMart parking lot. Get away from it, fast. And Miles. Keep your head down. This never happened. You never saw me."

"Don't worry." Miles's gaze wandered over Sean's blood-streaked face and torso. "You look like shit. Anybody good enough to do that kind of damage to you would run me over like a tank. I don't want to die."

"Good man," Sean said. "Have you thought of a cover story?"

"I lent my car to Keira, the cute backup singer in the Howling Furballs," Miles said. "The one with the pierced clit."

Sean clapped him on the shoulder. "That's my boy." He stopped, eyes narrowing. "How'd you know that girl's clit was pierced?"

Miles rolled his eyes and looked martyred. "She told me."

Sean was cast down. "Oh. So you never, uh . . ."

"Nope," Miles said dolefully. "Girls just tell me things. All kinds of crazy shit. It's always, 'Oh Miles, you're such a great listener. I wish my asshole boyfriend was just like you, but all he wants from me is sex, sex, sex.' It's, like, the story of my life."

"That sucks, buddy," Sean said sympathetically.

"We've all got our crosses to bear. At least nobody tried to kill me today." Miles pointed out philosophically. He stuck his hands in his pockets, rattling the Jeep's keys. "OK, I guess I'd better disappear. Let me know what's going on, OK? This shit's weirding me out, big-time."

"I'll be in touch," Sean promised. Miles's worried look made him want to bear-hug the kid and tousle his hair. He suppressed the impulse with difficulty. Miles was finally developing spine-stiffening machismo and male dignity. Sean didn't want to impede the process.

Miles nodded politely to Liv. She nodded back. "Thanks for the shirt," she murmured.

Sean unlocked the dead bolt for him. "You saved my ass."

Miles gave him a quick grin. "Anytime."

Sean watched the kid climb into the Jeep through a crack in the door, his stomach hollow. It was only two minutes on the strip mall to get to the BiMart parking lot, but he hated exposing his little buddy to the risk of attracting any attention from those murdering fuckheads. Miles was smart and talented, but a hopped up gorilla like T-Rex would smear him all over fifty yards of asphalt. Having Miles on his conscience, too . . . Christ, that would be the final nail in his coffin.

He shut the door, slammed the bolts and locks and chains home. The deed was done. No point stressing over it. He unzipped the duffel part of his kit bag that he'd dragged out of his truck, and rummaged through the jumble of spywear prototypes until he found a pair of squealers, Seth's portable alarms to fix on the door and windows. They weren't much, but they might give him that split second advantage that meant the difference between life and death. If everything went to shit.

Finished with that, he turned to find that Liv had dumped the contents of Miles's bag onto the bed. First aid supplies, soap, shampoo, combs, a three-pack of white XXL T-shirts, all good. There was food, though he was still too buzzed to think of food. Granola bars, chocolate, sardines, Ritz crackers, pepper-jerked beef sticks, standard convenience store fare. Miles had thrown in a couple pairs of cheap sunglasses and some baseball caps. Great. That would help, with anonymity.

His gratefulness evaporated when Liv held the caps up for him to see. One had a cartoon female body wearing only a skimpy pink thong on her prominent ass, turning a seductive kitty-cat face over her shoulder. Pussy Kat was stitched above the bill in pink cursive letters.

The other one read simply Sex Machine in big, white letters.

That snide, smart-assed cretin.

Then Liv held up a package of condoms in her other hand. He actually blushed. "I did not tell him to buy those!"

"You didn't have to," she said. "He knows you well. What's the Sean McCloud credo? The desire to get laid is the fuel that powers the universe?"

"I'm rearranging his teeth when I see him next," Sean growled.

Judging from the look on Liv's face, it looked like the screaming, pounding, wall-shaking fuck-fest had been indefinitely called off.

Just as well. The kiss had him on the verge of bursting into tears, begging her to love him forever. He hated to think of what extremes screwing her would have reduced him to. Particularly since she thought he was a fluff-brained gigolo that would pork anything with a pulse.

It made his face burn like a hot griddle.

The aftereffects of that kiss made him itchy and restless. He wanted to kick down doors, put his fists through walls. He should probably jack off in the shower, wrangle the savage beast down to reasonable proportions. Liv had been through enough this morning without having to do a whip-and-chair routine with his unruly dick.

He peeled off the filthy, bloodstained shirt, flung it on the floor. Bent down to pry off his shoes. He pulled out the Ruger, checked the cylinder out of habit. Still fully loaded. He cocked it, and placed it in Liv's hands. She looked up at him, wide-eyed with alarm. "What's this?"

"I'm taking a shower," he said. "I want to wash the mud out of these cuts before I put disinfectant on them. You're on guard duty."

She sputtered with protest as he unbuckled the holster and the knife sheath. "But I don't know how."

"You did great with that Beretta," he said. "You rocked."

"But . . ." Her voice trailed off helplessly. "Isn't this a bit excessive? I mean, nobody know's we're here but Miles, right?"

"Right. It is excessive. It's totally ridiculous. So is what just happened to us with T-Rex up at the lake. Any more questions?"

He shoved down his pants, which had the desired effect of choking off whatever other protests she might have made, as his hard-on sprang out, in all its undignified glory. Swaying back and forth, the flared tip as big as a ripe plum. Adorned with a drop of pre-come.

"Good Lord, Sean," she said. "Talk about excessive."

"Excess is the road to the palace of wisdom. Watch that door." With that parting shot, he stalked into the bathroom, stepped into the plastic tub, and set the water running, as hot as he could stand it.

It stung in all his scrapes and cuts. It felt like getting flogged. He gritted his teeth and went at himself with the cheap deodorant soap.

He soaped and rinsed, soaped and rinsed, watching mud and blood and grit swirl around his feet and down the drain. He took his aching cock in his soapy hand, but he was too conscious of Liv out there, holding his gun in her shaking hands. Unguarded, while he panted in the bathtub, yanking on his tool. Nah. Didn't seem right.

He rinsed the soap off, toweled off. The threadbare towel got smeared with pinkish bloodstains almost immediately.

Liv let out a sigh of relief when he came out, as if she'd been holding her breath the whole time. He followed her gaze as her eyes darted down to register if he was still—yep. Sure enough. Still was.

He took the gun from her. "Go take your shower," he told her.

"You're covered with cuts and scrapes," she said. "Let me—"

"First, shower. You'll feel better," he said. "You can do the Florence Nightingale routine when you get out." She fled into the bathroom, and he ripped open the gauze and the surgical tape. Most of his cuts were from his falls in the fight with T-Rex, the glass on the deck, the bouncing over granite on the fall to the lake beach. A couple bullets had scored him, too. He was damn lucky. Oozing all over, but still lucky.

She exited the bathroom in a cloud of perfumed steam, eyes downcast, face red, having managed to tuck the scroungy little towel around her luscious curves. Her hair was wrung out, hanging down in damp, tangled locks. He was going to comb that for her again, whether she knew it or not. Combing her hair soothed his soul.

"Ladies first," he said. "Come over here, and let me fix you up."

"Oh, no. I hardly have any—"

"Shut up and get your ass over here."

She jumped, stung by his drill sergeant voice. "I don't have bad ones. Not like you."

He ignored her, and started with her hands, smearing antibiotic ointment on the nicks and cuts. Then the marks on her wrists from the plastic strapping. The cut beneath her ear, the angry teeth marks. She had marks on her arms that were going to bruise. He should have asked for some ice. He contented himself with smoothing them with his hands. Her worst injuries were the ones in her head. Nightmares, anxiety. The shame, the fear. Injuries to the soul where the hardest ones to heal. He knew all about that. He wished she didn't have to.

But Liv was tougher than he'd ever imagined. A freaking goddess.

"Any spots I missed?" he asked.

She shook her head, red-faced.

"I'd better do a more careful check." He tugged the towel loose. She tried to hold it over herself, but he wrenched it away, ran his hands over her cool, trembling skin. Got lost staring at her naked body before he remembered the script. "Uh . . . let me check your ribs," he said.

She closed her eyes tight as he touched her breasts. They had red marks from that filthy bastard's squeezing fingers.

T-Rex was going to die for that. Squealing in pain.

He spun her around, raising up the heavy ropes of dripping hair, running his hands down the curve of her back, her waist. Drops of water dripped sensually down into the cleft of her ass. There were small blue marks on her thighs. He realized that he'd inflicted those himself.

He flushed with lust and shame, and sank to his knees behind her. He stroked them. "I gave you those, didn't I?"

She nodded, mutely.

"I'm sorry," he said. "I didn't mean to hurt you."

"It's OK." Her voice trembled. "I didn't care. At the time."

He slid his hand between her legs, the edge ever so slightly touching the tender hidden folds of her pussy. He kissed every mark, one by one. Then he kissed them all again. She swayed in his hands.

"Don't you want me to, ah, deal with your cuts and scrapes?" she asked, her voice breathless and unsteady.

"Whatever," he said. He sat back up onto the bed, and jerked her towel away when she started trying to wrap it around her body again.

"No way," he said. "Do it naked."

She made that breathless giggling snort that he loved. "That doesn't sound like a practical idea. I'm not sure how far I'd get."

"It'll be therapeutic," he assured her. "You'll be amazed."

"I don't doubt that," she murmured. "I always am."

She started with his back. He scoped her with his peripheral vision, marveling at her flawless skin. Kissably smooth, fine grained as a baby's. He hardly noticed the sting as she dabbed with cotton balls and gauze and butterfly bandages. "You should go to the emergency room," she told him. "You need stitches. Some of these are deep."

"Nah," he said. "I'm not worried. I heal fast."

"They'll scar," she warned.

He snorted. "So they'll be in good company."

Her cool, soft hands petted him tenderly. "You've got scratches and bruises all over." She sounded adorably worried. It was cute.

"It's been an intense couple of days," he said. "Some are from T-Rex, some are from a fight I had with my brother—"

"Your brother? What on earth?"

"We had a knock-down, drag-out fight last night," he admitted.

She peered around at him, fascinated. "Really? Why on earth?"

"Long, complicated story. I don't have enough blood circulation going to my brain to tell it," he hedged. "Some of them are from you."

Her hands, wielding the cotton balls, stopped moving. "Me?"

He laughed at her horrified squeak. "Yeah. You," he said softly. "You were a wild woman. I'm lucky I got out of there in one piece."

She slid off the bed and tilted his face up. "Let me get this one."

She worked, slowly and intently, on the scrape on his cheekbone, the split on his lip. Dabbity dab with the ointment, her eyes solemn and focused. Naked Nurse Liv. Her tits were right at eye level. Plump and full, with that ripe peach swell he lusted for, but all the jiggly, pointed softness of homegrown tits. Not the perfect round silicone variety.

Not that he'd ever been fussy about tits. Nosirree, he loved them all. Even the surgically enhanced ones had their place in his heart. Tits existed to be passionately appreciated, in all their wonderful varieties.

But when confronted with divine perfection, he could not but fall to his knees to worship. Or in this case, drag her forward so he could wallow in those soft hot curves, nuzzling like a man gone wild. He rubbed her nipples against his face, and drew one into his mouth.

She arched in his arms. "Sean! I'm not done with you yet!"

"No?" He leaned away from her and wiped his mouth. "Sorry."

She sank down to her knees in front of him. Fabulous scenarios spun through his head. She started dabbing at a long scrape on his thigh with the ointment. His heart sank. Huh. Whatever.

She wiped her fingers with gauze, and gazed earnestly into his face, like she wanted to say something that he wouldn't want to hear.

Like that she wanted him to stop bothering her, probably.

He braced himself to put his dick in a cage and leave her the hell alone. She'd had a terrible experience of assault, and here he was, slobbering all over her tits like a teenage boy in the backseat of a car.

"What?" His voice was harsher than he meant it to. "Spit it out."

She leaned forward, giving him just enough time to wonder if this was really happening before she took his cock right into her hot mouth.

Hot, wet, gliding pleasure caressed him, enveloped him. He panted, red-faced, speechless. He who always had a smart, funny, seductive line of patter to turn a girl on, or soothe, or zing, or titillate.

Without it, he was a blank, grunting idiot, just hoping not to do anything clumsy or rough that might make her change her mind.

It started torturously slow, as she got used to his size. She licked his glans, bathing him until he gleamed while she figured out what to do with all of him. Didn't take her long. She loosened up into the sensuous, red-hot sex kitten that she was, using those cool, soft hands on the part of his cock that wouldn't fit, petting and squeezing.

She deepened her stroke, taking him deeper into her mouth than he'd ever dreamed she could, and then doing a tight, tongue-swirling clutch and suck and pull on the outstroke. Again, the gliding plunge, again the long pull, her pink lips distended around his shiny cock, her face pink and dewy, her eyes so dilated, heavy-lidded, and again, that long, hot, wet pull—oh, God. Again, again, again. Please. Forever.

But it wasn't going to be long at all. He was going to explode.

He didn't have enough self-control to live up to the question, but it was still good form to ask it. "Can I come in your mouth?"

She did another mind-blowing suck-n-swirl, and nodded, rubbing the tip of his cock against her cheek. "Wouldn't miss it."

"Are you sure you don't want me to—oh, fuck . . ."

The words broke off as she sucked him into her mouth again.

He sagged forward, hair dangling around his face, breathing in the sweet scent of shampoo. Racked by shudders of pleasure. God, she was good. She brought him so close, and then eased him down again.

Then she started stroking his balls with her fingertips. Little, ticklish caresses. Flower petals. Butterfly wings. That was it. That did it.

A herd of wild horses was stampeding towards him, thundering across the plains. Tossing their heads, snorting. Knife-sharp hooves churning, mud and turf flying. He waited, body straining, taut as steel cable, and waited for those suckers to mow him down. They did.

His eyes flickered open some time later. He'd tumbled back onto the bed. Boxes, tubes, plastic packaging crinkled, jabbing his sore back.

He heard the sink running in the bathroom. His limbs were made of lead. The bed shifted. Things slid around, rearranged themselves as Liv sat down beside him. The give of the mattress beneath her made his head flop bonelessly to the side. She fished a comb out of Miles's bounty, and worked it through her hair. She looked like a sixteenth-century painting. The alabaster-skinned mythical goddess at her toilette.

"That's my job," he said softly. "Stop it. I wanted to do that."

Her lips curved. "It'll get tangled again. You'll get your chance."

He subsided, reassured, and lay there marveling at her beauty. Enjoying his floating, empty state. It didn't last long, though. It came rushing back all too soon, the anger and the ugliness and the mind-fucking incomprehensible mystery of it all. Kev, T-Rex, Liv.

He couldn't deal with it, and there was only one thing in the world compelling enough to drag his mind down another track. He slid off the bed and onto his knees, and pushed her perfect white thighs apart.

She blinked. "Sean?"

"Just let me look," he begged. "I need it. I need you."

She laid down the comb and touched his face with her hand. Made a soft, sighing sound, but she didn't resist as he pushed her open.

God, she was beautiful. That long pink secret slit, the shiny folds of silky girl flesh. Little puffy bits that pouted out. Her pussy was hot and bright and swollen. Glistening with lube. Sucking him off had excited her. Awesome. His mouth watered. His cock sprang to attention, ready for action and adventure, after less than, what, ten minutes?

Unreal. He was prodigiously oversexed, for sure, no arguments there, but even he had his limits. Just not when it came to Liv.

Liv reached down and parted her labia, sliding two fingers down on either side of her clit and pressed so it popped out of its hood, pink and taut and shiny. He put his mouth to her, suckling gently. She jerked in protest, supersensitive. He softened up the contact, licking tenderly, circling it with his lips, trilling at it with his tongue.

He stiffened his tongue and thrust it deep into her pussy. She flopped down on the bed in her turn for the long, lavish tongue-fucking.

He pushed her up, up, eased her down, just as she'd done to him, on and on. When she was on the rise again, he slid two fingers into her cunt to find that melting hot place just inside, freeing up his tongue to do a delicate, fluttering tremolo across her clit. It was like flashbulbs popping in his face when she came. She writhed, clutching at his delving fingers with her cunt. Her pleasure nourished him, and at the same time, created an insatiable craving for more.

He reached for the condoms.

Chapter
13

Liv didn't know what set her off. Maybe his matter-of-fact air, as if he were taking what was due to him. He wrenched the covers down, scattering the stuff Miles had bought over the floor, and caught her under the armpits, tossing her onto the middle of the bed. He shoved her thighs wide, mounted her.

"Hey!" She shoved at his chest. "I didn't say you could do this!"

He fitted the broad, blunt head of his sheathed penis to her opening, and nudged it inside. "Nope," he said. "You didn't. So?"

"What do you mean, so? So stop it!"

"No." He shoved himself inside her, wedging deep. His body pinned her to the crumpled bedclothes, breathlessly big and hot and heavy. His chest pressed against her breasts, squishing them flat.

He just went at her, that huge thing of his plunging and sliding, making her hot and frantic. His hard, heavy strokes jarred her across the bed, jolting her up until she was crammed against the headboard and had to reach up and brace herself. "Stop it," she hissed, wiggling and squirming. "Get out of me. You're making me crazy."

"Yeah, I know," he said. "You love it."

Relax. Hah. She wrenched her hands free, swatting at his face.

Sean caught her arms again, and pinned them to her chest, hips pulsing sensuously against her. "What the hell is the matter with you?" he demanded. "Is it the position? Do you need to be on top?"

"No!" she yelled. "It's the look on your face that I can't stand!"

He looked startled, and stopped moving, staring down at her with a frown. "Uh, that's a tough one," he said warily. "I don't even know what look was on my face, baby. Being as how I'm behind my face."

"Do not smart-mouth me." Her voice shook. "It's that 'I'm entitled to this' look. Like, you saved me from T-Rex, so now it's your God-given right to fuck me, however, wherever, whenever you want, right?"

He looked horrified, and withdrew instantly. "Whoa." He rolled to the side, still holding her. "I didn't mean to make you think about him. I'm sorry."

Her face dissolved. She covered it with her hands.

Sean leaned closer and nuzzled her, kissing the side of her face over and over with soft, pleading kisses. They stayed that way for a long time, silently cuddling, until she managed to speak.

"He was going to cut me," she whispered. "He was going to do horrible things to me, and then stick my dead body in the ground."

His arm slid around her. "Yeah, but he didn't. Because you're strong and brave and quick. He's in my sights, believe me. I'm sorry he got near you. I'm sorry he breathed the same air as you."

"No." She shook her head violently. "Don't make me out to be some big heroine. I'm only alive because you came after me. Not because I'm so great or smart or brave. That's bullshit."

He petted her hair. "Wrong. I saw you bite that guy when he was holding a gun to your head. You don't fool me for a second."

"You don't understand." Her voice quavered, broke. "I was so scared. I would have told him anything. Anything, you get me? I told him I brought Kev's note to you. I could have killed you by doing that."

He pried her hand off her wet eyes and frowned, earnestly. "Babe. Everyone breaks under torture. Read my lips. Everyone. Human beings are not designed to withstand that kind of abuse. Don't bother feeling guilty about it. It's a big waste of time."

She yanked her hand back, hid her face again, shook her head.

"I caved, when it happened to me," he said. "In a nanosecond."

She jerked up onto her elbow, startled. "You? What? How?"

"See these?" He lifted his arm, and pointed at the silvery lines slashing along his ribs. "That was in Sierra Leone. I had a job guarding a diamond mine. There was this rival warlord who wanted to . . . well, to make a long, boring story short, this was done with electrical wire."

She gasped. "Oh, God. Oh, that's horrible."

"It pretty much sucked," he agreed. "I'm not much of a stoic, to tell the truth. I was crying for Mama in no time. I fucking *hate* pain."

That was so ironic, after having witnessed his outrageous heroism in action, that she started to shake with laughter, eyes watering.

"Gee. I'm glad that my heart-wrenching tale of physical and mental anguish is so amusing for you," he said dryly.

"Shut up, you idiot," she wheezed, between peals of laughter.

His smile creased the sexy crinkles around his eyes. "That's much better," he said. "You're scolding me. It's kind of comforting."

She laughed herself right back into tears again and rolled onto her stomach, burying her face in the covers. The storm moved through her, leaving her exhausted, but somehow cleaner. She lifted her head.

The white-hot anger in his eyes chilled her to the bone.

"I'm going to hunt down that sadistic piece of shit and rip him to pieces for doing that to you," he said evenly.

She was unnerved. "Um, isn't that vigilante justice?"

"Yeah." His eyebrows quirked up. "So?"

"It has no place in a civilized society," she said.

He leaned back and folded his muscular arms behind his head. "If civilization is civil to me, I'm civil to it."

She thought for a moment. "I'd rather kill the bastard myself."

He gave her a wary, sidelong glance. "Ah. I'm afraid I can't make any promises about that, babe. We'll see how it goes, OK?"

She snorted. "See how it goes, my ass."

He smooched her butt. "It's a wonderful ass," he said.

"Don't try to distract me with sex." A fresh blaze of anger flared up, and she rolled over and lashed out at him, swatting at his face.

He parried the blow easily, and all the ones that came after it. She lost it completely, and flung herself at him, in a frenzy of frustration.

He pinned her onto the bed and held her squirming body down.

"You want me to teach you to fight? For real?"

"Yes!" she shouted, writhing. "You bastard! Get off me!"

"It's a long, slow process," he warned. "I'm a tough teacher. I kick ass. Just ask Miles. I taught him. Me and my brothers."

She heaved and bucked beneath his weight. "I said get *off*!"

"You'll always be at a disadvantage in a fight with a man," he went on. "No matter how hard you train, no matter how good you get. It's a fact of biology, muscle mass, upper body strength. The one thing I can promise is that you'll have more of a chance than you had before."

She collapsed, panting. Tears of frustration leaked out of her eyes. "Yes," she said, swallowing hard. "Yes. I want more chances."

"Done," he said.

"Guns and knives, too," she added.

He looked alarmed. "Uh, OK," he said. "If you say so."

"Bombs, too. They say you know all about bombs. I want to know everything that you know. Everything."

He stared at her, wide-eyed. "You're scaring me, baby."

"Good. Be scared." Her eyes dropped to his erection. "I see fear doesn't affect your sexual enthusiasm."

He glanced down at himself. "Right," he agreed. "Do you want me to fuck you now, Liv?"

She stared up into his face, and tugged, in vain, at her hands, still pinned against the bed. "No," she said. "I want to fuck *you*."

"Uh . . . what exactly do you mean by that?"

"I want something I can't have!" she yelled. "I'm sick of being tied up and jerked around. I want to throw you on the bed and show you who's boss. I want to fuck you until you learn some goddamn manners!"

He looked perplexed. "So does this mean you want to be the boy? Or what?"

"Don't be so damned literal about it," she grumbled.

"You want to strap on a big, scary dildo, and bend me over and—"

"No!" She jerked up on to her elbows, her face going hot. "For God's sake. I told you I wasn't into that kinky weird stuff. Ick!"

"Just trying to get the parameters straight." The dimple flickered in his lean cheek. "You just told me you wanted to kill a man, and learn how to build bombs. What's a strap-on dildo compared to that?"

"Stop teasing me," she snapped. "I imagine you've done it all?"

"No," he admitted. "I like being on top. But when it comes to you, I'm flexible. I'll take turns. I'll submit, to a sublime sex goddess like you. Maybe not all the time, maybe not for very long, but . . . sometimes."

"Oh. I see." Her face felt like it was on fire.

"I would go to incredible lengths to satisfy you," he said, his voice silky. "I would bend over backwards. Or even frontwards."

She exploded into shaking giggles. "Gee, thanks. I doubt I'll take you up on it, but I appreciate the sentiment."

"Just be gentle with me, princess. Go easy, OK? Take it slow." He shot her a sideways look. "I hate pain, remember?"

"Shut up, you clown." She grabbed the pillow and swatted him.

He grabbed it back from her. "The problem is right now."

"And why is now a problem?" She tried to yank it back, in vain.

"Because after that fight, and that suckfest, and this incredibly weird conversation, my cock is about to explode. And I'm not feeling submissive. At all. I know you want to fuck me, but I want to fuck you first. And I'm bigger." He flipped her onto her belly. "So deal with it."

She wriggled. "That's not fair!"

He knocked her thighs apart, fitted his penis to her, and drove inside, with a deep, jarring thrust. "No, it isn't," he said. "Try to buck me off, if you can. It'll be fun."

She did, and it was. He pounded into her, deep and hard. She struggled against him, her hot face pressed hard into the pillow to muffle the shrieks that jerked out of her with each heavy, slapping lunge. He rubbed over a secret spot deep inside her that bloomed hotter and brighter with each stroke. She shoved back to meet him, reaching.

The climax was long and wrenching. He nuzzled her ear as it jerked through her, endlessly. "I want to try something," he whispered.

She was barely able to turn her head. "What?"

"Something I've never tried before." He eased out of her and rolled her over, pulling her up. No small task, she was such a wobbly rag doll.

"Come on, babe," he coaxed. "Just one little thing. Just for fun."

She squinted at him, suspicious. "What could you possibly have never tried that I would be willing to do?"

"You gave me the idea yourself. Being as how you're a dominating bitch goddess who wants to fuck good manners into me. Thing is, I'd have to take off the condom, and we haven't had that conversation yet."

"What conversation? Oh, wait. You mean—"

"The safe sex conversation," he supplied. "So let's get that part of it over with. I've been very sexually active, no denying that."

"That's for sure," she muttered sourly.

"But I've always been safe. I swear, I shrinkwrap myself every time. Religiously. Never done it without latex. Never done IV drugs. Rigorously hetero. Always tested negative for HIV, and everything else floating around out there. Plus, I don't propose coming inside you—"

"So what the hell are you proposing?" she demanded.

"Let's finish the tough, awkward part of this conversation first, and then move on to the fun, sexy, erotic part. Your turn, sweetheart."

"Oh. I'm fine," she admitted. "I haven't been with anyone for two years. I've had bloodwork since then, for my annual exam. Negative."

"Great." He rolled the condom off, tossing it into the trash beside the bed. "Then do that excellent thing you were doing before. Put your hand on your pussy, and press your fingers down so your clit pokes out. Wow! You've got such a gorgeous, aggressive looking clit."

She did as he asked, struggling not to giggle. "So? And?"

"A clit is like a vestigial cock, you know?" he said. "And yours has got a hard-on right now. So fuck me with it."

She still didn't understand, until he slid his hand the length of his penis, letting just the broad flared tip poke out of his clutching fist. The slit at the end glistened with a shining, slippery drop of pre-come.

Her neck, her face, all went even redder and damper than they already were. She swallowed, tried to get a grip on herself. "What makes you think this is a vestigial penis?" she demanded. "It depends on your point of view. We could as easily say that you've got a ridiculously oversized clitoris bouncing around in front of you."

A slow, delighted grin spread lazily over his face. "So this is, like, a lesbo fantasy? Wonderful. Girl on girl—I go for that."

"Shut up, you dog. I do not want to hear about your depraved previous sexual adventures. They make me want to beat you."

His eyes widened. "Mmm. Scold me," he murmured. "Show me who's boss." He grabbed her free hand, wrapped it around his thick shaft, and brought it up, presenting it with an exaggerated sigh of surrender. "Go for it. Teach me some manners, sweetheart."

She pressed the tip of her clit against his penis, slid it inside.

They both gasped. It was a tiny movement. Intensely erotic and tightly focused. Their bodies shook. The stimulation was almost too intense to bear, but Sean was groaning, his big shoulders shaking. He liked it. So did she. She ground his glans harder against herself. Her excitement coiled up, tightening to a sharp, shivering point.

Sean leaned his damp forehead against hers. He shook with laughter, and excitement. "Take me," he whispered.

She dissolved into giggles right as her orgasm pulsed through her, wrenching through every limb. He grabbed her other hand and wrapped it around his penis, squeezing her hand beneath his own. Hot jets of semen spurted over their clutching hands, onto her breasts, her belly.

He rested his hot forehead on her shoulder, trembling violently.

The creamy liquid seemed to burn her skin. Liv stared down at it, touched the white drops with her fingertips. She felt breathless, moved.

Semen had always struck her as an unfortunate and somewhat comical by-product of sex. Something sticky and icky to deal with. Usually safely contained in latex and conveniently ignored.

This was so different. This was his body's offering. A tribute to life, poured out on an altar of passion and desire. A magic potion.

She wanted him to fill her with it, feel it trickling hot between her thighs. She wanted him to give her a child with it.

She'd been in free fall ever since she'd seen him standing in the ashes of her bookstore. Her chest ached and throbbed like her heart had been torn apart. He could destroy her with a wave of his hand.

He raised his head. She kept her watery eyes averted. She couldn't bear to look at him. She extricated her hands from his strong grip and clambered off the bed. "Have to wash," she mumbled.

When she swept the shower curtain aside, Sean stood there waiting. She felt melted and blurry, unfit for scrutiny. She stepped out of the tub, tried to walk past without looking at him.

"Goddamnit, Liv." He spun her around and kissed her.

It was a dominating kiss, but her need flared right up to meet it. She clung to him and kissed him back. He lifted his lips from hers. "Don't do that. Tear me to pieces, and then give me the cold shoulder."

"What do you think you did to me last night?" she flung back.

"Let's make a deal. You don't do it to me, and I won't do it to you."

It's never that simple, she wanted to scream.

"Let's kiss on it. Look me in the eyes, Liv. And kiss me."

"We just did," she pointed out. "Very thoroughly."

"That was before we made our deal." His voice had that soft, unguarded tone that tugged at her heart. She couldn't resist him.

She put her hands on his hot, scratchy cheeks, and stood up on her tiptoes, pressing a soft kiss to his lips.

"Promise?" His voice was hoarse.

"Promise," she assured him.

He dragged her out of the bathroom, stretched out on the bed and held out his arms. It felt so sweet and perfect, sliding into them. She hid her face against his chest, let the deep thudding of his heart soothe her.

She must have slept. Bizarre images paraded through her mind, from the violent to the erotic. She woke to find Sean gazing into her face. His expression brought her to instant wakefulness. "Yes? What?"

"Tell me everything T-Rex said to you, Liv," he said quietly. "I'm sorry to make you think about it, but I have to know."

She closed her eyes, and tried to remember the sequence, the wording. "He told me that he saw me in his rifle scope that day that I met Kev," she said. "He recognized me from a TV interview I did when the bookstore opened. That's how he found me. He saw Kev give me that sketchbook. He wants the tapes. What tapes?"

He shook his head. "Kev mentioned tapes in his note. He must have coded the information into his sketches, but he coded it too well. He overestimated us. We couldn't crack it. We tried. For months."

"Where is that notebook now?" Liv asked.

Sean rolled onto his back. "My brothers ripped out the pictures and framed them. Davy said he'd be damned if he'd waste Kev's last sketches. I didn't take any. Can't even stand to look at them when I go to visit. Those guys are made of tougher stuff than me."

She kissed his hard belly. "You're plenty tough."

He grunted. "You should see my brother Davy. Talk about tough."

She frowned. "Is he the one who gave you those bruises?"

"Oh, don't blame him. I provoked him on purpose," Sean said absently. "Davy's a pain in the ass, like any McCloud, but he's great. You'll like him. And Margot, his wife, is fabulous. You're going to love her. Con's wife, Erin, too. I can't wait for you to meet all of them."

That gave her a warm, tingling glow in her chest.

"Tell me again exactly what Kev said to you," Sean said.

"Not much," she said regretfully. "That he was being chased. That some guys wanted to kill him. He scribbled that coded note, and told me to take it to you and run like hell, or they'd get me too. Scared me half to death." She shrugged. "That's all. I wish I could help you more."

He nodded, his eyes miles away as his brain crunched data.

"What was in Kev's note?" she asked. "I've wondered for fifteen years."

Sean's gaze flickered away. He let out a sigh, as if he were bracing himself. "It said if you didn't disappear that night, you were dead meat."

She stared at his averted face. The silence in the room swelled, as his meaning sank in. "Wait. You mean to tell me the horrible things you said were to drive me away? You did that deliberately? To *protect* me?"

He nodded. She slid off the bed, onto legs that would barely hold her. Stared at him as if she'd never seen him before.

"That's not possible." Her voice shook. "You're kidding."

He shook his head.

Fury, grief, built up inside her like steam. She covered her shaking mouth. "You *bastard!* How could you do that to me?"

"I don't know." His voice was flat. "Still don't. It almost killed me."

She lunged towards him, and slapped his face. He barely flinched.

"For fifteen years I thought it was just a crazy fuck-up," he said. "But if I hadn't done it, T-Rex would have killed you. You're alive, right? I have that much satisfaction. I did the right thing."

"The right thing?" Her voice cracked with outrage. "Did it occur to you for one second to tell me what was going on? Did it occur to you to trust me? It didn't cross that thick rock that passes for your mind?"

He shook his head. "You would have resisted. You wouldn't have wanted to leave me in the lockup. You might not even have believed me. I made an executive decision. But I hated hurting you."

"An executive decision. To totally destroy me, emotionally." She let out a peal of hysterical laughter. "Wow. Cool as a cucumber."

"It was the only way I could be sure you got on that plane," he said. "I was locked up, Liv. I couldn't protect you. There was no one to call for help. Davy was in Iraq. Con was on a stakeout somewhere. Kev was in trouble. The police were already pissed at me. I did what I had to do. And for the first time in fifteen years, I can stand by that decision."

She pressed her hand against her face, like it might fall off. "It never occurred to you to contact me after?" she whispered.

"Only every single fucking minute of my life," he said savagely. "First I thought it was safer not to get near you, while we were puzzling it out. Convincing ourselves that Kev had gone nuts was a long, gradual process. I looked for you after, but you were in Europe. Then I ended up going into the military. I looked for you when I was on leave. I saw you, once. You were out with some guy you were seeing. In Boston."

"Oh, God." She covered her face, shaking her head.

"I followed you around for a while, like your standard obsessed maniac," he went on. "Then I got embarrassed at myself, and left."

"Without ever contacting me," she whispered.

He shook his head. "Didn't seem right. To freak you out, disrupt your life, after years had already gone by. I figured you'd be furious. That you hated my guts. And that you'd hate them even more when I explained what I'd done. Surprise, surprise. Looks like I was right."

She couldn't get her quivering throat to calm down. "My whole life, my parents have jerked me around. When I met you, I thought, finally someone who's straight with me. How ironic. When it comes to lying and manipulating, you give my mother a run for her money."

"I'm sorry you're so offended." His voice was clipped. "I thought you'd be glad to know that all the nasty shit I said wasn't true."

"Oh. Yeah. That." She shook with painful, ironic laughter. "Like, the pool you had going with the construction crew? Did you invent that right off the top of your head? Like, how bored you were at the prospect of deflowering me?" She grabbed the phone, dialed for an outside line.

He yanked the receiver out of her hand. "Who the fuck do you think you're calling?" he snarled.

"A cab," she shot back. "I'm out of here. I've had enough of this."

He slammed the phone back, and shoved her down onto the bed. "I did what I did because I loved you. Does that count for anything?"

She shivered, staring into his fierce gaze. "If that's what it means to be loved by you, I don't know if I can survive it," she whispered.

He shook with tension. "No. You promised you wouldn't go cold on me. I hold you to that goddamn promise. You owe me that much."

It was an impossible demand. He couldn't hold her to that stupid promise. Feelings were feelings. Anger was anger. The past could not be changed. "What are you trying to accomplish by squishing me flat?" She demanded, struggling to keep her voice from shaking. "Using sexual intimidation to bully me into not being angry?"

"Sexual intimidation is as good a plan as any I can think up," he said. "Would it work? I'll do anything that works."

The blaze of predatory energy from him took away what little nerve she had left. She shook her head. "Won't work," she whispered.

"Let's see." He pushed her thighs apart, fitting himself to her tender opening, and shoved himself deep inside her. "Does this work?"

She turned her crumpled, tear-blurred face away, but her body answered to his, helplessly, instinctively. Opening, yielding, rocking.

"It sure feels like it's working," he muttered, against her ear.

She shook her head against the crumpled wad of sheet. She would have screamed, but her throat vibrated too hard. The charge was already building, stoked by his hard, pounding rhythm. The molten eruption burst through her, wrenching jolts of dark pleasure.

Her lungs couldn't expand, she realized, when she could think again. The solid weight of him was collapsed across her body.

She shoved at him. "Air," she croaked. "Can't breathe."

He rolled off. The air was cool on her body, where the sweat had glued them together. She struggled up, reached between her legs.

Whoa. Holy crap. She was a lake. They hadn't used a condom.

Or, to be fair, he hadn't. She hadn't had a thing to say about it.

Sean shot her an uneasy glance. His eyes slid away. "I didn't mean to do that. I never . . . fuck." He sounded almost bewildered.

Liv slid off the bed, struggling to remember how long it had been. She'd gone without sex for so long, she'd stopped paying attention to her cycle. She was somewhere smack in the middle. Right in the danger zone. Great. Another element of uncertainty to jazz up her life.

She felt big hands behind her, hoisting her up to her feet. He swept her up, which made her squeak with alarm, but he held her against his hard, sinewy chest as easily as if she were a child. He set her down on the tub, grabbed the detachable showerhead and set the water running. He pushed her legs apart, lathered her up. Apologizing with his hands. She stared at the top of his head, relaxing into the soothing, tender caresses. "I don't know what to think," she said. "Fifteen years of nothing. Then my life falls to pieces, and you come out of the woodwork, and get all intense about me. I don't know what to feel."

"Me neither." He blotted her dry with the last remaining hand towel. "I think I got imprinted by you, or something. You know, how some dogs bond with one person, and that's it? No one else will do?"

She snorted. "Um, yes, you do have many doglike qualities."

"What?" He grinned. "Loyalty? Steadfastness? Selfless courage?"

Yes, and yes. "I don't think you're imprinted, though," she said crisply. "I think you made do just fine."

"Because I slept with other women?" His voice hardened, and his hands stopped moving. "Do you think for one instant that what's happening between us is not important to me? It rocks my world."

"I'm not on the pill," she blurted. "I could get pregnant."

He kissed her hands. "For some reason, that doesn't scare me."

She pried her hands away and covered her face with them. "Don't say stupid things like that. It's irresponsible. It messes with my head."

"I'm sorry," he said. "You turn my brain into mush, you know."

"Oh, my. How gratifying to have such a powerful effect on a man. Don't you think the timing is bad? On the run from a bloodthirsty murderer while urping with morning sickness. Cool."

"We can talk about it more rationally if we eat something," he said. "Anyway, there's that morning-after pill, too. But you're wiped out. You need fuel."

The first bite that hit her mouth made her gasp with delight. It was just a honey-nut granola bar, but it tasted like heaven. So did the crackers with peanut butter, the oily sardines, the can of warm Coke. They sat cross-legged on the bed together and went at it like wolves.

"I can't believe I'm eating this crap," she said. "It tastes so good."

"Convenience store haute cuisine." He handed her another loaded cracker. "Stick with me, babe, if you want to live large."

"So what are we doing here, anyhow?" she asked. "We can't hide in this room eating crackers and having wild, crazy sex forever."

"Wish we could," he said, sounding wistful. "But I have a friend we can crash with. She's expecting us late tonight."

Liv went tense, and was angry at herself for being so. "She?"

Sean lifted his hands defensively. "Not an ex-lover, as God is my witness. I would never dream of getting it on with Tam. She intimidates the living bejesus out of me. She's just a really unusual, ah, friend."

"Intimidated? You?" She snorted. "Oh, please. Get real."

"I'm kind of a wuss, if you want to know the truth," he confessed.

"Right. Big lily-livered wuss." She rolled her eyes. "Unusual how?"

"You have to meet her to understand. Tam is indescribable."

"Whatever," she said. "I need to contact my parents first."

"Davy's done that. They know you're safe," he said.

She shook with a burst of dry laughter. "Um, no, Sean. They know that I'm with you," she corrected. "They don't know that I'm safe."

He handed her his cell. "Be my guest. If you have the strength."

She took a deep breath, and dialed the number of Endicott House. It was snatched up on the first ring. "Hello?"

"Mother?" she asked. "It's me. I'm—"

"Oh, my God, Livvy. Have you gone insane? Where are you?"

"I'm with Sean," she soothed. "I'm fine, I'm safe."

"How could you do this to me? Come home this instant!"

"Um, actually . . . no. I'm going to disappear for a while. I—"

"The police need to talk to you, Livvy! That man is dangerous!"

Huh. Her definition of dangerous had gotten a sharp adjustment lately. "You've got the wrong idea," she explained. "Sean rescued me."

"Are you trying to punish me, Livvy?" Her mother's voice cracked. "When will it be enough pain to satisfy you? When will it stop? When?"

Liv swallowed back all the rest. No point. Nobody was listening. "Give Daddy a hug for me," she said. "Bye, Mother. I'll be in touch."

"Livvy! Stop! Don't you dare hang up that—"

Click. She broke the connection and stared down at the phone in her hand. She felt empty, light. She could float away, like a dry leaf.

"Well," she whispered. "I've done my duty. For what it's worth."

She set the phone down. Sean was rifling through his big, heavy olive green duffel bag full of mysterious equipment. "There's something I need to tell you," she said. "Something that's going to be hard to hear."

He went motionless for a moment, then straightened up, gripping the mattress on either side of him. "Yeah?" he said warily.

"Remember how you told me that everyone breaks under torture?"

He jerked his chin in assent, and waited for her to go on.

"It's not always true." She tried to swallow over the stone hard bump in her throat. "T-Rex said . . . that Kev never told them anything. Where the tapes were, where the notebook was. Who I was. No matter what they did to him. He didn't tell. So . . . I owe my life to him, too."

Sean looked away. He got up and circled the bed. He sat down with his back to her and sagged forward, leaning his face on his hands.

Liv crawled across the bed and draped herself against his back.

They stayed like that for a long time, waiting for night to fall.

Chapter
14

"Hold still," Osterman growled. "I'd already be done if you would just stop that goddamn twitching. Idiot."

His nostril flared with distaste as he swabbed the puncture wound on Gordon's furry buttock. The man's body stank. Yeasty and rank. This type of intimacy was repulsive to him. It was coming back to him, why he had abandoned the idea of practicing medicine, and chosen the realm of pure research. Fewer revolting odors.

He would have enjoyed the power that being a famous surgeon would have given him, but human bodies were disgusting. Particularly a sweaty animal like Gordon. He simply did not have the stomach for it.

"Spray on more anesthetic, you fucking sadist," Gordon barked.

Osterman ignored him. The slices on Gordon's back, the jagged puncture wound on his cheek, the teeth marks on his wrist, had been duly taken care of, but Osterman had not been gentle.

Idiot. Jerking off, at Osterman's expense. Correction. At Osterman's huge, crushing, exorbitant expense. He dug the needle in.

"Fuck!" Gordon hissed.

"Keep your voice down. A professional with years of experience, trounced by an unarmed research librarian. The mind boggles."

"I told you. Sean McCloud kicked my gun out of my hand while that crazy bitch was stabbing my face and biting my arm!"

"I don't want to hear excuses," Osterman fumed. "I don't understand why they aren't just *dead*, damnit."

"I don't get it." Gordon's voice was a rasp of frustration. "I waited on a rock right over that goddamn road. I was going to take them out when they came down, but they never did. That road dead-ends on Garnier Crest. I checked. The only way out of that place was down. They must have taken his truck off-road, or maybe they—"

"I was paying you to think about all that before the job," Osterman fumed. "You should have put a bullet through her eye."

"That wouldn't have been in character," Gordon said grumpily. "That's what a professional does. Not a sexually obsessed maniac."

"Yes, and you identify so intimately with the role, hmm? You have no end of excuses for wallowing in your trough. You medicated yourself before you picked her up, too, didn't you? I can tell from your stink."

"I wanted to be sharp," Gordon muttered. "I took some ZX-44."

"It's supposed to give you an edge in a high-stress situation," Osterman lectured. "You may as well have popped barbiturates."

"I didn't think McCloud was going to turn up out of nowhere—"

"You didn't think at all." Osterman swabbed and bandaged as quickly as possible, trying not to inhale. "You stopped thinking a while ago. You are degenerating. As of now, our contract is null and void."

"Shut the fuck up, Chris." Gordon swiveled his head around. The whites of his eyes were bloodshot, the lids puffy. His face was beaded with cold sweat. "There are lots of reasons to reconsider that decision. Most of them I don't have to say out loud. Like how popular you'd be in prison with that pretty face of yours, for instance."

"You can't expose me without incriminating yourself." Osterman's body was gripped with tension. His worst nightmare was coming true. Held hostage by a crazed, malodorous thug.

It made him so angry. That he, a gifted scientist who had given so much to humanity, who had given up all hope of a personal life, who had poured all his strength into selfless work to improve the quality of peoples' lives, should be forced to deal with such filth. Such squalor.

He braced himself. "You've gone beyond any reasonable—"

"But the most important reason is one you don't know yet." Gordon's voice took on an oily, insinuating tone.

Osterman set his teeth. "And what might that be?"

"I once heard you say that you made more progress in your research in those four days that you had Kevin strapped to your examining table than the rest of your entire career. Before or since."

"I fail to see how that is relevant to—"

"The most promising lines of research. The most innovative product designs and ideas." Gordon's grin froze, as it pulled at the blood-spotted gauze taped to his cheek. "And you never had so much fun in your life than you did dicking around with that freak's overdeveloped brain. You were on fire. You played him like a fine instrument."

"Make your point, and be done with it," Osterman snarled.

"One," Gordon held up a thick finger. "Back off on the lectures about self-indulgence. Two," he waggled another finger, "consider this before you have me waste Sean McCloud. He's Kevin's identical twin."

Osterman's breath froze in his lungs. "Identical . . ."

"Yes." One side of Gordon's lip curved up, in a grotesque smirk. "Are you still sure you want me to turn that brain into a bucket of pink slop before you have a chance to play with it? Think about it, Chris. An exact, identical genetic copy of your favorite toy."

Osterman stared at him, his palms sweating. "Why didn't you tell me he was Kevin's twin?"

Gordon shrugged. "I didn't know 'til now. They didn't play up the resemblance. Sean was behind Kevin in school, because Kevin kept skipping forward and Sean kept getting expelled. I found out they were twins when I questioned the girl. When I checked my obit collection—"

"Keeping a string of scalps on your Palm Pilot is a disgusting, twisted, barbaric practice," Osterman cut in. "Dangerous, too."

"Sure enough," Gordon pushed stubbornly on, "the obit said 'survived by brothers Davy McCloud, aged 27, Connor McCloud, aged 25, and Sean McCloud, aged 21.' Same age as Kevin. Take a look at the photographs from their file. If you study them, you can see it."

Osterman stared at the wall, clenching down on an excitement so intense, it was like sexual lust. "I want him alive," he said hoarsely.

He could feel Gordon's triumphant smile behind his back.

"All right," the other man purred. "You can strap down McCloud and play your dirty games, and I'll have my fun with the girl. Everybody gets their rocks off. Deal?"

Osterman gave him a short nod. He swallowed the excess saliva that was pumping into his mouth. He was trembling with eagerness.

"I'll need to hire some backup," Gordon said.

"Of course. It's clear you can't handle him alone."

Gordon's eyes sharpened. "I thought you wanted me to play it safe," he said slowly. "To cover your ass. To cover Helix's soft, pimply white corporate ass, too. If you want me to go mano a mano with that crazy fucker, I'll do it. But you'd be rolling the dice right along with me. The guy's extremely dangerous. And he'll be on his guard."

"Hire whoever you need," Osterman snapped. "Just keep it contained."

"I'll need people for surveillance. The McClouds would notice us watching, but the Endicotts are idiots. I'll tap their phones . . ."

Gordon droned on, but Osterman was no longer listening. He was lost in the memories of those four amazing days he'd spent playing with Kevin McCloud's brain. Released from any responsibility not to injure his subject, since thanks to Gordon's machinations, the young man had already been officially dead. Ashes, floating on the breeze.

Which meant that the unhappy creature strapped to that chair had belonged, completely and utterly, to Christopher Osterman.

What a feeling it had been. Utter power, total freedom. Bliss.

He'd been trying ever since to repeat the experience. In vain. He hadn't found a brain with anything near that capacity to diddle with.

This was dangerous. Gordon was nuts. Things were slipping out of control. He was risking everything he'd spent his whole life building.

But this temptation Osterman could not hope to resist.

"I can't figure out what we're doing wrong." Cindy fast forwarded through the homemade audition tape to see if that wobbly wah-wah sound was constant throughout. It was. She tried not to groan.

"It sounds like I'm playing underwater," Javier said glumly. "I can't send in that piece of shit. They'd laugh their asses off."

Cindy couldn't deny it. The tape sounded horrible.

She really wanted for Javier to get into the Young Artists' All Star Jazz Program. He was more than good enough for a scholarship, even if he was barely thirteen. He played the hell out of that sax.

It wasn't his fault that the recording wasn't great. Her mike sucked, the acoustics sucked, and the recording device sucked, to say nothing of what she herself might be doing wrong. She needed a decent mike, a soundproof room, a digital recording device. Someone who knew what he was doing. In short, she needed Miles.

Too freaking bad, honey. He thinks you're a brainless snow bunny.

"I'll ask around, see if I can find a better recording setup," she offered. "We'll try again. Don't get discouraged."

"Nah. The application said it had to be postmarked by tomorrow." Javier was downcast. "Thanks for trying, though. Don't sweat it." He gave her a smile that hurt her heart. He'd been disappointed so often, he'd come to accept it, with an adult grace that put her to shame. She was ten years older. She bitched and moaned ten times as much.

"No, really. Don't give up yet. I have a friend who's a sound magician. I'll see if he can help us out," she promised rashly.

Javier gave her a "whatever" shrug as he took his sax apart and lovingly laid it in the nest of crimson fuzz inside the case.

She wanted that scholarship for him so bad, she could taste it. She'd bonded with Javier at the beginning of band camp. They were about to throw him out for fighting, and she'd taken him aside to figure out what the deal was. Turned out that the spit-shined mama's boys in the brass section had been ragging him because his dad was in jail.

"No kidding? So's mine," she'd said. "Sucks the big one, huh?"

Javier's eyes had narrowed to liquid brown slits, hyper-wary of being messed with. "No shit," he said. "How long's he in for?"

"Life." Her throat still clamped down painfully on the word. It had been years, but she just couldn't get used to the idea of Daddy in jail.

"No parole?"

She shook her head. "Not a chance. They slammed him but good."

"What's he in for?" Javier demanded.

"Murder, mostly. Some other stuff, but that was the biggie."

That had impressed the hell out of Javier. "Wow," he breathed. "Bummer. Mine's just in for pushing dope."

She'd won him over with that little bit of one-upmanship. She'd had a sharp word with Mike, who led the brass section, and things had evened out. She discreetly gave Javier twice as many lessons as camp curriculum called for. It was no chore. He wasn't so hot at reading music yet, but who the hell cared? His improvisations blew her away.

She was so pleased with herself for wrangling him a great deal on a professional quality used sax. She'd used tits, mindless giggling, and judicious blackmail on Dougie, the proprieter of Doug's Music. She'd given Dougie to understand that she knew what had gone down at his piggy bachelor party, and with who. His bride, Trish, did not know. Nor should she, ever, if Dougie knew what was good for him.

Maybe Cindy had been a bad girl, but Javier got a good instrument, Trish remained blissfully ignorant, and Dougie was an oinking piglet who deserved to be slow roasted with an apple in his mouth. So whatever.

Javier deserved that scholarship. She didn't have time to find someone else to bully into helping her. It had to be Miles. The dojo where Miles taught was close by, and it was early evening, class time. She would just pop down there and hope he didn't bite her head off.

Being on Miles's shit list truly sucked.

She hopped on her bike and sped past the ruins of the bookstore. It was still shrouded with lingering smoke. What a drag. Endicott Falls had needed a good bookstore. It had been too good to be true. Typical.

Speaking of drags. Of all the things currently getting her down, Miles topped the list. It was so hard to accept, that he was definitively blowing her off. They'd been friends forever. He knew her embarrassing secrets, all the crazy shit she'd done, and he'd accepted her anyway.

Not anymore. He'd abruptly cut off the total acceptance part.

She'd known that he had a thing for her, of course, but what could she do about that? She'd never led him on. She'd been clear from the start that he wasn't her type, that she just wanted to be friends.

Call her shallow, but when it came to romance and sex, she went for big, gorgeous, muscular guys. Like, duh. So shoot her, already.

It was so hard. She kept on wanting to talk to Miles about all her problems, all the weird stuff that happened. She missed his sarcastic, funny take on things. Life was flat, without Miles to bullshit about it with. And he was so freaking brainy, too. It had been super convenient, having a crazy smart, insanely competent best friend. Like being smart herself, but without the effort and the bother. How awesome was that.

At least she had the satisfaction of knowing he still missed her. Or why would he have used her for his Mina profile?

That had given her an idea. A favor she could offer him, in return for helping record Javier's tape. She wasn't asking any more free favors.

Not while she was still smarting from that crack about her being a concubine, when she was not.

That had stung. Months of working eighteen hours a day, keeping her nose clean, saving up for first, last and security on the Seattle house in September, and he thought she was just a slut any guy could buy for a couple of lines of coke. Ouch.

She peeked around to see if Miles's new wheels were parked outside the dojo, but she didn't see the car. She ran up the stairs, nose wrinkling at the overpowering odor of sweat. A karate class was taking place, she saw through the glass window, kids dressed in their white outfits, going through a sequence of kicks and punches.

She pushed the door open and leaned on the frame, spotting Miles off to the side, correcting the posture of a kid with a green belt knotted around his gi. Miles knocked the kid's knees out to widen his stance, tugged his arm out, nudged the back arm higher, and said something that made the kid laugh. He held up his hand at shoulder height and jerked his chin, *go*. The kid swung his leg back, and kicked at Miles's hand, over and over. Sometimes he hit, sometimes he missed. They tried it from the side, from the front, from the back again.

Cindy was startled. Miles looked different. She hadn't gotten the full effect in the dark basement. Hair in a ponytail. No glasses. He grinned at the kid, said something encouraging. He didn't look like the vampirish Goth geek freak she knew and loved. He looked, well, cute. He had a black belt knotted around his waist, too. Wow. Who knew?

He spun around, kicked. *Tap*, he touched the kid's chest with his toe, ever so lightly. She was no expert, but that looked awfully graceful.

Then, predictably, disaster struck. He caught sight of her, and did a big fat double take just as the kid threw his leg back again.

Smack, the kid's foot connected with Miles's face. Down he went, on his ass. There was yelling, screaming. A bunch of people scurried towards him. Blood streamed from his nose, dripping all over his gi.

Cindy sprinted towards him, horrified. "Shit! Miles? Are you OK?"

"Get off the tatami with your shoes, Cin." Miles's voice was razor sharp, even burbling through the blood.

She retreated, chastened, to the door, and waited. People clustered around him. Someone brought him a towel. His eyes kept darting over to her. They did not look friendly.

Aw, shit. *Shit*. What was it with her? Was she cursed, or what?

Miles got up and stalked towards her, stripping the bloodstained gi off with a hiss of disgust. "What the hell are you doing here, Cin?"

"Uh . . . I . . ." She gaped at his naked torso, struck dumb.

Holy cow. Miles was, like, ripped. Big, thick, meaty deltoids that a girl could just sink her nails into. Cut pecs. Serious ab definition. She wanted him to turn around, show her his lats, his traps. His ass.

Um, no. That was asking a bit much, under the circumstances.

"Uh, Cin?" he prompted. "Hello? Why are you here?"

She opened and closed her mouth, helplessly, like a beached fish.

"Just thought you'd help me make an unforgettable first impression on my first day of teaching, huh?" His voice dripped sarcasm. "Thanks, Cin. This does great things for my credibility."

"I didn't do it on purpose! I was just standing there!"

"Yeah, that's all it takes." Miles took the towel away from his face, and grimaced at the gory smears. "Jesus. I need ice."

"Can I go get you some?" she asked, eager to redeem herself.

"No. Just tell me why you're here, and get it over with. Come on."

He grabbed her arm, steered her into a room full of weight-lifting equipment. He shut the door, and dabbed at his nose. "So? Spit it out."

"It's really hard to talk to you while you're glaring like that."

Miles rolled his eyes. "A glare is the default expression of a guy who's just gotten his nose practically broken by a twelve-year-old. So have you thought of something you want from me after all?"

She gritted her teeth and pressed on. "Actually, yes," she admitted. "But not for me. It's for Javier. He's—"

"Forget it." Miles's scowl deepened. "I thought you said you didn't have a boyfriend right now. In any case, I'm not doing favors for him."

"Javier is twelve!" she snapped. "He's one of my students. I want to make him a decent audition tape. He's applying to the All-Star Young Artists Jazz Program, and he needs a scholarship to—"

"Bring out the violins." Miles clapped the towel over his face, giving her another chance to ogle his awesome body. Those biceps were to die for. She wanted to palpate them so bad, her fingers twitched.

"I'm out of the business of doing sound for free," Miles went on. "I spend all my time doing favors for my musician friends. That's why I'm broke. I've got to draw the line somewhere, so here it is. Don't cross it."

"Please?" she wheedled. "I know you think I'm pond scum, but this isn't about me at all. Javier's a great kid. His uncle Bolivar is the janitor up at the Colfax building, and I've been giving him lessons for free for almost a year now. His dad's in jail, and his mother—"

"I don't want to hear about his mother," Miles cut in. "I don't want to hear about her working double shifts in the factory to put food on the table, and poor Tiny Tim with his crutch in the corner. I do not care."

"It'll take you a half an hour," Cindy coaxed. "We'll come to your house any time it's convenient—as long as it's before the post office closes tomorrow. Javier's a really great kid. He deserves a break."

"Who's going to give me a break?" Miles's voice was plaintive.

"Well. Since you mention it." Cindy crossed her arms over her belly, pressing down on her nervous flutter. "That brings me to another thing. What do you intend to do when Mindmeld wants to meet Mina?"

Miles's face darkened. "I'll cross that bridge when I come to it. And it's none of your damn business, anyway."

Cindy rocked back, unnerved by the anger blazing out of Miles's brown eyes. "Well, I got to thinking last night about how the physical profile sounds, um, a lot like me."

"Goddamnit, Cin, I told you—"

"Shh! Just hear me out!" She held up both hands. "I thought that if you needed to set up a real meeting, you could use me."

Miles blinked at her. "Use you," he repeated.

"Yeah!" She gave him a bright, encouraging smile. "As bait, you know? It's, like, perfect. I'd be more than willing to help."

He was dead silent for almost a minute, his blood streaked mouth dangling open. "Are you fucking nuts?" he finally exploded.

Cindy jerked, startled at his vehemence. "Ah . . ."

"Do you have any idea how dangerous that would be? Did it occur to you that we're talking about a serial killer?"

"Uh, yes," she said cautiously. "So? People take risks to catch guys like that, right? Why not me? I just thought—"

"Don't think, Cin," he snarled. "We'd all be better off."

"I still think it's a good idea," she muttered, defensive.

"It's not a good idea. It sucks. And I don't know any polite way to tell you this, but I've been making like a physics whiz. Dazzling this guy with Mina's brain. That's what this asshole gets hot for. Understand?"

She put her hands over the hot red spots flaring in her face. "So what you're saying is that I'm not smart enough?"

Miles looked pained. "You said it, Cin. Not me. You play a mean saxophone. I talk shop about acoustic physics. We all have our gifts."

"Oh, shut up," she said, through the snot bubbling in her nose. "Don't condescend to me. How smart can these geeks be? They're dumb enough to get nabbed, aren't they? And when it comes to getting mixed up with the wrong kind of guy, I'm, like, unbeatable."

"Do not mention this to anybody." Miles's voice had a steely tone.

"Oh, no. Don't worry. I understand," she babbled, through her tears. "God forbid that Connor and his brothers should find out that you talked about their big manly business to a fluff like me."

"Stop feeling sorry for yourself, Cin. It's a really bad habit."

"Don't lecture me!" she shot back. "You're not my friend anymore, so you no longer have the right." She wiped her nose with the back of her hand, sniffing angrily. "OK, never mind me and my dumb ideas. I'll just hire you to do Javier's tape. How much do you want?"

Miles groaned, beneath his breath. "Cut it out, Cin."

"No, really. I've got some money saved. Quote me your hourly rate. Just don't tell Javier, because he'd be really embarrassed."

"I'm not going to let you jerk me around," Miles said.

"I'm not jerking you around!" she yelled. "God, what do I have to do to persuade you? What do you want from me, a blow job?"

The next fraction of a second was very weird. One moment she was standing there blubbering. The next, her back was flat against the wall, with Miles's surprisingly hard body holding her there.

Breathless. Squished. Startled . . . and scared.

"Do not ever, *ever* joke about that with me," he said.

Miles's hoarse whisper sent shivers up her spine. She made a sound like a rusty hinge. She noticed random, disconnected things. Like he had nice breath. A sexy mouth. And his nose was swelling up.

Yikes. Miles's nose had been really formidable to begin with.

"Ever again," he repeated softly. "Not. Funny. At all. Got it?"

She licked her lips, and nodded. "Sorry," she mouthed.

He didn't let go. Just loomed over her, vibing like crazy. Wow. Miles was freakishly tall, but he'd never loomed before. But then again, looming was a state of mind. The McCloud guys were all loomers, every last one of them. Miles must have learned the art from them.

He'd learned it really well. Her head flopped back so far to look up at him, her neck hurt. She'd never felt this quality of energy buzzing off him before. And intense heat was radiating from the hard bulge at his crotch. She sneaked a quick peek, and almost squeaked. Gosh. The old joke about long noses must be literally true. Miles was hung.

It was like there was a volcano inside him. Her geeky old best buddy was looking at her as if he were about to grab her and kiss her.

And for one wild, crazy second, she actually wanted him to.

He stepped back, broke eye contact, broke the spell. "Sorry." He looked away. "Didn't mean to scare you."

Her heart thudded. Her knees felt wiggly and weak. "Oh, puh-leeze. Give me a break. I wasn't scared," she lied.

"Bring the kid to record his thing tomorrow at noon. Don't be late. I've got things to do." He yanked the door open, and marched out.

Well, that settled that. His lats and traps were finger-licking good. And his ass was just as good as she had imagined.

Chapter
15

Besides being butt-ugly, the fogeymobile was a rattling, tubercular piece of shit. Sean tried to coax more speed out of the old monster, but when he hit sixty, it started to shimmy all over the road.

He eased down, cursing under his breath. It was taking longer than he'd anticipated to make it to Tam's. He was reasonably sure they weren't being followed, but he could use some sleep, in someplace secure. Tam's fortress was as secure as it got, after Seth and Raine's Stone Island hideaway. Seth had rigged it up for her himself. Pure, high-tech, state of the art paranoia. Just what the doctor ordered.

"What language was that?" Liv asked.

He glanced over, startled to find her awake, and dragged the incredibly filthy epithet he'd just uttered out of his short term memory bank. "Croatian," he said. "A regional dialect of it, anyway."

"What does it mean?"

He hesitated. "Uh, well, it was directed at the car," he hedged.

"Yes?" she said sweetly. "And the meaning?" Her soft, beautiful voice was froggy with sleep, but full of curiosity. She waited.

He sighed. "It was a crude, vicious attack upon the virtue and chastity of the mother, grandmother and great-grandmother of the mechanic who last serviced this piece of shit car."

She made that muffled little giggling snort that he loved so much. "How awful," she murmured. "Those poor women. How unfair."

"Yeah, right. My manners suck," he said sourly.

"So where did you learn Croatian?"

He shot an uneasy glance, but there was nothing to see in the dark but the pale glow of the oversized T-shirt she wore. He'd been pathetically grateful when the princess collapsed into exhausted sleep the minute they got on the road. She needed the rest, for one thing. And he needed space just as badly. Time to process what was happening.

He wasn't done with that processing yet, but Liv was done with her nap, and feeling fresh and chatty and curious. He was so in for it.

"In the Army," he told her. "Ranger Regiment. Mostly in the Balkans. After my stint in the military, I bummed around in eastern Europe and Africa. I got contract work through military contacts. The money was good. And it suited my mood, at the time."

"Contract work?" Her voice was delicately cautious. "What's that?"

"Mercenary," he said.

That shut her up. She was probably thinking that he'd been a hired thug. In some ways, he guessed he had been. It all depended on your point of view. Life was like that. Hard to define, hard to justify.

"Wow," she said faintly. "Isn't that, ah, really dangerous?"

"Yeah. I got lots of work because I pick up languages fast. I speak Croatian, and Farsi, and some Arabic, some Persian, decent French, and a bunch of obscure dialects you probably never heard of. That photographic memory about works aurally, too, if you program your brain right."

"Wow," she whispered. "Amazing. I wish I could do that."

He shot her a glance. "Why couldn't you?"

She gave him a derisive snort. "Get real."

"No, really," he protested. "It's just a trick. My dad taught us. You just have to set your mind to it. No biggie. Anyone could do it."

"Yeah, right." Her voice was heavy with irony. "I don't know how to break this to you, Sean, but what you describe is not normal. It is, in point of fact, what other people would describe as freak genius."

"You got the freak part right," he agreed. "You should hear my brothers talk. They think I'm an idiot savant. I can do tricks like a dancing bear, but I can't seem to stay out of trouble with the cops. What does that suggest about my intelligence level?"

She covered her face. He heard smothered giggles. It gave him a happy glow to get a laugh out of her, even if it was at his own expense.

"So you've been doing, ah, contract work ever since then?" she asked, when she got her voice back under control.

"Nah. I burnt out a while back. For a while, after Kev died—after Kev was murdered," he corrected himself. "I didn't care whether I lived or died. But after a while, I started caring again. And if you keep putting yourself in harm's way, it doesn't matter how lucky you are. Statistics will catch up with you. Besides, it was so freaking depressing. I would have ended up eating a bullet in the end. Just so I didn't have to keep seeing all that awful shit every time I closed my eyes."

"Oh dear," she whispered. "That's awful. I'm sorry."

"You know that diamond mine fuck-up I told you about? The electrical wire episode? That was the clincher, for me. I got this other scar in that incident, too." He put his hand over the side of his abdomen, against the throb of remembered pain. "I had lots of time afterwards to lie around watching a bag drip into my arm and ponder how fucked up my life was. I decided it was time to lighten up."

She was quiet for a while while she thought about what he'd said, but he knew he wasn't off the hook yet. Long car trips were the pits, when it came to curious women. It was like being chained to a chair.

"That summer that we met, you were saving up money to finish your degree," she ventured, her voice cautious.

And I blew every last penny on a rock for you, baby.

He stopped himself, just in time. No need to burden her with that. He touched the small gem in his ear, twirled it. His one nervous habit.

He'd worn it ever since he'd gotten the money together to set it into an earring, and never examined why. Masochism, maybe. A stern reminder not to get wound up about women. A perverse mix of both.

Maybe just because he was a vain peacock. The diamond looked sharp, which he liked, and it bugged his humorless brothers, which he also liked. Jerking Davy and Con around was one of the great joys of his existence. They considered his diamond an effete affectation. Fuck 'em. That was just dour old crazy Eamon talking. He'd be damned if he'd let the ghost of his dead father dictate his fashion accessories, too.

The shadow Dad had cast over his life was long enough as it was.

"So. I know you were interested in studying chemical engineering. Did you ever . . ." Her voice trailed off.

"No, Liv," he said gently. "I never went back to finish my degree."

She paused. "I didn't mean to seem as if I was criticizing you."

"Nah. A lot of things changed that summer. To tell you the truth, I forgot all about chemical engineering. It barely crossed my mind."

"I'm sorry," she said quietly.

"Don't be," he told her. "I'm not. In retrospect, academia or theoretical research or a think tank would have been all wrong for a spaz like me. I would have gone batshit. Adrenaline junkie that I am."

She twisted her hands together. "I'm so sorry," she said again.

He shot her a puzzled look. "What are you sorry for this time?"

She shrugged. "All of it. What happened fifteen years ago. The dent that it put in your life. What happened today, too."

"Ah. That," he said. "Don't be sorry about that on my account. I'm better off than I was before. It's easier to deal with Kev being murdered than accept that he'd gone nuts. Now I've got someone external that I can hunt down and kill. That's so much better, babe. So much."

"Well," she murmured doubtfully. "I suppose. If you say so."

He decided to deflect questions from his own twitchy self. "So what have you done with yourself in the past fifteen years?" he asked.

She let out a small laugh. "Compared to you, absolutely nothing."

"Oh, come on," he said. "Spill it."

She tossed her hands up. "Normal, dull, predictable stuff. Went to college. Went abroad. Studied art and architecture and literature.

Tried to learn some French and Italian. Didn't get very far. Got a masters in library science. Worked various places as a research librarian. Decided to try my hand at running a bookstore. And the rest you know."

"I thought your folks wanted you to go into the family business."

"Oh, yes. My mother was frantic. I wasted lots of energy opposing her. I guess that's the big war story of my life, but it's too sad and boring to tell. So that's it for me. No crossing the desert on a camel, or swashbuckling swordfights, or guarding diamond mines, or mortal combat with cruel warlords or suchlike. Just dull, normal living."

He rubbed the scar from his bullet wound. "Be glad," he said.

"I know, but it seems so tame. At least until yesterday. My normal life is mostly work. In my spare time, I read books, shop for groceries, do laundry, pay utility bills. I see lots of movies. I love to garden. I collect patchwork quilts. I enjoy making bread and jam. Being domestic."

He pictured it. Cooking with her, rattling around together in their homey, cluttered kitchen. Cuddling next to her underneath one of those quilts. Munching homemade bread and jam with her on her couch.

Gardening? Hmm. Maybe he could sprawl in a lawn chair and nurse a cold beer while he watched Liv garden. Bent sexily over her tomatoes at a ninety degree angle, in snug blue jeans. Yeah. Mmm.

"Sounds real nice," he said wistfully. "Can I come?"

She made a sound, like she was blowing air out of her lungs. "Stop it, Sean. I don't know what to think when you say stuff like that."

"I'm a simple creature," he said. "Take me at my word."

"Simple?" Her voice began to shake. "Oh, yeah, Sean. Sure. Look what your simplicity has done to my life. I was in therapy for years."

That perplexed him. She seemed so well-adjusted. "You? Why?"

"I wanted to stop thinking about you," she said, forcefully.

They both stared out straight ahead, watching the yellow line that divided the small highway curving to the right, the left, the right again.

"Did it ever work?" he asked quietly.

She shook her head. "No," she whispered.

"Not for me, either," he admitted.

"I don't want to think about it." Her voice sounded bleak. "Let's figure out what's going on here and now. You're not kidnapping me, last time I checked, so what's our status? Am I running away with you?"

He felt suddenly more cheerful. "I like the sound of that."

"And what do you plan to do with me?" she demanded.

"I can think of some real fun things right off the top of my head."

"Oh, stop it," she snapped. "Be serious, for once."

"I'll keep you safe." The words came out clear and decisive.

"Well, that's nice, Sean, but in exchange for what? A professional bodyguard comes at about two hundred bucks an hour. I have exactly nothing. And I do mean zip. Just a burned-up bookstore and a gargantuan mortgage. I'll get some insurance money eventually, but until then—"

"I don't care," he said.

"And don't think my parents being filthy rich will help." Her voice quivered. "They've cut me off. I'm out of the will."

"Good," he said, with quiet vehemence. "That's great news, babe."

"Is it? Really? So how am I supposed to recompense you?"

"Sexual favors," he said promptly. "Let's see, two hundred bucks an hour for twenty-four hours, that's forty-eight hundred bucks a day, princess. That's a lot of favors."

She snickered into her hands. "Oh, would you shut up."

"I'd be at you all the time," he said. "When I'm not defending you with life and limb, we'll be writhing around in bed. It'll be strenuous."

"It already is," she snapped. "I can barely walk."

"Sorry," he said meekly. "Bullshit aside, though. I don't need two hundred bucks an hour. I'll just do it because you're the princess. You deserve to be protected. You don't have to put out. And you don't have to pay me. All you have to do is exist. That's more than enough for me."

Her eyes gleamed at him, luminous with tears. She wiped her eyes, looked away. The silence got very thick for a moment.

"That's a very sweet thing to say," she said demurely. "But it's not very economically practical. We need a nuts and bolts plan."

"I'm working on it, babe. Now if you'll excuse me, this is where I have to start concentrating if I'm going to find Tam's place."

He had memorized the exact point on the fourth curve after the old stonework bridge where he had to stop, and slew to the left, bumping down into a narrow ditch and up again, straight into what seemed like a blank thicket of scrubby bushes. They scraped and brushed against the body of the car. He pushed on through the wall.

Once through it, they found themselves in a blind clearing blocked by the wall of a barn. The tumbledown roof was green with moss and full of gaping holes. The fogeymobile bumped over something metallic. Sean saw a flash of movement ahead and jerked to a halt right before the low, jagged metal spikes rising up at an angle out of the ground could puncture the front tires.

"Oh, God," Liv squeaked.

"Damn you, Tam," he snapped. "Snotty bitch. She did that to rattle me. I don't want to have to replace the tires on this heap of junk."

The row of spikes slowly, majestically retracted back into the ground. Sean grunted. "Gee, thanks. So generous of you."

A narrow beam of red light flipped on, swiveling until it focused first on him, then on Liv's face. It flicked back to him, lingered. Sean thumbed his nose, waggled his fingers, stuck out his tongue. "Yes, it's me, Tam," he said. "What do you want, a fucking DNA sample?"

There was a muted hum, and the wall of the barn divided into four parts and retracted, showing a road that led into the forest beyond.

"Good heavens," Liv said. "I've never seen anything like this."

Sean grunted. "Yeah, it's like Disneyland. But she's got money to burn." He acccelerated through the barn. The road wove through the thick woods, climbing and switching back, until it topped a crest.

"Look down, to your right," Sean said.

She did, and gasped. The road was on the crest of a hill that sloped down to the beach. The vast immensity of the Pacific Ocean spread out before them, illuminated with moonlight that cast the shadows of the stunted, wind-contorted trees. Wind-combed shreds of cloud moved across the sky. Surf washed over the broad, shining beach, in long swathes of white, bubbly foam, crashing against spires of black rock. It was beautiful, in a cold, aching, melancholy way.

"Tam's fortress is up top," he explained. "Architectural camouflage. You really can't see it until you're in it."

"It's like a James Bond movie." Liv's voice sounded nervous.

"Oh, you ain't seen nothing yet," he assured her. "Tam is like a bad Bond girl herself. The kind that'll do a backflip onto your head and break your neck with her perfect thighs if you don't look sharp."

She turned a worried gaze on him. "That sounds alarming."

"Oh, no. She's more fun than a barrel of monkeys. It's just that you can't ever relax with her. She's . . . well, you'll see."

"Who *is* this woman?" Liv demanded. "What does she do? You're driving me nuts with this 'you'll see, you'll see' crap. Tell me, already!"

"She's a mystery," Sean said helplessly. "I'm not being coy. We don't know much, and we're kind of afraid to ask. Nobody knows what all she's done, but it was against the law, that's for sure. And when you look around her place, you'll see that it was profitable."

"How do you know her? You don't mean to tell me that you . . . ?"

"Hell, no," he said hastily. "I'm squeaky clean, sweetheart. I don't need to go looking for trouble. I'm plenty busy enough with the trouble that comes looking for me."

"So how did you meet her?" Liv persisted.

"My brother Con met her a couple years ago. She was the mistress of this psychotic billionaire who was trying to rub out my brother's girlfriend. Who is now his wife, Erin. Anyhow, turns out Tam was trying to assassinate the guy herself, but he was a real tough bastard. She and Connor saved each other's asses."

"It does sound a tad stressful," Liv murmured. "So? Did she?"

"Did she what?"

"Kill the billionaire," Liv said impatiently.

"Ah, no, actually. It was Erin who killed him."

She shot him a wide-eyed glance. "You mean, Erin is a commando chick who breaks men's necks with her perfect thighs, too?"

"Nah. Erin is a sweet, demure antiquities nerd who wouldn't hurt a fly. But she stabbed that evil fucker right in the throat with a Bronze Age Celtic dagger." Sean's voice was proud. "Blood squirting everywhere. You should have seen the walls of the place. It was unreal."

"Thank God I didn't," Liv said faintly.

"Well, he was trying to strangle her to death," he added, defensive. "And then Con and Tam shot up all his evil henchmen. It was intense."

Liv shook her head. "I'm getting an inferiority complex."

"Why? It's no different from what you did to T-Rex this morning."

Liv let out a bark of laughter. "There's the difference that Erin killed the billionaire. Whereas T-Rex is still running around out there."

"Don't feel bad about it, babe. Practice makes perfect," Sean encouraged her. "I'm sure you'll get another whack at him."

"Whoopee," she muttered.

Sean pushed on. "So that was our bonding experience with Tam. She was maid of honor at Con and Erin's wedding, when she gave Margot, Davy's wife, this hairclip that sprays soporific gas. Which saved Margot's life when they were being hunted by this wacko scientist who was selling a lethal flu vaccine . . ." His voice trailed off. He gave Liv's averted face an uneasy glance. "Maybe now's not the time to share."

"It's OK." Liv's voice was hollow. "I'd rather know that the woman I'm staying with is a hard-core career criminal."

"Not now," Sean said quickly. "Retired career criminal would be more accurate. She just lurks in her fortress. Designs crazy jewelry."

"Yeah. She's as harmless as a patchwork granny, I'm sure."

"She's special, our Tam. Try not to let her get under your skin," he advised. "Check out this space age cloaking device over the garage."

"What garage?"

She gasped as the mountainside split, bushes and moss and rocks gliding smoothly aside to reveal a garage carved right into the mountainside. "My God," she whispered. "This is surreal."

"Yeah," he said, switching off the headlights. "Don't worry. Tam likes us, for some reason. I imagine that's why she hasn't killed us yet."

Liv stared, transfixed, at the rectangle of red-tinged light at the end of the dark garage. Light spilled out, reflecting in a long, ruddy streak on the gleaming stonework of the floor. A slender form appeared in silhouette, dramatically backlit. Hip cocked, leaning against the door frame. A gun dangled negligently from one hand. The other brought a cigarette to her lips. The tip glowed red. She tilted her chin up, blew out a stream of smoke. It looked like the opening of a dance piece.

Liv took a deep breath, and shoved the car door open. All she needed. Another challenge. Chatting up the beautiful bad Bond girl.

Sean slid his arm around her waist. "Relax," he whispered. "What's with the gun, Tam?" he demanded. "Lighten up."

"The day I lighten up is the day I get killed." Tam's voice was low and husky. "I know your face, but I don't know hers. She could have been holding a gun to your ribs, for all I knew."

"I don't do things like that," Liv announced.

"I can see that." Tam took another deep drag on her cigarette and sauntered towards them, hips swaying langorously, keeping Liv's face in the light and her own in the shadow. "Oh, God, look at you. Looks like I'll be doing some emergency shopping in the morning." She grabbed the flapping T-shirt Liv wore and twisted it, to reveal the shape of her body. "Nice tits. Thirty-six double D, size . . . twelve?"

Liv jerked away, hackles rising. "On a good day. But please don't bother. I'll manage."

Tam took another drag. "I can't let a sister with a figure like yours dress like that. It's a crime. Follow me. And take off those shoes."

Liv stopped on the threshhold, stepping out of her ruined sandals. "Do you have a no-shoes rule in your house?"

"I have a no-ugly-shoes rule in my house," Tam said coolly.

Sean made a smothered laughing sound, and turned his face away. Liv privately vowed to make him pay for that lapse. In blood.

"Look, lady, I've been on the run for my life," Liv told her, through set teeth. "I've had way more important things to think about than—"

"On the run for your life is all the more reason to look your best, cupcake." Tamara tucked her gun into the back of her jeans, and waved them on ahead of her. "Believe me, I know what I'm talking about."

Liv stared as Tam tapped in codes to reset the alarms.

"I've never seen you with brown hair and yellow eyes," Sean said.

"Enjoy it while you can," Tam said. "You may never see it again."

Tam was slim, muscular, and curvy, a triple combination which Liv took as a personal affront, it being so unfair. Her brown hair was braided, long wisps dangling around the sharp line of her jaw. She had the most astonishingly beautiful face Liv had ever seen. Everything was perfect; high cheekbones, full lips, straight, perfect nose. Her eyes were huge; golden brown, with curling lashes and winged brows. There were smudgy circles beneath them, but what would make another woman look tired and frazzled made Tam look dramatic and mysterious.

She was dressed in faded, low-slung Levis and a tank top that showed off several inches of taut belly. No makeup. Barefoot. Her only jewelry was a gold horn stuck through one ear that tapered to a point, like a fang. Anyone hugging her would probably bleed to death, stuck through the carotic artery. Maybe that was the idea.

Liv felt fat, frumpy and outclassed. She couldn't stop staring.

Tam ignored her, evidently used to it. She shooed them into a huge kitchen, and turned on a bright overhead light. Liv blinked as the light refracted off an uncountable number of gleaming reflective surfaces. Tam gave Sean a brilliant smile. "Your brothers will be here to kick you around, first thing in the morning."

Sean groaned. "Shit. Tam, I told you not to—"

"I didn't have to. Any idiot would guess that you would go to ground here. Let's just hope that no other idiots know about me."

Sean gave her a smile that was equally toothy. "Just us idiots."

"And no one followed you?"

"No." They eyed each other, like alpha wolves circling.

"Hmm," she murmured. "Come on, come on." She grabbed Liv by the arm, and shoved her on one of the stools in front of a big bar.

Her kitchen was amazing. Acres of black gleaming marble counter space, endless expanses of shining silver toned appliances, an enormous double-sized silver refrigerator. A knife block that would be the envy of a professional chef, racks of hanging copper bottomed pans. The place looked like a showroom. It had clearly never been used.

Tam opened the refrigerator, and took out a clear plastic box with several hypodermic needles. "Always prepared."

Liv blinked at them. "What—hey!" She squawked, struggled, but Tam had already yanked her T-shirt over her head and tossed it. Liv tried to slide off the stool, but Tam's hand clamped onto her shoulder.

"What the hell? Do you mind?" Liv hissed. "Give me my shirt!"

Tam's perfect brow tilted. "Sean said you had cuts, and a bite wound. I want to take a look. Allergic to any antibiotics?"

"No!" Liv glared at Sean, who gave her an apologetic shrug. Ineffectual twit. "And I've had enough of people ripping my clothes off today to last a lifetime. It is *rude!*"

Tam examined the bite mark, which was sore and red. "But you have great tits. Sit up straight and show them off." Tam swabbed Liv's arm with disinfectant, and stabbed the needle in without warning.

"Ouch!" She jerked, but Tam held her arm firmly in place. "What are you doing to me, anyway? What the hell is that?"

"Broad-spectrum stuff," Tam said. "Human bites can go bad." She spun the twirling stool around, swabbed the other arm.

"Hey. Wait. What's—"

"Tetanus booster. Had one lately?"

"Uh . . ." Liv hesitated, trying to remember.

"Then you need one." *Stab.*

Liv tried not to shriek as the stuff burned into her arm like a massive, awful bee sting. But it seemed ignoble to bitch about it.

Tam held up a third hypodermic. "Were you raped?" Her voice as matter-of-fact as if she were asking if Liv took milk in her coffee.

Liv caught her breath as an image of T-Rex squatting on top of her, flashed through her mind. "No," she said. "Close, but no."

Tam flashed Sean a quick, approving glance. "Good."

"What's in that one?" Liv asked, with some trepidation.

"A dose of morning-after juice," Tam said. "Do you need it? You did spend the day wrangling an oversexed gorilla who was hopped up on adrenaline. I doubt he exercised much restraint. Just say the word."

"God, Tam," Sean complained. "Would you back off?"

"Never," Tam said sweetly.

"Isn't that stuff available by prescription only?" Liv asked.

Tam's grin lit up her face, showing off blindingly white teeth. "Aw. Is she for real? She's cute, Sean. Where did you find her?"

Sean shrugged. "In Endicott Falls. Of all places."

Tam snapped her fingers in Liv's face. "So? You want this shot?"

Sean lifted his shoulders in a shrug that said "your call." She thought about it for a second and a half. "No," she said quietly. If it came to that, she and Sean could have The Talk.

Tam's eyes widened. She rummaged in the chest, and pulled out a string of condoms. "You hardly need these, but take them as a reminder not to take advantage of a girl's romantic feelings." She flung them.

He caught them one-handed. "I am tired of everyone throwing condoms at me," he growled. "I'm perfectly capable of getting my own."

"But not using them, hmm?" Tam's voice was sugary.

"Mind your goddamn business, Tam."

"Oh, but I was. Until I got your phone call. If you want my help, you'll just have to tolerate my character defects. Now get your own shirt off, big boy. It's your turn."

"Me?" he sounded aggrieved. "Why? Nobody bit me. And nothing's infected. I would know by now if it was. So don't worry about—"

"Shut up." Tam's voice was adamant. "If she gets it, you get it."

Sean let out a liquid string of words as he yanked his shirt off.

"Insult me any way you like," Tam said. "But if you ever talk trash about my mother and grandmother again, I will rip your guts out and tie them around your neck in a big, festive bow. Is that understood?"

Sean's eyes widened with shock. "You speak Croatian?"

Tam's face was an icy mask as she squeezed the air out of the syringe. "Assumptions get you killed. Filthy, shit-mouthed idiot dog."

"Uh, sorry," he said, chastened. "I didn't mean it personally."

She swabbed, and stuck him in the arm.

Sean hissed. "Fuck! I take it back. I'm not sorry. Not sorry at all."

"Crybaby." She swabbed the other arm, jabbed.

"Hell witch," he snarled.

She responded with something incomprehensible. Sean shot something back. The insults flew, picking up speed and volume and vicious energy, each in a new language she had never heard.

"Stop it!" Liv yelled.

They stared at her, startled into silence. Liv retrieved her shirt and tugged it on. "Stop showing off," she snapped. "It's really irritating."

"Sorry." Sean turned to Tam. "You have to teach me the one about the goat-fucking son of a lazy camel, though. What is that, Turkish?"

"Yeah. I liked the Corsican one about the sheep in the bushes," she said, faint admiration in her tone. "Very obscure. Very dirty."

Sean gazed at her for a long, thoughtful moment, his smile fading. "Where the fuck are you from, anyway, Tam?"

Her smile was brilliant and empty. "Nowhere," she said.

Tam opened the door of the vast refrigerator, which had nothing in it other than mineral water and a big box. "Here's your dinner. Take it up to your suite to eat it. I can't handle the smell of food tonight."

Sean frowned. "Not eating, huh? You don't look so good."

Her eyes flashed. "Your usual cheap gallantry has deserted you."

"You've lost weight," Sean persisted. "More than you can afford to lose. And you've got circles under your eyes. Have you been sick?"

"How about you mind your own goddamn business, hmm?"

Sean grabbed the box. "Whatever," he said. "Thanks for dinner."

Tam jerked her chin at him, with ill grace. "Take it and go. You're bothering me tonight. Take the north tower. You know the way."

Liv scurried to follow him. If that was how Tam looked when she wasn't looking good, Liv would be afraid to to see her looking fabulous.

Chapter
16

Something was wrong with Tam. She wasn't any pricklier than usual, but she had a strange vibe. Stranger than usual, that was.

He would almost describe it as vulnerable. Though he'd probably die a slow, horrible death if he ever said as much to her. A guy stepped careful around that chick if he wanted to keep his balls attached.

Still. She was too damn skinny. Shadowy-eyed. All muscle and rib and hollows under her cheekbones. And that bluish network of veins showing at her temples didn't look right. Someone should sound her out, see if she was OK. Maybe he'd get Margot or Erin to do it. Call him gutless, but he knew when he was out of his depth.

Liv made no sound behind him as she padded barefoot up the long staircase and followed him down the maze of corridors and clusters of dim rooms that led to the north tower. "Wow," she murmured, looking around herself. "This place is incredible. She lives here alone?"

He snorted. "Can you imagine anybody living with Tam?"

"Uh, no, actually. She's intense."

"Tell me about it. And this is the way she treats the people she really likes, too. Just imagine how it would be if she hated your guts."

She snorted. "Thanks, but I'd rather not."

They started up the spiral staircase of the tower. Liv stopped at every landing, gasping at the view. The tower had to be architecturally camo'ed too. Cool. Even the princess, who had grown up in multiple luxury homes, appreciated Tam's super-duper lair.

He himself, who'd had only a nodding acquaintance with indoor plumbing for his entire childhood, had been staggered by it.

Not that he was bad off, money-wise. He was doing just fine. His big condo had all the comforts of life. It was all a matter of degree.

The north tower was a tall octagonal room as big as an apartment in itself. Moonlight streamed in the horizontal diamond shaped windows. A spiral staircase led up to an airy sleeping loft above.

He flipped on a wall sconce lamp that gently lit the downstairs, showing blond wood paneling, the nubbly beige rug, plush off-white couches and chairs grouped around a huge entertainment console, the fully stocked bar. One side of the octagon was a kitchen and a dining area.

Liv spun, open-mouthed. "This is her guest room?"

"One of many." Sean set the box down. "The east tower is Tam's workroom, but there's the west and the south towers, and lots of other rooms." He pulled the lid off the box, and started reading off the labels on each package of food as he pulled it out. "Chicken sesame. Grilled salmon. Fresh pork roast. Filet mignon. Braised greens with vinegar and bacon. Greek salad, potato salad, taboulleh, sourdough rolls, asparagus quiche, roasted artichokes, stuffed three-cheese mushrooms, chocolate ganache, and fresh nectarines, honeydew and pineapple. And ah, Tam." He pulled out a six-pack of his favorite beer. "I can almost find it in my heart to forgive her for the tetanus shot."

"She's just like you described." Liv peeled open the chicken and sniffed with delight. "Everything she says puts you at a disadvantage."

"True, but she kicks serious ass in a gunfight." Sean pulled out a chair for her, popped open two beers and pulled the plates out of the box. "Come on, babe. Let's pig out like there's no tomorrow."

They went at it, making wordless, appreciative noises from time to time in place of dinner conversation.

Halfway through, Liv paused for a breather. "Other than the crackers and sardines, this is the first food I've eaten in two days. And I'm not the type who voluntarily goes without eating. On the contrary."

"Good," he said. "Nobody should."

"After looking at Tam, I want to eat bread and water for ten days."

He blinked at her, perplexed. "You've got to be kidding. Why?"

She lifted her shoulders, eyes sliding away. Her face reddened with embarrassment. "She has such an amazing figure," she mumbled.

He stared, incredulous. Liv was his gold standard for female perfection. Every rosy, luscious feminine detail, right down to the shape of her little pink toenails. He lifted his beer, a silent toast to voluptuous womanly bodies. "Bon appetit," he said simply. "You are stunning exactly the way you are. I would not want you any thinner. I am dead serious. I do not like stringiness, or bones that stick out. I like *you*."

"Hmph. It's very nice of you to say so," she murmured.

She didn't believe him. He felt suddenly desperate to make her understand. "I'm serious," he protested. "I like your body. It's ripe and juicy. I love those big, soft tits that fill up my hands. I love the way they move. I love your soft, sweet kissable white thighs. I love those cute dimples in your knees. All of it. Tam's got nothing on you, babe."

"Oh, don't even," she snapped.

"Really. She's a fine-looking woman, sure, but she's too goddamn skinny. It worries me. She should see a doctor, drink some Ovaltine, stop smoking, I don't know. And she's not my type, sexually. It's like she's made out of stainless steel. Steel doesn't turn me on. Neither does fighting a duel to the death every goddamn second. It's fun for a while, sure, but it's exhausting. I'm a lover, not a fighter, you know? I like cuddling, tickling, hugging. Who could cuddle with Tam?"

"I see your point." A cautious smile dawned in her eyes.

He followed up on his advantage rapidly. "I'd rather dance with a

beautiful woman than spar with her. And I want to dance with you."
He emphasized his point by leaning over the table with a forkful of
night-dark chocolate ganache torte poised on the end of his fork.

She accepted it, and made a low, approving sound that he felt all
the way down his back, like a warm tongue licking him. "I just want
to fall on you," he confessed. "Just grab you and lick you and nuzzle
you. You're so sweet and soft and luscious. I love grabbing that
round, rosy ass. I love kissing your tits. And that tight, slick little—"

"Stop." Her voice rang with royal command. "This is not dinner
conversation. I want to concentrate on my meal, thank you very
much."

He subsided. They finished their dinner in charged silence.

They leaned back in their chairs afterwards, shy and silent. The
lavish luxury was more inhibiting than the sleazy hotel room.

He couldn't stop staring. Her eyes shied away, but he knew she
was conscious of his eyes on her, as he stared at her profile.

She was more beautiful grown up, he concluded. Her features
had come into perfect focus. So elegant and fine. He shifted uncomfortably in his chair. "You're cute in that T-shirt," he ventured.

Liv giggled again. "Tell me a better one."

"OK," he said easily. "You look better without it. Take it off."

Her expression went wary, but he sensed the energy beginning to
hum. She was tired, wiped out . . . but tempted.

"You have got to be kidding." Her voice was crisp and austere.
"I've had more sex in the last twenty-four hours than I've had in the
last three years of my life combined. Don't expect me to start working off that forty-eight-hundred-dollars-a-day bill tonight, buddy. I
need sleep."

He gave her his best, seductive bad boy smile. She made a huffing sound and got to her feet, tossing her hair back. She marched to
the bathroom, disappeared inside. The oversexed gorilla inside him
who never knew when to give it a rest got up and followed her.

He was helpless to stop himself. How could he? He had a massive
crush on the princess. He'd been cooked since he laid eyes on her.
Fuck the forty-eight hundred a day. He'd pay good money to be her
bodyguard, lady's maid, masseur, stylist, comedian, sex slave. Hell,
he'd even iron. He liked his own shirts crisp and nice, so he wasn't

half bad at it. Though it was a skill he knew better than to brag about.

But he would iron Liv's underwear for an excuse to stay close to her. Carry her bags, shine her shoes, suck her toes. Lick her pussy.

Just looking at her nipples pressing against the thin, cheap white cotton of the T-shirt made his palms sweat. It occurred to him that, what with one thing and another, in the past two days, he hadn't seen her wearing any sort of restraining device on those tits yet. He'd only seen them swaying and bouncing, au naturel. Awesome.

If she were a different woman, he would think she was doing it on purpose to drive him mad with lust. Not that it mattered, on purpose or not. The mad lust result was exactly the same, either way.

He wanted to dig his fingers into that cloud of hair, lift it up and stare at the graceful line of her neck. He wanted her to turn those big, gray eyes on him. Let go and fall into them, sploosh, like falling into deep water from a great height. Plunging into a mysterious otherworld.

He wanted to see everything from her point of view. Find out what she thought about everything. Get inside her mind. It pulled at him, like a tractor beam. He leaned against the door, listening. Water running, toilet flushing. Was it kinky to listen through a door? He supposed it was. Too bad. He was too far gone to care.

The door opened, suddenly, and she squeaked when she found him standing there. She was still dabbing at her face with a towel, damp and soft, the hairs around her face and ears wet and clinging to her face. She smelled like honeysuckle and peppermint. Her jeans were draped over her arm, her underwear washed out and draped over the shower stall. So she was bare-assed, under that flapping T-shirt.

His boner went from hopeful half-mast to full, urgent salute.

"What are you doing, lurking out here?" she demanded.

He told her the blunt truth. "I can't stay away from you."

Her beautiful eyes narrowed to slits. She turned away, stomped towards the staircase. He followed like a hound, two paces behind.

She turned around at the foot of the stairs and gestured sharply for him to go up first. "I'm not letting you climb a flight of stairs behind me while you've got that look on your face," she said.

"Sure, babe. Grab my ass all you want." He started up the stairs, wagging his tush, and was rewarded by a smothered burst of laughter.

"I'm serious," she said. "No sex tonight."

He stripped off his shirt, stretching and flexing and showing off until he heard that giggling snort again. "I promise, I won't jump you," he said. "But I won't promise that I won't talk you into jumping me."

"Don't hold your breath." She marched around the big, king-sized bed, yanked back the maroon chenille coverlet, and slid between the sheets, tucking the coverlet up under her chin. "I am *resting.*"

He undid his jeans, kicked them off, and lay down naked on the bed, his dick high and thick and throbbing purple against his belly.

"Sure. Just pretend there isn't a naked man in bed next to you with a huge, aching hard-on from watching your tits bounce all day."

"You had plenty of opportunity to slake your lust. A normal man would be in a coma from the amount of sex we had."

"I'm not normal," he said.

"I noticed that," she retorted. "Maybe you should see a doctor."

"I can think of a quicker, yummier solution."

Her eyes flicked down to his cock. He stroked it for her benefit, with a rough, careless jerk of his fist. Inciting the beast.

She rolled onto her belly and buried her face in the pillow. "I am ignoring you," she informed him, her voice muffled. "Good night, Sean."

"Go ahead." He slid between the sheets. "It won't stop me from dreaming. Fantasizing. Like I've been doing for fifteen years now."

Her head popped up at that. "Oh, really?" she asked. "Like you've had the time to fantasize about me, what with the psycho billionaires and terrorists and mad scientists and evil warlords, and bullets flying? To say nothing of the hordes of women parading through your bed."

"You're still way up top, when it comes to my fantasy life," he told her solemnly. "Remember that day in the historic collection room?"

She made a muffled sound he couldn't decipher. He decided to take it as assent. "All I have to do is crack the spine of an old book, and I'm back there," he said dreamily. "Stone hard. With my fingers in your tight, hot, juicy cunt. Feeling you come."

She ignored him.

"The harder I pushed, the hotter you got."

She pushed her face back into the pillow.

"You used to get so red when I whispered sexy stuff in your ear." His voice lowered to a silky soft croon. "Turn around, Liv. Let me see your face. Look at me. Are you getting pink yet?"

She shook her head violently, face still hidden. "Not in the least."

"I bet nobody had ever talked dirty to the virgin princess before that, huh? But I've been able to keep my mouth shut to save my life."

"That's for damn sure." The words were muffled, but the note of quivering laughter reassured him. He pushed hopefully on.

"Remember how I used to talk to you on the phone? I always told you to touch yourself while I did, and you always told me no, no, no, you wouldn't. No, no, no, you couldn't. But I think, maybe . . . just maybe you were lying to me." He paused. "Were you?"

She didn't speak. A triumphant grin wrapped itself around his face. He tried to curb it. It was too soon to get cocky and over-confident.

"I thought so," he went on. "It was torture. All alone in a public phone booth, people all around me, so I couldn't even grab my dick. Imagining you in your lacy, virginal bed. Those soft white thighs, open wide. Holding the phone with your shoulder while I described exactly how I wanted to touch you, lick you, suck you. Put my cock into you."

She wiggled, restlessly, beneath the coverlet. He edged closer.

"I imagined your hand in your panties," he went on. "Touching yourself til your pussy was hot and puffy and slick. It was agonizing."

She nodded, her face still hidden.

"Tell me something, baby. Did you ever put your finger into your pussy and imagine that it was me?"

She looked up through a tangled veil of hair, a gleam of reluctant laughter in her eyes. "Duh."

"Yeah? Really?" He edged closer still, so that he could sniff that honeysuckle smell. "Can I ask you an incredibly personal question?"

She shook with helpless giggles. "Like the last one wasn't?"

He ignored that, intent upon his own curiosity. "Did you ever, ah, use a dildo when you thought of me?"

She hesitated. "None of your business," she said primly.

He studied her hot pink cheeks, her averted eyes. "I'll take that as a yes," he murmured. "Wow. That blows my mind, babe. I just can't picture you going into a sex shop and buying a—"

"I did nothing of the kind," she snapped. "It was a gag gift. From my girlfriends. We threw a renewed virginity party for me once. To celebrate a full year of celibacy."

He winced, at the very concept. A year? Ouch.

"We got toasted on frozen daiquiris, ate erotic pastries and trashed all the men we'd ever known," she said. "You were included, I'll have you know. After my third daiquiri, I went on and on about you."

"I'm honored to have been included," he said gravely. "So, uh, does it vibrate?"

She shook with silent laughter. "Of course it vibrates. You dork."

His eyes were wide with fascination. "Whoa. And did you use it?"

"Certainly I used it," she said tartly. "I hadn't had sex for ages."

He tried to wrap his mind around that for a while, and ended up squeezing a restraining fist around his cock, doing some deep breathing and muscle control to keep from coming then and there. The idea of Liv playing with a vibrating sex toy made beads of sweat spring out on his forehead. He couldn't stop himself from asking. "How do I measure up?"

"To the dildo?" She let out a crack of laughter. "Oh, please. It's much smaller than you, don't worry. Less problematic, too."

"Less problematic?" He scowled. "What the hell does that mean?"

She snorted. "It means that when I'm done, I switch it off, wash it with soap and water and put it back in its box. It doesn't follow me around, and manipulate me into endless marathon sex sessions."

"Mmm." He did the deep breathing trick again, tightening all the muscles in his groin, his fist squeezing his aching cock. "Princess? If we get through this, when things calm down . . . can we play with it?"

She was startled into another burst of laughter. "Why on earth? Like the one you've got on your body isn't enough for me to deal with!"

"I want to watch you use it on yourself," he confessed. "The very idea makes me practically explode all over the sheets."

She grunted. "Oh, please. What doesn't have that effect on you, Sean?"

"Aw. That's not fair." He flopped down onto the pillow. "I just go nuts at the idea of you pleasuring yourself. You're so sexy."

"Oh, stop. Don't overdo it."

He nuzzled her hair, lifting it up to see the bright red color of her cheeks. It was working. "Sweetheart?" he asked softly. "Do you want to touch yourself now?"

She let out a shuddering sigh, and shook her head.

"It doesn't mean that you have to have sex with me," he coaxed. "It doesn't mean that I won and you lost. It's just pleasure. I want you to have it. I love it when you're pleased. I love it when you take a bite of chocolate, when you laugh, when you come. It makes me happy."

She shifted under the covers, and he felt her yielding as he cuddled closer and draped his arm over her tense, trembling back.

"Do it. Put your hand between your legs," he urged, his voice a velvety caress against her neck. "I can't even see you. It's all under the covers. All secret, all hidden. Just do it. Give that pleasure to yourself."

It took her a long time to struggle towards her climax. He loved holding her, tuning in, feeling the tension as she strove for completion, but it was torture to feel that sexual energy vibrating through her beautiful body, and remain outside. Waiting patiently.

She finally got there. Pleasure jolted and shuddered through her body, and knifed right through his own, by reflex. It made him gasp.

Every time, he made the same mistake, made it worse, took it further. Every time he fucked her, his seductive bullshit backfired on him, pulling him deeper and deeper into a vortex he'd created himself.

He nuzzled her hair, parting it until his lips touched damp skin. Touched her with the tip of his tongue, tasting salt, sweet. Pretending to be the slick, confident seducer who had it all together. Not a desperate man who would fall into jagged, broken pieces if she turned him down.

"Liv," he said. "Do you want me now?"

He couldn't hide the need in his voice, even though it shamed him. All his stupid patter, and he was reduced to begging anyway.

She nodded. He almost wept with relief. "Tell me you want me," he demanded. "Say the words. I need to hear them."

She turned her face, and looked at him. Her eyes swam with tears. "I want you," she said simply.

He grabbed the covers, wrenched them down over her body. The T-shirt had ridden up over her magnificent ass. He tugged it up over her head, tumbling her hair over her face, and tossed it away. "Roll over?"

She shook her head, and pressed her face down into the covers again. He stared down at her luscious, plump backside, his breath coming fast. Great. This position would do just fine.

He fumbled with the condom he'd slipped under his pillow, rolling it on with fingers that shook. Positioned himself behind her, stroking her satiny smooth ass cheeks, sliding his hand tenderly between her thighs. She parted her legs for him, tilting her ass up with a sigh as he teased her plump, shining pink pussy lips open. His bold caresses made her jerk and shiver as he spread hot lube all around, to ease his way.

They moaned when he slid his cock heavily into her tight, plush depths. He braced himself, and pumped, giving it to her nice and slow, but the rhythm quickened anyway. It was Liv who was pushing him, shoving back with her ass, wordlessly demanding it deeper, harder.

He gave it to her. He was helpless to do anything else.

"There's nothing else like this," he muttered. "There's no one like you in the world, princess."

She laughed at him, but the sound was punctuated by sobbing gasps with each heavy stroke. "Come on. In this position, I could be anyone for you. You could be Attila the Hun. I could be Sophia Loren."

That crack slid right under his guard and made him furious. He slid his arm around her neck, bending her head back. "It doesn't matter what position you're in. I know exactly who I'm fucking. I know the taste of your sweat. The taste of your lube. The smell of your hair. The exact curve of your ass, your waist, every bone of your spine. Every beauty mark. This one—" he kissed her shoulder blade, "and this one, and this group of three. I know the dimples over your ass—"

"OK, I'm convinced. Stop pulling my head back."

Her voice was choked and shaking, but she didn't seem upset. He eased off, but not much, sensing that the roughness excited her. He stirred his cock around. "You know me, too," he said. "You wouldn't mistake me for any other man you've ever been with. Would you?"

She tried to speak, failed. Shook her head.

"You like this position, don't you? I can tell, from that fluttery thing your pussy does when I rub this spot with the head of my cock."

"Sean . . ." She clutched handfuls of the sheet with shaking fists.

"It pulls me, like it's begging me to stay. Begging me to massage all those sweet hot spots until you . . . oh. *Yes.*"

She convulsed. He rode her out, eyes squeezed shut as he savored every little clutching pulsing wave of it, and pulled her face around to his. "You don't look like a china doll now," he told her. "All damp and soft and sweet. That hot rose color drives me fucking crazy."

"You're already crazy." The sound choked off into a whimper as he started moving again. He nuzzled her hair, breathing in hungry gulps of that hot, damp honeysuckle smell. Licking away the delicate salt tang between her shoulder blades.

He'd always been good at getting inside a girl's mind, intuiting what she needed to get off. Since he was thirteen he'd been good at it. But it had never cut both ways. Petting her clit was like touching

himself. Every stroke of his cock was a sweet lash of mutual pleasure.

He drove her to the edge, but he was right there with her, shivering on the verge of the abyss. She clutched his hands, begging with
every movement of her body for him to bring her off.

"Roll over," he said.

She stiffened, turning her head. "Why?"

"I want to kiss you," he said. "I want to look into your eyes."

She hesitated, but he pulled out of her hot, clutching sheath and
flipped her over onto her back. He mounted again, and slid deep
and hard into her slick depths, jarring a gasping sound from her
throat.

"One more," he said. "One more, and I'll come with you."

He pried her hands off her face and stretched them wide. It wasn't
a confinement, she just stretched voluptuously against the resistance. It opened her wider to him, her chest, her throat. Chest to
chest, heart to heart. A dam breaking, a geyser bursting forth.

Pleasure thundered, splintered through their fused bodies.

There was barely enough of him left afterwards to deal with the
condom and then crawl back between the damp, crumpled sheets.

He hugged her jealously tight. He was as exhausted as she, probably more, but all he could do was stare at the sooty fan of lashes
against the blush rose stain on her cheek. Awed, at how beautiful
she was. Terrified, that this incredible thing might go sour on him.

He could make some butthead mistake, let T-Rex through his
guard, and lose her. And even if he killed T-Rex, he had no clue who
held the fucker's leash. There was an endless supply of thugs for
hire.

He didn't even know where to start with this crazy shit. He hadn't
gotten anywhere with it fifteen years ago. He had even fewer ideas
now.

And even if he did resolve this mystery, that was no guarantee at
all that he could hang on to the princess. He was perfectly capable of
fucking this up, even without the help of a homicidal maniac.

He'd been a fuck-up since he could remember. He'd driven old
Eamon nuts with his nonstop chatter, his off the wall energy, his
shit-for-brains impulsiveness. But even the most severe punish-

ments his father came up with never calmed him down, or shut him up, or taught him sense. He just ended up bouncing off the walls that much harder.

Davy and Con loved him, he knew that, but they were always on edge, scared he would do something crazy. Hurt himself, or someone else. The only person he'd ever been able to relax and chill with, who wasn't always irritated and aggravated by him, had been Kev. And Liv, for that brief, fabulous interval. And then they'd both disappeared.

He'd been passed from one prison to another his whole life. His father's degenerating illness had been the first, then the hell of public school. The coursework had been a joke. It was staying square with the powers that be, keeping out of trouble, that he couldn't seem to grasp. No matter how he tried, he kept fucking up. Like college. Losing his scholarship, for some sweaty afternoon quickies with the dean's wife.

Then he'd met Liv. That had felt so effortless, so precious, so exquisitely right. Til he'd been forced to destroy it with his own hands.

Then Kev's death. Accepting lies for truth had put him in still another prison. A metal box in the dark for his mind. He'd huddled in that box for fifteen years. It was like he was under a goddamn curse.

But now the bonds were broken. The box was open. He felt so lost, so disoriented. Cut loose, scared shitless. *Liv.* His need for her was stronger than any bond he'd ever felt. So was the fear, that she might decide she didn't want him anymore.

He couldn't take that. He'd lost enough, suffered enough, fucked up enough for any one lifetime.

This time, losing her would kill him.

Chapter
17

Liv didn't want to wake up from this dream. She was awash in erotic sensations, every nerve kissed and caressed. Swimming in pleasure, like raw fresh honey, but something was pulling her to wakefulness. A sound that would not stop, a moaning whimper.

It was coming from her own throat. She opened her eyes, blinking in the morning light. Incredibly warm, held tight against a hot, hard male body. Her thighs were splayed, and Sean's skillful hand moved between them. His fingers made wet sounds as they stroked and delved and circled. She was sopping wet, squirming with excitement.

Oh, please. Again? This was beyond ridiculous. This was insane.

He smiled into her eyes. "Sleeping beauty," he whispered.

He was outrageously beautiful when he smiled. She was so dazzled, she just smiled helplessly back as he rolled on top of her, and entered her. Her inner flesh fluttered in protest at the slow stretch, sore from all the unaccustomed sex, but she was too aroused to care. He gathered her into his arms and moved, staring into her eyes with fierce intensity, as if he were trying to tell her something.

She wrapped her arms and legs around him, and moved with him, trying to listen.

It was a slow dance, a lazy, sensual heaven of tender intimacy. He started kissing her, his warm, soft lips coaxing hers open, exploring, claiming. The thrust of his tongue in her mouth echoed the thrust of his penis. She had never felt so alive. She was so present in her body it was almost frightening. Everything was so bold and sharp. She surged against him, rocking on heaving waves of delicious sensation.

She didn't want it to end, but the shimmering glow between her legs kept growing until it brightened and swelled to bursting. The wave carried her sweetly away. When she drifted back, she found him still inside her, still hard. She blinked at him. "Um, didn't you come?"

"I had more orgasms than I can count." He kissed her jaw, nuzzled her throat. "I just didn't ejaculate."

She lifted her head, blinking. "Don't you need to?"

"There's no law says I have to." His voice was soft with amusement. "And I'm not wearing latex."

"Oh. There is that," she murmured. "I didn't know guys could do that. Is this another one of your dancing bear tricks?"

He grinned his appreciation. "You could say that. It's just manipulating energy, controlling your breathing, knowing what muscles to squeeze, and when. It's a trick of concentration."

"And practice, too, right?" An edge crept into her voice. "Years of daily practice, I bet."

He slanted her a cautious look. "You always start whaling on me when we get anywhere near that subject. I'm tired of being pounded."

He dragged himself slowly out of her body, with a long, hissing indrawn breath of pleasure, and flopped onto his back. His penis lay stiff and hard against his belly. Gleaming wet from her juices.

She gazed at him, bemused. "You can just leave it like that?"

Mischief flashed in his eyes. "You want some more?"

"No, thanks," she said hastily. "I'm done for now. It just looks like you're, ah, not done. In the least."

Sean was enjoying himself hugely. "I'll live," he said, his voice offhand. He stroked his penis and brought his hand up to his face, inhaling. "Your smell makes my mouth water. Can I go down on you?"

"Um . . . actually . . ." She stared at him for a long moment, and gave in to the impulse. "I have a better idea."

She rolled over and reached for him, gripping the broad stalk of his penis, and took him in her mouth, tasting herself as well as his own hot salt tang. He groaned, shuddered. "Oh, God, Liv."

She murmured something soothing, petting and licking him.

It was by no means easy to perform fellatio on a guy of his proportions. Particularly since her jaw was still sore from her pit-bull imitation with T-Rex. She didn't care. She wanted this. She was hungry to pleasure him, to reduce him to a state of writhing desperation.

Hungry to wrest the sexual upper hand away from him, for once.

But he gave it to her generously, abandoning himself with his usual wholehearted sensuality. He curled his body over hers, clutching her hair, her back, shivering and moaning his incoherent appreciation.

He reached down and touched her cheek when she took a moment to breathe and relax her jaw. "Stop if you're tired," he said gently.

She milked him with her hands, smiling. "Gotta get going early if I want to make a dent in that forty-eight-hundred-dollar bill."

Laughter jerked in his chest, but he tilted her face up again. "You know that's just a joke, right?" His eyes looked worried. "I know I come on strong, but if you don't want it, it stops. Is that clear?"

"Um, OK," she faltered. "Does that mean you don't want . . . ?"

"Fuck, no." The words burst out of him. "I love it. I'll beg, plead, suck your toes. But you decide when and how much. Understand?"

"Um, yes, thanks," she said demurely. "Can I continue, now?"

He ignored the question, caressing her cheek with his fingertips. "This means a lot to me," he said. "I don't want to mess it up."

The earnest, worried look in his eyes made her heart swell with tenderness. "You're not," she told him. "Believe me, you're not."

She tried to scoot back down and pick up where she'd left off, but he grabbed her and spun his body around until they were sixty-nined.

"I can't wait," he said. "Let me play, too."

He pushed her thigh up and put his mouth to her.

Liv stiffened, at first. Sixty-nining was not her thing. Oral sex required concentration, and to have the guy bend her into a pretzel and stick his face between her legs, tickling and prodding while she tried to pull it off . . . um, no. In her opinion, a proper blow job, like driving an expensive sports car, or chopping vegetables with a sharp knife, was a thing best done without serious distractions.

But like everything else she thought she knew about sex, that turned on its head when Sean was concerned. Being twisted into a pretzel was great if a girl was relaxed to virtual bonelessness from multiple orgasms, and Sean's lapping, lashing, trilling tongue was so unerringly skilled at keeping her in a state of quivering delight.

It was perfect, twining and luscious and ravishing. Each inspired the other to more sensual, ravenous excesses with each suckling stroke, each voluptuous caress, his pleasure amplifying hers and vice versa until they melded into a shining whole; his hardness to her softness, his rough to her smooth, offering satisfaction to every secret, wordless yearning. They crested the wave, exploded into crashing foam together.

She lay incapable of moving while the light in the room slowly brightened, inhaling his warm man musk smell. She was petting the gilt tipped hairs on his muscular thigh when she noticed something that looked like a small, irregular bruise. She looked closer. It was a tattoo, written crookedly on his thigh in small, blurry letters. SEAN.

She traced it with her finger. "Did you do this yourself? It doesn't look like a professional tattoo."

He grunted. "It's not. Dad put that on me when I was about eight, with a hot needle and a ballpoint pen. Bottle of Scotch for disinfectant."

Liv froze, her hand tightening on his thigh. "Eight years old?"

"Yeah. He was pissed at me and Kev for playing tricks on him. That was back when it was real hard to tell us apart. Dad didn't have much of a sense of humor. I think that's the first thing to go, when a person is mentally ill. So he labeled us. He did Kev first. When I saw what was in store for me, I took off for the woods. Took him days to track me down, but I let him find me, in the end. I got hungry."

"My God." She stroked the mark with her finger, horrified. "Sean, that's awful. You poor baby."

He looked uncomfortable. "I've had worse experiences. I'm just glad my name didn't have more letters. Kev only had three. Cured

me of any impulse to get a tattoo, I'll tell you that much." He pondered for a moment. "Maybe that's why I hate Scotch," he added
thoughtfully. "Even the smell of the stuff makes me gag."

She wondered if he even knew how much that confession revealed about his childhood. She could see so clearly the little boy
he'd been, hiding in the woods. Hungry and scared. It made her
chest hurt, but she sensed that her sympathy would embarrass him.

She wiggled closer, and gently kissed the faded tattoo. Silently
grateful that all that pain, all that darkness, had not put out his light.

In spite of everything, he still shone so bright.

"How romantic. Nuzzling each other's genitals, like puppies."

The cool voice issuing from the stairwell made them jump. Liv
scrambled to wrap the sheet around her naked body, her face heat-
ing.

Sean sat up and glared at her. "Holy shit, Tam. You could knock."

"Where's the fun in that?" Her head and shoulders poked up over
the stairwell. She sniffed the air. "Hmm. I see you two have been
busy."

"Disappear, Tam," he snarled. "Wait for us downstairs."

She laughed, and vanished down the hole. "Since when have you
gotten so prissy?" her voice floated up from below. "My sources led
me to understand that you liked kink."

"Your fucking sources led you wrong." He yanked on his jeans
and clattered down the spiral staircase after her.

Liv hastened to pull on her T-shirt, longing in vain for her under-
pants. She started down the stairs, bracing herself for anything.

Tam propped a taut buttock on the edge of a couch as she lit up a
cigarette. She was dressed in black jeans and a silver-gray tailored
blouse. Her hair was swept into a roll that looked both careless and
perfect. She took a deep drag on her cigarette, nostrils flaring in disgust as Sean rooted through cold leftovers from last night's dinner.

"Garlic, at this hour?" She shuddered delicately. "God."

"Something tells me you're not going to serve us coffee and crois-
sants," he said, dropping a slice of filet mignon into his mouth.

He twitched the cigarette out of her mouth, and scowled at it.
"What is this, Tam? Your breakfast?" He ground it out in the empty
taboulleh container. "Are you trying to starve yourself to death?" He

grabbed a sourdough roll, smeared butter onto it and held it out. "Eat a goddamn piece of bread, already."

Tam recoiled. "Carbs. Ick. Back off."

"Why should I?" He took a bite of the roll. "If you're going to be rude and invasive and in my face, I'm going to return the favor."

She sniffed. "That's gratitude for you. I got up early and went shopping this morning, for your friend." She turned her gaze up, and ran it over Liv. "Morning sex becomes you," she said, her tone approving. "Makes your lips red and puffy. You barely need the makeup I got. There are your new clothes. Have fun."

She gestured towards a cluster of shopping bags near the door.

Liv stammered for a moment, bemused. "Um . . . thanks."

"No need." Tam shrugged. "I wouldn't have bothered doing it if I didn't enjoy it. Shopping is relaxing. Particularly when someone else is paying. Which reminds me." She pulled a handful of credit card slips out of her jeans pocket and held them out to Sean. "These, I believe, are yours," she said. "Pay me back in a timely manner, please."

Sean took the slips of paper, studied them. His jaw dropped. "Holy shit. What is this stuff? Is it cut out of cloth of gold?"

"Shame on you, you cheap bastard," Tam scolded. "Aren't you man enough to buy your woman some decent threads?"

Sean stared at another one of the charge slips. "It's not that I'm not man enough," he said. "It's that I'm not rich enough."

"Bullshit." Tam clucked her tongue. "You've just never stayed with any one woman long enough to be obliged to buy her clothes." She shot a glance at Liv. Her mouth curved. "I think you'd better get used to it."

"He doesn't have to get used to anything," Liv broke in. "I don't need a man to buy me clothes. Don't worry, Sean, I'll pay you back, as soon as I get the insurance money from the—"

"Stop!" Tam's voice rang with sharp command. "This is a teachable moment, cupcake. Don't spoil it for him."

"But I don't need anyone to buy me—"

"And besides, this extravagant boy is a walking fashion plate in his own right. I never see him but he's wearing Prada, Dolce e Gabbana, Armani. Custom tailored this, leather-tooled that."

"My wardrobe is none of your goddamn business," Sean growled.

"Don't let him tell you he can't afford it, either." Tam's eyes gleamed. "I've seen his tax returns, his investment portfolio, the income from his rental properties—"

"Hey!" Sean was outraged. "How do you know my private stuff?"

"Don't be stupid," Tam cut in, rolling her eyes. "Privacy is an illusion in today's electronic world. And I always investigate the people who interest me." She pulled out another cigarette, lit it. "And we haven't even gotten to his toys," she continued. "The motorcycle, jet skis, boat, hang glider, deep sea diving equipment. He's not as rich as he would have been if he'd participated in some of my projects, but he can afford decent clothes for you. Don't doubt it."

Sean peeked up at her, abashed. She tried not to laugh. He made a big show of rifling through the credit card slips. "Eight hundred bucks at one store? What the hell is Melinda's Intimates?"

"She needs sexy lingerie, don't you agree?"

Sean's eyes lit up. He strode over to the shopping bags and rooted through them til he found a pink one with tinted tissue poking out of it.

He reached in with both hands. When he pulled them out, several small, complicated garments dangled from them. An ivory bustier trimmed with a froth of antique lace. A black demi-bra and matching thong. A pearl pink baby-doll nightie. He looked up at Liv. "Oh, wow," he said reverently. "Good investment, Tam. Worth every penny."

Tam snorted. "Men. So predictable. It's sad, really."

Sean rubbed the pale green silk tap pants voluptuously against his face. "I don't suppose you picked up anything for me, did you?"

Tam blew out a stream of smoke, her beautiful eyes narrowed to golden slits. "No," she said. "I was far more inspired by her. You're perfectly capable of doing your own shopping, big boy."

"I figured as much," he said, looking resigned. "You'd rather be shot through the eye than give me a break, wouldn't you?"

"You're getting bodily fluids all over my sheets, insulting me, inconveniencing me. That's not enough of a break?" She turned to Liv. "You're in no condition to model this stuff until you've had a shower, so get to it. This clown's brothers will be in my face any minute. Hurry."

The door clicked shut behind her. Sean shook his head. "I shouldn't have brought you here," he muttered. "It's not worth the stress that woman puts me through." He reached into the pink bag again, as if seeking comfort, and soon found it, in the form of pink French cut satin panties, trimmed with black ribbon. "Ooh. Crotchless." He waggled his fingers through a slit in the gusset. "Wear these today."

Liv willed herself not to laugh. "Why on earth would I do that?"

He blinked innocently. "For spontaneous sex. You know. Bent over the hood of a car. Perched on the washing machine during the spin cycle. Up against the wall in the hall bathroom."

She decided that ignoring him was the best policy. "I'm going to pay for those clothes myself, you know."

He waved his hand dismissively. "Like hell. Even if that wasn't a direct affront to my manhood, it wouldn't be fair to you. You didn't ask Tam to drop five thousand bucks on clothes for you. She did it for fun, to bust my balls. It's between me and her. Besides, she likes to see girls looking good. I think maybe she goes both ways."

"Five thousand?" Liv's mind snagged on the sum, stupefied.

"More, actually," he said, with martyred calm. "But it's OK, babe. The numbers were just a shock, first thing in the morning. I might have to cut back on the servants in my sixty room mansion. Run my own bath in the solid gold tub. Cut my own toenails with the diamond encrusted platinum clippers. No biggie."

"Stop teasing for just one second and be straight with me," she said. "Just how do you make your living, anyhow?"

He shrugged helplessly. "Little bit of this, little bit of that."

"You're avoiding the question," she snapped.

"I'm not," he protested. "My professional life is a grab bag. I get bored easily. If something starts feeling too much like work, I drop it and move on."

"Wow. Lucky you." She tried to picture that kind of flexibility, but it was hard to imagine. "And you can afford to be so fussy?"

He looked embarrassed. "Yeah. Like Tam said, I've got some interest income. My brother Davy's a financial whiz. He did some

good investing for me over the years. Lately, I've been doing consulting gigs for war films. My brothers think it's fluff, and maybe it
is, but I've had enough heavy shit to last a lifetime. I like to keep
things light."

"With us, too?" She couldn't help but ask.

The smile vanished from his eyes. "No, babe." He reached up,
and gripped her wrist. She stumbled down the rest of the stairs to
meet him.

Sean lifted the T-shirt up over her head, and claimed her mouth,
in a slow, possessive kiss. "When it comes to you, I'm dead serious."
He shoved the crotchless confection into her hand, closing her fingers around it. "Wear these for me today. Every time I look at you,
I'll think about slipping my fingers through that hole, finding you
wet. And when I finally get you alone, you'll be so ready, I won't
have to do cartwheels and backflips to persuade you. I can just
mount up and ride."

She stumbled back, pulling away. "I have to take a shower."

He gave her his sexy fallen angel smile. "Can I come?" He
popped open the top button of his jeans. They strained over his
erection.

"Absolutely not." She fled to the bathroom, locked the door, and
sagged down on the edge of the bathtub, trying to breathe.

When was she going to get used to him? It didn't matter that she
was traumatized, bitten, bruised, penniless, jobless, in danger for
her life. All he had to do was whisper in her ear, and hey presto, she
was a knot of mindless yearning. Helplessly aching and throbbing
for him.

Bits of pink and black satin poked out between her fingers. She
looked up at the wrinkled cotton briefs that hung stiffly over the
shower rod, and collapsed with her face to her knees, shaking.
Maybe it was a blessing that Sean took up so much space in her
mind.

It kept her too busy to bother with the screaming panic.

She put on her boring undies after her shower and stared into the
mirror. *On the run for your life is all the more reason to look your best.*

She peeled them off. Pulled on the pink and black panties.

Wow. They were . . . well, bold. She took a deep breath and hesitated at the door. She was so accustomed to privacy, solitude. She just didn't know how to cope with the intensity of his attention. His sexual energy knocked her backwards. Her fantasy Sean had never reduced her to stammering idiocy like this. Her real Sean was cocky, off the wall, larger than life. So much fun. She had to learn how to get dressed in front of him without tripping, or blushing. Or ending up flat on her back, road-testing those crotchless panties.

She peeked as she walked to the shopping bags. The intensity in his slitted eyes made her stumble into a chair. She rummaged 'til she found the bra that matched her panties. Another bag held jeans. A third held an assortment of tops. She snatched one out, at random.

"Isn't there a miniskirt in there?" His voice was silky.

"Dream on, buddy," she said. "I haven't got miniskirt legs. And even if I did, hah. Like I'd wear crotchless panties with a skirt. That's just begging for trouble. I've got enough trouble right now."

"But jeans sort of defeat the purpose, don't they?"

"Cope," she said tartly.

He laughed, under his breath. "Is that a challenge?"

"No, it's not, you sex-crazed idiot. It's just a pair of jeans. Get your mind out from between my legs and get dressed."

"But my mind feels so good down there, between your legs." He petted her wet hair as he walked by. "You look gorgeous, princess."

He disappeared into the bathroom, to her profound relief.

The jeans fit perfectly. So did the red wrap top. Sexy and fitted, but not vulgar. The price tag almost made her hyperventilate.

She rooted through the bags, found a pair of sandals. Delved into the cosmetics. She almost never wore makeup, but these were strange days, and a girl needed all the help she could get. Back off, T-Rex. Bring on the terra-cotta shadow and the scented *noir* mascara.

When Sean came out, she was as ready as she would ever be.

He held out his arm. "Come on. Let's go meet my family."

A rumble of male voices issued from the kitchen door as they approached it. Tamara's husky voice cut through it, razor sharp.

". . . a cop, to my house? You stupid, selfish, arrogant *bastards!*"

"I'm not a normal cop," a voice soothed. "I have no intention of—"

"Of course you're not normal. No cop is normal," Tam snarled.

"Come on, Tam. Lighten up. I was a cop once, remember?"

"You are a special case," Tam spat out. "You're a McCloud first, cop second. But this is the brainless asshole who almost got you killed two years ago. And you bring him to my home? Do you never learn?"

There was an uncomfortable silence. Liv and Sean glanced at each other and stopped short outside the door.

"Yes," the first voice said quietly. "I am that brainless asshole, but I'm trying to make it right. I'm here because I want to help."

"Bullshit. I know why you're here. You're still under the delusion that I'm going to help you get closer to Zhoglo, right?"

An embarrassed silence followed.

"Dream on," Tam said. "When he catches you and puts your balls in his custom-made vise and starts turning the screws, you think you're not going to tell him where to find me before your testicles explode?"

"He's not going to catch me," the guy said doggedly.

Tam said something in a foreign language that sounded like nails spitting. Liv gave Sean a wide-eyed, questioning glance.

"Remember Kurt Novak? That psycho billionaire I told you about?" he whispered. "Vadim Zhoglo was the guy's business partner. Russian mafia. Real bad-ass. He and Novak's father are two of the reasons Tam's so paranoid. He and Daddy Novak wants to chop her into little bitty pieces for betraying Kurt. Nick wants to bring Daddy Novak and Zhoglo down. He's been bugging her for inside info ever since Davy's wedding. Tam's bummed about it. Can't say as I blame her. Those guys are crazy mean fuckers."

"For God's sake." Liv covered her face. "You people are all nuts."

"It's not our fault." Sean sounded aggrieved. "Vadim Zhoglo is a—"

"Don't tell me about Vadim Zhoglo," she broke in. "I can only wrap my mind around one psycho murderer at a time."

Their whispering had caught Tam's ear. She flung the double doors open. "The lovebirds have clothed their nakedness and deigned to grace us with their presence! Behold, gentlemen. The beauty who has held our fickle Sean's attention for, what? A record of three days now?"

Liv blinked. It was like being in a spotlight, having four big, intense looking men, checking her out. Two she could identify as Sean's brothers from their looks. Both very tall, both extremely handsome. Each with bright, tilted green eyes. The other men were dark, and equally big. One was rough, with beard stubble and long wavy brown hair, tattoos adorning his muscular shoulders. The other was even darker, golden skinned, with flashing black eyes, and a smile that turned slowly into a huge, white-toothed grin as he looked her over.

"Nice," he said, staring at her breasts.

"Stop drooling, Seth," Sean said coolly.

"How can he help it? Isn't she tasty?" Tam sounded pleased with herself. "Don't you just love those hourglass curves? Wardrobe courtesy of me, I'll have you know. I can't wait to see you in the red halter dress, honey. You're going to cause car accidents in that thing."

"Three days, you said?" Seth looked impressed. "That's a long term relationship for Sean. He goes through chicks like French fries, two, three at a time. So have you gotten her a rock?"

"None of your business," Liv cut in, in her sharpest, most authoritative voice.

Seth looked chastened. The men shot each other significant glances. Sean cleared his throat. "So. The guys with the dirt blond hair are my brothers. The clean cut one is Davy, the furry one is Con."

The two men nodded warily. She nodded back.

"The smart-ass lech is Seth Mackey, Davy's business partner. And that tattooed low life scumbag over there is Nick. He's—"

"He's a fed. And he shouldn't be here," Tam broke in, her voice harsh. "He's not welcome. And he's not leaving this place alive."

"Aw, come on. We can't just let you kill him, Tam." Connor's voice was mild and conciliatory. "He used to be my colleague. It wouldn't be right. And besides, sometimes he's even a little bit useful."

"So I won't kill him. I'll give him a massive head injury. Cause irreparable brain damage." She turned to Sean. "They had him hunch down in the backseat when they went past the cameras!"

Sean's mouth compressed, trying not to smile. "That's terrible."

"I'm getting a thermal imager installed," Tam fumed. She swung her furious gaze on Seth. "You got a decent one in your catalogue?"

"Top of the line," Seth said cheerfully. "Costs a fucking fortune."

"E-mail me the details. I'm going to price check, and I expect a fifty percent discount, as an apology for this violation of my privacy."

Seth's grin faltered. "Aw, come on, Tam. Get a sense of humor."

"Let's get breakfast going before we get started," Davy said briskly.

"What do you think this is, a diner?" Tam lit up another cigarette. "I don't have breakfast stuff. Go to town if you want to eat. Better yet, don't come back at all. You dickheads are pissing me off. Good-bye."

Davy pointed to a big box that sat on the floor by the door. "We brought food," he said, a hint of triumph in his voice.

Tam sagged down into one of her bar stools, knocking her forehead against the gleaming black marble countertop. "I should have shot the whole mangy pack of you years ago, when I had the chance."

"Too late." Connor slapped butter down onto the counter.

Tam lifted her head. "It's never too late," she said darkly.

Liv sat in the center of a hive of activity while Sean briefed the others on their adventures. Ham sizzled on a griddle, panfuls of omelet cooked up, fluffy and tempting. Toast, bagels, butter and jam appeared. Orange juice was opened. Coffee made. Tam's kitchen had never seen such disarray, judging by the delicate revulsion on the woman's face.

Davy loaded a plate and slapped it down in front of Tam. "Eat."

She gave him an are-you-kidding look, and blew out a lungful of smoke. "Not hungry," she said, her voice sullen.

"I don't care," he said. "Eat anyway. You've lost fifteen pounds since we saw you last. You need food."

Tam shoved the plate away from herself. "Don't dictate to me."

"Who will, if we don't do it?" His voice could cut steel. "I look around this place, and I don't see anybody else to tell you to eat."

Tam tilted a brow. "What does that have to do with anything?"

"So it falls to us." He nudged the plate towards her. "You wouldn't let us near this place if you didn't want us here. So deal with us."

"I'm rethinking that rash decision," she said sourly.

"Fine. Rethink it while you eat your fucking breakfast."

Tam picked up a triangle of toast, sighed, and nibbled the point.

They ate til they could eat no more, and then plates were cleared, fresh coffee poured, and everyone took a place at the table.

"So," Sean said. "The only starting place I can think of is the notebook, so we need to get those sketches off your walls."

"We're ahead of you." Connor pulled out a battered cardboard file. "We've been studying these all night. Knock yourself out, bro."

Liv pulled the file towards herself, fingertips buzzing. The key to this torturous puzzle lay somewhere in that cryptic sheaf of papers.

It was a series of simple, graceful pen and ink sketches. Landscapes, animals. A lake, with wild geese flying over it, golden eagles, owls, gulls, ducks on a pond. Tucked in their midst was Kev's coded note, the one he'd scrawled in front of her fifteen years before. The page was crumpled from when she'd stuffed it into her bra.

"Does anyone remember the order they were in?" she asked.

Sean spread them out over the table with a gentle circular sweep of his hand, and put them into sequence. He pushed the ordered pile towards her. "I'm sorry to make you repeat yourself, but please tell us, one last time, exactly what Kev said when you saw him that day."

Liv let out a sigh as she stared down at the coded note. "I was coming out of the library. I heard him calling, from the rhododendron bushes," she started, dutifully. "At first, I didn't think anything of it. I ran into him all the time, but when I got closer, I saw that he—"

"Wait a sec." Sean cut in. "Why did you see Kev all the time?"

"I was volunteering two hours every weekday afternoon in the library," Liv said. "Don't you remember?"

"Sure I remember, but Kev wasn't working at the library."

"I saw him on his way up to work," she explained. "He always headed up there the same time. It coincided with my volunteer hours."

The silence was so charged with tension, Liv stopped breathing. Her eyes darted around the table. "What? Was it something that I said?"

"Work?" Davy said softly. "What do you mean, work?"

"That . . . experimental thing," she faltered. "You don't remember?"

The brothers exchanged grim glances.

"Kev was doing research for his thesis that summer," Sean said. "He didn't have any other job that we knew about. Unless you're talking about the summer school chemistry teaching."

She shook her head. "No, it was something else. Experiments he was participating in," she said. "He got paid for each session. He told me about it once. Brain function, human cognition, that kind of thing."

"Where?" Con asked.

She swallowed nervously. "The Colfax Building. Above the public library."

"I know the Colfax." Connor said. "It houses the music department. Erin and I have been up there to see Cindy's concerts."

"Do you remember anything else?" Davy asked. "Anything at all?"

Liv squeezed her eyes shut and racked her brain. Reluctantly, she shook her head. "It never occurred to me that you all didn't know that, or I would have said something sooner," she whispered. "I'm so sorry."

"Don't sweat it," Sean said. "It's more than we ever had before."

Davy broke the long, reflective silence. "Maybe this is the door."

Liv looked at him, puzzled. "What door?"

"We spent a year banging our heads against a wall. This is the door. It's locked, and maybe there's nothing behind it, but it's a door."

"So let's dynamite that son of a bitch down," Sean said.

"I recommend a more subtle approach," Davy said dryly. "Miles is up in Endicott Falls already. We can have him ask around about—"

"No," Sean broke in. "I don't want Miles involved."

Con grunted. "The kid's got to get some experience. He's bright, and hungry, and already in place. I think he's even taken classes from that chemistry professor, what was the guy's name? Beck?"

"No," Sean said vehemently. "He can hack. That's all. I do not want him seen asking questions. T-Rex would wipe Miles out."

"Speaking of getting wiped out. We raided the gun safe in your condo and brought you a few pieces of your arsenal," Connor said.

"That's great news," Sean said fervently. "Oh, yeah. Nick, could you run some prints on T-Rex's Beretta?"

"Do I have yours for comparison somewhere?"

"Actually, it was Liv who got hold of his gun and emptied the clip. You'll need her prints, too."

The silence was broken by an appreciative snicker from Tam.

Davy cleared his throat, and gave Liv an appraising glance. "She does look a hell of a lot better than you, now that you mention it."

"T-Rex looks pretty bad, too," Sean said defensively.

"Bad enough so he would seek professional medical help?"

"No more so than us," Sean replied. "Some stitches and he'll be ready to rock. He got my blade in his ass, a bad bite on the wrist—"

"You bit a guy?" Con grimaced.

"Not me." Sean jerked his chin at Liv. "Her. Stabbed him through the cheek with a rusty nail, too. I'm telling you, the chick is lethal."

"Was this before or after she emptied the clip at him?" Nick asked.

"Before." Sean grinned, proudly. "Don't get on her bad side."

"I missed," Liv broke in. "By a mile. So it doesn't count."

"Bullshit," Tam said briskly. "You just need the right gun."

Chapter 18

"What do you mean, no? Why not?"

Miles realized that he was yelling into the phone. He shoved against the stained basement wall with his feet, sending the wheels of his desk chair bumping and rattling angrily across the concrete floor.

"No means no." Con's voice was steely. "Sean doesn't want—"

"Sean thinks I'm a snot-nosed idiot. We're not talking about rescuing hostages, or rappeling out of a helicopter! We're talking about asking fat-ass Professor Beck what Kev was doing at the Colfax! I aced the guy's classes. I know how he likes his ass kissed. What's the worst that could happen, if I mentioned this Midnight Project to him?"

Con snorted. "And how do you propose to justify your curiosity?"

"I could say I found Kev's research notes," Miles improvised. "I could say I'm reconstructing some work he was doing for his thesis."

"A two-hundred-and-fifty pound gorilla stuck a sharp knife under Sean's girlfriend's ear yesterday and asked her questions very closely related to the ones that you propose to ask Beck," Con said. "Look into who sold the building. That's all. Take this dead serious, hear me?"

Miles blew out an explosive breath. "Sure, I hear you," he said.

"I hear that you all think I'm a fucking infant. And I'm fed up with it."

"No, we don't, and I'm sorry you feel that way." Con's voice was calm and even. "How's the other project coming along?"

"OK," Miles said sullenly. "Jared's hot to meet Mina, but she wants to get to know him better before she risks a face-to-face. She's wary, been burned before. Shy fawn, and all that. I emailed you a transcript of last night's chat. Seen it yet?"

"No. I was at Davy's all night, working on this other thing."

Miles practically snorted. Typical McCloud, to refer to an investigation into his brother's murder as "this other thing."

"Gotta go, Miles," Connor said. "Watch yourself, OK?"

"Why should I bother?" Miles said bitterly. "No one ever lets me participate." He slammed the phone down.

"Wow, aren't you sweet tempered today."

He spun around with a yelp. Cindy leaned in the door. A bombshell, in cutoffs that showed off an endless expanse of tanned thigh. A pink halter top that showcased her pointy little tits. Her hair hung loose and glossy down her back.

His mouth went dry. "Could you knock, for once in your life?"

"I would have, but the door was open," she said. "Your mom told us to come on down. You should clue her in as to my status in the doghouse. She still seems to think that I'm your good buddy."

A gangling kid with curly black hair and huge black eyes peeked in after her. "This is Javier," Cindy announced, dragging him inside.

"Oh. Yeah." *Shit.* He'd been so wound up arguing with Connor, he'd forgotten all about giving in to Cindy's bullying yesterday. He waved them in. "Go sit down," he said sourly. "I'll get stuff set up."

"Were you, uh, in a fight, or what?" Javier asked.

Miles touched his sore, swollen nose. He looked pretty scary, with his nose all puffed up. He rummaged through his equipment, gathering cables, mikes, jacks, DAT. "I guess you could say that," he mumbled.

"I assume, from the incredibly frustrated tone of that conversation, that you were talking to a McCloud?" Cindy inquired.

Miles stiffened. "How much did you overhear?"

"Enough to wonder why the McClouds would ever be interested in anything old Professor Porky Pig Beck might have to say," she said.

Miles groaned inwardly. "Could we not talk about it now?"

"Sure, whatever," she murmured. "Let's get going, then. Get out your sax, Javier, and warm up your reed while Miles sets up."

The recording went smoothly. The kid was good, Miles had to concede. Cindy put him through some major and minor scales, and then he played through the tunes all the applicants were supposed to learn. On the final rep, he inserted a thirty-two-bar blues improvisation. In less than an hour, he was writing Javier's name and number on a good demo CD. He handed it to Javier. "Good luck. I hope you get it."

Javier slipped it into his sax case, and flashed a grin with his big, white, overlapping front teeth. "Thanks!" He grabbed Cindy and gave her a hug. "I'll go get this to the post office right now."

"You've got money for postage?" she called after him.

Javier rolled his eyes. "Duh. See you back at band camp!"

They listened to the kid's sneakers thud up the stairs. He peeked at her, and his gaze slid away. He couldn't bear to look at that smile.

"Thanks for doing that," she said. "He really deserves that scholarship. It was sweet of you to help."

He shrugged. "No big deal. Um, Cin? I've got a whole lot of work to get done today before I go up to the dojo, so—"

"So take my bunny tail and go twitch it in somebody else's face?"

Miles winced. Cindy made no move to leave. "I looked around, but I don't see your mom's Ford," she said. "I thought she gave it to you."

"I, uh, lent it to Keira for a few days. You know, one of the back-up singers for the Furballs? The one with all the piercings?"

Cindy looked blank, and her eyes narrowed. "That is a big, fat lie. Keira flew to Reno yesterday to visit her sister. She doesn't have your car." She paused, sucking her lip between her teeth. "So who does?"

"It's none of your goddamn—"

"Business, yes, I know. You gave it to Sean, didn't you? Erin said that Con was in an unholy snit yesterday. It was because Sean took your car and gave everybody else the slip, right?"

"No," he lied, through gritted teeth. "You're way off. Light years."

"That would explain why your face is so red and you can't look me in the eye." Cindy stretched so that her little tits strained against her halter top and the ends of her hair tickled the tattoo at the small of her back. "So what's up with Kev and the Colfax Building and old Porky Pig?"

"You shouldn't eavedrop on other people's conversations."

"I didn't do it on purpose, and in any case, I've already talked to Erin. So I know that Sean McCloud's paranoia is flaring up big-time. I heard he's freaking out, saying his twin was murdered after all."

"You wouldn't call it paranoia if you'd seen him yesterday," Miles snarled. "They ripped the shit out of him! They practically killed his girlfriend—" His voice trailed off. His stomach sank at the triumph in Cindy's eyes. Snookered into babbling his private business.

Pussywhipped asshole.

He sighed. "Forget it," he said wearily. "Just leave, OK?"

"OK. So don't tell me how those McCloud dudes don't think you're grown up enough to ask Porky what Kev McCloud was up to at Colfax. So don't tell me how they're blowing you off, like an idiot child."

He conceded that much. "Drives me freaking nuts," he growled.

Cindy's eyes were soft with understanding. "I know exactly how that is," she said. "I feel that way with those guys all the time."

Part of him shrank from the chummy, bonding moment that Cin clearly wanted to have. Another part was desperately eager for any crumb she might drop. No. He was done with this soul-killing bull-shit.

"I think the situations are pretty different," he said coldly.

The smile faded from Cindy's face. "And that difference is what? That I actually am just an idiot child, whereas you are not?"

He spun the chair around. "I did your favor. Don't make me re-gret it by making me listen to your poor-me routine. It's a big bore."

The silence behind him stretched so long, his neck started to itch.

"Weird, that old Porky could ever have anything to do with the McClouds," Cindy said softly. "Slobbering old lech. Did Kev know him?"

"Kev was student teaching Beck's summer school courses," Miles said stiffly. "Con said Kev taught the whole course, lectures and all. Beck just kicked back and got a paid vacation out of it."

"Sounds like Porky. Did I tell you about the time I went to his office? I wanted to do the midterm as a take-home exam—"

"So I could help you with it?"

She ignored his interruption. "You know what he did?"

"Cindy, I'm serious. I have to get back to work."

"He said he could tell from my face that I was carrying lots of tension in my shoulders. So he started massaging me. Like this."

She stepped right up behind him, and started petting his shoulders. Every nerve was desperately aware of her caressing touch. Pleasure shuddered through him, even while the thought of Porky's damp, puffy pink hands touching Cindy's skin nauseated him.

Her hands slid down in front of his chest. "Then he started creeping his slimy way slowly but surely towards my tits. That was when I realized what the deal was. If I just pulled my pants down and bent over his desk, I could get an A on that midterm exam."

The question burst out of his closed throat anyway. "So did you?"

Her hands tightened, her nails digging through his T-shirt. "No, Miles. I flunked that midterm," she said. "Egregiously, I'm proud to say. I may be a dog when it comes to chemistry, but I'm not a whore."

She spun his chair around, and before he could stop her, she'd swung that perfect thigh over his lap and sat down, straddling him.

He froze. He didn't know what to do with his hands. He was scared to death. And so aroused he was in danger of passing out.

Cindy wiggled her tight, perfect ass right against his hard-on. He shrank away from her, but she leaned closer. No escaping her seductive honey-and-vanilla scent. "Don't be scared," she said. "I won't bite."

Yeah, like hell. "Jesus, Cin. Are you on drugs?" he demanded.

She laughed. "I drank a bunch of killer java this morning down at the Coffee Shack. I'm feeling really strange, actually. Wired. Like, I don't give a shit. I'll say what I think. I'll do what I feel. Why shouldn't I?"

"Oh, God." His terror was heartfelt. Cindy in a manic mood was dangerous. He grabbed her waist, and his hands skittered off her like he'd grabbed a red-hot coal when they encountered hot, velvety bare skin. "Cin—"

"Shhh." She put her finger over his mouth, then grabbed one of his flapping, useless hands and pulled it up to her neck. She wrapped his fingers around one of the ties of her halter top, smiling that secret, dangerous, sexy-wild smile that he saw in his hottest fever dreams.

Then she tightened her own fingers around his, and pulled, until the knot slipped and gave. The halter fell down, the material snagging on her nipples. She shrugged, a graceful ripple of her slender body, and the top flopped all the way down over her belly, baring her breasts.

They were just like he'd imagined. No, better. Creamy triangles of soft, untanned skin against the darker freckles of her throat, her shoulders. He was transfixed. Gaping. She was so fucking beautiful.

"Touch them," she invited him.

He shook his head, every system on red alert, throat shaking, eyes stinging. On the verge of shooting his wad in his pants, right underneath the weight of her squirming ass. But Cindy was not to be denied. She grabbed his hand, and pressed his palm against her breast.

He gasped. So soft. Dewy skinned. So pale. The tight bud of her nipple tickled his palm. Her scent was making him dizzy.

She wrapped her arms around his neck, tugged his head towards hers. He yanked her close, and buried his face in her tits, rubbing his cheek against her. Kissing, licking. He'd wanted this for so long, even though his chest felt like a hot blade was turning inside him.

This would blow up in his face sooner or later. Probably sooner. More like, instantly. He had zero experience, zero technique, but Cindy seemed to like it anyhow. Her face was pink, and she was pressing her crotch against his erection with an insistent, grinding rhythm. She went motionless, and made a sobbing sound as a ripple shuddered through her body. Then she sagged over his shoulder.

He nuzzled, memorizing the taste of her sweat, for later. When she'd blow him off again.

The question rose out of the depths of his anger and sadness. "Why are you doing this?" He couldn't stop his voice from shaking.

She lifted her head. Her eyes were glowing with arousal. "Why not? I've got nothing to lose. It's not like I have to worry about ruining our friendship, right? It's already ruined. So why not cop a feel?"

He pushed her off his lap. She stood there, flaunting her body. "So, Miles?" she taunted. "Are you going to do the nasty with me? You got me all hot. It would be mean to send me off without nailing me."

"Get out, Cin." The wobble in his voice was getting bad.

"I could sit right here." She perched on the table, parting her thighs so he could see a flash of lace. "The table's the right height. Or we could do it on the chair. I love playing horsie. Or I could lean against the wall, and stick my ass out, like this." She turned, demonstrated.

He shook his head. She laughed at him. "Liar. Don't you want to see my Brazilian wax job? I had the girl trim my pussy hair into a heart shape. Want to see?" She put her hands on her waistband.

"Out!" he bellowed, surging to his feet.

"Not without checking you out." She grabbed the waistband of his sweatpants, yanked. His dick sprang up, bobbing and waving.

Cindy pursed her lips in a silent whistle. "Whoa. You've been keeping this big, bad thing hidden in your jeans for all these years?"

She gripped his cock, stroked him. He tried to suck air into his shuddering lungs. "I told you not to joke with me about this—"

"Who's joking?" She sank to her knees and took him in her mouth. He sucked in a shallow gasp, and stopped breathing altogether.

He didn't last long. A few excruciating strokes, a few teasing swirls, and it was a landslide, an earthquake, a catastrophic explosion, molten lava spurting. He was startled to find himself still on his feet.

Cindy was wiping her mouth, gazing up. She looked startled.

"Uh, wow," she whispered. "That was explosive."

He yanked his pants up. Turned his gaze away.

"You're a virgin, aren't you?" she asked. "I always wondered."

Right. Like he could admit that to her. He knew how that would play. She'd have been all worried for poor sex-starved Miles. She would have tried, out of sisterly compassion, to get him laid with one of her sluttier girlfriends. Whichever of them was game for a mercy fuck.

His eyes stung. "I don't need your pity. Just leave me alone, OK?"

Cindy rose to her feet. "I don't pity you. You don't deserve pity. Don't think I did this for you. You don't deserve it, you nasty prick."

"Then why'd you do it?" he asked, though he knew he would hate the answer. Her nonchalant shrug made her tits bounce tenderly.

"Because I felt like it. You know what a selfish bitch I am. Have a nice life, Miles." She turned. The door to the stairs slammed shut.

He sank into his chair, and burst into tears.

Cindy sprinted through the kitchen, pretending not to hear whatever Miles's mom called after her. She couldn't make out the words. She was blubbering too hard. Bone deep, shivery shaking.

That had been so weird, so kinky. Out of nowhere. The impulse to come on to him had been so strong. So wrong.

She grabbed her bike and swung her leg onto it. She wobbled and swerved, dashing hot tears from her eyes. The taste of him was still in her mouth. She needed a drink of water in the worst way, but it wasn't like she could ask Miles's mom for a glass. *Gee, thanks, Mrs. Davenport. You know how it is when you swallow.*

She was so wound up. Her crotch tingled against the bike seat. She'd genuinely wanted him to yank her cutoffs down and go at her like a stallion with that thick, excellent thing. Like, who knew? The best kept secret in Endicott Falls, hidden in Miles Davenport's baggy pants.

Why did she keep doing this? Throwing herself at him, begging him to be her friend again. Lashing out like a spoiled baby when he shoved her away. She was a glutton for punishment. Well, she'd definitely made an impression with this stunt. Whatever he thought of her, he wasn't going to forget this in a hurry.

She laughed bitterly to herself, trying to keep her eyes wide open so the wind in her face could dry the tears leaking out.

She was so sick of being treated like a bimbo. Granted, she wasn't the superbrain that her big sister Erin was, but her scores on all those tests back in school had always put her up in the top tenth percentile.

Not in the same egghead club as Erin or Miles, maybe, but not a drooling vegetable, either.

She'd just gotten too comfortable playing the cute 'n sexy card. But what did she have to show for it? A string of badass ex-boyfriends, one of whom she'd barely escaped from with her life. An ex-best friend who hated her guts . . . even when he was coming in her mouth.

Yeah, being cute had enhanced the quality of her life, big-time.

She should tone her looks way down, maybe. Wear horn-rimmed cat-eye glasses, big baggy sweaters, combat boots. Ditch the makeup. Might as well go all out, and just shave her head while she was at it.

But the idea made her so anxious. If she wasn't getting attention from the guys, what did she have going for her? What was she, any-how?

Not much. Just a random girl. Not real special. Not real bright.

Miles would tell her she was doing her poor-me routine again. She snuffled with soggy, ironic laughter. Thank God for her sax. At least she could do one thing that was cool, and real, and all hers.

She started down the long descent into Edgewood Circle, a super wealthy enclave of Endicott Falls, and coasted past the manicured Victorian home of the college president. She'd played receptions with the Vicious Rumors there, back in the good old days when Miles was doing sound for them. Back when he still liked her.

She was so curious about these mysterious projects Miles was working on. He got off on the dark, creepy vibe, Goth freak that he was, and there were always plenty of creepy vibes to go around when those McCloud guys embarked on one of their bizarre adventures.

Weird, that they'd forbidden Miles to ask Porky questions. Too bad he couldn't take her along. She'd be his secret weapon. If she wore her stick-on silicon boob pusher-uppers and a micro-mini, she could pry anything out of old Porky. That type went nuts for bubbleheads. Bubbleheads made them feel so godlike and smart by contrast.

The impulse came to her out of nowhere, just like the impulse to jump Miles's hot bod had done. Almost as stupid, no doubt, but still.

The McClouds had forbidden Miles to ask Porky questions, but nobody had forbidden silly Cindy to do anything. And they might be surprised at what a simpering sex object might pry out of a man like Porky. For all their charisma and experience, she had something they didn't have. Two somethings, bouncing on her chest, and all the bells and whistles that went with them. She knew how to use them, too. It was her most highly developed skill. Other than playing sax, of course.

She swerved at the next corner, onto Linden Street. Porky's house was famous for how garish it was in a town full of fussy Victorians. She peeked at her watch, buzzing with excitement. She could do this and still have time to spiff up for her gig with the Rumors tonight. They were opening for Bonnie Blair, at the Paramount. A super important gig. She had to look stunning, and that took some time.

Speaking of which. She glanced down at her skimpy attire, and concluded that she was perfectly dressed for this little adventure.

She leaned her bike on the stone wall that bordered the lawn, and walked down the drive towards the house, trying to ignore fluttering in her belly. An attractive Hispanic lady in her fifties dressed in the uniform of domestic staff answered the doorbell. She looked Cindy up and down, and gave her the Death Star look. "Yes?"

"Is Professor Beck at home?" Cindy attempted a friendly smile.

The lady's mouth tightened to a grim line. "What's it about?"

"I'm a former student," she explained. "I wanted to ask some questions about a project of mine."

"Wait here." The door closed smartly in her face.

Cindy shrugged inwardly. No point in getting uptight about it. Dress like a devil slut, get treated like a devil slut. Simple.

Her musings were cut short when the door was yanked open

again. This time, Porky was behind it. His initial puzzlement quickly warmed into an appreciative leer, but there was no recognition in it.

Just as well. She didn't really want him to remember her D+.

She zapped him with her incandescent bubblehead smile, and he waved her right on in. He flung a fleshy arm around her shoulders, fingers in position to start their sneaky downward creep, and led her through a series of luxurious rooms. She wondered how a place could stink of money and still be so butt-ugly. The place had a cold, professional vibe that suggested a decorator's high concept design, not a home. Like the lobby of a wealthy lawyer's office.

He led her down broad marble steps into a sunken living room, and plunked her down on one of several plushy, cream-colored leather couches, grouped around a low, gleaming ebony table which was longer and wider than a queen-sized bed. A stark, spiky red flower arrangement was perched in the exact middle of it.

"So, my dear, what can I help you with? And would you refresh my memory again? I have so many students, you see. I remember your lovely face, of course, that's unforgettable."

"I'm Cynthia Riggs." The eyelash treatment, a tit-enhancing tilt to the rib cage, and a slow, deliberate recrossing of the legs, a la Sharon Stone. "I just graduated this June. I took your course two years ago. It was totally great," she gushed. "I'm not a science type, but you made it so interesting somehow. Even kind of beautiful. That may sound dumb to you, but I just don't know how else to describe it."

"Thank you." He sat down close to her so their legs almost touched. "But you didn't come here just to give me compliments."

She giggled. "Um, no. It's about a personal project of mine."

His knee made contact. "I love personal projects." His eyes glowed with fascinated curiosity, lit up from behind by plain old lust.

"I could probably have asked other people these questions, but I decided to come to you, first." She gave him a fluttery sidelong glance. "You're so, like, approachable, you know?"

His arm shifted so that it touched her bare shoulders. "You can't imagine how much pleasure it gives me to hear that, Cynthia."

She let her lashes sweep down. "I've been doing some writing lately, and I'm getting really into, like, biographical projects? And I got to thinking I could, um, write a biography of a local person?"

He frowned. "A historical personage, you mean?"

She shook her head. "Oh, no. Modern day."

"That's fascinating, but it's not my field," he said regretfully. "If you like, the director of the Young Writers' Workshop at the Arts Center is a personal friend of mine. I would be delighted to introduce him to such an attractive, well-spoken young woman."

"Oh, thanks!" she burbled. "That would be fabulous! But actually, I didn't want to ask about writing. I wanted to ask about the person I mean to write about, because you actually, like, knew him."

Porky's eyes widened. "You tease me. Who is this mystery man?"

Here it was. The deep end of the pool. She took a deep breath, and dove. "Kevin McCloud."

Everything changed. The temperature of the room plummeted. The smile on Porky's face flash-froze in the meat locker chill.

Suddenly, his fingers weren't inching down below her collarbone anymore. His arm was up on the back of the couch. His knee was a full two inches from hers. His mask of fascinated curiosity was gone, along with the lust that had animated it. His eyes had gone totally blank.

She was spooked. She felt very young, and very alone, and very stupid to mess with stuff that wasn't her goddamn business.

He cleared his throat. "You might be mistaken about my knowing this person, Cynthia. That name doesn't ring any bells in my mind."

Yeah, right. Liar, liar, pants on fire. It rang car alarms in his mind. She widened her eyes. "I heard you guys knew each other," she said earnestly. "Back when you were doing research at University of Washington? And he was student teaching for you for a while, right?"

His eyes flicked away. "Ah. So we're talking a good long while back? It is a somewhat common name, after all . . . oh, wait. Are you by any chance referring to that poor young man with the mental problems? The one who took his own life some years ago?"

"Yeah, that's him!" Innocent, blinky-blinky puppy dog eyes. "God, it was, like, so incredibly sad, huh? So you did know him, then?"

"In a way." He frowned. "But that's a terrible story. The waste of a promising young man's life . . . it's better off left in the past. Don't dwell on it, for God's sake. What got you interested in that person?"

She grinned, teeth clenched. Damn. She'd been afraid he was going to ask her this, and she had no good answer ready, so she just used the one she'd overheard Miles suggest to Connor on the phone.

"Actually, I found one of his personal notebooks," she explained. "I've been studying it. It's incredible. He was such a genius, you know?"

"That he was," Porky muttered.

"Anyhow, I thought there might be a book in it," she went on. "I thought I might investigate into why he might have offed himself."

"Oh. Well, I'm sorry to disappoint you, but the truth is sad and obvious. I suspect he might have been afflicted by his own extreme intelligence. Many geniuses are, sadly. History abounds with them."

Porky was relaxing, warming up again. Back in the saddle.

"Oh, so, you remember a lot about him, then?" She beamed.

Porky blinked rapidly. "It's, ah, coming back to me. You know how it is. Pull a memory in the database, and you find the connected ones."

Dewy, hopeful eyes. "So could you answer some questions, then?"

His smile faltered. "I hate to disappoint such a lovely creature, but I don't know what else I could tell you. He's been gone for a long time."

"Well, a couple things in the notebook puzzled me," Cindy said. She steepled her hands and put on the cute-little-girl-recites-her-lesson look. "It referred to work he was doing at the Colfax Building."

Porky's brow looked shiny. "Ah. Well. I . . . I don't really know what he did with his time when he wasn't teaching."

"Have you ever heard of anything called the Midnight Project?"

His Adam's apple bobbed. "It, ah, might have had to do with neurological research. I believe the project folded long ago. Dried up due to lack of funding. The Colfax belongs to the college now."

"Oh, I know that. I'm working up there this summer," she confided. "Band camp. I teach saxophone to the kids."

"Really?" He rallied, grinning weakly. "So you're a musician, as well as a writer. A young woman of many talents. I'm dazzled."

Cindy glowed and fluttered for as long as she could string it, and gave it one last college try. "Do you know who funded the research?"

"I'm so sorry, Cynthia. I'm afraid I don't." Porky grabbed a device that was clipped to his belt, and pushed a button. "Emiliana? Would you bring us some iced tea and a plate of your pecan puffs?"

He replaced the thing on his belt, and cleared his throat nervously. Cindy cast around for some bubbly noise she could pump into the silence before the guy freaked out on her. "Love your house," she offered lamely. "Gorgeous place. It's so big."

He looked around, like he'd never seen the house. "Ah. Yes."

The Hispanic lady appeared, tightlipped as ever, bearing a tray with a frosty glass pitcher, two glasses and a plate of cookies. Porky was grateful for the interruption. "Ah, thank you." He held out the plate. "Emiliana is new to me. Her predecessor just retired, but not before finding someone excellent to replace herself. There's a network of people out there that you would never find at an employment agency. Try the pecan puffs. It's clear you don't have any problems with your figure."

The cookies were fab, the tea was cold and sweet and good, and Porky kept gamely on with the sticky stream of compliments, but she could tell his heart wasn't in it. He almost leaped for joy when she said she had to scoot. He saw her promptly out, not touching her at all.

She hopped on her bike and took off for the campus. She wasn't sure what, if anything, that she'd gleaned from that, other than that the mention of Kev McCloud made old Porky so tense, he actually stopped hitting on her. Which was to say, severely tense. Hmm.

She stopped at the Colfax to get her sax from the practice room, and turned when she heard somebody calling her name. It was Bolivar, Javier's uncle, the janitor at the Colfax. He had a huge grin on his face.

"Javier came by here a little while ago. Told me you got him a good demo recorded," he said. "He just sent off his application."

"That's great," she said. "Keep your fingers crossed. He's got a good chance at the scholarship. It would be great experience for him."

Bolivar beamed. "The music, it's good for him. Keeps him steady. He's a good boy, Javier." He paused. "Thank you for helping him."

She was embarrassed. "Nah. It's no big deal, really—"

"You helped him get the sax. You give him extra lessons free. His lessons go two hours sometime, he tells me. He's a lucky boy, and you are a nice lady," Bolivar announced, as if daring her to contradict him.

Lots of people might take issue with that statement, but still, it was awfully nice to hear someone say it. He was turning to continue on down the hall when a thought came to her, of what Porky said about Emiliana, and the unofficial network of workers. "Ah, Bolivar?"

He turned, still smiling. "Hmm?"

"This may sound weird, but would you know anybody who was on the janitorial staff of this building fifteen years ago? Around August."

Bolivar's smile faded. "Depends on why you want to know."

"Oh, I just want to talk to the person," she assured him.

Bolivar's eyes went very cautious. "Is this about the curse?"

Cindy's stomach fluttered. "Curse?"

"When I took this job, people said the place is cursed. But Javier needed a dentist, his mama was having another baby. I didn't have time to worry about no curse. Didn't want to know. Still don't."

Cold fingers were doing the creepy, tickly dance up and down her spine. "Never mind," she said. "I don't want to cause you any—"

"I'll ask around," Bolivar said. "It was a long time ago."

Cindy felt guilty that Bolivar felt obligated to do something that made him nervous, but gee, a curse? She dug in her pocket, found a dog-eared business card. It was simple, just her name, a sexy picture of her playing the sax, and her cell number. Miles had taken the picture.

Miles had typeset and printed up the cards for her, too.

"Call me if you find anything out, OK?" she said.

Bolivar nodded, tucked it into his pocket. Cindy loped towards her room, wishing she had something to show for this stunt. All she had were feelings, vibes, rumors. Tickles on the back of her neck.

It was frustrating. Maybe that was what real detective work was like. It would drive her nuts. Thank God she was a musician.

Man, she hoped the band would be blazing tonight. It was going to take a serious, exalted groove to play all of today's worries away.

Chapter
19

Professor Sidney Beck stared through the glass at the willowy seductress's beautifully presented ass as she rode away on her bicycle.

Then he shuffled back to the living room. Sat down, heavily.

He drank several glasses of tea. Ate the remaining pecan puffs, crunching them mechanically. He poured the last half glass, took it to the bar, topped it off with rum. He felt steadier after gulping that down.

He went to the bathroom, when the call of nature became too urgent to ignore, and pissed. His heart raced, but the thumping felt feeble, insignificant and faraway. Mice, skittering on tiny feet. The pumping action didn't get as far as his brain, his leaden limbs.

He stared at his heavy slab of a face. His double chin. The broken veins in his cheeks. Emiliana's pecan puffs had transformed into corrosive acid sludge that churned and frothed, burning his esophagus.

McCloud. Dead fifteen years, and still forcing him to look at the corrupt, mediocre fraud that he was. Not that he'd ever rubbed Beck's nose in it. Kevin hadn't been arrogant about his genius. He had not the slightest need to be. It had never occurred to him to look down on other mortals less gifted than he, because everyone was less gifted than he.

All that genius, calm self-assurance, and youth and good looks, too. He'd been so jealous of McCloud, he could have murdered him.

Maybe he had.

Oh, no. No need to take on that burden. All he'd done was give him Osterman's number, told him that the research might intrigue him. That there was money involved. Minimal time commitment. That was the extent of his responsibility. He hadn't known what would happen.

He hadn't forced Kevin to call, to get embroiled. To get hurt.

True, Osterman had asked specifically for highly intelligent young people without a lot of family ties, but Beck hadn't taken that to mean the man was up to no good. Why should he?

He could never have guessed how sick the whole thing would become. His career, his house, the stock options in Helix, the toys, the indulgences, hot tubs filled with smiling young women—all of it built around one unspeakable secret. If that crumbled, everything crumbled.

After all. The damage was done. The milk was spilled. If he was going to hell anyway, why not cut his losses and try to enjoy it?

His face looked so blank. Slack. Old, though he was barely into his fifties. He stumbled into his office, the one overlooking Endicott River. If he opened the windows, he could hear the roar of the falls.

He saw and heard none of this. Just booted up the computer, picked up the phone, and dialed.

"Office of Undergraduate Studies," said a crisp, female voice.

"Eileen? Hello, this is Sidney Beck," he said, in his best hearty, jovial tone. "I hope you had a lovely summer."

"Hello, Professor! I did, thanks. Anything I can do for you?"

"Yes, in fact. Would you e-mail me the academic records of one of my former students? I have a friend who's interviewing her for a job."

"Why, certainly, Professor. What's the name?"

"Cynthia Riggs," he said.

"One moment." He listened to Muzak, foot tapping compulsively.

Eileen came back on the line. "Professor? Are you sure you've

got the right person? This girl was a music major. And on her transcript, I see that she barely passed the course she took from you."

"Actually, ah, my friend is a musician," he improvised.

"Ah. I see. Well, I'm sending the file. Do you want the photo?"

He was startled. "You have a photo?"

"We have a photo on file of all our students. Do you want it?"

"Uh, why, yes," he said distractedly. "Please, send it along."

And there it was, in his inbox. He opened the jpg, and stared at
Cynthia's pretty face. He thought of how warm the skin of her shoulders had been. How in a couple of days, that warm skin would be
stone cold.

That curvy, slender body, laid out on a coroner's table.

He was going to hell anyway. It didn't matter anymore what sins
he committed. And besides, no one had forced that idiot girl to ask
her stupid questions. He'd done nothing. She'd brought it all on
herself.

He dialed. The phone was promptly answered. "Beck?"

"Yes! Dr. Osterman? How are you? I haven't heard from you in—"

"Cut right to it, Beck," Osterman said. "I'm very busy."

Beck swallowed his anger at the man's arrogance. "Ah. Yes." He
cleared his throat, and laughed nervously. "I thought you might like
to know about an odd visit I got, from a former student of mine. She
was asking questions about Kevin McCloud."

Osterman waited. "What questions? Who is she? Spit it out."

"She asked about the Midnight Project," Beck blurted out.

The quality of Osterman's silence changed. It made Beck feel
guilty. As if this mess were his fault. "She said she found his notebook. She wants to write a book." He laughed again. "I doubt her
interest runs very deep, knowing the young lady in question," he
babbled. "Not the brightest bulb, though she does compensate in
other ways—"

"Her name, Beck. Don't waste my time."

He stared at the girl's bright smile and took another step towards
the crackling flames. "Cynthia Riggs. She's teaching up at the Colfax. Probably staying in student summer housing. I . . . I have a
photo."

"Send it. What else do you have?"

Beck studied the files. "Academic records, parents' address—"

"Send it all." Osterman had a smug, satisfied tone. "I don't have to tell you how important discretion is, do I?"

Beck forwarded the files to the appropriate address, hit send and gulped back a rush of bile. "No," he said hoarsely.

Osterman paused, sensing the conflict in the other man. "You are contributing to crucial, life-enhancing research," he lectured. "There are always ethical conundrums to be faced. Hard decisions to be made."

"Of course." Beck's voice felt strangled.

"You do enjoy your tenure? Your position? Your interest income?"

"What a question." Beck tried to laugh. "I'm very appreciative of—"

"Good. Have a good day, Professor."

The line went dead. Leaving him sitting there, empty, staring and staring at the smiling face of the girl who was about to die.

Far off, in the back of his mind, he could hear her screaming.

Osterman studied the photograph, then clicked through the files. He was buzzing with excitement. About time that sack of lard he'd invested so much money in made himself marginally useful.

So she'd found his notebook, had she? Colfax Building, Midnight Project, it had to be the famous lost notebook at last, but who else had seen it? And who was she? How could McCloud's notebook have fallen into the hands of some random female? It was incomprehensible.

He would normally have called Jared to do the Internet research, but he couldn't wait. He typed her name into the search engine and began to sort through the hits. *Spin*, a music review mag. ". . . the third cut, "Wild Card," an exceptional solo flight by sax player Cynthia Riggs, creating a blazing counterpart to the lead guitar . . ." *Folk Music Today*, ". . . of particular mention, the title song, "Falling Away," by Cynthia Riggs, is the strongest piece in this overall strong debut album . . . the Vicious Rumors have shown themselves to be a band to watch . . ."

Yes, yes. Beck had mentioned that she was a musician. He flicked

over the other references to her musical career until he found La
Pineta Folk Festival, which had a photograph attached. He clicked
to enlarge.

It was a shot of the band playing on stage. He recognized the girl
in Beck's photo instantly, blowing into her instrument with almost
sexual abandon.

Hmm. Gordon was going to enjoy this assignment.

The next hit caught his eye, from the Endicott Falls *Sentinel,*
dated last year. He clicked on the article and read it, heart pounding.

". . . Erin Riggs, daughter of Edward and Barbara Riggs of Seat-
tle, to Connor McCloud, son of the late Eamon and Jeannie Mc-
Cloud of Endicott Falls. Attending the bride was her sister, Cynthia
Riggs . . ."

He clicked to enlarge the attached photo, and started to laugh.

The girl in the photo was an older, plumper version of Cynthia.
And the grinning man who clutched her bore a striking resemblance
to Kevin McCloud. The girl was the sister of Kevin's sister-in-law.
Well, then. Perhaps the matter was still more contained than he had
feared.

Still, Cynthia could not be allowed to run around babbling about
the Midnight Project. She had to disappear. And if all else failed,
she was an excellent lever to draw in the real prize. Sean McCloud.

He dialed Gordon. The man picked up. "What?" he barked.

"Don't sulk, Gordon," he purred. "I have a juicy piece of meat to
throw to you. You're going to absolutely love this job."

Proof on the tapes in EFPV. HC behind count birds B63.

Liv tried to make her brain soft and receptive. Looking for that
relaxed, creative place where insights came from. She stared at one
of Kev's pictures. The lake, with ducks swimming on it.

The rumble of male voices in the background had blurred. She
no longer heard individual words. She fought discouragement. The
McClouds guys had spent months poring over this stuff, they'd
known their brother since birth. Plus, they were all brilliant. If
they'd had no luck, what the hell did she think she could accomplish?

Then again, what else did she have to do? It was all she had to offer. Not being a commando warrior like everybody else around here.

She rested her eyes and stared out the huge window that looked out over the cliffs. The fog had rolled in, so they seemed to be floating in the clouds. Insubstantial wisps of mist were woven and braided through the dark trees of the mountains that thrust through the mass of white.

The door to the room slammed open. Tamara stormed in, and placed her fists on her hips, glaring at the men who sprawled on her couches and chairs, guzzling coffee and muttering amongst themselves.

"Your womenfolk have arrived, gentlemen," she announced. "Have you invited anyone else to my secret hiding place without asking my permission? Should I call the caterers?"

Seth sat up, scowling. "We told them to stay on the island today!"

Connor flopped back on the couch. "It's like talking to the wall."

Tam stomped out of the room, muttering under her breath.

Sean noted Liv's bewildered face. "Don't worry," he assured her. "She likes Raine and Margot and Erin. Way more than she likes us guys. She just has to make a fuss, on principle. Pay her no mind."

"Uh, OK." Paying Tam no mind was a real toughie. "Whatever."

"Come on." He slid his arm around her waist. "Let's go down and meet them. I want to introduce you."

They crowded into the foyer as Tam disarmed the security. The pieces of the space-age door retracted. A square of greenery quivered at the end of the long garage. A sporty little silver Volkswagen pulled in.

Three women climbed out. A pretty dark-haired woman who was clearly pregnant, a voluptuous freckled beauty with a bushy red mop of hair, and a slender blonde, her fuzzy cloud of pale hair pulled back into a loose braid. Their eyes fastened on to Liv, alight with interest. She braced herself as they crowded into the little room, looking her over.

"Were you followed? Did you bother to check? Did it minimally occur to you?" Tam barked at the tall redhead in the fore.

The woman beamed, and gave her a bear hug. Tam stiffened, holding out her arms like she didn't know what to do with them.

"Great to see you, Tam. We miss you." She frowned, spanning Tam's waist with her hands. "You've gotten teensy. What is up with that? You been sick?"

"Sick of hearing about it, that's for sure." Tam's eyes narrowed as she returned Margot's scrutiny. "Oh, God. You're pregnant."

Margot's eyes widened. "But we're not sure yet."

"Be sure."

"How?" Margot demanded. "Did Davy say something to you?"

"No. He didn't have to. It's written all over you. Like neon."

Liv studied the redhead's amazonian body, but she didn't see any neon. Just strong, sexy curves. The brunette, who had to be Erin, grabbed Tam as well, hugging her with the same fearless abandon.

Tam returned the hug, albeit somewhat stiffly. "How's gestation?" she asked, patting Erin's rounded belly in a gingerly way.

Erin's smile was complacent. "Cowlike. Blissful. A boy."

Tam smacked her forehead. "As if the world needed another McCloud male." She turned to the blonde, and suffered patiently to be hugged a third time. "You're not breeding yet, are you? Say you're not."

A pained smile flitted over the woman's face. "Ah, nope. Not yet."

Tam's eyes sharpened as she looked her over. "Hmph," she murmured. "Not from lack of trying, I bet." She spun around and indicated Liv with a flourish of her arm. "Well, ladies, here she is. The main event. The mild-mannered librarian who sent a contract killer running with his tail tucked. Our kind of girl. Cute, isn't she?"

"She sure is," Margot said, her eyes flicking up to Sean's with a delighted twinkle in them. "Nice work, buddy. She's yummy."

"I didn't, really. Send him running, I mean." Liv hastened to clarify. "It was just, you know. Dumb luck."

The women looked at each other. "That's all it ever is," Erin told her solemnly. They chortled, as if at some private joke, and smirked at Sean, slapping his ass as they filed by. He suffered this with a look of stoic martyrdom, and followed them down the hall towards the kitchen.

Margot flung an arm over Liv's shoulder. "Excuse the invasion," she said. "We were practically peeing our pants from curiosity. Any woman who could wrangle this spaz into shape must have an amazing set of ovaries. We just had to come and gawk."

Liv blushed. "After the stories Sean tells, I'm gawking too."

"Oh, Sean talks too much," Erin said cheerfully. "Don't listen."

Tam spun around and blocked the parade. "Erin. I finished a new piece recently," she announced. "I want to name it for you. May I?"

Erin looked startled. "I suppose. Wow. Could I see it?"

Tam's smile took on a catlike satisfaction. "Certainly. Right this way." She led them down a corridor, and up into the octagonal tower, a workroom paneled in dark wood, the effect both stark and lavish.

Entire walls were covered with tiny catalogued drawers. Bars of powerful lighting hung from the high ceiling. Mysterious chunks of machinery were bolted to the heavy worktables. Strange, twisted metal things like tormented mobiles from a goblin's dreams spun lazily in the breeze from the window. With the tree poking through the clouds, the smell of metal and chemicals, and the backdrop of the sound of the heaving surf down below, it seemed like an ancient alchemist's lair.

"The finished pieces are here." Tam led them to a table draped with black velvet and lit with its own bar of lights. Several polished wooden boxes sat on it. Tam flipped one open, and presented it to Erin.

Liv's breath stopped, the piece was so startling, although upon second glance, the design was simple. It was a torque, meant to be worn around the neck, of twisted white gold, smaller threads of subtly colored gold woven through it. The finials were an intricate snarl of golden knotwork, with glowing red stones.

"It's like Novak's torque," Erin said. "Except . . . different. Oh, Tam. It's gorgeous."

Tam looked pleased. A flick of her thumb opened the torque. She fitted it around Erin's neck. "Watch carefully. If you're ever in a tight spot, press the garnet, push on this lever here, and there you go." The finial came off, proving to be the decorated hilt of a small, curved blade.

"Wow," Erin stared at the wicked looking knife. "I'm honored."

"You should be," Tam said. "Asking price is two hundred K."

Liv's jaw dropped. "People pay that kind of money?"

"You bet." Tam dug into her pocket, and passed the cards around. *Deadly Beauty: Wearable Weaponry. Tamara Steele.* "Most people capable of paying that much money for a piece of novelty jewelry are very insecure. Take your standard mafioso mistress whose lover could be mowed down by a rival boss from one day to the next. An item like this will make her feel safer. Even if the safety is totally fictitious."

"Are there a lot of mafioso mistresses out there?" Liv asked.

"Plenty. Mafioso wives, too. Lots of money and fear in the criminal underworld. Perfect market for Deadly Beauty. I call this series 'Margot.' With your permission, of course."

They gasped at the assortment of hair ornaments. They seemed to pulse with trapped light. The designs were intensely sensual; feminine curves, slashing angles. Simplicity juxtaposed with tormented intricacy.

"Where did you learn how to do this stuff?" Raine asked.

"My father was a goldsmith. I was his apprentice 'til I was fifteen."

There was a startled silence. Liv looked at the glances flashing between the other women, and realized that Tam volunteering details about her mysterious past was a first time event for all of them.

"What happened when you were fifteen?" Erin asked.

Tam waved her hand, fanning the past away from her as if it were a bad odor. "He died," she said curtly. "I got apprenticed to somebody else. Look at this one." She held up another pin. "Based on the spray model that you all know and love, but if you press this topaz . . ." She held it up. A needle glinted, so fine it was barely visible. "Load it with poison, or a sedative, depending on your needs. And there's the old classic." She picked up a horn shaped clip, twisted the knob, and pulled out a blade. "You can treat the blade with poison, if you don't trust yourself to hit a vital organ or artery on the first stab."

"Is this grisly exhibition necessary?" Sean cast an uneasy glance at Liv. "You're freaking me out."

"Leave the room, if you have a weak stomach," Tam said.

"Is that blade longer than four inches?" Connor's voice came from the open door. "Any longer than that, and you're carrying concealed."

"Certainly it's longer. What a foolish question, Con. Four inches plus one millimeter." Tam's voice was smug. "It's a matter of principle."

The menfolk jostled Con aside and filed into Tam's studio, looking around themselves with wary fascination.

"You guys were supposed to stay at the island," Seth complained.

Raine gave him a cheerfully apologetic shrug.

"Actually, I came to get you," Erin said to Connor. "Cindy called to invite us to her gig at the Paramount. I want to keep an eye on her, if she's on stage with this psycho out on the loose. She's staying with us, after. I don't want her at Mom's all alone while Mom's on vacation."

Connor groaned. "You couldn't just tell her to blow off the gig?"

"I tried," Erin said. "She said I was insane for even suggesting it."

"But I already told Miles to stay with us tonight," Connor complained. "He'll be furious with me if he finds Cindy there."

Erin rolled her eyes. "Miles will survive."

Tam cleared her throat. "Have you finished boring us with your irrelevant personal business? Oh, good. I'm so glad. This is the 'Raine.'"

Tam flipped open the box. The women sighed, in unison. The pendant was stunning, an oval as large as a flattened egg. An opal flashed with deep blue-green fire in a setting of woven open-worked gold.

Earrings accompanied it, smaller pendants dangling on slender, braided gold thread from a whorl of colored gold in the earlobe.

"Like the Dreamcatcher," Raine said. "Except . . ."

"Except," Tam said. She twisted the knob where the chain was attached. The thing clicked open in her hand, revealing a dense tangle of wires and circuits, and a wad of what looked like grayish clay.

Sean sucked in a sharp breath. "Is that what I think it is?"

"A bomb," Tam said proudly. "It has a limited blast range, but it's very effective. Place it next to the target's pillow while he snores in postcoital bliss, go to the next room, take off your earring, twist . . ." she demonstrated, pulling off the jeweled bulb, "and voilà." She revealed a small button. "Your detonator. Ka-boom. Your life has been simplified."

Seth made a rude sound. "Did it occur to you that some women might be sleeping with men that they do not necessarily want to snuff?"

Tam shrugged. "Things change," she said. "Men grow tiresome."

Seth muttered something in Spanish that sounded insulting.

"It's a waste to blow up something so beautiful," Liv commented.

"There is that to consider," Tam agreed. "Which is why I have a simpler version, with poison beads. Tasteless, odorless, with a helpful chart to help the novice poisoner get the right dosage based on body weight and timing issues. There's a version with inhalants, and a tiny hypodermic, too. But I think my bomblet might have some takers. There have been moments in my life when I would have sacrificed jewelry worth millions in exchange for some man's sudden death."

T-Rex's bloody grin flashed through Liv's mind, making her feel nauseated and cold. "Amen to that," she said.

Erin, Margot, and Raine all nodded.

Tam stared at Liv with narrowed golden eyes. "Now what kind of piece would be the perfect 'Olivia,' I wonder?"

Liv looked at the scabbed marks around her wrist. "Something to cut through ropes or plastic, even if your hands were tied," she said.

Tam's eyes lit up. "I have just the thing." She chose another box, and flipped it open, revealing several rings. Some with glowing stones clutched in tangles of golden wire, some with simple metallic braided bands and stripes. Tam picked out one of the simpler designs, variable bands of colored gold swirling around a square-cut piece of jasper.

"Pry out this lever, and press the stone," she directed. "I made it hard to trip, because I don't want a blade popping out at the opera while you're clapping after the overture. Sean, would you demonstrate?"

Sean looked dubious. "Is the blade poisoned?"

"If I wanted to kill you, I'd have done it long ago," Tam snapped.

Sean did as she had directed. A very small but efficient looking blade snapped out, less than an inch long, and serrated near the base.

"You could slice off your own fingers," Davy commented.

"Yes, in fact, it's a nice little surprise weapon," Tam said. "And as a last resort, you can always use it to open a vein."

A nervous silence followed her words, quickly followed by a grunt of disgust from Sean. "Yeah, over my dead body."

"Just so, my friend," Tam said softly. "Just exactly so."

Liv shuddered. She looked into the woman's big, golden cat eyes, and found herself caught in them. Tam's mocking laughter was gone. Somber shadows had taken its place. A silent understanding, beyond words. Tam had been in that place where T-Rex had almost taken her the other day. Where death would be a mercy. She knew it well.

Some part of her had never quite come back from it.

Liv took the ring from Sean's hands, and examined the sharp little blade. Yes, this would have come in handy yesterday. She pushed the chunk of jasper with all her strength. *Snick*, the blade snapped back.

Too bad she didn't have tens of thousands to spend.

She held it out to Tamara. "It's a wonderful piece," she said, with total honesty. "Beautiful, as well as useful. You're very talented."

Tam slid it onto her index finger. It fit perfectly. "It's yours."

Liv gasped, and pulled the ring off, holding it back out to her. "Oh, no. I couldn't. It's so valuable."

"One of the nice things about being rich is that I can afford to indulge my sentimental impulses." Tam slid the ring back onto Liv's hand. "I don't have sentimental impulses often, so don't waste it. And your man hasn't gotten you a special ring yet, has he? Cheap bastard."

"Hey. I resent that remark," Sean said vehemently. "Excuse me if I've been too busy engaging in hand to hand combat with psycho maniacs and running for our lives to stop at a fucking jewelry store!"

"Excuses, excuses," Tam scoffed. She lifted Liv's hand to her lips and kissed the back of it. "It tickles me to beat him to it. Besides, never count on a man to give you jewelry. They usually suck at choosing it."

Sean's jaw was tense. "You are a cat bitch from hell, Tam."

"Ah, how deeply my little barbs sink into your tender places," she taunted. "You give good sport, Sean. I've always liked that about you."

Raine cleared her throat. "Ah, Tam? Why haven't you ever gotten together with Seth to discuss a line of jewelry with beacon trasmitters?"

Tam shook her head. "It's contrary to my philosphy. Beacons presuppose that other people give a shit whether you live or die, which has not been my experience. Besides, I prefer to be unfindable, as do most of my clients. Thirdly, a trasmitter is no good if someone's holding a knife to your throat. That's what wearable weaponry is all about. An extra something when your back's to the wall, and you're on your own."

"You're depressing the hell out of me," Davy said.

"Take a pill," Tam said. "They've got great mood stabilizers now."

Sean glared down at the ring, and slanted Liv an uncertain glance. "I hope you know you're not wearing that thing to bed with me."

"Feeling insecure?" Tam peered into the box, and chose three rings, similar to the one she had given Liv. She grabbed Erin's hand, Margot's, then Raine's, and bestowed a ring upon each of them.

"A token of my regard, ladies," she said, with a wicked grin. "I never miss a chance to annoy a man."

Chapter
20

Miles tossed and twitched on the daybed in the studio. He felt hot, sticky and irritated. Wrangled into his worst nightmare: stuck under the same roof as Cindy Riggs. She was right upstairs, wearing only a chemise and thong set. He wondered if her pussy hair really was trimmed into a heart shape. He imagined sneaking into her room and demanding that she prove it. He'd showed her his. It was only fair.

Nah. She might tell him to piss off, at which point he would be obliged to fall into a yawning crack in the ground and die.

Worse yet. She might get that sultry look in her eyes that made him terrified and crazy, pull her panties off . . . and prove it to him.

Yeah, and then? His mind ran up against a wall of stark terror.

Having sex with her would be incredibly exciting. And the inevitable aftermath would kill him. He knew it. He fucking *knew* it.

Every time he closed his eyes, he saw her slender body twined around him, writhing. Coming, while he nuzzled her incredibly tender, soft tits. He'd had no idea it could be so easy to make a girl come.

Unless she was faking, of course. But why would she? It wasn't like she gave a shit about his poor tender virginal ego, at this point.

It sure hadn't felt fake. He'd felt every tremor, reverberating through his body. Every gasp, every clutch of her long nails.

And when she took him in her mouth, oh, God. Oh, God.

Connor was a sneaky asshole for getting him into this. He used every trick he had to stay out of that wacky little headcase's way, and everywhere he turned, there she was. Shaking her tits in his face.

He groaned, rolling up onto the edge of the daybed. He'd whipped himself into such a frenzy, there was no point trying to sleep. He might as well make himself useful. He booted up his laptop, and clicked his way into the chat forum where Mina had been hanging out with Jared.

Hi anybody out there Im bored, he typed.

A handful of people responded. He exchanged banalities with them, letting time creep by. Deliberately not thinking about Cindy's heart-shaped pussy hair. Jared finally appeared, oh thank God.

Mindmeld666: hey Mina lets do a u2u

They got into a private room. Jared got right to the point. **Ive been authorized to offer you an invitation.**

2 what?

A special place. The Haven. Heard rumors?

He had, in fact. Some mythical secret place where people learned amazing brain control techniques. He'd taken it for sci-fi bullshit. There was so much preposterous crap floating around in cyberspace.

Tell me more, he typed.

Dont want 2 talk about it online, Jared typed. I wanted 2 meet u and talk in person, but ur so shy I had no choice. My job is to recruit people like u.

Blushing, Miles typed coyly.

Don't. Most people who come here pay huge money. We hand pick special ones like u. The guy I work for is a genius. U have 2 xperience it 2 believe it.

Who is he? Miles typed.

Mindmeld hesitated. **Im not authorized to tell u that. I havent met u so how do I know if u r who u say u r?**

Fair enough. Thats my problem 2, Miles typed.

Only 1 way 2 solve ur problem. Meet me?

The question scrolled out across the bright screen and waited.

A knock on the study door sent his heart off on a tizzy.

Fuck. What to do? Hide under the bed? Stop breathing and pretend to be dead? Shit.

"You awake?" Connor's gruff voice sounded from the other side.

Not Cindy. Miles almost slid off the chair, unmanned by a combination of relief and disappointment. "More or less," he called.

Connor opened the door. He was fully dressed, a SIG in his hand.

"I just got a call. The SafeGuard alarm in Erin's mom's house tripped. Thank God she's in Hawaii. I called the cops, but I'm going to take a look. I want you to stand guard. Can you handle one of these?"

Are you kidding? I'm just a clueless gearhead, he wanted to yelp, but the part he'd been relentlessly training swallowed hard and nodded.

"I've put in some hours with Sean and Davy at the gun range. Let me just finish this." Miles leaned over the keyboard and typed,

gotta go. Check back in 2 hrs?

Ur a tease, Mindmeld666 typed. **Will check back. Bye4now.**

He followed Con downstairs, and took the gun.

"Heads up," Con said. "I'll be back as soon as I can."

Miles paced the foyer. His brain buzzed like a hive of bees. He couldn't sit still. The house was dim, just the orange glow of streetlamps from the window. The gun felt heavy and strange and alien in his hand.

"Oh. There you are." The soft voice made his heart jolt and skip in his chest. "I was just looking for you."

He turned. Cindy's body resolved out of the infinite shades of gray in the kitchen entrance. Just as he'd thought. A tight string tank. Not a thong, but those low-slung form fitted shorts were just about as bad.

"You should be sleeping," he said.

"Can't." Her voice was fretful. "I'm wound up from the gig. We were hot tonight. Too bad you weren't there. Holy cow, Miles. What the hell are you doing with a gun?"

"Guard duty," he replied. "Connor's gone off to check on your mom's place. Somebody tripped the alarm."

She tossed her head back, making her hair do that seductive swirl thing. "Someone has to protect us against the fanged monsters, right?"

He refused to let himself be needled. "The monsters are real, Cin."

"You're as bad as they are." She sauntered close enough so he could smell her honey-vanilla scent. The details of her body came into focus in the dimness. He gulped, and looked out the window.

"Can I hold that gun for a sec?" Her voice was teasing.

"No," he said.

She folded her arms over her belly and slouched against the wall. "Are you afraid I'll sexually assault you, or something?"

"Connor asked me to guard this house until he got back," he said tersely. "I'm goddamn well going to do it. So don't bug me."

Cindy slid down the wall until she sat on the floor, hugging her knees tightly to her chest. "Are you ever going to stop hating me, Miles?"

He let out a long, careful breath, trying to choose amongst the hundred thousand completely contradictory replies he could give to that statement. "I don't hate you, Cin. I just hate the way you made me feel. I hated being your personal slave while all your dickhead boyfriends treated you like shit. I really, really hated that."

"I'm not with any dickhead boyfriend right now," she protested.

He shrugged. "It's just a matter of time. I've got better things to do than run errands for you while you track your next dickhead down."

She covered her face with her hands. "Nobody forced you to do all that stuff for me." Her voice was small. "You could have just said no."

"That's true. That's what I finally did, Cin. I just said no."

She sniffled. "You hate my guts because of this morning, right?"

Oh, yeah. Right. He almost exploded in hysterical laughter. "No, Cin. I told you. I don't hate you. I wish you well. All the best. Really."

She chewed on that. "Wish me well," she repeated. "I wish Great-Aunt Martha well. I wish all the poor children in the world well. I wish the humpbacked whales and the bald eagles and the panda bears well."

He shook his head. "I've got nothing against whales or eagles or pandas, or Great-Aunt Martha. And I've got nothing against you."

She covered her face with her hands. He was appalled to hear soggy sniffling sounds again. He clenched his teeth. "What do you want to hear? That I love you? I'm not going to say that. I had a crush on you, but I'm over it. I'm not letting you wipe your feet on me anymore."

"I wouldn't," she whispered. "Ever again."

"Wouldn't what?" His voice hardened.

"Wipe my feet on you." She brushed tears out of her eyes, sniffing hard. "I'm sorry if I ever did. I never meant to."

The soft invitation in her trembling voice tore him to pieces. He wanted it so badly. His fantasy of Cindy, just how he wanted her to be. Grown up, chilled out, feet on the ground. And wanting him.

Fantasy, though. The key word here was fantasy.

He stood there, throat frozen with fear and pain, until the question in the silence between them became a flat, implacable answer.

Cindy let out a shaky sigh and got gracefully to her feet, padding through the kitchen. She stopped at the foot of the stairs. "Miles?"

He braced himself. "Yeah?"

"I wish you well, too," she said. "I really, really do."

She had a tone in her voice he had never heard before. She wasn't trying to sock in a zinger, or impress him, or shock him. She wasn't trying to jerk the world around until it was the way she wanted it.

Her voice was sad and flat. Facing reality. Dealing with it.

It almost made him change his mind. Having Cindy be real and straight with him was all he had ever wanted from the universe.

But she'd already vanished up the stairs. The fleeting moment was lost. He'd probably imagined it anyway, knowing how fucked in the head he'd always been about that girl.

Miles stared out at the lightening dawn. His heart felt heavy, a dead weight in his chest just like the gun in his hand, and a cruel, searing tightness in his throat, like someone was pulling a knot tight.

God help the fool who tried to assault that house on his watch. He would blow the fucker full of holes without a shred of remorse.

* * *

"He looks just like Connor." Erin sounded smug.

Cindy squinted her eyes, still gummy from last night's mascara, and took another swig of coffee as she tried to make sense of the grainy sonogram images of her little nephew. "I still don't see what you see."

"Imagine that you're looking straight up, under his chin," Erin explained. "See? There's his lips, that's his little nose . . . see it now?"

It finally slid into place. She got a sweet, shivery thrill of wonder.

"Wow. Oh, yeah. I see it!" She peered at it again. "Like Connor? Everything about this little guy is round, Erin. Nothing about Connor is round. I'll concede that he appears to be a recognizable member of the human species, but he doesn't look like Connor."

"Oh, you're hopeless." Erin got up, and scooped French toast out of the skillet and onto a plate, slapping them down in front of her sister.

"You'll make me fat," Cindy complained, out of reflex.

"Don't even start," Erin warned. She set the butter and maple syrup down in front of Cindy with a sharp, eloquent thud. "Miles? How many slices of French toast for you?"

"Not hungry, thanks." Miles's remote voice floated to the kitchen.

Erin fixed Cindy with a speculative gaze. Cindy's eyes slid away. She felt herself blush, for no reason she could figure. She hadn't done anything to Miles last night except give him one more spectacular opportunity to reject her. Which he had done. So thoroughly, she had finally gotten a clue. Charm, tears, even sex, nothing worked with that guy. Her usual tricks had bombed out, big-time. Looked like she was going to have to bite the bullet. Get a dignity implant, or something.

There was a rumble of male voices in the foyer, and then Connor appeared in the door to the kitchen. He looked tired and grim.

"What's up?" Erin asked.

"Nothing good," he replied. He grabbed her, kissed her.

Erin poured a cup of coffee, which he took with a sigh of thanks. He sank down into his chair, rubbing his leg. "I got there right after the cops. I parked in the alley, so I almost cut him off when he bolted."

Erin scowled. "Did you chase him?"

Con didn't meet her eyes. He sipped his coffee.

"You macho idiot!" she scolded. "You'll limp worse for a week!"

Connor sighed. "Couldn't stop myself," he said dolefully. "I got so close. But then he vaulted the Sizemores' fence, and I was fucked." He massaged his leg. "My days of chasing those bastards are over."

"So? Did you see him?" Cindy asked. "Is he Sean's guy?"

Connor shrugged. "Might be, might not. He was big, dressed in black. That describes a lot of lowlife scum who engage in B&E."

"What did he take?" Erin asked. "Did he get Mom's jewelry?"

"No. That's what worries me." Connor met her eyes. "He didn't take anything. He'd deactivated the old alarm, but he didn't cop to the SafeGuard one. He was there for twenty minutes. He didn't take a thing. I think he was hunkering down. Waiting for somebody to come home."

Erin shuddered, hunching down over her rounded belly and wrapping her hands around her coffee cup. "Why would he go after Mom, if it's Sean's guy? And not, say, us? Or Davy and Margot?"

Connor shook his head. "She's an easier target."

Cindy squirmed uncomfortably as she thought of her adventure with Porky yesterday. Her cell phone rang. She fished it out. The unfamiliar number made her belly twist. She picked it up. "Yeah?"

"Yes, is this Cindy? This is Bolivar."

"Oh! Hi, Bolivar." She padded into the living room, rummaging for pen and paper. "What's up?"

"Look, I don't want you to tell nobody I tell you this, OK? This is some bad shit here, and I don't want no part of it." He spoke so rapidly in his accented voice, she could barely make out what he was saying.

"Uh, yeah, I understand," Cindy said. "Yes, of course."

"That summer, there was three janitors. One was Fred Ayers. He died July, heart attack. There was another guy, Pat Hammond, a drunk. Died in a car accident. Then there was a Vietnamese guy, Trung. He left when the building closed, relocated up the coast. Town called Garnett. His daughter runs a grocery store there. I never talked to you. OK?"

Cindy scribbled it down on a Post-It note. "Sure," she said. "The last thing I want is to make any trouble for you. Thanks, Bolivar."

She hung up, and stared down at the square of paper. Her belly clenched. The moment had come to own up. And it wasn't going to be pretty. Everybody was going to have a cow. Right in her face.

She walked towards the hum of conversation in the kitchen, and stopped in the door, gathering her nerve. Eventually, they fell silent.

"What have you got there?" Con gestured at the Post-It note.

She swallowed. "It's a lead."

Connor looked blank. "Huh?"

"The janitor at the Colfax. I teach sax to his nephew. I, um, asked him if he knew who was on the janitorial staff of the Colfax the summer Kev died. He asked around. Two of the men died that summer, weirdly enough. This guy," she held out the paper, "is still alive. In Garnett."

Connor took the scrap of paper, frowning at it.

"Bolivar told me that when he took the job, some people told him the place was cursed," Cindy said. "I thought maybe that curse might have to do with what happened to Kev."

Connor propped the scrap of paper up against the syrup. "I'll be damned. What made you think of doing that?"

This was it. Into the valley of death rode Cynthia. She plopped her butt in the chair, breathed deep, and clenched her belly. "I, uh, thought of it yesterday, after I went to see Porky. He told me his housekeeper—"

Smash. Miles dropped the glass French press coffeepot. It cracked into several pieces, spattering scalding coffee all over the tiled floor.

"You did *what?*" Miles hissed.

"Who's Porky?" Connor's gaze flicked rapidly between them.

"Professor Beck," Cindy supplied, in a small voice. She bit her lip, wrapped her hands around her belly, and braced herself.

Miles crouched in the deafening silence, gathering up shards of glass. He kicked open the kitchen screen door, went out into the yard. Nudged the lid of the metal garbage can open with his knee.

He lifted the chunks of glass high and hurled them with all his strength into the bottom of the empty can. *Crash.*

Cindy squeaked, digging her teeth into her lip almost till she broke the skin. Oh, boy. This was bad. And it was about to get worse.

Miles stomped back into the kitchen. He leaned over her, making her cringe back. "It's a good thing I didn't fuck you last night," he said. "Or I would be that much more angry than I am right now."

There was a shocked silence. Connor and Erin exchanged shocked, wide-eyed glances. Cindy pressed her trembling lips together.

Connor turned his glare on Miles. "What the hell were you thinking, telling your business to her?" he demanded.

"He didn't," Cindy whispered. "He wouldn't. I overheard him, talking to you on the phone. I thought . . . I knew old Porky . . . so I went and asked him about Kevin. And the Midnight Project."

"Oh, Christ." Miles stormed out. The door to the study slammed.

Connor covered his eyes with his hand. "Sweet, holy Jesus. I cannot believe it. I just cannot believe it."

Erin clutched her cup, staring into her coffee as if she were afraid to speak. She wouldn't meet Cindy's eyes. No moral support there.

No support anywhere. And no one to blame but herself. As usual.

"Do you want to tell me just what the fuck you thought you were doing?" Connor's voice slashed across her rattled nerves, making her jump. "Were you, what, bored, Cin? Amusing yourself?"

"No," she said. "I just . . . I know Porky. He's a slimeball lech whose brain melts whenever he sees a pair of tits, so I just thought—"

"Thought? You?" Connor's laughter was cruelly sarcastic. "You are aware, just for starters, that going alone to the houses of lecherous slimeball men and attempting to use your tits to influence them is a really excellent way to get sexually assaulted?"

"Oh, but I didn't think that Porky would ever . . . the guy is really essentially harmless, so I thought—"

"Harmless? Yeah? And the mysterious visitor to your mother's house this morning? Does that strike you as harmless?"

Cindy's insides froze solid. "No way," she whispered. "That can't possibly have anything to do with—"

"Beck had access to your mother's address through the school records. What did you tell him? How did you present yourself?"

"I—I just said, um, that I wanted to write a book about Kev," she faltered. "I said that I'd found one of his old notebooks."

"Notebook?" Connor clapped his scarred hand over his face. "She told him she had his *notebook*. No shit they came after her. Do you have any idea what you've done?"

"Um . . . evidently not," she squeaked.

He dropped his hand. His glare made her cower back in her chair. "You've put yourself on a hit list. You just made our lives that much more complicated. What's this all about, Cindy? Do you need more attention? Did you think we needed more of a challenge?"

She shook her head. "No. I'm sorry."

Connor slammed his scarred hand down onto the table, making the dishes rattle and bump. "Sure. Aren't you always?"

"Connor? Cool it," Erin said. "Back off."

"Don't even try to defend—"

"I'm not defending anyone." Erin's voice was sharp. "But I will not tolerate one of your temper tantrums, either."

"You call this a temper tantrum?" he roared.

She glared at him, her soft lips primly compressed, arms folded over her protruding belly. "Yes," she said, in her snippiest voice.

Con limped to the door and stared out onto the back lawn, his back to them. His long, lean frame was tense, vibrating. Radiating fury.

Erin cleared her throat. "OK. Well, Cin, since the damage is done, you might as well tell us what the man said."

"Yeah, Cin. Tell us." Miles's voice came from the doorway, icy and sarcastic. "I'm twitching with curiosity as to what your tits can do."

"Oh, but I think you already know, Miles," Cindy retorted.

Miles's face reddened, but at least that shut him up. Cindy wound her fingers together and squeezed til her knuckles went white. "Well, um, he didn't tell me much. He said he didn't know Kevin well. That the Midnight Project had to do with neurological research that folded due to lack of funding. That he didn't know who funded it. That's all. It's just . . ." She hesitated, unsure if her feelings were worth sharing.

Erin made an exasperated sound. "What, Cin?"

"It was the vibes I got from him, more than anything he said," she offered hesitantly. "When he first saw me, he came on real strong—"

"Fuck, Cin," Miles burst out. "Are you insane?"

"No, just a slut," Cindy said sweetly.

"Don't get sidetracked," Con snarled. "Keep your mouth shut, Miles. So? Go on. He was sliming you, and then?"

"And then I said the name Kevin McCloud," she faltered. "And it switched off. Like, I mean, gone. I swear, the room got instantly colder. He stopped playing kneesies, stopped staring at my chest, stopped giving me compliments. It just . . . stopped. Boom, like that."

Connor kept staring out the screen door, shaking his head.

Cindy pushed doggedly on. "So, I got to wondering what would make a really turned on guy suddenly switch off?"

"Fear," Erin said quietly. "Guilt."

Connor nodded. "We'll be paying another visit to Beck. Real soon."

His tone made her shiver. Sometimes her brother-in-law scared her.

"I want to know what that janitor in Garnett has to say," she said.

"You'll have to wait to find out," Connor said. "You're going to Hawaii to meet your mom. I'll make some calls and arrange for twenty-four-hour bodyguard coverage for both of you while you're there."

Cindy's mouth flapped. "But band camp hasn't finished and I've got a wedding to play this weekend with the Rumors, and—"

"Forget band camp. Forget the Rumors. Forget anything written in your datebook. You canceled it all out when you provided an assassin with your mother's home address. Miles, get onto the computer. Now."

"Just a sec. I was just going to go have Mina tell Mindmeld to—"

"Forget Mindmeld," Con snarled. "We're working full time on this, all of us. I am sick of having assassins breathing down my family members' necks. It makes me fucking *tense*."

The savagery in Connor's voice made Cindy cringe even further

down into her chair. She felt small and stupid. "Sorry," she whispered.

It was a mistake to have spoken. Con rounded on her.

"You have two things to be grateful for. One, that your mom is in
Hawaii. Otherwise she would be dead. And two, that you stayed
with us last night. Or you'd be dead, too. Or else begging for death."

He flung open the door that led down to his basement workroom
and stomped down the stairs. Miles stood there, probably trying to
come up with his own parting slap, but he couldn't top Connor's, so
he just dove down the stairs himself, leaving her alone with Erin.

She couldn't meet her sister's eyes. She wanted to disintegrate,
on the spot. Erin never got into trouble like this. Or at least, when
she did, it was never her own fault. She was smart, brave, sensible.
All the stuff that her clueless little fluff-bunny sister wasn't.

Cindy's the beauty, Erin's the brain, her mom said, but Cindy had
seen through that crap from the start. Erin was pretty in her own
right, which meant Mom's statement was just a trick to make Cindy
feel better about being, well, less brainy. At least she was cute, right?

Small comfort now. She buried her face in her hands.

Erin cleared her throat delicately. "Cin? Um—"

"Please. Don't. You don't need to scold me, too. I got the point."

Erin's chair scraped as she got up from the table. She walked out
of the kitchen, leaving Cindy to dissolve alone.

She'd put Mom in danger? God, was it possible, that just going to
bat her eyelashes at old Porky could have unleashed all this may-
hem?

It would be a relief to everyone if she just disappeared.

She got up, with a vague notion of going up to the bathroom, to
make that French toast sloshing around in her stomach go away.

She stumbled past the studio, saw the rumpled daybed where
Miles had slept. She drifted in the door, staring at it. She'd come to
his room last night. Not a plan, just a random slutty impulse, to slide
into that narrow bed, just to see what those hard-muscled, hairy legs
would feel like, twined through hers. Just to see what he said. What
he did.

But he hadn't been there. Just his laptop, glowing in the dark.

She sank down in front of the desk, wishing she were a better person. Smarter, less self absorbed. She wished she hadn't hurt Miles's feelings so badly. That she were the kind of person that Con could respect. Maybe even like.

She blinked at the computer screen. Letters typed themselves across the page. She got a ghostly shudder til she realized the screen was open to a chat room. Someone thought they were talking to Miles.

Mindmeld666: Hey Mina u still there? Want 2 meet me and C the Haven?

She ran her eyes up the screen, scrolled up, read the previous conversation. The Haven. That mythical place she'd heard of, like the school for mutants in the X-Men movies. It was real. How totally wild.

It occurred to her. Here was a place she could go where the assassin she'd unleashed upon her luckless family would never find her. No one would. She had no idea where it was, and Mindmeld had no idea who she was. Double blind anonymity. It sounded great right now.

She could lift the dead weight from her long suffering brother-in-law. Get away from all those scowls and scolds and disapproving glares.

And just maybe even make herself slightly useful in the process.

Her mind raced, excited. She could meet this guy, check out the place, suss out the vibe. If they were up to no good, she would send an SOS to Miles, cross her fingers and take her chances, like other grown-ups who did risky things. Dad had risked his life all the time to catch bad guys, before he'd gotten wound up with that scumbag Lazar. He'd done some good along with the bad. That didn't cancel out the bad, of course, but maybe, in the end, it tilted the scales in his favor a tiny bit.

She wanted to do good mixed in with her bad, too. At least, she could try. They would worry, and be furious, but so what else was new?

If she got wiped off the face of the earth, it wasn't like the world would stop. Her mom and Erin would be sad. Miles would be relieved. The Rumors would find another sax player. Life would go on.

Chances were, Mindmeld and the Haven were exactly what the guy said they were, in which case, well, bully for her. The Haven was all about expressing dormant brain potential, right? God knows, her brain was as dormant as they came. Who knew? She might even learn something. Stranger things had happened.

She reached out, poised her fingers over the keyboard. Hesitated.

Me again. I decided. Would luv 2 meet with u. Where?

Chapter
21

"Please slow down," Liv asked him for the fourth time.

He didn't ease off the accelerator on the car Davy had rented for him. He was showing admirable restraint by staying below ninety.

"If you don't like how I'm driving, tough shit," he said. "You should have stayed with Tam, where you'd have been safe."

"I don't want to sit on the shelf like a china doll," she said. "So far I've contributed exactly nothing to the solving of our problem. Other than servicing you sexually, of course."

He gave her a sidelong glance, caught the teasing gleam in her eye. "Not that it's such a chore," she added. "It's excellent. Even so, I don't want to spend this whole investigation with my legs in the air."

He started to speak, but she cut him off. "Yes, you're the super commando whiz with a zillion languages, but I have some ideas, too."

"I never said you didn't." He slowed down as they entered Garnett. "I think you're brilliant. Which is why you should be working on Kev's drawings. I stared at those suckers until I went batshit fifteen years ago. I have no ideas left. You might see something fresh."

"I'll study them all you want. I would have studied them all night, if you hadn't kept distracting me."

"Distracting you? There's a brand new euphemism. Actually, it was you who distracted me. I remember lying helpless, flat on my back, with a sweaty, dominating bitch goddess riding me hard."

"You were hardly helpless. And that was after over an hour of being distracted by you, Sean," she pointed out. "But I suggest we don't discuss it now. This is a dangerous road, and we're almost there."

"We could pull over in the woods," he suggested hopefully. "I could distract you up against a tree. Or we could try the backseat."

"I want to talk to Trung, and so do you," she said. "Concentrate."

He appreciated her attempt to lighten the mood, but it just didn't seem right to him, wandering around under a big, open sky with Liv beside him and no squadron of Special Ops soldiers flanking her.

He didn't know how to deal with this fear. Usually he faced danger with the what-the-fuck attitude of a guy who wasn't particularly afraid of death. He was afraid for Liv, though. Pissing himself afraid.

He was nervous as an alley cat, constantly checking the rearview. Peering into the sky to check for helicopters, for fuck's sake. This was the flip side of what happened when a guy allowed himself to give a shit. It clouded his brain, made him stupid and thick and useless.

"It's not safe," he said. "I can't concentrate. I could get us killed."

She reached over, touched his thigh. "I feel safest with you."

His throat went hot and hard as a fist. "Please, don't say that." He forced the words out with difficulty. "Don't set me up."

"I'm sorry if it makes you nervous, but we got into this thing together, and we need to figure it out together."

He forestalled the rest of her bracing inspirational lecture by tossing the e-mail from Con onto her lap. "Read me the directions."

"Why should I, Mr. Photographic Memory?"

"You wanted to make yourself useful? Be useful," he growled.

They pulled up in front of a seedy-looking grocery store. Sean parked and got out, turning a slow three-sixty. He grabbed Liv and hustled towards the store. He didn't want her out in the open. Not that she was recognizable in that blond wig, but even so.

A pimply teenaged boy manned the counter. Sean gave the kid a bland smile. "I'm looking for a man named Mr. Trung."

The boy went motionless, eyes big. He scampered out of the room.

That was unnerving. He slid his arm around Liv's waist while he waited. She was so soft and warm and vibrant. It made his breath snag, his chest tighten. Awareness of her throbbed in his groin. In spite of how tense he was. In spite of the fact that he'd been at her all night. He couldn't get enough. He craved that sensuous dream world they slid into when they got it on. He could live in that world with her forever.

A middle-aged Vietnamese man came out, followed by a fortyish woman. They regarded Sean and Liv as if they were poisonous snakes.

The woman spoke mechanically, as if she'd rehearsed the words. "I am Helen Trung. This is John, my husband. My father is not here. He is gone back to Vietnam six months ago. He is not come back."

Sean looked at the blank wall of the couple's faces, tightening his arm around Liv, and followed his first impulse. "Fifteen years ago, I believe there were people who threatened Mr. Trung," he said. "These same people killed my brother, and are threatening me, and her." He nodded at Liv. "I want to find them."

The man and woman looked at each other. The woman turned back. "My father is gone. He is not come back," she repeated.

Sean waited, letting the silence speak for him.

The woman began to mutter angrily in Vietnamese. He dredged up his memories of the language that Crazy Eamon had drilled into him and his brothers, the language his father had learned in the four tours he'd served, in the war that had broken his mind.

"Please help us, if you know about these men," he said, in halting Vietnamese. "My wife is in danger from these men. We will not endanger your family. You have my word."

The couple's eyes widened. He was startled at the impulse that had moved him to identify Liv as his wife. "Girlfriend" sounded frivolous. And he didn't have a word for that concept in Vietnamese anyway. He hadn't used the language since he was twelve, when Dad died, and the word girlfriend had not entered his active vocabulary, in any language.

The word wife had such a different weight to it. "Wife" made it sound like her welfare and safety was his, by God, business. He liked it.

He was just about to give up and leave when a wheezing voice came through the curtain that divided the store from the back room.

"Bring them in to me," someone said, in Vietnamese.

They followed the woman through the curtained door, through a cramped hall and into a small kitchen. A swift glance around revealed a oneway mirror to monitor the shop outside, and a wizened guy in his late sixties, sitting at the kitchen table, smoking a cigarette. He flicked an appraising glance over Liv, and then fixed his gaze on Sean.

Sean waited patiently for the older man to speak first.

"I thought they had killed you," he said slowly.

Sean suppressed a surge of wild excitement. "Perhaps you mistake me for my twin brother," he said. "He was killed, fifteen years ago. I wish to find this killer, and avenge my brother."

Trung's face twitched. "You sound like my old great-aunt from Khanh Hung," he wheezed. His laughter turned to a coughing fit. He rapped a command to his daughter, who hurried in with a fresh pack of cigarettes. She looked like she was trying not to smile, too.

Liv nudged at him. "What's so funny?" she asked.

"Me, I guess," he said ruefully. "My backwoods yokel accent."

"Those who are curious about death often find more than they wanted to know," Trung intoned, his head wreathed with smoke.

"So be it," Sean replied quietly.

The daughter whispered furiously into her father's ear. He shook his head. "Sit down," he said to Sean, gesturing at the table.

There was only one chair, and Sean gestured for Liv to sit. The man's daughter made some explosive comment under her breath, and disappeared into the other room, coming back with folding chairs.

She crowded them into the narrow space around the table.

"Coffee," Trung said to his daughter.

The old man hunched over the table, staring at the smoke curling up between his gnarled fingers. "I never saw you," he said slowly.

"I understand." Sean shot a reassuring glance at Liv, wishing he could translate for her, but he needed all his concentration for this.

"I thought you were your brother," Trung said. "He always spoke to me courteously, in my own language, when he saw me. He was a good boy, kind and polite. I will tell you what I saw, for his sake."

"I thank you," Sean said, inclining his head.

"I worked for three weeks at that building," Trung said. "One day, I go into one of the rooms, and I find the table broken, chairs on the floor. Glass, everywhere. No one told me what had happened. I did not ask. I seldom saw the people who used the building. I did not know what they did." He finished his smoke. "One morning, I went in early." The old man stopped, his eyes far away. He groped for the cigarettes.

Sean pushed them across the table into his hand.

He shook another out, lit up. His fingers had a constant tremor. "I was going down the hall," he resumed. "The light was on in one of the rooms. I thought I had forgotten to turn it out. I opened the door."

He paused. "There was a man," he went on. "A big man. His hands were red. There was a body on the floor. He had been putting it into a plastic bag. There was blood leading to the door, where another body had been dragged before." Smoke trickled between his fingers. "Then he said, 'Since you are here, come help me. This one is heavy.'"

The room was quiet for several seconds.

"I helped him." Trung's voice was flat. "We dragged the body to a van. There were other bodies in the van. Then he pointed a gun at me, told me to clean up. I could hardly work, my hands shook so." He held up his hands. "They have not stopped shaking since that day."

"I am sorry," Sean said. "And after?"

The man sighed, papery eyelids fluttering. "He put a knife to my eye. He said, 'Leave this place. If you tell anyone, I will eat the liver of the youngest member of your family while you watch. Then I will cut out your eyes, your tongue.' He cut me, under my eye." He indicated a scar that distorted his lower eyelid. "My grandson was two years old. We left that day."

"This man spoke Vietnamese?" Sean asked.

Trung's mouth twitched. "No, he did not," he said, in English.

Sean nodded, grateful to switch from Vietnamese. "Did you see others? Did you know their names?"

Trung's smile vanished. "I had no reason to be curious before. I had many, many reasons not to be curious after."

"Could you identify the man you saw?" Sean asked.

The old man had another coughing fit. Helen Trung poured him a glass of water. He gulped it, wiped his mouth with a shaking hand. "No, you fool," he said. "Have you not heard anything that I said?"

"If you were asked to testify, you would have protection."

The man leaned across the table, touched a thickened yellow fingertip to the scab on Sean's forehead. He gestured toward the bruises on Liv's jaw. "If these people can beat a man like you and his wife, what would they do to her?" He gestured towards his daughter. "Or him?" He waved towards the teenager lurking in the door. The kid ducked out. "You are only one man. Look to your wife. Now go, please. You are not welcome to return. I want no more visits from anyone."

His wording made Sean pause. "Wait. I'm not the first person to ask you about this?"

Trung's shoulders jerked, in a short, angry shrug. "There was a reporter, soon after we came here. He wanted to write a story about boys who had disappeared at that place. I told him nothing."

"I am grateful for what you have told us, for my brother's sake," Sean said. "But who was the reporter?"

The elderly man frowned at his persistance. "I don't remember. He wrote for a big paper. Maybe the *Washingtonian*. He wanted to become famous." He snorted. "Writing in the blood of my grandchildren. Fool."

"When exactly did he come to see you?" Liv asked.

Trung gave her a startled glance. "I don't remember."

"He bought a pumpkin," Helen Trung spoke up. "To carve, for Halloween." She came forward, and began clearing the coffee cups.

Sean thanked the man, nodded to his daughter and son-in-law.

He and Liv took their leave, gulping oxygen. He bundled Liv into the car, seeing that van door yawning wide in his mind's eye, plastic-wrapped bodies piled inside. Liv was speaking, so he shook himself out of his grisly reverie. "Huh?"

She made an impatient sound. "I said, the next step is obvious."

That stumped him, being how nothing in his entire life since birth had ever been particularly obvious. "Oh, yeah? And what's that?"

Her smile was brimming with satisfaction. "We go to a library."

They stopped at the first decent-sized library they found. Liv engaged in shop talk with the librarian, and they were soon ensconced in the microfiche room and alone. He was grateful Liv was taking over, because his brain had gone into hiding.

The older editions of the newspapers were not digitally stored, and that meant doing research the hard way. But Liv scrolled through microfiche with a speed that made his eyes water, keeping up a soft patter to chill him out, make him feel included.

". . . October fifteenth through November fifteenth, and if I have no luck, I'll keep going forward. I don't think anybody ever carves a pumpkin before the middle of October."

"Yeah. Sure," he muttered distracted.

There was only one functioning microfiche reader. Just as well. All he could do was contemplate the ache in his stomach. So like, and yet so horribly unlike the ache he usually had when staring at a woman he'd been boffing for a few days. Usually by now he was casting around for a gentle, non-hurtful way to extricate himself. Though he knew, in practical terms, that no such thing existed. It always hurt.

But looking at Liv's elegant back seated at the microfiche reader, he realized it was backwards. He wanted to handcuff her to his body, he was so anxious to keep her safe. He was so afraid of failing.

His track record sucked, so far. He'd never gotten there on time to save anyone. He'd been too small, when Mom died. He still remembered his fury. He'd dreamt of saving her with some act of glorious heroism. Woken up crying because it wasn't real.

He'd been the one to find his father lying in the crushed bean vines, staring up at the sky. Eamon's body had still been warm.

Kev had been burned to ash by the time he galloped to the rescue. He'd been too late to help his older brothers when they got into their messes, too. Thank God, they'd pulled themselves out of the shit with their skins largely intact. No thanks to him.

"Sean." Liv's voice vibrated with excitement. "Take a look at this."

He leaped up, and stared over her shoulder at the screen, displaying an editorial, by Jeremy Ivers, dated November 2.

The Brain Drain: Young Geniuses Vanish.

Micky Wheeler was puzzled. Sunday morning, bright and early, his friend and classmate, Heath Frankel, a doctoral candidate in applied physics at the University of Washington, didn't show for their climbing date. Messages were unanswered. His apartment was deserted. When Micky tried to get in touch with Heath's only close relative, an uncle in San Diego, he found the uncle away on business. After days of worry, Micky went to the police and filed a missing persons report.

That same day, he heard of another acquaintance, Craig Alden, a computer engineering student at University of Washington. According to Alden's girlfriend, he'd disappeared at the same time. Coincidentally, Alden also had little family to sound the alarm. As one friend put it, "He's a genius, but he parties hard. He's probably sleeping off a bender in a hotel in Reno."

Sean skimmed the rest, pulled out his cell, and dialed Davy.

"Yeah?" Davy demanded. "So? What did the janitor say?"

"He saw bodies, blood, and a guy who threatened to eat his grandkids' livers. He doesn't want to be involved. Find me a guy named Jeremy Ivers. Reporter. Wrote for the *Washingtonian* fifteen years ago. Have Nick check on the status of these missing persons. Heath Frankel and Craig Alden." He hung up, before Davy could bust his balls.

Liv blinked up at him. "And now?"

"Now Davy does his magic thing and finds the reporter."

She looked up through her eyelashes. "I don't suppose we could do anything so mundane as get some lunch in the meantime?"

He opened his mouth to say no when his stomach growled.

The seafood restaurant Liv picked had a great view of the surf. There was something surreal about ordering food in a restaurant with a woman. Like they were playing make-believe at being a normal couple.

He felt much more anchored to the ground after his combo platter. Lobsters in drawn butter, plus smaller portions of barbecued shrimp, pan fried oysters, grilled swordfish and batter fried halibut, with baked potato and Ceasar salad for sides.

Afterwards, Liv tried to drag him down to the beach, which is where he drew the line. "No way," he told her. "We're lying low."

"Oh, come on," she coaxed. "We're just another couple on the beach. No one knows we're here. We didn't even know we were coming."

That was when he saw it, and practically broke his own neck twisting to look. A stunt kite, the kind that could pick an unwary man off his feet on a blustery day and carry him to his death. He had several himself, but this one made his heart jump out of his chest. He recognized the hypnotic mandala on it. Kev had painted that design onto their bedroom ceiling the year their father had died. He'd spent hours lying on his cot, staring at it.

He took off after it, feet churning in the sand, dragging Liv behind him, his hand clamped like an iron manacle over her slender wrist.

"Sean? Sean!" she protested. "Hey! Ouch! Where are you going?"

He couldn't answer. His heart was going to explode like a grenade. The guy flying the kite had a pointy goatee. He wore tie-dye, baggy canvas shorts. He saw Sean heading towards him. His eyes went big.

"Where did you get that kite?" Sean gasped out.

The guy's jaw flapped. "I didn't steal it—"

"I never said you did." Sean could not control the snarling edge in his voice. "Just tell me who you got it from."

The guy kept backing away to keep his kite aloft. "Uh . . . uh, at a sporting goods shop, in San Francisco. They specialize in—"

"Who designed it?" he barked out.

The kite sagged, and the guy scuttled backwards to take out the slack. "I dunno. I'd, uh, have to look at the packaging. Some outfit in the Bay Area. Hey, dude. I gotta catch this breeze. Take it easy."

He darted away, casting nervous glances back over his shoulder.

Sean stared after him, heart pounding. Liv was saying something, but he could only make out the soothing tone. He hugged her fiercely.

"It's OK, it's OK," she was murmuring, over and over.

He shook his head. It wasn't OK. He was losing it.

". . . was that all about?" she was asking him gently.

He took a deep breath, and blurted out the truth. "That kite," he said, exhausted. "That black and orange design. It's one of Kev's. He painted it on the ceiling of our bedroom when we were kids."

"Ah." Her arms tightened. She pressed her warm, soft lips against his shoulder. "And did you think that—"

"No," he broke in savagely. "I didn't think. Kev's been dead fifteen years. And I still didn't think. See? That's my problem. I never think."

"No." Her soft voice was stubborn. "You don't have a problem. You think just fine. You just think . . . differently. But you're brilliant."

The burst of laughter hurt his throat. "Brilliant. Freaking out over a kite while I'm supposed to be protecting you? Yeah, babe. Genius."

He stared into those black-fringed gray eyes. Felt sweaty-palmed hunger grip him, revving his engines. Adrenaline, shifting into lust.

She sensed it, and stiffened. "Don't you give me that look, you sex freak. You're not going to get lucky with me on a public beach in broad daylight, so get it out of your head."

He saw a solution. Made for it, towing her behind him.

"And just where do you think you're taking me?" she asked.

He jerked his chin at the building. "That hotel."

Liv stumbled into the hotel room, backing up as Sean advanced on her. She circled the bed, putting it between them. He pulled the drapes closed with a hard yank. They stared at each other in the dimness.

That predatory look in his eyes made her feel like a quivering virgin who could barely guess what was in store for her. Heart hammering, belly tightening, breathless excitement. Her lips, her breasts, her crotch, all tingled and buzzed. Her laughing, teasing, playful Sean who wheedled and coaxed and patiently, skilfully seduced her into sex was nowhere to be seen.

This man would not coax. He would take what he wanted.

He made her stammering and stupid; his big, gorgeous body, the stark beauty of his battered face. Those eyes. He could ignite desperate yearning inside her with just one smoldering look.

And it was all the more potent for the silence, the waiting.

He ripped off the shirt he'd bought that morning. She just couldn't get used to the lean, sinewy perfection of his body.

"You're wearing some of that sexy underwear under that dress?" The seductive rasp of his voice dragged over her nerves like silken fur.

She tried to reply, but her breath was too uneven. A stuttering squeak came out. She opted for a nervous nod.

"Strip," he said softly. "Show me."

She leaned down, began unbuckling the delicate ankle straps.

"No," he said. "Leave on the shoes."

She straightened, running her hands over the curves of her body, modeling the stretchy sheath dress for him. It was sexy, comfy, a blend of rust, orange and brown. The nine hundred dollar price tag that had dangled from the sleeve was a blatant provocation. "Do you like my dress?" she asked shakily. "I hope so, because you paid enough for it."

"I like it fine," he growled. "Get it off."

She took her time, tugging up the clinging skirt, in no hurry to reveal the lingerie she'd put on that morning. The thigh-high brown stockings, trimmed with brown and gilt lace that by some freak of masterful design actually stayed up. The chiffon panties, the sheer, clinging chemise. The transparent demi-bra, which hoisted her boobs up to unheard-of heights while still managing to look delicate.

She pulled the dress over her head, careful not to dislodge the wig, and shook the unfamiliar wavy locks loose over her shoulders.

"Take off the wig," he commanded.

Liv ran her fingers through the curls. "I kind of like it. Pretending to be someone else is freeing, you know? I'm just some anonymous blonde in a hotel room. Who knows which way I'll jump?"

"I've fucked lots of anonymous blondes in hotel rooms," he said. "I'm bored with it. I want to fuck you. Lose the wig. *Now.*"

She peeled the wig off, muttering under her breath as she

plucked out pins, and shook the dark mass of hair down into a kinky, tangled cloud over her back. She lifted her chin. "Happy now?"

"I'm getting there," he rasped. "Soon. I'll be happy very soon."

She backed up against the vanity. He loomed over her, stealing all the oxygen, blocking all the light. Her bottom pressed hard against the cool, varnished wood. He kicked her legs apart and stood between them. The fine chiffon snagged on the rough spots on his hands.

He sank down onto his knees in front of her, took one of her feet, caressing it in his big, warm hands before draping it over his shoulder.

"Pull the crotch away," he directed her. "Show me your pussy."

She shivered with dizzy excitement as she tugged the damp scrap of chiffon out of the way. She was so aroused, puffy and pink and wet.

He let out a long sigh of delight. "Wow. So shiny and pink. You glow. Put your finger inside your pussy. Show me how wet you are."

She bit her lip, shaking uncontrollably as she parted her labia and slid her finger inside herself. She wanted to do it seductively, like a strip tease, but she was too aroused to choreograph herself.

She pulled her finger out. Sean seized her hand, dragged her finger into his mouth. The hot, tight suction sent delicious shivers of longing through her. He pulled her finger out of his mouth.

"Hold your panties out of the way while I get my fix," he ordered.

She couldn't speak, or breathe, or do anything but watch. Her arm trembled at the strain of supporting her body while her other hand held the gusset of her panties aside so that he could have at her with his skillful, ravenous tongue.

He gripped her hips while his tongue lashed and thrust into her juicy folds, swirling around, stabbing deep, then trilling deliciously with his tongue. His position was submissive, but he was anything but. He took what was all his, laying claim to her pleasure. Every time demanding more from her, every time a deeper, wider surrender.

She quivered in his ruthless grip, pushing herself eagerly against his face. The mirror was cold and hard against her back, the edge of the vanity cut into her bottom, she didn't even know anymore which way gravity was supposed to be pulling her except closer to his hungry, sucking mouth, closer, whipping her up to a screaming intensity—

Wave after wave of sweet hot pleasure throbbed through her, lapping over every nerve.

Far too soon after that, he pulled her up onto her rubbery legs, turning her so they both faced the mirror. She caught herself with her hands on the edge of the dresser, panting through flushed, shaking red lips as he kicked off his jeans. Naked and hard and huge.

"I like the mirror," he said. "I want you to watch your own face while I fuck you. I want you to see how hot you look when you're sighing and moaning and coming. Pull your panties down, Liv."

She shook her head. "I can't do it like this, standing up," she said breathlessly. "No way. I'm . . . I'm jelly. I'll melt. I can't."

"Yes, you can." A merciless smile curved his mouth. "You will. You'll do whatever I want. You like it that way. You like me this way."

He had her, the arrogant bastard, but there was nothing she could do when he touched her like that, nuzzling the hair away from the nape of her neck while he yanked her panties halfway down her thighs.

"You jerk. You're b-being ridiculous," she forced out.

"Works for me." He tugged her arms until they folded. "Prop yourself up on your elbows. I love your ass at that angle. I can see your pussy lips kissing my cock. I like to see your legs shake. I want to fuck you until you're tottering on those heels." He kissed her nape. The scorching contact of his skin against her body made her gasp.

"I love to make you tremble," he murmured. "I love to make you weak, to make you wet." His voice was hypnotic, almost chanting. "I love to make you moan and whimper." He fitted the blunt head of his penis against her, easing it with licking, back-and-forth strokes between her labia. "Make some noise when I shove my cock into you."

He followed words with action, driving himself deep, and jolting a gasping cry out of her. He waited, motionless, until she could feel his heartbeat throbbing deep inside her against her womb, until she started moving, twitching her bottom against his groin to get him going.

He let out a soft sigh. She realized that he'd been holding his breath, afraid that he'd hurt her. Not that he would ever admit it while he was playing his macho caveman games. She wanted to smack that arrogant look off his gorgeous face, but she needed that injection of heat and energy he was giving to her even more. His deep, thrusting strokes, made her feel so female, so alive. Their eyes were locked in the mirror. He slid his hand between her leg and stroked her clit as he pumped, pulsed, stoking that yearning glow with slow, sure skill.

On and on, until still more unbearable pleasure wrenched through her.

When she looked up, he'd withdrawn from her shaking body, and was waiting, massaging his rigid member with a rough fist. He scooped his arm around her belly and spun her to face him, leaning his damp forehead against hers. His thick erection prodded her thigh, insistently.

"Make me come," he begged.

She sank to her knees, pulling him into her mouth, clutching his hips. She sucked him hard, flicking her tongue along the sensitive flare, swirling, teasing. Just a few long, voluptuous strokes, as deep as she could take him, deeper than she'd ever dreamed she could.

He exploded, pumping his salty male essence into her mouth.

He sank to his knees and wrapped his arms around her, giving her something to cling to so she wouldn't melt into a puddle.

Some minutes later, she felt him shift and move, pawing at the bedclothes. He got up, and pulled her body down on top of his on the bed. Still in her shoes and stockings. Panties wound around her thighs.

She must have slept for a while, and woke up disoriented. Her only point of reference in the world was Sean's big, hard body, holding her tightly against him. It felt so safe, so warm. But nature was calling.

He protested sleepily as she extricated herself, but she insisted, murmuring something soothing. She pried the sandals off and padded into the bathroom, took care of her business, and stood there staring at herself in the mirror for a long time. As if she'd never seen that woman before. Makeup smeared, hair big and wild and tangled. Tricked out in whorish lingerie. Private parts throbbing and hot and slippery, from hard, prolonged use. Badly in need of a wash.

She set the water running into the big tub and peeled off the underwear. The panties were a lost cause. Unwearable.

She went back to the bed and tugged Sean's arm. "I ran us a bath," she told him. "Come on."

He followed obediently enough, and climbed into the tub. She shut off the roaring tap, sudsed her hands up and started in on his chest, his muscular arms, his long, gorgeous hands. Loving the way the soapy water made his streaks and whorls of dark blond body hair so sleek, so deliciously touchable, strokable. Kissable.

His penis rose up again, indefatigable. She gazed at it, impressed. He shrugged, gave her a what-do-you-want-from-me look, and closed his eyes. Well, fine. If he could ignore it, so could she.

She stepped into the tub, sank down and wound her legs around his. "So did you get your ya-yas out? Do you feel better now?"

He opened one eye. "Fucking you definitely helped," he said blandly. "Do you mean, am I going apeshit? I don't know, Liv. That kite was a dirty trick. I swear to God, it was the exact same image."

"I believe you. But maybe Kev saw the image somewhere else."

"Our father never let us off that place, except to go to town for supplies," Sean said. "It's not likely he would have seen it elsewhere."

"That kite cannot have anything to do with Kev," she persisted gently. "You do know that, right?" She waited. "Don't you?"

"Yeah." He covered his eyes. "I just wish I could make it stop."

"Make what stop?"

"This feeling." He shook his head. "It was a twin thing. When one of us was in trouble, the other one knew it. It was like an itch, inside my mind. Fire ants, crawling through my nerves."

"Brr," she murmured. "Sounds uncomfortable."

"Yeah. Anyhow, you'd figure that when he died, the feeling would die with him, right?"

She felt a shivery rush of goose bumps. "You mean . . . it didn't?"

He closed his eyes, shook his head. "I feel it all the time. Not so much now as in the beginning. It drove me stark raving nuts the first few years. I had to distract myself by pulling crazy shit like jumping out of airplanes, blowing up buildings, getting tortured by warlords. That was what it took." He leaned back against the tub, staring up at the ceiling. "They say people still feel pain and itching in limbs that have been amputated. Phantom pain. I guess that's what I've got."

"I'm sorry it hurts, but I envy you. I have good friends, but I've never been as close to anyone as what you're describing."

A faint frown creased his brow. "Guess what? You are now, babe."

She blinked at him. "Hmm?"

"How do you think I knew to come after you? I woke out of a sound sleep full of adrenaline right before T-Rex stopped your car."

Her mouth opened, closed, opened again. "Ah—I—"

"Get used to it." There was a possessive gleam in his eyes. "You can't hide anything from me."

"I have nothing to hide," she said. "Not from you. You always get uptight when I say things like this, but that makes me feel . . . safe."

Predictably, his smile faded. "Oh, God. Don't jinx me, babe."

"Why are you so twitchy about that?" she asked crabbily. "I couldn't imagine a guy more protective or vigilant or heroic than you."

"My father was, too," he said. "But my mom wasn't safe with him."

"Tell me."

"He didn't hit her. Fuck, no. Dad would sooner have drowned himself than hit a woman. She was everything to him. But he fucked up. Kept her up there, pregnant, in the winter. Impassable roads. She paid the price."

Tears stung her eyes. She blinked them away. "That's terribly sad, but I don't see what that has to do with us," she said cautiously.

"Look at us, Liv. I'm doing the same thing to you that my dad did to her. I whisked you away, hid you, decided I'm the only one on earth who can keep you safe. Where have I heard this song before?"

She shook her head. "No. It's not like that."

He shrugged. "I'm scared shitless those bastards will get you if you go back to your folks. I don't think the cops have the resources to protect you, either. They're spread too thin to intercept anybody

as focused as T-Rex. That's my gut instinct, but I can't trust it completely. Not after watching what happened to my dad."

"You put all the responsibility for what happened on your dad,"
she said. "What about your mom? Did she have any opinions?"

His shrug was eloquent. "You didn't know my dad."

"No, but I know you. Besides, you're my responsibility now,
too."

His eyes widened. "Hell of a responsibility. Ask my brothers."

"High maintenance," she teased. "Like a Ferrari. Or a fighter
jet."

"Speaking of high maintenance . . ." He leaned forward, and
grasped her hips, pulling until she straddled him. He prodded the
head of his penis against her, and let her sink down, enveloping him.
"I've got a part that needs some focused attention."

She wiggled in his grasp, giggling. "But I'm exhausted."

"So rest." A lazy grin made his dimple deepen. "You don't have
to do a thing. But if we're going to lie around reminiscing and telling
secrets, I'd just as soon do it with my cock shoved way up inside
you."

She wiggled around him. "You can converse in this condition?"

"Best condition there is. Hugged and kissed by the princess's
tight, cushy pussy. I can't believe how good it feels."

"I can't think a coherent thought," she confessed, shivering.

"So don't think." Sean jerked her down so her breasts dangled in
his face. Her hair created a mysterious perfumed veil around them.
He blew a lock of hair out of his mouth. "This is all your fault, you
know."

She giggled at his hot, tickling mouth. "Oh, yeah? How is that?"

"You keep saying sweet things to me." He suckled her nipple
into his mouth, swirling and pulling. "Makes my dick hard."

"Get real. You get equally hard when I scream and pound on you."

He pondered that. "Well, hell. That's true," he said, in a tone of
mock discovery. "I'll be damned. That's remarkable. Angle yourself
so your clit's rubbing up against my . . . yeah. Just like that. Perfect.
Ah."

She gave in, moving over him, stretched taut between two poles of melting pleasure, the greedy suckling of his mouth against her breasts, and his thick phallus massaging inside her, with that slow, skillful glide and plunge. Her hair fanned out in floating clouds of suds. There was no sounds but the lap and splash and slosh of the water, the wet sounds of his suckling mouth against her, her gasping breaths.

The climax was long, and liquid, and endlessly lovely.

When her eyes fluttered open, he pulled her up and out of the tub, scooped her up into his arms. She clutched his shoulders with a squeak. She just couldn't get used to this being swept up routine.

He carried her into the other room and laid her down on the rumpled bed, dripping wet. He spread her legs, smoothed the clinging wet hair back off her face. "I want to fill you up with my come."

She tried to speak. The jerky hiccups were shaking her apart.

"Shake your head, if you don't want it." His voice was raw.

She caressed his face. He made a harsh sound, and let go of his control. Oh, God, she loved it when he went wild, when the tendons on his neck stood out, when he lost himself, ramming into her with deep, hard strokes that satisfied some crazy savage primordial urge.

The explosive rush of life-giving delight fused them together.

When she started noticing things again, she saw him rolling something small between his fingers. It glittered and flashed.

She peered at it. "Your earring," she said. "Did it fall out?"

He held it out to her. "It's yours."

She shrank back. "Oh, no. I've never seen you without it."

He shook his head. "No, it's always been yours. I bought this stone for you fifteen years ago."

She gaped, the protest she was about to make evaporating.

"I spent every dime I made that summer to buy it," he said. "It was the biggest one I could afford. I opted for just the stone. Anything I could have gotten with a setting would have been just a pinprick of a thing." His eyes slid away. "I know it's not a huge rock, but it's good quality." He pushed her wet hair back, fastened it into her earlobe.

Desperate questions welled up. She was afraid to let them out. Was it like an engagement ring? Was it just a sweet postcoital impulse?

She opened her mouth to ask, when his cell phone rang.

He flicked it open and barked into it. "You got something? . . . Grissom? Yeah, I know it. What's the address? . . . I'm on it. Later."

He clicked the phone shut. His eyes had focused, sharp and cool. "Get dressed, princess," he said. "Davy's found our reporter."

Chapter 22

The trade of journalism had not been prosperous for Jeremy Ivers. That was Sean's first impression when they pulled up in front of the chain-link fence that surrounded a shabby single-wide trailer home.

Two ferocious pit bulls were chained to a metal pole in the center of the yard. They snarled and lunged when Sean and Liv got out of the car. A garbage pail had been overturned long ago, and its contents were becoming one with the lawn, which had been dug up and excreted upon until it was just a few diseased patches of brownish yellow stubble.

The length of the chain and the ferocity of the dogs made it impossible to approach the door, but the dogs served as a doorbell, so he just twined his fingers through Liv's and waited. He lifted up the heavy mass of damp dark hair to admire the diamond winking in her ear. She was so damn pretty. He wanted to drape her with jewels.

It pleased him, to see that rock on her. It was about fucking time.

The screen door of the house squeaked. The man who came out was thin, eyes hollow and reddened. What hair there was on his head was greasy and straggling. His jeans hung on him, his limp T shirt was stained and grayish. He hacked, spat. "What do you want?"

"Are you Jeremy Ivers?" Sean asked. "The reporter?"

The man's eyes bulged. "Who wants to know?"

"My name is Sean McCloud. I wanted to ask you about an article you wrote for the *Washingtonian*, fifteen years ago."

Jeremy Ivers had begun shaking his head before Sean finished speaking. He shrank in the door like a turtle retracting its head into its shell. "I never wrote any article," he said. "You got the wrong guy. I'm not a reporter. I don't know what you're talking about. Go away."

The door was closing, the dogs flinging themselves frantically against their chains, barking madly with big, hoarse, hollow voices.

Sean pitched his voice to punch through the noise. "I'm going to kill those murdering sons of bitches," he said.

The door stopped closing. It opened a crack. Ivers's eye appeared.

"What murdering sons of bitches?" he called out.

"The ones that did this to you." Sean gestured at the yard, the dogs, the garbage. The festering despair that permeated the place.

Ivers opened the door and stepped out onto the tiny crooked porch. "What the fuck do you know about what they did to me?"

Sean thought about the nightmares, about staring at the ceiling with a hole in his belly every four AM for fifteen years. About what he had done to Liv, in the jail. "They did it to me, too."

Ivers looked him over, slowly, and snorted. "Yeah. Sure they did."

"I mean to rip those murdering motherfuckers limb from limb for what they did." He held the man's gaze. "But I need your help to do it."

Ivers rubbed his stubbly face. He looked lost. "I can't help you with anything," he said. "I'm no good to anyone anymore."

"We'll see," Sean said. "Please. Let us come in and talk."

Ivers shrugged. "Aw, what the fuck." He shuffled down the steps, and grabbed the dogs' collars. "Get inside. I'll hold them until you're in."

The interior of Ivers's home was much like the exterior. Dingy, reeking, with tattered thrift store furniture, an unbroken mass of clutter. Every surface was coated with a skim of oily dust and grime. There was a sour-sweet smell of spilled beer, dog urine and pot smoke.

Liv nudged a heap of junk mail gingerly off the cleanest looking sofa cushion, and perched right on the edge. Sean sat next to her.

Ivers shuffled in, and stared at them for a moment, as if two space aliens had sat down on his couch. "Uh, want a beer?"

He fetched himself one when they declined, and fell down with a crinkle onto a sliding heap of magazines on his sofa. He popped open his beer, glugged half of it down, and wiped his mouth. "So. What have you deluded yourself into thinking that I can do for you?"

"You wrote this article, fifteen years ago," Sean said, holding up the photocopy. "I just want you to tell me what happened afterwards."

Ivers closed his eyes, shook his head. His larynx bobbed in his lean, stubbly throat. "Look, you've got to understand. They can do what they want to me, I don't give a fuck. But I've got kids."

"I won't put your kids in danger," Sean promised quietly.

Ivers rubbed his wet, trembling mouth. "I was working on a follow-up article," he said. "I'd poked around, found two more names. One kid from Washington State, the other from Evergreen."

"How did you find out about the Colfax Building?"

"Ah. That was a stroke of luck." He laughed. "Good or bad, depends on how you look at it. If I hadn't talked to Pammy, maybe I'd still have a family. Maybe I'd still be a man. Not a piece of shit."

"Tell us about Pammy," Sean suggested gently. He had practice steering disturbed people gently away from the dead-end grooves in their minds, after all those years of trying to manage Crazy Eamon.

"She was the girlfriend of one of the missing boys. Craig Alden. She told me that he'd been doing drug experiments, getting paid good money for it, three hundred bucks a pop. She was into mind-expanding stuff like that, so he brought her up to the Colfax to see if he could sign her up. Double their money. To support her other drug habit, I expect."

"And?" Liv prompted. "Did he? Did she?"

"No," Ivers said. "The guy running the experiments didn't want

Pammy. She said the guy was pissed at Craig for bringing her there. Not surprising. She was a meth head. I wouldn't have wanted her, either."

"Did she remember the doctor's name?" Sean asked.

Ivers let out a derisive grunt. "Like it could be that easy. All she remembered was that he was tall, dark and handsome. Helpful, huh?"

Sean shrugged. "It narrows it down a little. Go on."

"So a couple weeks later, Craig didn't come home. She figured he'd gotten bored, run off with some girl. I was curious at that point, so I followed up. The building was closed. I tracked down the janitor who'd worked there, but he didn't know anything. I kept digging, found out the building was owned by Flaxon Industries. Big pharmaceutical company. I tracked down the local company rep. Guy told me there had never been any drug trials conducted there to his knowledge, so I figured Pammy had been dropping acid. But that night . . ." He stopped, rubbed his mouth. "Jesus," he muttered. "I'm slitting my own throat."

"No, you're not," Sean said patiently. "What happened that night?"

Ivers covered his eyes. "I woke up," he rasped. "A guy with a mask was holding a knife to my wife's throat. He told me I was going to stop writing articles, stop asking questions, or he'd cut her in front of me. Then he'd start in on my kids. Make it look like I'd done it. Three and six years old, sleeping down the hall. Those sweet, innocent little kids."

Liv leaned forward and put her hand on the guy's arm, making him jump. "I know how you felt," she said.

He yanked his arm away. "How would you know?"

"He had that knife at my throat two days ago." She nodded towards Sean. "He saved me. Or I'd be in a hole in the ground now."

Ivers's sharp laugh sounded bitter. "Whoop-de-doo for you, honey. Got you a big macho man, huh? My wife wasn't so lucky. She was gone in less than a month. With the kids. Bye bye to the ball-less wonder."

"I'm sorry," Liv said quietly.

"She married again," he said dully. "The kids have her husband's name. The only thing I can do for them is stay away. I haven't seen my kids in ten years." Ivers sagged, putting his face in his hands.

Sean waited for Ivers to get his boozy weeping under control, and pressed on. "Do you remember the name of the Flaxon rep?"

Ivers mopped his face, gulping snot. "Charles Parrish. But I don't recommend calling. Unless you want a nighttime visit from Godzilla."

Sean hesitated a couple of beats. "Bring him on," he said.

Ivers stared at him. "Fuck you," he said. "I hope you get those filthy bastards. But fuck you anyhow." He glanced at Liv. "No offense."

"None taken," she said.

Ivers got up, and yanked the door open. "It's time for you to take your extra load of testosterone and get lost," he said. "I'll hold the dogs."

Sean nodded, unoffended. The guy's shame and anger made perfect sense to him. He and Liv got through the gate, but he stopped before getting into the car. "Hey," he said. "If I get lucky and nail those guys, I'll contact you. Give you the all clear. You can go find your kids."

Ivers stared at him, his mouth turned down. "Too late," he said. "I'm wasted now. I'm all fucked up. They're better off without me now."

"It's not too late." He had no idea where the intensity in his voice came from. "Those bastards put it to you for fifteen years. Do not bend over and let them do it to you again. It's not too goddamn late."

He got into the car, started it up. Ivers stood like a statue in the yard, the dogs snapping and lunging on their chains. His big, hollow eyes followed them as the car pulled down the street.

Liv was startled to see Nick at the bar, along with Sean's brother Davy, when they walked into Tam's kitchen.

"What's with him?" Sean asked Tam. "What, haven't you gotten that thermal imager installed yet?"

Tam grunted sourly. "He knows where I live. The only remedy

now is to put him through the woodchipper and feed him to the pigs."

Nick rolled his eyes. "You don't keep pigs. You don't chip wood, either. And you need to do something about that irrational hostility."

"Where's Con?" Sean asked hastily, before the bristling Tam could gather herself for a cutting reply.

Davy made a disgusted sound. "Scouring the streets for Cindy. He bawled her out for jumping into this investigation. She got her feelings hurt. Pried the beacon out of her phone and skipped out."

"Oh, man." Sean winced. "She picked a tasty time for it."

Davy shook his head. "Glad it's not my job to run herd on that hellcat. Poor bastard. What the hell have you guys been doing all day?"

"That's easy," Tam broke in. "She left this morning with a blond wig, and unfortunate panty lines. I meant to tell you to go with the thong, but it slipped my mind." She lifted up the mass of Liv's tangled hair. "She comes back with smeared mascara, whisker burn, no wig, and no panty lines." She winked. "You do the math, gentlemen."

Sean made a growling sound, not unlike Ivers's chained dogs. Liv blushed fiery hot, and Davy spat out some incomprehensible epithet.

"Sean, do you think you could possibly redirect some small percentage of your blood flow from your dick back to your brain?" he snarled. "I know sex is your number one coping mechanism, but—"

"Shut up, Davy," Sean broke in. "Do you want to hear about the janitor and the reporter, or do you want to waste time giving me shit?"

Davy subsided, his face furrowed with concentration as Sean recounted the details of their two interviews. He passed the photocopy of the article to his brother. Tam and Nick read it over his shoulder.

"I checked those names in the missing persons database," Nick said. "Just like Ivers said. All male, all between the ages of nineteen and twenty-three. None have ever been found. None had much family. Some reports were filed weeks later. No one noticed they were gone 'til the rent came due. There were no prints on that Beretta, other than hers and a couple of yours. Guy must have wiped it down."

"He was wearing leather gloves," Liv said.

There was a chilled silence. Sean took a deep breath and shook himself. "So," he muttered. "What's next?"

Davy steepled his hands together. "We squeeze Beck again. Cindy rattled him when she mentioned Kev, Con said. That makes me think we should go rattle him again. Harder. See what falls out."

"Beck? You mean that chemistry professor that Kev—"

"Was teaching for, yeah. We talked to him fifteen years ago. You were still locked in the drunk tank," Davy said. "He was worse than useless. A total zero. Makes you wonder how he became head of the chemistry department. You'd think a functioning brain would be a prerequisite." He smiled thinly. "Let's go ask him how he pulled it off."

"We need to track down Charles Parrish," Sean said. "Ivers's contact with him is what touched off the hit man who attacked him."

"Let's leave for Endicott Falls tonight," Liv said. "Then we can go see this guy first thing in the morning."

Sean turned on her. "We? What's this 'we' business? You're staying right here. I thought we had an understanding."

"Ah, no," Liv said delicately. "I want to—"

"You are staying right here, and that is fucking final."

Everyone flinched. Davy cleared his throat. "Ah, could you guys maybe have this particular conversation in private?"

"Forget it, Liv." Sean ignored his brother completely, still staring into her eyes. "Just get it out of your head."

Nick broke in. "Weird, how they were all science geeks, huh? And all short on family. So sad to be all alone in the world."

"The guy must have been licking his chops when he met Kev," Davy said. "Crazy brilliant, no parents, no money. But he didn't factor us in. Maybe Kev didn't even tell him he had brothers."

"Why should he factor us in?" Sean said. "McCloud boys are easy to manage. Just tell them their brother went bonkers, and they'll fall right into line. Yes, sir. No, sir. Anything you say, sir."

"Hey." Davy's face hardened with anger. "Cool it, punk."

"I did," Sean replied, his voice bitter. "I did cool it, and it was a bad call, Davy. I should have known. I should have stayed hot."

"What difference does it make now?" Davy roared. "If we set it straight now or then? Kev's gone. Timing is nothing to a dead man."

"But I'm not dead," Sean spat back. "I've been playing dead for fifteen years. I'm fucking sick to death of it."

Davy shot to his feet. Nick backed away from the bar, keeping a wary distance. "Watch it, boys," Tam said, her voice a warning hiss.

"Stop it right now, both of you." Liv's voice was not loud, but its crystalline crispness sliced right through the red haze in the room.

Everyone looked at her, startled into silence. She glared at Sean. "This carrying on is not useful," she told him sternly. "Not to Kev, and not to you. Control yourself."

Sean flinched. He got up, and stomped out of the room.

Davy just stared at Liv. "I've been lecturing that spaz since he was born," he said. "How come I never get that kind of results?"

"Cunt power," Tamara purred.

Nick snorted with smothered laughter. Tamara turned her tilted amber eyes on Liv. "Our business is concluded. If I were you, I'd go after him and remind him that you're not wearing any panties. Turbocharged sex is so much more fun than a screaming argument. And men are so much more reasonable when they've just ejaculated. Try it."

Liv felt her hackles rise. "You are out of line, Tam."

Tam's laughter was deep and throaty. "That's high praise, for me."

Liv slammed the door as she left the room. She was appalled with herself as she followed in Sean's footsteps. And after her snarky little lecture to Sean too. She'd never slammed a door in her life.

She found him in the north tower, looking up at the last faint bit of twilight in the skylight above. His body radiated suppressed emotion.

She hesitated, intimidated, and forced her spine to stiffen. This hot-headed jerk was her man, and she'd be damned if she'd tippy-toe around him like a scared little girl. That was no sort of life.

She slid her arms around his waist from behind. "Sean—"

"You're staying right here," he snarled.

"Ah, yes," she murmued. "Right here. While Vadim Zhoglo and Daddy Novak with their testicle tongs comb the globe for my prickly hostess. Really safe, Sean."

His muscles jerked under her hand. "It's the best place I know of."

"If you don't want me to participate, I'll just take my chances with the police. I'm sure they'll be interested to know what we've been doing."

He rounded on her with violent swiftness. "You can't tell them what we did today. Not unless you want to read about Ivers and the Trung family in the obit pages. I promised them."

"OK," she said quietly. "I won't tell anyone. Just let me go with you. I helped you today. And I could help again."

"Oh, you helped. You fulfilled one of my fantasies. The Endicotts' perfect china doll daughter, on her knees. Sucking my dick."

She flinched, hurt clouding her mind, but something behind it whispered to her in a constant, steadying stream. Reminding her of the look in his eyes when he made love to her. The diamond in her ear. Intimacy like she'd never imagined it. He could throw up all the smoke screens he wanted, and she would see right through them.

"You can be as nasty and ugly as you like." Her voice was small, but steady. "I won't fall for it. Not a second time."

"Oh no?"

"No. You're in my head. You can't lie to me. I know you, Sean."

"You think so?" He backed her up to the wall. She stumbled as her high heels caught in the weave of the rug. Her back hit the wall.

"You think you know me?" His voice was a hiss of menace. "You have no idea of the shit I've done, the men I've killed, the women I've screwed, the things I've been paid to do. I fucked your brains out, so you think that means you know me? I've fucked a lot of girls' brains out. They'd run screaming if they knew me."

She shook her head. "It's not working. All I hear is blah di dah. Sean's having a tantrum. Freaking out because he can't get his way."

He shook his head, unbelieving. "Can't get my way," he repeated. "What are you going to do, Liv? Give me a lollipop to shut me up?"

"That's what Tam suggested," she said.

"The day you take Tam's advice will be a scary day for you, babe."

"I'm getting used to scary days. They're the new norm." She grabbed her skirt, and tugged it up, high enough to see her nakedness. The puff of hair between her thighs. "Want a lollipop, Sean?"

Sean stared at her body. His hand reached out, as if of its own volition, cupping her. His finger pressed against the damp, hot seam hidden in the silky curls. "Might work," he said hoarsely, fingers curling to grip her mound. "But don't jerk me around. My sense of humor's gone AWOL."

"Then don't set yourself up for it," she retorted. "Silly jerk."

The liquid rush of her arousal moistened his hand. His growl vibrated through her body as he thrust his fingers inside her. "Fine, babe." His breath was hot against her throat as he wrenched open his jeans and hoisted her against the wall. "Don't come crying to me if you don't like it. You begged for it. You drove me to it."

"I'll beg. I'll do what I have to do. Take what I have to take."

He drove inside. She knew that some part of him wanted to punish her, but his body wouldn't let him. They were too attuned to each other, every clutch and stroke, every thrill of pleasure. He couldn't make good on his foolish threats. He could do nothing but pleasure her. She wrapped her arms around him.

Hell and heaven broke loose together.

She clung to him, digging her nails into his shoulders. The jolting rhythm might have seemed violent if it hadn't been precisely what her body craved, to drive her to that magic place where boundaries melted, where lies became meaningless. She felt his need, his desperation, his fear. She wanted to soothe him, heal him, but all she could do was cling to him, offer up all her yielding sweetness.

His climax wrenched through him. She could not distinguish his pleasure from her own. It melted her down. She knew the second Sean registered her weeping, and the next second, when he misinterpreted it.

He pulled out, stepped away. She slid down the wall and thudded onto her bottom, stockinged legs splayed wide. She curled her legs up.

It shattered her, how huge this feeling was. How small she felt in its grip. How completely her happiness hung on the thinnest of threads.

He tilted her face up. "When I get these guys, and rip their guts out, you'll be free to leave. Until then, you stay where I put you. Nod if you understand me."

She nodded. He got to his feet, and headed for the door.

"I'm not a ch-china doll, Sean," she forced out, voice shaking.

He paused. "That doesn't mean you're not breakable."

The door closed. His footsteps faded down the stairs.

Chapter
23

"Run it all by me one more time," Sean said, tapping his fingers against the armrest console in a frantic staccato rhythm.

"Pay attention. Don't make me repeat myself like a fucking idiot," Davy growled. "And stop the finger drumming thing. Drives me nuts."

"He had a fight with his girlfriend," Miles said laconically.

"He must have gone without sex for more than twelve hours," Con said. "Didn't she take Tam's advice and show you her muff last night?"

Sean's hand shot out, fastened over Con's throat, bonking his brother's head back against the car window, hard. "Ow! Jesus, Sean!"

"Talk about her like that, and I'll break your bad leg. Again."

Con blinked, wide eyed. "You'd do that to a pathetic crip who spent the night driving all over Seattle looking for Erin's goofy sister?"

"Try me," Sean said, pitiless.

He took his hand away, ignoring as his brothers whistled and exchanged glances. He rubbed his sore neck, stiff from a night on a cheap motel mattress, to say nothing of the bruises and contusions.

"Sorry," Con said, sounding anything but. "It's just a shock. You never minded me going off about your babe du jour before, so I—"

"She's not my babe du jour. I don't want to discuss my woman problems. I want to talk about this investigation. If you don't mind."

"Huh. You're starting to sound like Dad. Humor-challenged."

"Bite your tongue," Sean said. "Tell me about Charles Parrish."

Miles spoke up. "All I could find out last night was that he rose in the ranks of Flaxon Industries for a few years, then left and formed the Helix Group. Pharmaceuticals, biotechnology, nanotechnology, what have you."

"Corporate headquarters are in Olympia. We squeeze Beck, and then drive down there," Davy said. "We have an appointment at noon."

"An appointment?" Sean was startled. "You silver-tongued son of a bitch. Who are we today? Zillionaires with scads of money to invest?"

Davy grinned. "I'm the zillionaire. You guys are just henchmen. We have to pretty up after we go to Beck's. I had Miles go to your condo and pick some pimp suits out of your closet for you guys."

"Which reminds me," Miles piped up. "Somebody's been through your place. They took your hard drive."

Davy swiveled back, glanced at him. "Did you have a password?"

"Uh . . . yeah," Sean said.

Davy's eyes narrowed at his tone. "Don't tell me. Let me guess. It was something stupid and obvious. Like Olivia, right?"

Sean didn't answer, abashed. Miles answered for him. "Right."

"Whatever. It's the least of our worries right now," Connor said.

"Speaking of worries, who's guarding the ladies?" Sean asked.

"Seth's on it," Davy said. "He's driving them all over Seattle today, and feeling very sorry for himself."

"They should be up at Stone Island," Sean said, scowling.

"Yeah, but Cindy's run off, and Erin didn't want to leave town without her," Con said. "Plus, Margot had to drop off a big proposal, and Raine had a meeting with the board of directors for Lazar."

"Here it is," Davy said, pulling over on the posh, treelined avenue.

They got out of the car, gazed at the house.

"What a godawful eyesore," Con commented.

"Must have cost a shitload of money," Davy said. "Who would have thought that academia was so profitable?"

The uniformed Latina lady who answered the door gave them a suspicious frown. "Can I help you?"

"We'd like to speak to Professor Beck," Sean said.

Her dark eyes narrowed. "Who are you?"

Davy opened his mouth to reply. Sean cut in, on impulse. "A ghost from his past," he said. "Tell him that."

The door slammed. Davy and Con and Miles stared at him, open-mouthed. "That's no way to get in the door," Davy pointed out.

Sean looked at the ornate, carved monstrosity of a door. "Oh, I'll get in there," he said softly. "If I have to shoot off the hinges."

Con gave him a quelling look. "It's early in the day for you to be having one of your meltdowns. Keep it together."

The door opened just a crack, the security chain fastened across it, and the lady's face peeked through. "I'm sorry, but the professor doesn't have no interest in talking to ghosts. Have a good day."

"Step back from the door, ma'am," Sean said.

The whip crack in his voice sent her darting back. Sean spun around and flung up his leg in a vicious back kick that broke the chain and sent the door flying open to crash against the wall.

The lady shrieked and cowered against the opposite wall. Davy and Con gave each other despairing glances, and followed him on in.

"What is the meaning of this?" A portly, balding man appeared at the end of the foyer, his face red with fury.

Sean walked towards him, arms out as if he were going to give the man a bear hug. "Hey, Professor. Remember me?"

The man staggered back, put his hand to his throat. His face went an ashy gray. Sweat popped out on his brow. "How . . . who . . ."

"What?" Sean put on a mock wounded expression. "Don't you like visits from the Great Beyond? Aren't you happy to see me?"

Beck made a choking sound. Put his hand to the wall for support.

"Shut up, Sean," Davy muttered. "We won't learn anything if the guy croaks from fright."

Beck's eyes darted back and forth between them. He sagged with relief. "Sean? Oh."

"Yes," Sean said. "Kev's identical twin. Kev's very pissed off, very fed-up identical twin. Good to meet you, Beck."

"Professor, I call the police for you." The Latina lady's voice rang out. She clutched the phone in one hand, a fireplace poker in the other.

Wow. That was one tough lady. Beck didn't deserve her.

He turned to Beck. "I suggest you stop her. Or I'll be forced to tell them everything I know about the murder of Kevin McCloud, and the Midnight Project. And you will go down, Professor. In flames."

It was a wild gamble, but Sidney Beck's eyes darted around. He moistened his trembling lips with his tongue. "Ah, don't make that call, Emiliana. These gentlemen and I just need to have a talk."

She scowled, not buying it. "I call the police anyhow."

"No! I don't want to waste the police department's valuable time, and really, it's fine. Why don't you take the rest of the day off? At double time and a half wages. My apology for the unpleasantness."

Emiliana muttered under her breath in Spanish, yanked open a wall closet, grabbed out a large patent leather purse and a sweater.

She elbowed her way out between Miles and Con, not gently, and pulled the door shut behind her with a resounding slam.

Beck crossed his arms across his chest, still blinking quickly. "So who's been telling you lies about this so-called Midnight Project?"

"Nobody," Sean said quietly. "We didn't have any proof at all that you were involved. Until now, that is. It was just a bluff. Worked, huh?"

Beck blinked frantically.

Sean took a step closer. "Let's cut right to it. Tell us everything."

"About, ah, what?" Beck sidled back against the wall.

Davy blocked him. "Kev, the Midnight Project, the Colfax Building, drug experiments. Flaxon. Charles Parrish. Helix. Missing college kids. Body bags."

Beck shook his head. "I don't know. About any of it. I swear."

"No? Then why didn't you let Emiliana call the cops?" Sean leaned closer and sniffed, smelling fresh alcohol on the man's breath. "You've been at the hard stuff, bright and early. Trying to calm the demons?"

Beck's eyes watered. "I don't know what on earth you're talking about. Please, keep your distance."

Thud, rattle, the letter slot emitted a slice of sunlight. A wad of envelopes was shoved through. They scattered around Miles's feet. Miles picked up a handful of envelopes, sorted through them. "You guys." His voice vibrated with excitement. "This is from the Helix Group."

Davy twitched it out of Miles's hand and ripped it open.

"Hey! That's my private correspondence!" Beck squawked.

Davy leafed through the papers. "From a guy who knows nothing about Helix, you own a lot of stock in it."

"My financial affairs are none of your business!" Beck blustered.

"Is that where you got the money? From Helix?" Con wandered down the corridor, peering into the next room. "Wow. Check out this solarium, guys. That's a thirty-foot plate glass window. Pricey."

"Yeah. How about that money? We're curious, Beck," Sean said. "Do you have family money? Or is this Helix money?"

"Helix has nothing to do with your brother." Beck's voice shook. "Helix has only existed for ten years, and it's only become a prominent player in the last eight. Poor Kevin has been gone for, how long now?"

"Fifteen years, five days and approximately six hours," Sean said.

Beck's mouth worked. "Ah. Just so. I'm very sorry for your loss, Mr. McCloud, but I think that you should be talking to a qualified psychotherapist about these issues, not to me. I'm sorry I can't help—"

"Where did the money come from, Beck?" Connor repeated. He strolled back from the solarium. "This is a five million dollar home."

"I hardly think that is an appropriate—mmph!"

Sean gripped the guy's throat, shoving him against the wall. Not hard enough to throttle him, but hard enough to shut him up.

"Appropriate?" he hissed. "Nah. Hit men, secret drug experiments, bloated, self-interested slugs sitting on top of piles of money, my twin brother's charred body—things like that make me mad. So talk to us. Give us names, dates, addresses. Or else . . ." He squeezed, and Beck let out a strangled squeak. "I move on. To Plan B."

Beck's mouth worked, soundlessly. Sean eased up. "That better?"

Beck coughed. Tears leaked out of his eyes. "I just know . . . a name. It might not even be his real name. And it may have nothing to do with this."

"Spit it out, Beck."

"I gave his number to Kevin," Beck babbled. "He needed intelligent research subjects. There was a fee involved. I knew Kevin needed cash, so I passed on the name. That's all. I swear, that's all I ever did."

"Except for keeping your mouth shut when people started dying?" Sean snarled. "Except for raking in the dough for decades afterwards? You're nothing but a turd with arms and legs, Beck. You make me sick."

"The name, Beck," Connor reminded him.

Beck started to sob. "O-O-Osterman," he stammered.

"Where does he operate?" Davy asked.

Beck shook his head in frantic denial. "As God is my witness, I have no idea. It's been fifteen years since I spoke to him, and I—"

"Bullshit. You talked to him the day before yesterday, to sic a hit man on my wife's sister. Give us the number you called," Con said.

Beck kept shaking his head. His body shook with sobs. A puddle of urine pooled around one of his shoes on the gleaming blond parquet.

Sean sighed, and dropped him. The guy fell to the floor with a heavy plop, like an overripe fruit. He wept noisily, covering his face.

"This one's played out," Sean said wearily. "Let's go."

Davy got the SUV in gear and accelerated away from that place. "Christ, that was depressing," Connor muttered.

Davy shot a furious glance back at Sean. "You pushed him too hard. You need to use a lighter touch. Unless you're practicing up for when you get tossed into a maximum security prison, of course."

Sean was too lost in thought to respond. "Drunk off his ass, at nine AM," he mused. "He smelled like fear. I scared him bad, but he still held back. Which means that this Osterman guy scares him worse."

Miles swiveled around, his eyes big. "What was Plan B?"

Sean looked at him blankly. "Huh?"

"You told Beck that if he didn't give you a name, you were moving on to Plan B. What were you going to do to him?"

Sean grimaced. Hard-core intimidation was tense, nasty work. He didn't really have the stomach for it. "Fucked if I know," he grumbled. "I don't even have a Plan A, let alone B. Let's get gussied up for Parrish."

Cindy gulped her coffee, and tried again to plow through an article about general plane wave solutions to sound wave equations in *Sound Spectrum Journal,* an egghead rag if she'd ever saw one. She'd even bought some intellectual horn-rimmed glasses, but she longed for a *Marie Claire.* An article on the cover had caught her eye. *When He Just Can't Forgive: Real Life Stories of Women Who Commited the Unforgivable Sin.* Hah. Bet those real life women had nothing on her.

She was nervous, scared, and buzzed out of her mind on caffeine, but if she bagged now, she'd ruin all of Miles's careful social engineering for nothing. This stunt might be monstrously stupid, but she wanted it to count for something. Especially if she was risking her life.

Her flop sweat was a clammy strip down her back. She was a pretty good liar, but how long could it take for that guy to figure out that she did not have Miles's brain in her head?

She thought about how angry Miles would be if he knew where she was. She wished she'd managed to seduce him. At least once, before . . . well, before whatever was going to happen happened.

Things looked really poignant when a girl was going undercover to hunt down a killer—with no backup, no safety net, nothing in her purse but a cell phone, a deactivated radio transmitter and lip gloss.

A guy walked into the Starbucks, and looked around like he was supposed to meet someone. She gave him a sideways once-over.

Nice looking, in a bland sort of way. His nose was too small and pointy for her tastes. She preferred nice, big, hooked honkers. Same with his brown hair. Too short. He had an OK body, for a nerd.

His face looked nice enough, but then again, so had Ted Bundy's.

His eyes slid towards her. She redirected her gaze at the magazine. He was coming her way. Oh, shit. It was him. She was on.

She missed Daddy so bad, she could have bawled. Daddy would have stopped her from doing such a stupid, butthead thing. She'd be sulking in her room at home right now, if Daddy hadn't screwed up and gotten himself incarcerated. She tried to breathe. She felt dizzy.

"Mina?" the guy asked.

She looked up, into guileless hazel eyes. No blaze of festering hatred in them. No skin-creeping vibe. No bloodstains under his fingernails. Just a guy in a buttoned down blue cotton shirt and jeans. He could have been a manager in a stereo store. "Jared?" she asked.

The guy smiled. A nice smile, not a maniacal Green Goblin grin.

He slid into the seat opposite, and peeked at the cover of *Sound Spectrum*. He chuckled. "Picked up a little light reading, huh? I get that one sometimes, too, just for kicks. It's good for the bathroom."

Cindy tried to laugh. Black spots danced in front of her face.

"Oh, yeah," she said, her voice hollow. "It's a real hoot."

Liv leaned over from her cross-legged position on the rug in front of one of Tam's big windows, stretching sore muscles. Banging her head against a wall, was how Davy had described it. Good metaphor.

She'd never liked puzzles. Her opinion was that communication between human beings was already difficult under the best of circumstances.

Of course, in this case, Kev had had a good reason.

The quiet was oppressive. Tam had gotten bored with "your boyfriend's tedious little project" long ago and had retreated to her tower workroom, leaving Liv to wring her lonesome, stressed out brain alone and unassisted. Liv could hardly blame her. This was hell.

She wanted to make a significant contribution to this godawful puzzle. To be something other than a dead weight slung around Sean's neck, or alternately, his sexual plaything. And as far as that went, she still couldn't get used to herself cast in the role of a sexual plaything.

She wasn't the type. She was a serious, independent, hardworking woman who favored baggy dresses, cotton leggings and flat shoes. Here she was, legs shaved, made up, dressed up, lotioned and perfumed. Wearing a frilly green bra and underwear set. Getting all hot and bothered imagining what Sean would do if he saw her in it. Whew.

Eyes on the prize, she lectured herself. Concentrate.

She studied the key Sean had scrawled for her. A no-brainer, he'd explained. Kev had used the code they'd cut their teeth on as babbling babes. He'd written out the alphabet, and working back to front starting with Z, had written under it the names of the McCloud family with no letter repetitions. Jeannie, Davy, Connor, Kevin, Sean McCloud. That yielded JEANIDVYCORKSMLU, which left ten unused letters to insert into the key in back to front alphabetical order. Thus, her own name was written KLFIFZ QST-FWKVV. Numbers remained unchanged.

Clear as day. Easy as pie. Go for it. Knock yourself out, babe.

Bwah-hah-hah. Those McClouds could take their damn babbling baby code and stick it where the sun didn't shine.

Proof on the tapes in EFPV. HC behind count birds B63.

Damn those difficult, convoluted McCloud men. EF had to be Endicott Falls, but PV? She didn't have a clue. The urgency in the faded, coded scrawl made her uneasy and sad.

Count the birds. The first sketch was a lake, with nine wild geese flying over it. Then two eagles, perched on a branch. Then a waterfall, no birds, but she'd decided that the lack of birds signified zero. A mountain crag, no birds. Seven swans. Nine gulls on a beach. Seven ducks in a pond. Nine two zero zero seven nine seven. OK, she'd counted them. So? Anyone? And what the hell was HC? Or B63?

Some crucial bit of info had to be missing. It made her crazy.

She got to her feet with an angry sigh, pacing the rug til she found herself in front of the picture window, looking down at the waves as they washed creamy foam over the sand. The clouds were high, the sky a brilliant white. She put the paper flat against the glass, smoothing the torn edge she'd ripped so long ago, so as to shove only half a sheet of thick folded paper into her bra.

The window illuminated a paler border where a strip of the fi-

brous paper had been torn away. The border of thinner paper ex-
tended higher than she'd thought, all the way up to the line of code.
She took it off the window, examined it from above. It looked like
normal paper again.

She spread it on the glass. Her stomach tightened as she stared at
that paler stripe. She rummaged for the folder, and pulled out the
waterstained cover of Kev's sketchbook. Inside those two pieces of
battered cardboard was the other half of the sheet of paper Kev had
written his fateful note upon. The one she'd ripped in two.

She pried it out, smoothing out the fibers at the extreme edge,
longing for a magnifiying glass. But there was no need, she realized,
when she put the pieces together. She could see with the naked eye
that some loose, fluttery fibers were stained with ink. Her heart
thudded.

She'd done paper restoration work in libraries in eastern Europe
on her studies abroad. She had a good eye, and a delicate touch.

She placed the two pieces together, smoothing down the feathery
curling layer over the bottom sheet, into what she hoped was their
original conformation. The smudges of ink corresponded to the last
character in the last word. QPRI, which, decoded, had become
EFPV.

There was a faint, broken line on the bottom of that I. It was, in
fact, not an I at all. It was an L. She had ripped off the bottom of
Kev's L, fifteen years ago. She almost wanted to scream as she
groped for Sean's key. The code L, coincidentally, corresponded to
the L in the alphabet. So it was not EFPV. It was EFPL.

That was an acronym she knew. It tickled her brain, maddening
her. It was stamped on the insides of her eyelids. She could see it,
floating there. She could smell ink, paper. Hear the ka-chunk sound
of a date stamp, coming down on a card with a lot of other dates on
it.

The kind of card that got stuck in a library book. Kev had flagged
her down outside the library. The Endicott Falls Public Library.
The EFPL. Oh, God.

She put her hands over her mouth and burst into tears.

Count the birds. She had, with endless speculation as to what that
seven digit number could refer to: an address, a telephone number,

a safe deposit box? But if EFPL was the library, Kev must be talking about a call number. 920.0797. HC had to be Historic Collection. Which meant it was an old book, from Augustus Endicott's original library, which had been donated to the town upon his death. Which made perfect sense, since B63 was the book's old Cutter number. Of course.

Oh, God, how simple, how banal. How wonderful and awful. All these years, all this pain, for a few lost paper fibers. How could she not have recognized the configuration? How could it have escaped her?

She was as embarrassed as she was elated.

She clapped her hands over her mouth, muffling shrieks of triumph into crazy keening squeaks. She grabbed the phone Sean had left her, and dialed Sean's number. Out of area. She could have howled.

All jacked up, full to bursting, and no one to share this exalted, euphoric moment with. She paced the room, still squeaking, jumping up and down. Clutching the phone, trying to breathe. She wished she had the kind of family she could share a giddy triumph like this with.

Which reminded her. Three days had gone by without any report to her parents. That was a bit harsh. And she felt much more kindly disposed to the world on the wake of her triumphant breakthrough.

She braced herself for a screaming lecture as she dialed.

"Endicott House," her mother's voice responded.

"Hello, Mother? It's me," she said. "I wanted to let you know—"

"Oh, Livvy. I thought you'd never call." Her mother's voice disintegrated into hitching sobs.

"Mother, I'm fine," Liv assured her. "I told you, the last time, that I'm just lying low while we—"

"It's your father, Livvy," her mother said brokenly.

An icy cold slice of fear cut her in half. She sank down onto the couch, her knees rubbery. "What about Daddy?"

"He had a massive heart attack, the day after you disappeared." Her mother stopped, to drag in a long, jerky sobbing breath. "The shock . . . it was just too much for him. You know all those episodes he's been having. That was the straw, Livvy. The last straw."

"How is Daddy now?" she demanded. "Is he conscious?"

"I've been with him, night and day," her mother said faintly. "I haven't eaten, haven't slept. I came home to see if you'd called."

"Mom?" she said more sharply. "Daddy. Tell me. How is he now?"

"Blair's with him now," she said, her voice taking on more strength. "Blair's been a rock for me. An absolute rock."

"What's Daddy's condition now?" she repeated desperately.

"Come home. Please, Livvy." Her mother's voice choked. "I'm begging you. He drifts in and out, but he keeps asking for you."

Liv leaned forward, doubling over. "OK," she whispered. "I will. I don't know if I'll be able to make it today, but—"

"Then you'll be too late. I understand that . . . *person* is more important to you than your own family, but Daddy is dying, Livvy."

Liv's mind raced in circles. "I'll get there," she promised rashly. "As soon as possible. Where is he?"

"He's in the critical care unit of the Chamberlain Clinic. North wing, second floor. When can you be there, Livvy? So I can tell Daddy."

"Not less than maybe four hours. Mother, listen carefully. There are people after me, people who are trying to kill me. Sean's been helping me figure out who and why, and we're making progress, but—"

"Livvy. Listen to yourself. I cannot believe that at a time like this, all you can think about is yourself. It's just me, me, me, and meanwhile, Daddy is hooked up to life support, gasping his last."

"Please, Mother," she said, with forced patience. "Stay with me, here. I will get myself to the clinic, but I need for you to arrange for a police escort to meet me there. Please, take this seriously. Please."

Her mother harrumphed. "Shouldn't be hard to convince them to come," she said acidly. "They're extremely interested in talking to you."

"Got to go, Mother. I'll be there as soon as I can."

"Livvy! Wait! At least tell me where you—"

She hung up, and sat rocking back and forth. A plan, a plan.

Tam was absorbed in her work, and might not notice if she slipped away. Assuming Liv could disarm the security system and open the garage, that Sean had left the keys in the ignition, that he'd left a full tank of gas, or even a half tank. That she could scrounge up some cash. That was a whole lot of hopeful assumptions.

Her license, IDs, credit cards, bank card, gas card, checkbook, were all lost. Comical, that she was wearing over a thousand dollars' worth of clothes on her body, and she didn't have a cent to her name.

Amazing, how helpless a person was without her wallet.

She stumbled up to the tower, tear-blinded. Good old gruff, benevolent, closed-minded, pig-headed, tender-hearted Daddy. He'd been using his clutch-the-chest trick for a decade. For a while, it had worked, but she'd gotten wise, hardened herself against his wiles.

She'd hardened too much. She felt like crap for dismissing all his "episodes." If he died before she could say goodbye—

No. She wasn't going to deal with that 'til she absolutely had to.

She rummaged around. Found thirty dollars in Sean's muddy cargo pants. If the gas tank was full, she just might make it. She wound her hair up, tugged on the blond wig, perched sunglasses on her nose.

Now for Sean. She poked out a text message on the cell phone.

found tapes i hope EF Public Library
Historic Collection Room
Look behind book with call# 920.0797 B63
knock yrself out love liv

Telling Sean about her father was pointless. He'd be frantic at the idea of her going alone. She felt like she was betraying him by running away from the haven he'd found for her, but that was too bad.

Saying goodbye to Daddy was worth the risk.

It shouldn't even be that much of a risk. She was in a car no one knew she had. On a road no one knew she was using. Arriving at a public building in broad daylight, met by a police escort, surrounded by her family. She was in sexy designer clothes. Blond, for God's sake.

Her own mother wouldn't know her.

Chapter
24

Sean cast an approving glance over Miles and his brothers as they waited in the muted, hushed elegance of the Helix reception area.

Not bad, he thought. They cleaned up nice. Sean's Ferragamo suit was too wide in the shoulders for Connor, but only a gay man would notice. Davy in his own Brooks Brothers suit had a stodgy, don't-fuck-with-me-or-I'll-club-you-over-the-head-with-my-stock-portfolio style happening, and Miles looked hot and hungry in Sean's gray Armani. With his hair gelled back and the mirror sunglasses, the kid looked like a cross between a prosperous young gangster and a human sports car.

With all the crap eating at his nerves, still it did his heart good to see those slobs spiffed up. The only false note in this pageant of male sartorial splendor was the scabby bruises on his own battered mug.

The phone in his jacket pocket let out a soft chirp. He pulled it out to check. Message from Liv. He pulled up the text. Read it. Stared.

"Holy fucking shit," he said, in a loud, carrying voice.

"*Shhh*," Davy hissed, as the receptionist gave him a snooty look.

"What is it?" Con snapped, under his breath.

"Liv's cracked the code. She's found Kev's tapes." His low voice felt strangled in his throat. "She says they're at the public library."

Everybody's jaws flopped, in the direction of the mauve rug.

In the stupefied silence, the receptionist spoke. "Mr. Urness? Mr. Parrish will see you and your party now. Marta will show you the way."

A stunning trophy secretary, blond, of course, greeted them with a brilliant smile, and gestured for them to follow her through the plush office complex. Wow. Deep carpets, picture windows, aromatherapy. Mosaic this, feng shui that. A fake waterfall bubbled away in a wall alcove.

The muted tones of mauve and cream made him feel sedated.

The blonde was twitching her taut, perky ass in the pencil slim skirt for their benefit. He fastened his eyes onto its jerky, back and forth sway, thinking about the peachlike contours of Liv's ass. How he loved to grip her hips, sink his aching prong into that slick heaven between her thighs. And she was a freaking genius, as well as a sizzling sex bomb. She'd solved the puzzle. Hot damn. What an amazing woman.

He jerked himself back to reality as the blonde gestured them into a big corner office, like a game show hostess displaying their prize.

Charles Parrish was a distinguished guy, with silver hair. He shook Davy's hand, then Con's, then Miles's. Sean hung back, avoiding the guy's gaze until the very last moment. Then he gripped Parrish's hand and stared into his face. "Hello, Mr. Parrish. Remember me?"

He saw it, in an instant. The smile went rigid, the flutter in the eyelids, the change in lip color. The involuntary tug as the guy sought to free his hand. Sean let him go. He'd learned what he needed to know.

"What are you . . ." Parrish looked around at the rest of them, confused. "Who are you? I'm sorry, but I don't remember you from anywhere, Mr . . . ? Please, refresh my memory."

Sean sighed. Another lying rat bastard with something to hide.

"My name is McCloud. So's theirs." He jerked his chin at his brothers. "I believe you met my twin, Kevin, when you were a company rep for Flaxon. I see from your face that he made a big impression on you. I want to know the exact circumstances of that meeting."

Parrish backed up, sidling to get on the other side of his desk.

Davy caught his wrist. "You're not going to call security," he said. "This is a friendly conversation, Mr. Parrish. We don't want to mess with your corporate empire. We just want to know about our brother."

Parrish's jaw tightened. He stared wildly around, from face to face. "Well. I did have a rather odd incident, back then, if that's what you're referring to, but it's so long ago, I really don't know if—"

"Just tell us." Sean's voice was getting sharper.

"All right. A mentally disturbed man got past the security in the Renton office of Flaxon, and attacked me. It was a terrible experience."

"What did he tell you?" Con asked quietly.

"He was raving," Parrish said defensively. "He was convinced that a mad scientist was conducting illicit experiments. Murdering people in one of our buildings. All kinds of absurd stories."

Sean's skin crawled. "I see," he said slowly. "What did you do?"

Parrish threw up his hands. "What could I do? I did what anyone would do! I called for help, I got security in, I had him confined!"

"And then?"

Parrish frowned, perplexed. "What do you mean, 'and then?'"

"What happened to him?" Davy growled.

Parrish shrugged. "I let Flaxon's corporate security do their job."

"You mean, you delivered him back into the hands of the people he was running from." Sean's voice was flat. "He risked everything to come to you and expose what they were doing. And you sold him out."

"What for, Parrish?" Connor asked. "For a corner office?"

"I had no reason to think that his stories were true! And I resent . . ." Parrish's voice trailed off. "My God, you're as crazy as he was."

Sean gave him a big, wide smile. "Oh, yes. At the very least."

Parrish started backing away.

"Helix is worth about two point five billion," Miles commented.

"Yeah," Sean said. "Interesting. Looks like the people who fucked Kev over are doing real well these days. Makes a grieving brother wonder. I guess karma hasn't caught up with them yet, but you know what? I think payback time is coming around. What do you say, guys?"

"I think you're right. I smell payback," Con agreed, his voice soft.

Davy just gave Parrish his thinnest, most menacing smile, all the scarier for the stodgy business suit. The man shrank against the wall.

"What in God's name do you want from me?" he demanded.

"We have one name," Sean said. "Osterman. Who is this guy?"

"I have absolutely no idea what you're—"

Thunk, he was pinned to the wall. Sean held him there, one hand twisted into the lapel of the man's costly suit jacket. He dug his finger into a sensitive bundle of nerves beneath his ear. Parrish shrieked.

"Watch it, Sean," Davy said, in the low, even warning tone he'd used during Sean's freak-outs since he was a little kid.

Sean ignored him. "Listen to me, you greedy buttfaced asshole," he hissed. "You fucked up my brother. I am not kindly disposed towards you. I am going to get to the bottom of this. I am going to find every last one of the shit-eating worms who did this to him, and I am going to rip their guts out. Decide right now if you want to be on that short list."

His finger dug imperceptibly deeper into that nerve bundle.

Parrish flailed and struggled, mewling. "Please," he whispered.

Sean eased up. "You got something helpful to say?"

Parrish managed to nod. Sean lifted his hand. "Let's hear it."

The man rubbed the spot, surprised it was not a bleeding hole. He gasped with each indrawn breath. "I had no idea—no idea—"

"Of course you didn't," Connor said. "No idea about what?"

"Osterman," the man gasped out somewhat more slowly. "He's . . . he's a researcher. I would never have dreamed . . . he's an extremely distinguished scientist. Brilliant. I can't believe that . . . the Haven is a legitimate research facility, in spite of being so secret, and—"

"The Haven?" Miles broke in, his eyes big. "You're kidding!"

Sean swiveled his head. "What? What's the Haven?"

"The guy who's been recruiting me," Miles said. "Mindmeld666. The Haven is his outfit. Which means that Osterman must be—"

"The Geek Eater," Con finished softly.

Parrish's breathing sawed heavily in the appalled silence.

"Where is the Haven?" Sean asked him.

"I don't know," Parrish replied. He shrank back as Sean raised his hand. "No! Please, no. I swear. The facility moves around, and the only people who know where it is are the people in the brain potential program. They specialize in product design, and those designs are realized by our development team. My own daughter participated in the program some years back. It produces spectacular results—"

"I don't want a promotional brochure. I want to know where that murdering psychopath *is*," Sean snarled. "And I don't believe that you don't know. Just like I don't believe that you never checked Kev's story. You were in on this from the very start, weren't you, Parrish?"

"No! You have to understand how crazy it sounded!" Parrish was getting desperate. "It was wild paranoid jabbering! He claimed to have been strapped down and tortured for days, but he was strong enough after his ordeal to pick up a security guard and throw him through a plate glass window! The man needed thirty stitches!"

Parrish's yammering receded as Sean's mind seized one detail, and focused on it. "Shut up," he said, cutting through the babble.

Parrish's voice cut off abruptly. "Huh? What?"

"Clarify something for me," he said. "You said Kev claimed to have been tortured for days. Kev wasn't missing for days. I saw him the morning of the seventeenth. Right before I got locked up."

Davy and Con exchanged startled looks.

"Where are you going with this, Sean?" Davy asked softly.

"What day did he come to see you?" Sean persisted.

Parrish blinked rapidly. "I don't remember."

Thunk, back Parrish went, flush to the wall, Sean's finger putting painful pressure on the now bruised nerve center under his ear.

"Think harder," he suggested, his voice deceptively gentle.

Parrish sucked air. "Ah . . . let me s-s-see. The day he came, I had a b-bicycle in the office. For my daughter's eleventh birthday party."

"What's your daughter's birthday?" Davy asked.

"The t-twenty-third of August. Tomorrow, actually."

Sean let go of the man so abruptly, Parrish stumbled forward and fell to his knees. Miles took the guy's elbow, helped him to his feet. Ever the sweet nice guy. Somebody was going to have to slap some mean into that kid, because the McClouds couldn't seem to manage the job.

That and other random thoughts ricocheted senselessly through his head while paralyzing shock rolled over him. August *twenty-three?*

They had buried their brother on the hill, near the little waterfall that he loved, on the twentieth of August. Twenty-three? What the *fuck?*

He put his hands on his knees, tried to get some blood back into his head. Swooning dead away in front of Parrish would not do wonders for his hard-core, meaner-than-shit intimidation machine.

Fortunately, Con and Davy's meaner-than-shit machines were in fine working order. He just hung on, concentrated on staying conscious.

An ungentle hand stabbed him hard between the shoulder blades some time later, to get him marching down the corridor. Past the red-hot blonde with the take-me eyes. No security personnel stopped them, no police were waiting. Parrish was going to play both sides until he could tell which way to jump. Prick.

When they got to the parking lot, Davy seized him by the scruff of the neck and slammed him against the SUV so hard he almost howled.

"I told you we weren't going to get physical," he snarled into Sean's face. "And you lost it. Both times. We do not need this kind of trouble, punk. If you cannot hang on to your shit, I will tie you and gag you and stuff you into the trunk, I swear to God."

Sean glanced to Connor for support, and got just a twitch of his mouth and a shrug. "I'll hold you down while he ties you," Con said.

He looked at Miles, who gave him his what-the-fuck-do-you-want-from-me look. He grunted, shrugged. Whatever. He was too boggled to get his feelings hurt. He rubbed the lump on his head as he got into the vehicle. "The twenty-third of August," he murmured.

Davy pulled out of the lot. "I knew that would set you off," he said grimly. "It was fifteen years ago. The guy could be lying. Or just wrong."

"And if he's not?" Sean said. "We put a body in the ground on August twentieth. If this guy saw Kev on the twenty-third, then . . ."

"Who's lying up there on the hill?" Connor finished.

There was a stony silence in the car while they pondered this.

"Didn't you . . . aren't there . . . dental records?" Miles faltered.

Con shook his head. "None of us ever went to a dentist until we were adults. Dad was dead sure they'd implant transmitters in our teeth."

"Oh. Uh, never mind," Miles mumbled. "Maybe DNA?"

"Forget it," Davy said harshly. "It doesn't matter. Kev is *dead*, Sean. There's no other reason he would not have contacted us. They got him. Face it, deal with it. We can't spend our whole lives like this."

Sean shook his head.

"Fuck," Davy's voice was bleak. "This means another freak-out?"

Sean met his brother's furious eyes in the mirror, and stared into them calmly. He said nothing. Nothing needed to be said.

Con looked miserable and worried. He massaged his bum leg.

"Great," Davy muttered. "So now what?"

Sean shrugged. "That's obvious," he said. "We go to the library."

"First, we run you through a series of tests to identify your learning style. Dr. O personalizes each subject's program," Jared explained, as he merged onto the interstate. "The tests are the hard part, but it's just the first couple of days. Then the fun begins."

Cindy stared out the windshield, bug-eyed. Tests? Her goose was cooked. To a crunchy crisp. "Wow." Her voice strangled. "Super cool."

Jared waited for some enthusiastic, intelligent, intellectual com-

ments from her, but anything she said would betray her for the bub-
bleheaded idiot that she was. In over her head. And going down.

"Uh, OK," Jared tried again, gamely. "So. I liked that abstract
you wrote about predictions of formant-frequency discrimination in
noise based on model auditory nerve responses. I even showed it to
Dr. O. I was thinking, maybe we could try combining temporal and
rate information for a smaller population of model fibers, and tune
them—"

"Um, could we talk about non-technical stuff?" Cindy rubbed
her damp palms over her jeans. "I really prefer to get to know people talking about, like, you know. Normal stuff."

"OK." Jared looked baffled. "What's normal?"

"You know. Everyday life. Movies. Current events. Fashion. I believe in being well-rounded. You can't sit around obsessing on plane
wave solutions all day, you know? You gotta make space for red cow-
boy boots, and espresso brownies, and the Howling Furballs."

Jared frowned. "Who the hell are the Howling Furballs?"

"They're an acid punk band that's doing some cool multimedia
stuff," Cindy explained. "They've got a totally wild sound, and the
engineer uses the signals the musicians generate in real time to create a freaky interactive light show. I'll show you their website, if you
want."

"OK. Great. Sounds interesting." He sounded bemused. There
was an uncomfortable silence that Cindy wanted desperately to fill,
but she didn't dare push her luck. Then Jared spoke again.

"I get the impression that you're not happy to be here," he said.

Duh. "Look at it from my point of view," she said. "I'm a girl all
alone with a guy I just met, going to a place I've only heard of on the
Net. Anybody would tell me I'm brain dead." *Yeah, like her entire
family.*

"You're not," Jared said. "I know you've had bad experiences."

She had? Shit! She hadn't read the transcripts of Mina and Jared's
chats, so she didn't even know her own back story. Yikes!

But Jared was talking earnestly on. She tried to concentrate.

". . . wanted to tell you that I understand where you're coming
from," he said. "I'm an orphan, too. In foster care since I was seven."

"Really?" She looked at him, wide-eyed. "Get out."

"I did high school at Deer Creek."

She blinked. "You mean the reformatory?"

"Drugs," he confessed. "I set up a meth lab in my foster father's barn, all by myself, when I was in the ninth grade. Dr. O heard about it. He came to meet me. He thought any kid who could get into that much trouble at age thirteen had to have potential."

"Wow. That's totally wild," Cindy said weakly.

"When I got out, he invited me to the Haven." He paused for a moment, and added "It's the only real home I've ever had."

"Wow," she said again, feeling totally inane.

"Maybe it could be, you know. A home for you, too."

She tried to smile. He seemed like a genuinely sweet guy. But the corners of her mouth felt like they had weights attached to them.

"So where is the Haven, anyhow?" she asked.

Jared chuckled. "I could tell you, but then I'd have to kill you."

He must have heard the thud as her stomach froze into a solid chunk and hit bottom. His gaze darted to her face. "That was a joke," he said. "You know, jokes? Hah, hah? Very funny? Irony, and all that?"

"Hah, hah, hah," she echoed thinly. "Very funny, Jared."

"I didn't mean to freak you out. We never tell new recruits where the Haven is until we get there. It's part of our mystique. You'll see."

"Oh. Yeah," she muttered. "I can hardly wait."

A six-foot-three blond guy in a Versace suit with a black eye attracted more attention than he wanted today, he reflected as he strolled through the library. Con and Davy agreed that only one of them should go in, and they'd opted for Miles, but this moment was a turning point in his life. He was goddamn well going to be present for it.

The two librarians were checking him out. The older one, an iron-gray lady shaped like a pigeon, was giving him a disapproving look over her bifocals. The cute younger one, with the bobbed strawberry red hair, was blatantly scoping him whenever the older one's back was turned.

He heaved an internal sigh. No quick in-and-out, then. He had to do the leisurely browsing masquerade for Strawberry Red's benefit.

He made a big show of flipping through the card catalog. Then he wended his way through the library, making stops at the magazine racks and the local newspaper, moseying with elaborate casualness toward the Historic Collection Room.

Through the glass doors, into the paneled room full of cracked leather sofas, brass reading lamps, hidden alcoves. This was where he'd had his historic tryst with Liv. The first time he'd made her come.

A feeling of foreboding took him by surprise, twined together as it was with the surge of lust and longing that came over him whenever he thought of Liv. Prickling his face, his balls. An urgent, *go go go* feeling.

This wasn't about Kev. Something was up with Liv. The certainty buzzed in his head. He had to finish up here, and check on her. Quick.

He snapped open the clasp on Davy's briefcase, scanning shelves for the reference number. The distinctive smell of old books was heavy in his nostrils. Anxiety pricked him, harder. Hurry. Hurry. *Go go go.*

Closer . . . almost there . . . and there it was. 920.0797 B63. It was a thick red leather tome, stamped in gold. He reached for it, with a hand that trembled—

"Can I help you with anything?"

He practically jumped out of his skin. He turned with a gasp.

Strawberrry Red stood there, smiling at him. "Hi."

He let out a shaky breath, and smiled back. "Whew. Startled me."

"So sorry," she said demurely. "Can I help you find anything?"

"Oh, not really. I was just, ah, poking around," he said helplessly. "I'm a history buff."

The wattage of her smile went up a few notches. "A history buff? That's funny. So am I. There are some beautiful historic sites in Endicott Falls. Are you just passing through?"

"Yeah. Sort of," he said.

"If you have the time, I could show them to you. I get off at four.

You see so much more with someone who knows the place intimately."

Sean swallowed. "Ah, wow. That's tempting, but I'm afraid I'm busy later," he told her. "I'm having dinner with my fiancée and her family." He gave her a you-know-how-it-is shrug.

She took it well. There was a brief, awkward moment while her smile stiffened, and she stepped back. "Well then. Another time. I'll just leave you to browse. Let me know if you have any questions."

Her heels clicked across the room. The door creaked open, fell to again with a sharp little thud, and he was alone again.

He almost sagged to the ground. From the adrenaline rush, from dumb relief for having gotten rid of her so easily, but mostly from blank, jaw-dropping shock, at having actually done that to a pretty woman.

He'd never turned down a cute girl before. No matter what was going on in his life. No matter how double or triple or quadruple booked his dick was. He had always, *always* managed to slot them in somehow.

Jesus. He hadn't even gotten her phone number.

And his improvised excuse made him snicker. Dinner with his fiancée's family, his ass. Talk about wishful thinking. They'd only shoot him on sight, and bury his carcass in the municipal dump.

He gripped the big book, lifted it out and peered into the shadows. Nothing. His heart fell. He groped. Still nothing. His heart thudded, his stomach clenched. He reached further, scrabbling with his fingers.

There was a niche in the wall. Something loose tucked into it.

He pulled out two dusty videotapes. Saw Kev in his mind's eye, clapping. *About time, Einstein. Give yourself a medal, why don't you.*

August twenty-third, Kev? What in the *fuck* . . . ?

No. One thing at a time. If he let himself think of Kev's post-death appearances on earth, he'd blow a fuse. He stowed the tapes, and pulled out the book with the fateful call number, leafing through it, just in case. It was titled *The Founders of Endicott Falls: A True and Faithful Chronicle of Those Heroic Personages Who Forged Our Fair Township from a Savage and Ferocious Wilderness. By* Joseph Ezekiel Bleeker.

Huh. Some ass-kissing scholar type, trying to score points with old Augustus. Probably wanted to marry the guy's daughter.

He shoved the tome back into its space and beat hell out of there.

He had to call Liv, tell her he'd found the tapes. Thank her for being a genius, a goddess. Tell her that he wasn't worthy to lick her perfect feet, and he was sorry he'd been such a rude dickhead.

And that he loved her, madly, till the end of time. Why hadn't he said that last night, instead of all his macho, blustering bullshit?

Strawberry Red discreetly turned her back so she wouldn't have to see his apologetic smile. Classy chick. He appreciated her delicacy.

He had his cell out before he was out the door. Liv's phone rang, and rang, and rang. He got into Davy's SUV, tossed the briefcase onto Con's lap and ignored the questions while he pulled up Tam's number.

She picked up instantly. "Sean," she said crisply. "Brace yourself."

"What?" he yelled. "What happened? Where is she?"

"I have no idea. She deactivated my alarms, took the car and left."

"When? Oh, fuck. No. When?"

"Stop yelling in my ear. My alarm was deactivated almost four hours ago. Leaving me wide open in my studio, wearing head phones. I'm going to have a talk with her about that."

"You were supposed to keep an eye on her!" he bellowed.

Tam snorted. "I was her host, not her jailor. If you'd asked me to confine her, I would have told you to go fuck yourself."

"I do not have time for your crap, Tam—"

"So don't call this number. I bet you were oh-so-masterful last night, right? Put your foot down, did you? Liv's a real woman, not a dance club sex doll. A real woman has her own agenda. Get used to it."

Sean hung up on her, tried Liv again. No luck. "*Shit!*" he hissed.

"Don't you just hate it when they do that?" Con slanted a sympathetic glance over his shoulder.

Davy let out an eloquent grunt. "Tell me about it."

Sympathy was not what he needed. He needed to see Liv, scream at her for scaring the shit out of him, and kiss her until she passed out.

"Is she wearing a beacon?" Davy inquired.

"There's one in her cell," Sean said through his clenched teeth, drumming his fingers. "Where's the nearest X-Ray Specs set-up?"

"I've got an old Specs receiver Seth told me I could mess around with in my folk's basement," Miles offered. "I think I can make it work. I've got the software, too. I can install it."

"Good," Sean said curtly. "Let's go."

Chapter 25

It went against her good girl instincts, leaving a car in a tow zone, but Daddy was on life support, a killer was hunting for her and she'd been running on fumes for miles. It was a miracle she'd arrived at all.

She parked the car outside the sliding glass doors, and bolted. So she'd pay the fee if they hauled it away. Um, yeah. Right. With what?

Ah, what a happy dream, to be capable of dealing with her own parking violations again. She scurried into the bustling lobby, looking for signs for the north wing. Wondering if Daddy was . . . no. Stop.

One thing at a time. One thought at a time.

She started out walking, but anxiety kicked her into a clumsy lope, and by the time she hit a straight stretch, it was a dead run.

Everyone shrank away from the crazy blonde sprinting down the hall in spike heels and the scanty, sexy red halter dress. She was too anxious to wait for the elevator. She dove for the stairs. Screeched to a halt outside the nurse's station when she saw Dr. Horst, her family doctor from Seattle. Oh, God. His being here could not be a good sign.

"Dr. Horst?" she called out, gasping for breath.

He frowned, no recognition in his eyes. She yanked off the diva sunglasses. "It's me. Liv. How's Daddy? Is he—is he—"

"Liv. My dear." He walked towards her, giving her a gingerly embrace. The grave look on his face terrified her.

"Tell me quick," she begged. "Say it, if it's bad news."

"Come on in here," he said. "Try to calm yourself. We have to talk." He towed her towards the doorway of a small waiting room.

"Please, just tell me if Daddy . . ." Her voice trailed off.

Her father was standing right there. Fully clothed, looking very much as he always did. No life support, no IV drip, no oxygen mask. He looked fine, but for the nervous, hangdog look on his face.

Her mother stood beside him. Her chest was puffed out, chin high, her face flushed. Blair stood there too. Wearing his pompous face.

"Mother?" Liv looked around at them. "Daddy? What's going on?"

"Lord," Amelia said. "You look like a hooker in that silly wig."

Her father mumbled something inaudible, and stared at his feet.

"I'm sorry it came to this, Livvy, but you left me no alternative," her mother said.

Hot anger flooded through her. "No alternative but what? To put me in danger for nothing? To put me through hours of hell thinking that Daddy was dying? You think you can actually justify that?"

"Try to calm yourself, Liv," Dr. Horst soothed. "Your mother truly does have your best interests at heart."

"As if." Liv looked around. "I don't see any policemen here. You didn't take me seriously. Why am I not surprised?"

"Liv, please," Dr. Horst said gently. "I promise that you will be absolutely and completely safe where we are taking you."

"Taking me?" Alarm bells jangled in her head. She backed away. "No way. You're not taking me anywhere."

"I know you've had a terrible ordeal, Livvy, but it's over now. And we're going to see that you get the help you need," her mother said. She grabbed Liv's wrist, her long red nails digging in with nervous strength.

"You haven't heard a word I've been saying!" Liv wailed. "I was attacked four days ago! A man tried to kill me! Sean saved me!"

"You see?" Her mother fixed Dr. Horst with big, imploring eyes.

"It's something like Stockholm Syndrome. She's so broken down, she's actually bonded and identified with her abuser. God, Livvy, just look at you. Bruises on your arms, your face. You've been beaten!"

"Mother, I told you—hey! What are you doing?"

"You're right." Dr. Horst had grabbed her arm, and was frowning at it. "Rope burns, knife cuts, hematomas. It will be necessary to document all signs of sexual violence for when you press charges."

"Oh, dear God." Her mother let out a theatrical sob of anguish.

"Press charges? Against who?" Liv stared wildly around herself.

"Oh, please, honey," her mother said. "Don't tell me you really believe these silly stories about an attacker. It's just a fantasy, to justify your unhealthy obsession with that horrible man."

Her jaw dropped. "You mean, you still think the bad guy is Sean? But I'm telling you right now that it wasn't! Mother, listen to me—"

"What is this?" Her mother lifted the blond curls off her neck, and gasped. "Oh! God! Livvy? What has that person done to you?"

"A human bite." Horst's mouth tightened with distaste. "You did the right thing, Mrs. Endicott. We probably got her back just in time."

"No. Wait. That wasn't Sean. He didn't do that. You're all crazy." Liv backed towards the door. "To hell with this bullshit. I'm leaving."

She bumped into Blair, who had sidled around behind her. He looped his beefy arms around her waist, pinning her arms.

"Livvy," Amelia said. "The police searched McCloud's apartment, and guess what they found? Look at this. Just look, honey."

"Let go of me!" she shrieked, struggling, but Blair's arms were strong. Her mother came over with a folder, and opened it up.

"Look," she said triumphantly. "Hundreds of photos of you, Livvy. They span years! This man has been stalking you for over a decade!"

Liv stared at the folder. Her mother leafed through the photos, displaying them in quick succession. Liv in college. In New York. Outside the library where she'd worked in Baltimore. Outside the apartment where she'd lived in Madison. She stared at them, stunned.

"See?" her mother said. "He's obsessed, Livvy. Face the facts."

Not. The pictures were startling, but she was almost immune to shock by now. Sean's passionate interest in her was intense and unusual, but not criminally violent. Not crazy. Not T-Rex. She knew the difference.

She shook her head. "The man who attacked me was not Sean, Mother. You have to believe me. I'm not crazy. And neither is he."

Her mother looked sadly up at Dr. Horst. Shook her head.

Blair's arms tightened. "Sorry, Liv. Remember, I am your friend."

She struggled, panicked. "Like hell you are. You guys can't do this to me! It's not legal!"

"I'm afraid you're wrong about that." Amelia's voice had a taunting tone. "We can prove you've been kidnapped and brainwashed. That you've been physically and sexually abused. You are a danger to yourself and to those around you. The paperwork is drawn up. It's incredibly painful for us, but we have to do what's best for you, honey. All that remains is to get that person behind bars, where he belongs."

"You idiots!" she shrieked. "Sean didn't kidnap me! He *saved* me! Let go!" She flailed, stomped, tried to knee Blair in the groin.

She felt a sting in her arm. Horst was pushing down the plunger of a hypodermic. The effect was instantaneous, cutting her loose from her frantic desperation. She floated, detached. She couldn't remember why it was so important to keep her knees locked, so she let them sag.

Blair hoisted her up against his chest, with considerable effort.

"Put her into this wheelchair," Dr. Horst directed. "We'll let her rest in the examining room while I go over some details on this paperwork with you. I want to get her settled into Belvedere by evening."

Belvedere? The mental health clinic for depressed, drug-addicted socialites? The rich bitch looney bin? Part of her wanted to shriek with laughter, but it wasn't a part of her that had any motor control.

Blair tucked her into the wheelchair, straightening her lolling head. She stared into his eyes, in silent pleading. He lifted her fake blond hair, looked at T-Rex's bite. He shook his head, and left.

Under the influence, she watched the wall grow wider, until it was as big as the sky.

She floated in the blue, longing for someone whose name she couldn't remember. She remembered his face, though. How he shone.

The door to the main corridor opened, letting in a slice of light and noise from outside. A large cart with big canvas linen bags creaked in. She saw its bulk approaching. She could barely keep her eyes open, or her mouth shut. Let alone turn her head to look at it.

And then she smelled him—T-Rex. That bitter, awful stench.

Fear bloomed inside her, faraway but terribly real. So was the grief. Sean. The name came to her. She clutched at it, desperately.

So sad. That all of Sean's heroic efforts should come to nothing, because she'd been so stupid, so credulous. The monster had come, and she'd never even thanked Sean for what he'd done. For his bravery, his passion, his sweetness. The lovely, shining truth of him.

The monster bent over her, dressed in hospital scrubs. His foul breath washed over her face. He bent close, gave her face a sloppy lick with his meaty red tongue. She was paralyzed, unable to flinch away.

"Oh, Olivia. I'm so glad to see you." His voice was a raspy whisper.

He scooped her out of the wheelchair. Dumped her headfirst into the canvas bin, half full of dirty sheets. Wrenched one over her body.

The sound of the wheels creak-creaking below her head was the last thing she heard as she faded away, buried alive in the airless dark.

Miles's Specs revealed that Liv's phone was in the Chamberlain Clinic. Sean was baffled, but glad that it was a public building where she would be relatively safe. At least the icon wasn't blinking forlornly in a ditch somewhere. "Give me your keys," he said to Davy.

Davy looked dubious. "If things go the way they usually do, you'll get hauled off by the cops, and I'll have to bail your useless ass out before I can retrieve my car keys. Don't you want to see the tapes?"

"I've waited fifteen years to see the tapes. I can wait another half hour. Hand 'em over." He waggled his fingers imperiously.

Davy sighed, flung the keys at him. Sean caught them, and bolted up the stairs and through Miles's mom's kitchen, deftly evading her as she tried to flag him down and stuff a sandwich into his face.

He called Liv's phone repeatedly, as he speeded through town. His nerves were crawling so bad, he could barely keep from screaming.

Answer it, he willed her. *For Christ's sake. Have mercy on me.*

He was so startled when a voice answered, he practically rear-ended the vehicle ahead of him. He screeched to a stop just in time.

"Liv?" he bellowed. "Where in holy hell are you?"

After a moment, an acid voice replied, "She's right where she should be, Mr. McCloud. Safe with her family, and away from you."

"Who is this?" he roared, and then realization hit, like an anvil in his face. "Oh, Christ, no. Don't tell me. Is this Liv's mom?"

"I am Olivia's mother, yes. Please do not try to get anywhere near my daughter, ever again. The police are ready to intercept you."

"I cannot believe this," Sean hissed. "What did you do? Lure her in by saying that one of you was sick? Is that why she's at the clinic?"

"My husband's frail health is none of your business."

"Frail health, my ass. I can't believe she fell for it, but then, she always cared more about you guys than either of you ever deserved. Put Liv on the line. Let me talk to her."

"No," the woman said, her voice triumphant. "She is resting. She's had a terrible experience. I will not let her talk to you. Ever again."

"How do you intend to stop her?" Sean asked. "She's thirty-two."

"Yes, and very fragile. Easily led by a dominating personality."

An image of Liv charging through the forest topless, screaming bloody murder as she emptied the clip of the Beretta at T-Rex, came to him. "Uh, yeah. Right," he muttered.

"Wait. Just a moment, Dr. Horst, I'm on the phone with that person, and I'll be with you in a . . . what? She's *what?*"

Crack. The phone had dropped to the ground.

A hole of fear yawned open in his belly. He listened to the still open line. People were yelling in the distance. Amelia was screaming.

Already. He'd fucked up. He should have stuck to Liv like glue.

"Mr. McCloud?" Amelia shrieked into the phone. "What have you done with my daughter? *Where is she?*"

Relief made him giddy. T-Rex had nabbed her, had not simply murdered her. There was still a chance. He laid on the gas.

"Nothing," he said. "Don't tell me. She's disappeared, right? Someone abducted her. You mean you're surprised? Where have you been for the past four weeks? Jesus, lady! Hello! Wake up!"

"It's not possible! She wasn't—you're not—"

"I'm not the one!" Sean yelled. "Bet she tried to tell you, huh? Bet you didn't listen. You've never listened to her in her entire life."

Her incoherent response suddenly diminished in volume. "Mr. McCloud?" said a gruff male voice. "Where did you take my daughter?"

"Nowhere," he snarled. "I'm trying to keep her alive, and you and your stupid wife are making it hard. How long ago did she disappear?"

"We saw her just fifteen minutes ago—"

"Tell the cops to block all the roads leading to the clinic. Stop everyone from leaving." He hung up the phone, and gunned the engine.

The cops would be all over his ass in no time. He had to catch up with T-Rex before they caught up to him. Think, goddamnit. *Think.*

He pounded the steering wheel. If he were a kidnapper sneaking a drugged woman out of a hospital and into a vehicle . . .

Basement. Laundry. Back entrance. Definitely.

He slewed the vehicle around just in time to take the lefthand road that looped up and around to the back service entrance and the employee parking garage. He jerked to a stop outside the garage, and left the SVU running as he sidled along the wall towards the entrance.

He definitely couldn't count on those brain-dead Endicotts to tell the cops to block the exit roads, so he yanked out his phone and dialed 911 as he peered into the entrance, sidling down. A pair of headlights flicked on in there. His heart kicked up a notch, his stomach did a no-hands cartwheel. The lights came slowly towards him.

He pulled out the SIG Con had brought him, held it discreetly behind his thigh. He couldn't make out who was in the driver's seat. He was still in the chute that led up to the outside lot. It was a white van, stenciling on the side, hospital supplies or something. His nerve endings prickled. The engine roared. Was it T-Rex? *Fuck.*

The dispatcher spoke into his ear. "Endicott Falls Police."

If that was T-Rex, the only solution was to shoot the driver right now, head-on. But he couldn't see who was driving. Couldn't risk it.

The van picked up speed, swerved. The door swung open. Sean leaped back, turning so that the spine-snapping lethal blow was downgraded to mere searing white-hot pain. The ground swooped up and slapped his body sidewise, knocking out his wind.

A bulky, familiar body dressed in hospital scrubs leaped out of the van. Sean lifted the gun that was still, miraculously, in his hand.

Pfft, a flash of light, a hard, shocking pressure to his upper arm. That cold, sinking feeling that he knew too well. He'd sprung a leak.

T-Rex scooped up the SIG Sean had dropped into his latex-gloved hand, and slammed his boot into Sean's kidney. A fireburst of pain.

"I thought you'd be more of a challenge." The guy crouched, fixing piglike eyes upon Sean. "It's pussy does it to you, you know? Makes a guy weak. You've been at her night and day, right? Made yourself as weak as a limp, floppy dick. Lucky I'm here to take over, huh?"

It would take too much energy to reply. He gathered himself in stillness, waited for his chance.

"I'm supposed to keep your brain in one piece until Chris is done playing with it," T-Rex went on. "But if there's anything left, I get to take you home, to play. Olivia, too. Chris promised I could have her for a toy if I brought you in. " He grinned. "I've got a meathook in my garage. When I'm bored with fucking her, I'll slide the point between her ribs, hoist her up. Use her for a punching bag. You can watch."

T-Rex hauled back, preparing for a spine-crushing kick. Sean's good arm shot up like a spring, stabbing two fingers into the guy's balls.

An instant's shock, a guttural howl as the pain hit the guy. Sean braced one leg against the wall, swept his other leg around to knock the guy off balance. There wasn't enough time to roll away before T-Rex landed on him, splat, like a half ton of shit.

Then, a hot burning sting in his thigh. Oh, no. Oh, fuck, *no*.

T-Rex rolled off him. The hypodermic stuck out of Sean's thigh.

"Hey! What's going on? Where have you taken Liv?" bellowed a loud male voice. Sean turned his head. Blair Madden was in the door.

He opened his mouth to yell "Run." He kept opening it, and opening it. His mouth had become a huge vast space in which his tongue was too small to be found. T-Rex aimed the SIG he'd taken from Sean, in slow motion. The gun blast reverberated endlessly.

Madden's eyes went wide, his hands went to his throat, clawing at the dark blood welling out. He dropped to his knees, face squished to the side. Wide eyes, looking straight at Sean. Astonished to be dead.

T-Rex grabbed Sean's bloody hand, slid Sean's fingers through the trigger, squeezed. His giggle was incongruous, from such a big man. "I love it when shit like this happens. I am a genius. Am I not a genius?"

You are a festering shithead, he wanted to say. *A hot pimple on the ass of the universe*, but he was too far away, his voice couldn't make it across the gap. The guy heaved him up, flung him into the van.

He landed on top of a soft, female form. He could smell her scent.

It broke his heart, and yet he was grateful for even that much to hang on to, like a glowing silk thread of light. The thread got thinner as he floated further, until thin became nothing, and it was all distance.

Miles plugged in the dusty dinosaur of a VCR into the outlet. He turned to Davy and Con, both leaning against the table, identical expressions of dread on their faces. "You guys ready for this?" he asked.

They both gave him are-you-kidding grunts. He hit play.

The recorder had been hidden behind a potted plant. The slice of white was the wall, the slanting blades of green were leaves. Minutes passed. Miles gnawed his nails. He'd never known Kev, but he was as invested in this as if the guy were his own long-lost brother. He was about to suggest fast-forwarding when they heard voices. A flash of movement. They leaned forward. Miles turned the volume up.

". . . just relax," said a low, soothing baritone voice.

Another flash, and they saw a face. A dark-haired man in a lab coat. A younger man, acne spots on his face. Shaggy hair. The lens was too low. They could only see the bottom halves of both men's faces.

"How long is it gonna take?" the younger guy asked.

"Oh, not long at all," the dark guy said. "A half hour, forty-five minutes at the most. Did you take the pills I gave you?"

"Exactly at ten o'clock AM just like you said."

"Perfect. Sit down, please. You haven't eaten, have you?"

"Not since last night." The guy sat down. "I could eat a horse."

"Hang on a little longer, and I'll buy you a steak," Lab Coat said.

Kev had framed the vid to record the face of anyone seated in that chair. Lab Coat leaned over. They got a good look at his close-set dark eyes as he adjusted a helmet on the guy's head. "Put your wrists here."

The guy obliged him, and blinked when the man wrapped on the heavy velcro wrist restraints. "Hey," he said. "What the hell?"

"Just procedure," Lab Coat soothed. "Don't turn your head. I have to adjust the sensors." The kid sat still while Lab Coat, who had to be Osterman, rearranged the helmet. There were several quiet minutes while he hooked up a tangle of cables to a machine. Craig tried to chat, but Osterman brushed his attempts off with vague, absent replies.

Osterman lifted a helmet onto his own head. "I'll be wearing one too. I'll feel everything you feel. It won't be uncomfortable." He rolled up Craig's sleeve and yanked over an IV rack.

Craig looked perplexed. "I've already taken the drug, right?"

"No, that was just a mild hypnotic, to prepare you. This is the real stuff. X-Cog Three. The drug that creates the interface." Osterman taped the needle in place, and winked at him. "Down the rabbit hole."

Craig's eyes slowly went vacant, but Osterman's smile remained, stamped on his face as if he'd forgotten he'd left it there. He snapped his fingers in front of Craig's face some minutes later. "Can you hear me?"

"Yes." Craig's voice was soft and vague.

"Relax, and follow any impulse that comes to you."

After a moment, Craig fumbled for the pen that lay next to his restrained hand. It slid from his clumsy fingers. Osterman nudged it back into his hand. "Good boy," he crooned. "Whatever comes to you."

Craig jerkily began to write. He dropped the pen, whimpering.

"You're doing well," Osterman praised. "Let's try one more thing."

Craig's head flopped from side to side. "No, no, no, no."

"One more thing, Craig," Osterman insisted. "Look at me."

Craig lifted his head. His eyes swam with tears. A thick thread of drool hung from his lips. He shook his head helplessly. "No, no, no."

Osterman adjusted the IV drip, turned several knobs. "Let's try this again, Craig. Say whatever comes to you. Just follow the impulses."

Craig's fingers scrabbled at the armrests. He looked bewildered. "F-fourscore and seven years ago, our fathers brought forth from this continent a new nation," he said, voice slurred.

"Very good, Craig," Osterman purred. "Very good. Go on."

"In the beginning was the word." Craig's voice was clearer. "And the word was . . . and darkness was upon the face of the d-d-deep . . ." His voice stuttered off. "Darkness!" he shrieked. "Darkness! Darkness!"

Osterman made an irritated sound, and adjusted a knob.

Craig began to twitch and wail. Osterman bent over him, soothing him. He began to scream. They couldn't see Craig's face, just his hands jerking against the restraints, the chair shaking, Osterman's elbows in the air, doing something they couldn't see. He straightened to reach for something. Miles almost screamed himself.

Craig was bleeding from his eyes, his nose. He shrieked, writhed. Osterman jabbed a syringe into Craig's upper arm, and the boy flopped forward, eyes blank and blood rimmed. Festoons of blood and snot dangled from his mouth and chin. Osterman stripped off his gory coat, and flung it to the floor. The petulant gesture was bizarre, against the backdrop of Craig's ravaged face.

A voice offscreen asked a question. Osterman shrugged. "There's nothing wrong with the machine," he replied. "The interface is perfect. He responded to my motor impulses. It's the drug that's not right yet."

The garbled voice said something else.

"He can't handle the side effects," Osterman snapped. "None of them can." He touched the boy's wrist. "His heart's stopped. Goddamn adrenaline spike. I need a shower. Get this place cleaned up. I've got another subject coming in an hour. I want this smell gone."

Footsteps, a door slamming. Craig's head dangled at a pathetic angle in the awful helmet. Miles stared, his hand pressed to his mouth.

He was used to TV action that came on fast and furious, afraid their spectators would get bored, change the channel. This video wasn't afraid of boring them. It was a stern, implacable witness. It stared at the dead boy until the blood dripping off his chin slowed . . . and stopped.

A shadow moved across the screen. It flickered, and went blank.

Miles hung on to himself. He was not going to cry in front of Con and Davy. Or barf. He was cool, he was fine. When he opened his eyes, Connor's face was buried in his hands. His shoulders vibrated.

Davy's broad, motionless back was as eloquent as Con's tears.

Miles ejected the tape, and laid it on the table. Gently, as if it were a wounded, living thing. He picked up the other one, and cleared his tight, swollen throat. "You guys, uh, ready for this other one?"

Connor made a sound, like a laugh, or a sob. "Oh, Christ."

"Play it," Davy said harshly. "Get it the fuck over with."

Miles pushed it in, hit play and braced himself.

It was a forest. Dappled green, sun. The handheld camera jerked with every step. The camera swung up, showing a curving bridge.

"That's the Korbett incline. The old Korbett Bridge," Miles said.

The camera swung left, focusing on a rock formation. It swung around and plunged into the woods, alongside a barbed wire fence.

"He's fixing the location," Davy said.

Whoever held the camera got down and wiggled through the

grass on his belly. The image came to rest, and the lens zoomed in. A black van in the woods, back doors gaping. A large man was digging a hole, his T-shirt plastered to his big body. His hair was crewcut, high and tight like a marine. He flung the shovel down, and headed to the van. He pulled out a body, trussed in black plastic, dragged it by the feet, head bouncing over rocks. He flung it into the hole. Went back for the next. The camera moved as the guy's back was turned. Wiggling closer.

"Oh, shit, Kev," Davy whispered. "You idiot. You had him."

The next time the image stabilized, the guy was tipping another body into the grave. They heard the thud as it hit. The lens zoomed in, gave them a leisurely look at the lantern jaw, the blue eyes. The guy leaned to grab the shovel. He froze, eyes fixed in the direction of the camera. "Hey!" he yelled. He yanked a gun from the back of his jeans.

The image swirled, spun, jerked. A confusion of green, of sky, of earth, of shouts, thudding feet . . . and the screen went blank.

They stood there for several minutes, mired in speculation.

"I want to talk to Professor Beck again," Davy said. "If Sean would ever come back with my damn car." He grabbed his cell, dialed. "Pick up your phone, punk," he muttered. "Sean? Where the hell—" His voice broke off, listened. When he spoke again, his voice had changed.

"I see. Yes. My name is Davy McCloud," he said. "I'm the brother of the man who owns this phone. Is he there? I need to speak to him."

He listened. His lips went white. "How long ago?"

They all heard the questioning tone of the next burst of words.

"Of course," Davy said. "I'm aware of that. I'll come down as soon as I can." He held the phone away from his ear as the guy reiterated his demand. "As soon as I can," he repeated. He snapped the phone shut.

"Detective Wallace, from the police department," he said. "They found Sean's phone, in a pool of blood. At a murder scene."

"Murder scene?" Con's voice sounded strangled. "Whose murder?"

"Blair Madden," Davy said. "Shot in the throat, in the parking garage. No Sean. No Liv, either. The filthy son of a bitch got them."

There was a moment of blank disbelief, and Miles spun around to check the monitor. "Wait. Don't we still have Liv on the Specs?"

Liv's icon blinked away, its position unchanged. "It's just her cell," Davy said. "She doesn't have it on her."

"Who do we squeeze?" Con said grimly. "Parrish? Or Beck?"

"Beck's closer," Davy said. "Stupider. If he hasn't skipped town."

Miles's mom bustled in, with her usual kick-ass timing. "I have some sandwiches." She looked around, smile fading. "Is everything OK?"

Miles took the tray, set it down, and gave her an impulsive kiss on the cheek. "Mom, I need the keys to your new car."

Chapter
26

"**I** am mortified that you were put through such an ordeal." Osterman was literally groveling, and it was not enough to smooth the feathers of Charles Parrish, the CEO of Helix. The man was hysterical.

"How did he connect me to you? Ask yourself that! Those thugs attacked me! I have bruises!" Parrish's voice cracked with outrage.

"I'm so sorry. I'm dealing with this little problem as we speak—"

"This *little problem*? Is that what you call it?"

Osterman winced. "I know that it's a serious breach of—"

"Your inappropriate methods of dealing with problems are what got us into this!" Parrish raged. "Every risk you take exposes Helix to bad publicity that could cost our sharehholders hundreds of millions!"

"I understand, but in my own defense, I must remind you that—"

"You have no defense," Parrish snarled. "What you have is a huge expense account. One or the other, Osterman. The next hint I get of any misconduct, we cut you loose. You take full responsibility for whatever mess you've created, and we will be shocked and sad."

"Mr. Parrish, I—"

"I thought your organization was legitimate! I trusted you, Osterman! I allowed my own daughter to participate in the program! Now I find that the person I entrusted her to is a violent criminal?"

"Lies," Osterman protested. "The McClouds have made me a scapegoat for their brother's death, and they are trying to ruin my—"

"I don't want to know the sordid details."

The connection broke.

Osterman slammed the phone down. How dare Parrish speak to him like this? If Helix was worth billions, it was due to Osterman. The cutting edge treatments for paralysis, spinal cord and brain damage, the immensely profitable weapons applications, all of it was fruit of Osterman's tremendous effort and sacrifice. He alone was strong enough to take the necessary ethical burdens upon his conscience, for the greater good of humanity. To create a legacy for future generations.

And the man had *scolded* him!

So it gave Parrish the shivers that his precious daughter had participated in Osterman's progam? He remembered Edie. Thin, big wary eyes. Artistic. A psychic component that made her family nervous.

Oh, how he'd longed to see what an interface with Edie might yield. But she was Parrish's baby girl. Her brain was off-limits.

Still, as it often happened, his fascination with Edie had launched a new avenue of research. He'd begun experimenting with artistically gifted geniuses, not just math and science types, which had widened the scope of test subjects nicely. The results were tantalizing, though not yet in shape to publish or patent. He'd found many talented Edie clones without rich fathers to protect them. In fact, the Edie experience had marked the beginning of his preference for working with girls.

And Gordon had been so happy about the girls. Keeping Gordon happy was a very important consideration. In fact, he was intrigued by the thought of playing with Cynthia, once Gordon finally reeled her in. She was quite gifted, if the online music reviews were to be trusted. He'd never tried an X-Cog interface with a musical talent before.

He had a vivid spontaneous fantasy, of putting the X-Cog crown onto Edie Parrish. Compelling her to kneel before him, open his pants and perform oral sex upon him, obedient and docile as a lamb.

, While Charles Parrish watched, of course. Tied and gagged.

He had conducted similar experiments, although he usually compelled the subjects to service Gordon, not himself. Using the X-Cog master crown required concentration. Sexual pleasure was distracting. The few times he'd tried it, he'd found it more irritating than exciting.

But for Parrish, he would exert himself. Oh, indeed he would.

Cindy huddled in the plush marble bathroom stall, and punched in a text message to Miles. The Haven had proved to be a luxurious complex set way back on a wooded hill in a little town named Arcadia.

She pulled the beacon out of her pocket, followed the printed instructions to start transmission. It had two days of battery juice.

No way could she keep up this charade for two days, but hey. Nobody had asked her to do this. If they felt like it, they could come for her. If not, tough luck for her. They might be too busy hunting down all the other bad guys, and she didn't blame them if they were.

And with that stern pep talk, she punched the beacon code into her SMS, and pushed send. She had no excuse, other than a nervous pee which produced about two drippy drops, not to go face Jared.

The common room was lined with books, couches and computers. Jared grinned when he saw her, and flagged down a handsome older guy in a flapping white lab coat who was striding across the room.

"Hey! Dr. O! Let me introduce you to—"

"Not now, Jared. I'm busy."

"But it's the new recruit I was telling you about," Jared persisted. "You told me you wanted to meet her as soon as I brought her in!"

Doctor O turned with a scowl, like he was going to bite Jared's head off—until he saw her. His face went blank. Then he smiled.

Cindy's neck prickled. She was used to attention from guys, but this felt different. And that toothy grin as he strode across the room did not reassure her one bit. *Oh, my, what big teeth you have.*

"And this lovely young lady's name is . . . ?" he asked.

She shook his hand. A warm, strong grip. A nice, manly man handshake, and yet, she suddenly wanted to pee again. "Um . . . Mina."

"Wonderful to meet you, Mina. I hope Jared's treating you well."

"Oh, he's been great," she assured him.

"I've been explaining the testing phase," Jared told him. "I figured, since it's so late, we'll have dinner and get started tomorrow."

"No, Jared. I need her today," Dr. O said.

Jared looked bewildered. "But she hasn't done any of the—"

"No need for pretesting," Dr. O said. "She specializes in acoustic physics, right? Give your cell phone to Jared, please, Mina."

She blinked at him. "Huh?"

His smile was stern, but charming. "House policy. It helps us all concentrate. You will have one half hour period every day to answer messages and phone calls. Don't worry. Jared will keep it safe for you."

She passed it over, with fingers that shook. Last hope lost.

"Come along, Mina. I'll show you the rest of the facility. We'll see you at dinner, Jared," Dr. O said.

Jared blinked at the dismissal, turned, and hurried out. Cindy was crushed to see him go. With her cell phone, too. Her last two allies.

Dr. O led her down a long breezeway, down a path through towering trees towards another building complex. Down several flights of stairs, into an underground building that had been cut right into the slope of the hill. They went in. The corridor seemed incredibly long.

Their footsteps echoed in the silence. Dr. O swiped a card, and put his eye up to a machine that shot a beam of red light into it.

The door hissed, clicked, opened. He led her into a big room with no windows, shut the door, and looked into the retinal scan thingamabob again. Big bolts slid, deep into the heavy door. *Ka-thunk.*

"My lair," he said, in a joking tone.

She tried to smile. "Uh, wow. It's an amazing place."

He perched on the edge of a table. "Welcome to the Haven, Cynthia."

The words sank in. She had to fight to keep from passing out.

Davy didn't bother to knock on Beck's door. He just turned the knob and yanked it open, using a tissue he'd gotten out of the car.

It struck Miles as strange that it wasn't locked, but the McClouds just pushed on into the house. He scurried after them. Davy stopped, turned, waved his hand at Miles to go back outside. Like hell. No way were they cutting him out of the action now. He sidled along the wall after Con, ignoring the squinty glares and the frantic hand gestures.

They rounded the corner. Marble steps led down into a vast sea of pale beige, with couch and chair islands adrift in it. The main island had a huge black coffee table. A vase was knocked over on it, pointy red flowers scattered across the light-colored rug—oh. No. Oh, shit.

A foot stuck out from behind the coffee table. Bare. Bluish.

They circled the room in absolute silence, and stared down at what had once been Professor Beck.

His head was half gone, and part of his face. His blood and brains were scattered in a dramatic, fanlike arc behind him.

Con let out a long, careful sigh. "This, we did not need."

"No," Davy agreed. "I don't think things could get much worse."

Miles swayed on his feet. This was the second violent, bloody death he'd seen that day. The first one, on tape, had been bad enough.

But at least he hadn't had to smell it.

His stomach lurched. He bolted out of the place in a stumbling run. Out the door, across the grass, and he tumbled onto his knees, heaving coffee-flavored gastric juices onto the ornamental shrubs.

He was trembling and tearful and embarrassed when his gut finally stopped spasming. He dragged himself up onto rubbery legs, wiped his eyes and nose on the sleeve of Sean's Armani. His phone chimed, in his pocket. He pulled it out and read the text message.

```
mina went 2 meet mindmeld. sorry.
haven in arcadia. took a beacon. code 42BB84
follow the bread crumbs if u feel like it
wish me luck pretending I have a brain
yrs cin
```

The world spun. Darkness slopped up over his mind.

A hand on his shoulder made him jump and shriek.

"If you're done depositing genetic material on Beck's lawn, could we get the fuck out of here?" Con said. "Before they haul us in?"

Miles straightened up, and held out his cell. "Davy. You know how you said you didn't think things could get any worse?"

Davy's eyes sharpened with dread. "Yeah?"

He passed over the phone. "You were wrong."

Pain, pain, and more pain. White hot screaming stabs of it, slicing right through him like a hot knife through butter. He was strapped into some sort of chair. Pain was everywhere, but the molten epicenter was in his right shoulder. A guy with a bloody lab coat was holding a scalpel and tongs. He went at Sean's shoulder with it. Gouging and rending.

"Fuck," Sean hissed, bucking and straining.

The guy displayed a dripping bullet clamped in his tongs. "Just a flesh wound," he said, his tone reproving.

Sean stared at the guy, baffled. "I've died and gone to hell?"

The guy grinned. "Not quite yet. Think of me as a preview, if you like." He moved to the side, displaying the room with a flourish.

Sean's chest clutched around his heart. Liv lay there, inert, hands and ankles fastened with tight leather straps to the frame of the gurney.

T-Rex stood there, fondling her. He licked his thick lips as he ran his hand up the inside of Liv's thigh. "Nice," he said. "Warm and soft."

"Not yet, Gordon," Lab Coat said sternly. "I have other plans for her. You can play with the other one. After we're done, of course."

Other one? What the hell? Sean could turn his head just far enough to make out a slender girl curled up on the floor. Her hands were fastened to the radiator, her hair hanging over her face. She looked up.

Cindy. That poor, silly chick. Fresh sadness welled up inside him. "Aw, shit, honey. I cannot tell you how sorry I am to see you here."

"M-me, too," she stuttered. "Right back atcha."

Sean strained in his bonds, rattling the chair. "So, then. You must be Osterman. The shit-eating maggot who killed my brother."

Osterman tipped a gallon bottle of alcohol, letting it glug out onto a cotton swab, and swiped the soggy thing, urgently, over Sean's arm. Sean convulsed with a fresh bolt of agony. "Yes, I am Osterman," the guy said. "Hold still while I stitch this up."

Sean struggled with that. "What's the point of stitching me?"

"I'm not killing you yet," Osterman explained. "I'll keep you alive as long as I can. I don't want you dying of a stupid infection."

That sounded ominous. "What the hell do you want from me?"

"Your brain." Osterman jabbed his needle through torn flesh. "I've refined X-Cog so much since I experimented on Kevin with it. He was remarkable, you know. He forged new neural pathways to bypass the nerve induction, right on the spot, just to spite me. Unbelievable."

Sean gasped with pain. "Before you murdered him?"

Osterman stabbed the raw meat of Sean's shoulder again. "I've been trying to duplicate those results ever since. And here you are, an identical genetic copy of Kevin McCloud, on a silver platter. The genes must have expressed themselves very differently in you. I hear you're quite a low achiever, compared to your twin brother."

Sean's teeth dug into his lip at the next savage poke. "That's a . . . a matter of opinion. I survived, right? Until now, anyhow."

Osterman chuckled. "Perhaps you're right. You might have a certain low cunning that Kevin lacked."

"What did you do to these kids?" Sean demanded. He was queasy with pain, and terrified out of his freaking wits, but so damn curious.

Osterman peeled off bloody latex gloves. "I got the idea years ago, trying out therapies in a mental health clinic. Controlled electrical stimulation to certain parts of the brain, coupled with a drug

I've named the X-Cog series, produces what I call an interface." He put a silver helmet on. "This is the master crown. You're wearing the slave crown."

Sean realized that he was wearing a helmet, too. His head itched.

"With these, I suppress the part of your brain that governs motor control, and send my own impulses directly from my brain to your body. I can make you do absolutely anything. You watch, conscious, but helpless. Hijacked." He stopped, his face expectant. Like he though Sean would exclaim in admiration at his brilliance. Sean just stared at the guy, struck mute. Dread swelled up, monstrous inside him.

"Anyway. You'll see soon enough." Osterman yanked an IV rack over, and slid a needle into the back of Sean's hand. "Let's get started."

"With what?" He didn't want to know, but he couldn't help asking.

"At first, I just thought that enslaving Ms. Endicott and having her perform degrading sexual acts with and upon Gordon would be entertaining, but it's been done, and sex gets so tedious, you know?"

"Chris prefers a good mindfuck to any other kind," T-Rex said.

Osterman's smile froze. "Keep your editorial comments to yourself, Gordon."

"Do whatever you want to me," Sean said. "Just don't hurt her."

"Oh, I won't." Osterman's smile looked almost jolly. "You will."

Sean's throat clamped down over the words. "I *what?*"

"You, Mr. McCloud. You will be the one to torture her. What better way to demonstrate what the X-Cog can do? I want to to see how far I can push the interface. If I can smash through all moral and ethical boundaries. Imagine the applications, if I can compel you to do something which is morally repugnant to you. I've never tried that."

Sean tried to shake his head, but it was clamped ruthlessly into place. "No," he whispered.

The phone on Gordon's belt rang. He picked up. "Yeah? I'll check on it." He clicked it shut. "Brice needs help wiping his ass. A car turned onto Schuyler Road, but didn't come out." He grabbed Cindy's hair as he passed, yanking it. "I'll be back, honey. Don't go anywhere." He swiped a card, peered into the retina scan machine, and left.

Osterman swatted Liv's cheek. "We've waited long enough."

"Yeah, I see. I'm handy when you guys need to borrow a car or do your computer shit work, but if anything important's happening, it's 'go suck your thumb in the closet 'til it's safe to come out, Miles.'"

"We don't have time for this argument," Con said. "You don't even have a gun. If we don't come back, you have to bring reinforcements."

"So that's when I can help," Miles snarled. "When everybody else has croaked, and it doesn't matter anymore. Just great. Thanks, guys."

"You can get over it and be of actual use to us and to Cindy, or you can get clubbed over the head and stuffed into the trunk." Davy's voice was steely. "Those are your options. Choose quickly."

Miles slumped down against the trunk of the cedar tree, defeated.

The two McClouds melted into the trees with the Specs handheld monitor, off to track down the signal from Cindy's cell while he sat here with his thumb up his ass. It didn't matter how hard he worked. No amount of training would ever get him up to par. And he was having a pity party, while Cindy chatted up a serial killer. Bat-brained, beautiful Cindy.

He wanted to howl like a chained dog.

He stared down at the grounds. The beacon in Cin's cell had been stationary, bleeping from the far edge of the complex. It made no sense for him to lurk up here. He should at least get closer to the main house.

There was a hedge down there. Good cover. Sean always talked about the importance of trusting your instincts. His own were biting his ass, with long pointy teeth, telling him to move, move, *move.*

A troll was looming over her. Blood-spattered, fanged, horrible, red flames flickering in the empty black sockets of his eyes.

Someone smacked her face. She blinked startled tears out of her eyes. The face was handsome, smiling, human, now, but the bloody coat he wore was the same. "I'm so glad you've woken up," he said.

Liv tried to lift her aching head. Memories drifted back. The clinic. Her mother's taunting voice. The needle. The monster. She peered around. "Where's T-Rex?" Her voice was a cracked whisper.

The man looked blank. "You mean Gordon? He'll be back. Gordon lives for my experiments. I let him participate, and in return, he cleans up my messes. It's a perfect symbiotic relationship."

"How did he know . . . where I was?"

"He's been monitoring your parents," the guy explained. "Gordon planted bugs in your mother's purses. We were sure you'd be foolish enough to contact them. They made our work so easy, reeling you in like that. But I won't wait for Gordon, though. I'm too eager to proceed. He can play with the other girl later. That should content him."

Other girl? Liv heard a whimpering sound. She craned her neck, saw the slender form huddled on the floor at the far end of the room.

She turned back to the man. "Proceed with what?"

The man rubbed his hands together. "With the experiments, of course," he said, his voice gleeful. "On your lover. I'm so excited."

"Sean?" She looked around wildly, pulling against the straps.

"Hey, my love. This shithead is Osterman. The guy who offed Kev." The voice came from behind her. She craned back, looked at him upside down. He was strapped into a chair, streaming with blood.

"Oh, Sean," she whispered. "Sweetheart. I'm so sorry."

His eyes were full of grief and pain. "Liv? Baby? Whatever happens now? I love you. Remember that."

The guy he'd called Osterman laughed. "I will be curious to see if she manages to remember it, after what you are about to do to her."

He grabbed a rolling cart piled with objects, and pulled it to the gurney. "Instruments of torture, gleaned from my kitchen and garage. Pliers," he displayed each item, "a scalpel, a handsaw, a nutcracker for fingers, a tire iron for breaking the larger bones, and this." He held up a bronze device that she didn't recognize until he flipped a switch. Blue flame hissed out of the curved pipe. "A blowtorch," he said proudly.

She started to shake. Thought of Tam's ring. *If all else fails, you can open a vein with it.* Well and good, if your hands were fastened together. Hers were strapped on either side of her. The worst she could do would be to stab a hole in the pad of her thumb.

Osterman peered into Sean's eyes. "Are you still able to speak?"

Sean's mouth worked. "Go fuck yourself." The words were slurred.

Osterman adjusted the knobs on Sean's helmet. He turned Liv's gurney around. "So you can watch," he said, as if conferring a treat.

Sean's face stiffened into a mask. Osterman stared, licking his lips. "He's mine. I'm command central of his brain. Isn't it incredible?"

"You sick fuck," Liv whispered.

He giggled. "Sean, you will feel an impulse to hold up a certain number of fingers." He leaned down, and whispered into Liv's ear as if they were playing a party game. "I'll tell him three. This is a direct impulse, from my brain to his hand. Watch carefully!"

Sean's hand twitched, clenched. The plastic tubing leading into the needle twisted around his wrist. He held up three shaking fingers.

"Very good," Osterman said.

Sean's hand kept moving. His index and fourth finger trembled, and curled down, leaving his middle finger sticking straight up.

Liv wanted to cheer at his desperate defiance. God, she loved him.

Osterman turned to the IV rack, adjusted the drip. "Most subjects would be in convulsions at this point. We'll try this again, Sean."

Sean's hand shook. Tears trickled from his eyes. A thread of blood ran out of his nose. Liv bit her lip, trying not to whimper.

"You learn more about the choreography of mental domination by working with the strong ones," he said smugly. "It's more complicated than you might think. But I've been practicing for decades."

Liv tried to moisten her cracked lips. "Why do you hate him?"

Osterman looked surprised. "Oh, but. I don't hate any of my test subjects. I just . . . happen to them. Like a stroke. If I want results which translate into rapid advances in medical treatments, and defense applications that contribute directly to the security of my nation, a price must be paid. And I sincerely believe the price is worth it."

"But you're not the one paying it," Liv pointed out.

Osterman blinked, and cleared his throat. "Ah. Well. Point taken. However, you can't get out of being tortured to death by your lover. Besides, I have a meeting later, and I'll need time to clean up. Let's see how Mr. McCloud is coming along."

Liv looked, and cried out involuntarily. Sean's nose bled from both sides now. His mouth and jaw were a gleaming crimson mask.

"Observe, if you will." Osterman had a lecturing, professorial tone as he unbuckled the straps that held Sean's arms. "He can't move a muscle, other than breathing, swallowing and suchlike, unless the impulse comes from me. Watch this." He picked up the tire iron.

"No!" Liv shrieked, as he whipped it down, smacking hard right against Sean's blood-drenched, injured shoulder.

Sean didn't move. Fresh blood streamed down his arm, dripping off the ends of his fingers and onto the floor. His eyes burned wildly.

Osterman dropped the tire iron, hands opening and closing. "See?" His voice shook with excitement. "He didn't even flinch, and that had to hurt. There's nothing wrong with his nerve receptors, you see."

She wanted to scream, but once she started, she wasn't going to be able to stop. If the blade on Tam's ring were longer, she would spare them what was about to happen. Without hesitation.

Osterman was undoing the restraints that had fastened Sean into the chair; wrists, ankles, arms, the belt around his waist. Sean began to move. He got slowly to his feet, and shuffled towards Liv's gurney.

"Good boy," Osterman crooned. "You're doing wonderfully." He glanced at Liv. "Just think of the applications for weapons defense."

"Stop," Liv told him, her voice cracking. "Just stop."

"Oh? Really? Should I?" His mouth stretched in a hideously cheerful smile. His eyes were utterly mad. "I don't think so. Let's start with the blowtorch, hmm?"

She shrank back. Sean awkwardly picked up the blowtorch. He flicked the switch several times before he managed to turn it on.

She stared into his eyes. It took several tries to get the words out. "Sean. Wh-whatever happens now . . . I l-love you."

"Aw." Osterman let out a sigh. "Brings tears to my eyes. And speaking of eyes. Let's start with one of hers." He patted her cheek. "Feel free to scream," he invited her. "The place is soundproofed."

The girl tied to the radiator started to wail. Osterman spun around. "Shut up, or I'll have him start with you instead," he barked.

The girl curled up with a keening moan, and began to rock.

Sean's body jerked, shuddered. He took a shuffling step closer.

Liv squeezed her eyes shut, cringing away.

Chapter 27

Osterman lied. This wasn't a preview. This was hell, here and now. Twisting in the flames, damned souls screaming, pitchforks jabbing. Every muscle was locked in a burning rigor of agony with the effort to resist the impulse Osterman sent through his nerves.

The impulse to lift the blowtorch, and burn Liv's beautiful, tear-streaked face with it.

He could sense Osterman's gloating pleasure. Fucking with him and liking it. The foul intimacy of the contact made him want to vomit.

Consciousness of who he was, what was happening, wrapping itself into a protective bubble, retreating from the horror . . .

He yanked it back. Pain roared through his body afresh. If he let go of that bubble, he was dead meat walking. Osterman's pet zombie.

Time warped, stretched. He hung on, shuddering to stay still while Osterman yanked the puppet strings. The room spun. He was trapped in the center, in a fiery pillar of agony. His father stood before him, his lean face seamed with pain and loss. He contemplated his lastborn son's distress as if he were all too familiar with it.

Do the hard thing, he advised, his voice dour.

Sean would have laughed, if he could. *Yeah, Dad. And what might that fucking hard thing be? It's all hard.*

Eamon nodded gravely. *Turn it around.*

Turn what around? How? I'm paralyzed!

Eamon was gone. Sean sat on the plank floor of the kitchen. A woman with blond hair sat with him. She had dimples. Beautiful green eyes. A rush of emotion made his heart leap. *Mom?*

She held a piece of gray plastic tubing, from the irrigation pipes his father was laying outside, tilted it down towards him, and poked something into it. A ball bearing rolled into his palm. A toddler's hand. Knuckles dimpled. Grubby, dirty nails. *Turn it around. Send it back.*

Then he was on the cot in his room, staring at the mandala on the ceiling. Its hypnotic curves sucked him up, tossed him in the air. He swooped with the stunt kite over a desert landscape. The colors of the kite were so bright against that vast, aching blue. *turn it around*

He followed the cord down to the figure far below. Tall, dirt blond hair, buzzed so short it was mouse brown. The man lifted his face.

It was Kev, but not the Kev that he remenbered. This was a Kev Sean had never known. His face was thin, seamed and hard. His eyes distant. The entire right side of his face was puckered with scars.

Sean opened his streaming eyes, stared at Liv, lying on that table. She told him she loved him. While he held a blowtorch over her.

turn it around

His mother held out the length of gray tubing.

He took it, held it to his eye. It was no longer gray plastic. He was looking through a throbbing red wormhole. He gathered his strength.

turn it around

He dove. The universe screamed with him as he raced through the wormhole, burrowed into the polluted place that was Osterman's brain.

He sank the talons of his will into the other man's mind, and reeled. These were not his hands, clutching the scalpel. Not his muscles trembling, not his limbs holding this body upright.

Not his, this dead, rotting heart, that somehow still beat.

He couldn't keep this up. Pressure was building. There was no valve to release it. He spoke, haltingly. Alien vocal folds vibrated, the pitch and timbre all wrong, and he fumbled with the wrong teeth, the wrong tongue, but still, the words came out, of Osterman's mouth.

"Goodbye, princess," he said thickly. "I love you."

His/Osterman's hand whipped up, slashing the scalpel deep into the man's carotid artery. Sean felt the awful pain of it. The heat of the arc of blood that sprayed, spattered across Liv. It welled over his/Osterman's chest. A series of soft explosions popped, in his head.

Darkness rushed in, and swallowed him whole.

Liv beat and flailed against her bonds as Osterman flopped down on top of her. His dead weight crushed her lungs. His hot blood pumped out, soaking into her blouse, trickling over her ribs. His face dangled over her ribs, wet mouth gaping, eyes white-rimmed like a mad horse.

She shrieked, bucking madly, bowing herself up in an arch until the heavy body shifted and slid into a heap on the ground.

Sean still stood, his face blank. She screamed his name, but his eyes no longer saw her. The blowtorch fell, bounced, still hissing.

Sean toppled, rigid as a tree crashing down. He hit the rolling table of improvised torture implements. It tipped, and the stuff clattered and crashed to the floor. So did the big, uncapped bottle of alcohol.

The liquid glugged out onto the floor tiles in a spreading puddle. Rivulets reaching out like tentacles, towards the blowtorch, hissing on the floor. The clear liquid inched closer to the tongue of blue flame.

Swoosh, fire found the volatile liquid, and a thread of flame raced its way back to the big mother puddle. *Whump*, the pool caught fire.

Heat crackled, roared. The air shimmered and shook.

The girl tied to the radiator began to scream.

The raggedy hole in the foliage of the rhododendrons was just big enough so that Miles could watch the guy approach. Big, muscle going to fat . . . that lantern jaw, those pale eyes, where had he seen that guy?

The tape. It was the grave digger from Kev's tape. Fifteen years older, heavier, thicker, but it was him. Even the rolling, apelike walk was the same. A knee-weakening rush of fear pulsed through him.

The guy slowed down, and grabbed a walkie talkie off his belt. He put it to his ear. "What the fuck is it now? You gotta learn to wank off by yourself, Brice. Don't ask me to jerk your willie for you, because I got my own—" His voice trailed off. "Fire? In C Building? What the *fuck?*"

He spun around, and took off at a dead run.

Miles scrambled to his feet and took off after him. Anything that made that guy run had to be Miles's business. He had to keep this guy in sight while staying somehow invisible himself.

Tough, for an unarmed, clueless geek dressed in fucking Armani.

Oh God they were going to die they were going to roast and fry—
"Hey! You! Girl! Shut up and listen to me!"

The sharp words somehow cut through the terror in Cindy's brain. She flipped her hair aside to peek at the woman strapped to the cot. Liv. Erin had told her about Liv, the goddess. Liv's head and shoulders were lifted off the gurney. Her eyes blazed with urgency.

"Do you want to live?" she demanded.

Cindy sucked in a sobbing breath. "Y-yes!"

"Good. What's your name?"

"C-Cindy," she chattered out.

"Listen up, Cindy. I've got a trick ring. Press hard on the stone and a tiny knife pops out. I can't use it, but you could. Understand?"

Cindy tried to swallow with her shaking throat, and nodded.

The woman worked the ring off her trapped hand with her middle finger and thumb. "I'm going to throw this to you. Cross your fingers."

Liv's wrist flicked. A small, shining golden thing flipped into the air in a long, low arc. It hit, bounced, bounced again. Rolled. It was like breathlessly watching a roulette wheel as it spun and stopped.

Three feet away from Cindy's sneakered feet.

"Oh, shit, oh hell, oh *fuck!*" Cindy shrieked. She flung herself out, stretching, rubber-soled shoes squeaking, groping and scrabbling. Liv bit her lip and closed her eyes, letting her head drop down onto the cot.

No way was she going to die like this. Not Liv, either. Or Sean, whom she liked. Sean was by far the nicest of the grim McCloud crowd. She kicked off her sneakers, gripped the hem of her jeans between her toes and started tugging. Thank God for low rise. She flailed, kicked, until they were long tubes of denim stuck to her ankles.

"Hurry," Liv begged.

Cindy lifted her ankles, and flung the wad of fabric out.

The waistband fell inches short of the ring. The next try hit, but sent the thing skittering a foot to the left and inches further away.

Cindy pried the jeans down until they were all the way off, then clamped the hem of the legs between her toes. She lifted. Flung.

The butt part of the jeans landed on the ring. She heard a voice chanting as she reeled it in. It was her own voice, whimpering *"please, God, please, God."* Liv was yelling, hurry, hurry. Tears and snot ran down her face. She bent herself inside out to get her bare foot onto the ring, to nudge it under herself. Her fingers groped, grabbed, slid it on. It was too big, but she twirled it around, shoved the stone.

The knife sprang out, bit her. Blood ran over her hand, but she still went at it, straining and sawing at the duct tape 'til it broke free. She struggled to her feet, stumbled across the room. Yanked at the buckle straps holding Liv's wrists down. Liv leaped off the bed, dove for Sean. She grabbed him under the armpits, but could barely move him. Cindy jolted into action, grabbed the other shoulder.

Liv hit the tire iron with her foot. Scooped it up. By the time they got to the door, the room was choked with acrid smoke. The door was locked. Liv flung herself at it, yelling and pounding with the tire iron. The thing barely scratched the varnish. Cindy tugged at her arm.

"We need that guy's body!" she coughed out. "We need his eye!"

"What?" Liv yelled. "What the hell are you talking about?"

"His eye!" Cindy croaked, louder. "The door's got one of those retina scan lock doohickeys. I think the card's in his pocket."

Cindy fell to her knees, took as deep a breath as she could, and scrambled over the floor. Flames roared against the back wall. The sicko doctor's shoes were smoldering. She grabbed his arm. Liv blundered out of the smoke, and grabbed the other arm. Somehow, they got the corpse to the door. Cindy rummaged in his pockets for the key card.

"We gotta get him on his feet," she panted. She and Liv hoisted up the dead weight of the guy's bloody, neck lolling, head-flopping corpse up to eye level. "Ohmigod, this is sickening! I want to barf," Cindy gasped.

"Later," Liv sputtered, coughing. "Barf later."

Cindy swiped the card. The machine beeped. She pried the doctor's eyelid open. Put his clammy, scummy dead eyeball up to the scanner. A red light shot in, turned green. *Click*, the lock popped loose.

The doctor's corpse pitched over the threshhold. They kicked him aside to make way to drag Sean. Stumbled towards the end of the smoky tunnel, hacking and spitting. They shoved open the door, tumbled out into sweet, fresh air. Smoke boiled out along with them.

Click. The sound of a bullet being chambered. They spun around.

"Just where do you ladies think you're going?" Gordon rasped.

Miles's shoe slipped on the branch. He grabbed the bough above his head. There was so much smoke in the air, he hoped that the leaves and twigs falling to the ground would go unnoticed.

He'd crawled off the roof of the underground building, and onto an overhanging branch. He was filthy from crawling on his belly through mud and leaves. His legs wobbled and shook. They could probably hear his heart thudding a half a mile away.

The grave digger's taunting voice floated up from below. ". . . one of you shall I shoot first? Tough choice. I wanted to bang you both before I snuffed you, but it looks like I'm going to have to pick. Eenie, meenie, minie, moe. Did you take your pants off just for me?"

A low, hacking cough. "No, I didn't." Cindy's voice was hoarse, but steady. "Fuck off and die, you sick asshole."

Miles inched further out. The slender bough he crouched on was bowing under his weight, but he wasn't over T-Rex's head yet. He was only getting one chance at surprising this guy. It had better count.

"Ooh. Naughty girls who use bad words will get punished," T-Rex crooned. "Turn around, sweet cheeks. Show me your ass."

"Not," Cindy said. Her voice shook.

"Let me restate that. Turn around or I'll gut-shoot you."

Miles took one more shuffling step. Another. Almost there . . .

Crack. The branch broke. Down he went, along with what felt like half the tree. He landed on top of the guy. Thuds, shrieks, shouts.

A gun went off. He was flung, like a toy. Concrete smacked him, conking his head. T-Rex came at him, screaming with rage.

Miles's body jackknifed. His dress shoes slammed into the other man's gut, lifting him, tossing him headlong. He rolled up onto his feet. So did the other guy. Miles's leg whipped out at T-Rex's gun hand, and he was astonished to make contact. *Smack*. The gun flipped, twirled. Miles lunged, but T-Rex jabbed in a frontal kick, right into his nose.

Blood squirted. Miles reeled back, saw stars. *Crunch*, he took another doozy to the ribs. He fell, saw the gun, reached for it—

T-Rex kicked it away, and stomped on Miles's fingers with a huge booted foot. "I don't think so, dickhead," he snarled.

There was a crackling, popping noise. Miles screamed as the boot crushed all the bones in his hand. He grabbed Miles's wrist, lifted his boot off. Wrenched the arm up, and violently back. *Snap*. Agony.

Then T-Rex stumbled back. Cindy was clinging to his back like a crazy monkey, clawing at his face with something sharp. He bellowed, and flung her off. She flew, legs flailing, hit the concrete. Lay very still.

Miles struggled up onto his knees, but knives were stabbing his lungs, and his arm, his hand, were a throbbing mass of fiery splinters.

He tried to get into guard. His legs wobbled crazily beneath him.

T-Rex wiped his bloody face. "Say goodbye to your face, pretty boy," he snarled, winding up for a kick. "I'm going to cave it in for you."

Thunk. A hollow, wet sound. T-Rex's face took on a surprised look. He toppled forward. A ton of malodorous meat crashed down on Miles's fucked-up arm and hand, and sweet bleeding Christ, it hurt.

Liv stood there, clutching a tire iron in shaking hands. Barefoot, eyes blank and staring, in her clinging, blood-drenched red halter dress.

Liv waited until Miles had wriggled out from beneath T-Rex's bulk before she staggered forward and prodded at the man's head with the tire iron. No more surprises for this woman today, thank you.

There was a bloody, gaping hole in T-Rex's skull. She stared at it, mouth dangling. She should feel proud. Triumphant. She felt nothing.

Miles was scooping up T-Rex's gun, and saying something to her. She couldn't understand him. She'd forgotten what words meant. Miles dragged out his cell phone. Calling for help. That was good. His face was streaked with blood, but he'd be OK. So would the girl. They'd all do.

The only one who wouldn't do was Sean. He wouldn't do at all.

She staggered to where Sean lay, half in and half out the door, and fell to her knees, searching for a pulse. His wrist was sticky with drying blood. She found one, a faint fluttering under her finger.

There was nothing she could do for him. He needed medical help, a team of neurosurgeons. She still saw Osterman's horrified eyes as Sean spoke through the man's lips. *Goodbye, princess. I love you.*

God, how had he done that? How the hell had he done that?

That touched her off. She'd found her feelings again. A tidal wave of them. She sagged over him, lifted his hand to her face, and wept.

Cindy rolled up onto her knees, dazed. Amazed to be alive. Stinky black smoke poured from the building. Wind sighed in the trees. Birds twittered. Liv was curled into a shaking ball over Sean's sprawled form.

Miles swayed on his knees, trying to peel the jacket over his poor squished hand. The arm of his shirt dripped crimson. She stumbled towards him, tearing off her blouse. "Ohmigod you're bleeding," she babbled. "Did he shoot you? Oh, shit! I gotta call someone!"

"Davy's on it," Miles forced out the words. "He's getting an ambulance. It's a compound fracture. No big deal."

"Oh, shut up. No big deal, my ass." She wadded up the blouse and pressed it against the dripping splotch. Miles howled. "Christ!"

"Sorry," she whispered. "Just trying to help."

"This is so fucking typical." His voice was thin and breathless. "You always end up buck naked in all your freaky adventures. Put on my jacket, for Christ's sake. It's bloody, but it'll cover your bare ass."

Cindy rolled her eyes. "I cannot believe that you can still give me shit about my underwear after what just happened to us."

"Underwear?" He hissed as she applied pressure. "That's a see-thru doily and some string. But at least one burning mystery is solved."

"Yeah?" She scowled at him. "And what burning mystery is that?"

"You were telling the truth about your heart-shaped pussy hair."

She tried to laugh. "Ah. Well. If you're all intense about my pussy hair, you can't be too bad off. Lie down before you faint. Macho dweeb."

Davy and Con barrelled down the hill. She and Miles got a quick once-over, and the McClouds went for Sean like a shot, ignoring the two of them. She eased Miles onto his back, trying not to look at his poor mashed hand. It made her want to hurl. "Thanks for coming after me."

His eyelids fluttered open. "Hmmph."

"Yeah, I know. It's nothing personal. You'd do the same for any whale, eagle or panda you met on the street. But still. You know what?"

His eyes narrowed. "What?"

She leaned down and kissed him. Blood, gore and all.

When she leaned back, he had a wondering look in his eyes.

"Don't you dare feel sorry for me, Cin." His voice vibrated oddly. "You don't owe me a goddamn thing. So don't think you have to—"

She shut him up with another kiss. A deeper, more demanding one. "Shut up, you big dork," she whispered. "You're bumming me out."

They stared at each other like they'd never seen each other before. Until the med techs came, and hustled them all away.

Chapter
28

Three months later . . .

Sean's fingers scrabbled for the spur of black granite. His numb hands were ragged and torn from days of climbing. Pain thudded in his head. Partly altitude, partly the lingering hematomas in his skull. There was a strange, constant hissing in his ears.

He'd ditched his pain meds. Anticonvulsants, too. He wondered, distantly, what it would be like to have a seizure while clinging to a cliff face.

His chest jerked, mirthlessly. At least it would be quick.

It was just past dawn, but the clouds didn't let much light down. Shreds of mist floated beneath his dangling feet. He clung like a spider to the bottom of a small overhang, hyperextended, muscles burning. Wind roared in his ears. Pellets of hail pinged at his face.

It was the closest thing to peace of mind that he'd found lately.

He heaved and struggled, supporting his weight on one set of trembling fingertips, then the other. Clawing upwards, hand over hand.

He felt no triumph when he flung his leg over the ledge. He flopped onto his back, stared into the sky, panting. Just blank stasis, and that constant hiss. No more desperate effort to expend. He needed another cliff. Quick, before he started thinking. Or worse, feeling.

He'd been up here for a week, with a bare minimum of survival gear. He hadn't bothered to bring much food, figuring he could hunt if he got hungry. He had, the first couple days, but the longer he stayed out there in the wilderness, the less interested he was in food.

He'd left behind the cell phone, doctors' advice, frantic fussing from family. Lectures, pep talks, stern talkings-to. Offhand comments about what Liv was doing, what Liv said, how Liv felt.

How devastated she was that he refused to see her.

He let out his breath in a harsh sigh, trying to exhale the pain that gripped him when he thought of her. Launched into his rationalization for the millionth time. It had dug a groove in his mind.

Nah. More like a fucking trough, at this point.

He'd done what he had to do. He couldn't bear to look at her, in the condition he was in. He hadn't been that much of a prize even before Osterman had mind-raped him. Add on the nightmares, the stress flashbacks of torturing her, killing her, and oh, Jesus.

It was a stain on his soul that he couldn't scrub clean. It scared him out of his wits. His mind shied away in horror from the thought of hurting her.

He couldn't risk it. Liv was alive and well. Miraculously. That was how she was going to stay. Without him, if necessary. Whatever it took.

Hey, princess, take a chance on me? C'mon. Live dangerously.

Hah. Right. He lifted his hand to the cord around his throat, the tiny leather bag that hung on it, like a totem. The diamond earring.

She'd stuck it in a padded envelope, and mailed it back to him after he refused to see her. No accompanying note. He didn't blame her.

It was like that scene in the jail, all over again. But far worse.

He put his hand to the buzzed-off hair, the indentations on his skull where they'd opened him up, fucked around in there. He was sure they'd done their best, but he felt like a jerry-rigged pile of shit.

He dragged himself onto his knees. His head spun. Every breath was a knife stab. He staggered up to the crest, and stepped up onto the highest point to look down over the long, curving sweep of gray shale—

The rock tipped, dumped him off. He did a crazy dance trying to scramble onto something solid, but everything was moving, he was—

falling down the rocks, thudding and bouncing, and no way would he make it back up in time to save Liv from T-Rex, he just kept falling, falling, with a terrible unstoppable momentum, past all hope . . .

He drifted back, some time later, to a vague awareness of cold. He put his hand to his face. Sticky. He wondered if he'd snapped his spine.

The hiss in the back of his head had gotten louder.

He pried his eyes open. Liv stood before him in the shifting mist.

Joy surged in his chest. T-Rex hadn't killed her. Her hair looked like a dark cloud. His hands ached to touch it.

"Get up, you idiot." She smiled at him, held out her slender hand.

He scrambled to her feet and seized her, starving to taste those soft lips, drink in her fragrant breath, fill his hands with her warm—

Her eyes froze wide. She made a choked sound, and the color in her cheeks drained away. She sagged, and he caught her. Liv slipped to one side, because he'd only caught her with one hand.

The other hand held the knife he'd just driven into her chest.

Stark horror spread through him like blood from a severed artery.

He lowered her down, but there was no place to put her on the steep slopes, the jagged, sliding rocks. Osterman's mocking laughter echoed through his head. The hiss became a deafening roar.

He finally recognized it. It was the blowtorch.

He staggered away, his howls swallowed by muffling fog, stumbling over stones, head dangling, sobbing for breath—

Stop it. You dumb ass.

He was so startled, he slipped, and clutched a spur of rock to keep from sliding further. He looked up. It was Kev. The older, scarred, grim-looking Kev with haunted eyes that he'd seen in that freaky vision. Kev's dimple was forever hidden in the grooves of his unsmiling face.

"Leave me alone," Sean said dully. "I can't take any more."

I see that. You can't take much of anything.

Sean was stung at the flinty judgment in Kev's voice. "What would you know about it?" he snapped. "You're dead. Stop criticizing."

Kev's cool expression did not change. *So put a gun in your mouth, already, if dead's what you want. Don't stage some pussy accident.*

"I shouldn't even talk to you. I'm just encouraging you." Sean shut his eyes, counted ten firebursts of pain, willing the apparition to be gone when he opened them. Still there. Stubborn pain in the ass.

If you go over the edge, Osterman's won. Kev's voice was harsh. *He'll be laughing in hell. You want to be the butt of his joke?*

"So what the hell am I supposed to do?" Sean roared.

Kev's tight mouth barely quirked. *The hard thing.*

That pissed him off, in a big way. "I am, butthead," Sean snarled. "What do you think I'm doing up here? Playing with my dick?"

Kev looked unimpressed. *Dying is easy. It's living that's hard.*

That logic struck Sean as dubious, coming from a dead guy, but he didn't have it in him to argue. He was too fucking miserable.

He buried his head in his arms. Might even have slept for a while.

The sound of his own teeth chattering woke him. The wind had picked up, whipping the thick fog away into fine, transparent shreds.

He blinked, focused . . . and gasped. His gut yawned with terror.

He was perched on a cliff. One foot dangled over it. One arm. An entire shoulder. He stared, gaping, a thousand feet straight down.

He froze, scared shitless. He'd been flirting with death for a week, but this was the first time that death had made a move.

He didn't want to die. The realization startled him. It would be all wrong. Broken off, unfinished. So stupid, to die now, after all this effort, all this drama. To never see her again. Never touch her, hear her sweet voice. The fear of that pierced him like a needle of ice.

It took forever to break the spell and creep back from the edge.

He rolled onto his face on the jagged rocks, his limbs as weak as water. He fell apart, for the first time since he'd woken out of the coma.

He cried, for all of it. Dad, Kev, Mom. For Liv. For all the pain and fear that Osterman had inflicted on all those poor kids. The loss, the grief, the waste. It thundered through him, on and on until he started to wonder if it would ever stop.

It finally did, leaving him exhausted. Limp as a rag, clinging to the mountaintop under the threatening gray sky.

But when he rolled over, the hissing sound was gone. All he heard was the wind, whistling through the jagged rocks and crags.

He felt light. Clean.

He tried to get up. His legs buckled, dumping him on his ass.

It made him laugh. Ironic, if he died now like a bozo asshole, just because his worthless legs shook too much to bear his weight.

Liv. He braced himself for the pain, but the pain had changed. It was hotter, softer. It was the pain of longing.

It was the sweet ache of dawning hope.

Liv stepped back from the scene she was painting. The last time she'd painted murals for the kid's section, she'd considered *Bluebeard* too scary. She was tougher now. Or maybe she was just warped.

Bluebeard's curious young wife crouched by the iron door of the secret chamber, clutching the key. Liv hadn't painted the room's contents, just a crack of utter darkness. Yeah. It was creepy. It worked.

"It looks real nice, honey."

She jumped into the air at her father's voice. Her nerves were still shot, after months. She glanced at the painting. Of all words she might have used to describe it, "nice" was not one of them. But hey. Whatever.

"Thanks, Daddy," she said. "What are you doing here?"

Her father looked around at the dusty chaos of renovation in her bookstore, and turned a manila envelope in his hands.

"Place looks great," he said, with forced heartiness. "Good job."

Liv shrugged. "I should be ready for business in a few months."

A tense silence fell. Her father blinked, shuffled. Cleared his throat. "Have you, ah . . . have you heard from Sean McCloud?"

Every part of her shrank from the pain that name invoked. She pressed her hand to her aching throat. "No. We're not together anymore, Dad. Please don't ever mention his name to me again."

"Ah. Well. Seems strange, after everything that happened—"

"Yes, but that's the way things are, so let's leave it," she said sharply. "What's in the envelope?"

He glanced down. "Oh. It's for you. A courier brought it. I saw him at the door when I was coming in, so I signed for it."

She held out her hand for it. Waited. "Dad?" she prompted.

He frowned. "I thought I should open it for you. Considering."

"Oh, stop." She twitched it out of his hands. "The people who were trying to hurt me are dead. I can open my own damn mail now."

He shrugged. "Open it, then."

"In private," she snapped. "Come on, Daddy. Spit it out. Say whatever she told you to say, but I warn you, I have no intention of—"

"I'm not carrying messages from your mother," he said abruptly. "I've been living in the apartment on Court Street for three weeks now."

Liv stared at him, dumbfounded. "Oh. Is it—"

"Permanent? Yes." He could not meet her eyes. "It's something I guess I should have done long ago. I just didn't want to wreck anybody's life. But after what happened, I got to thinking."

"Yes," she said quietly. "I can see how that might have helped."

Her father's face was seamed with lines of regret. "I'm real sorry I didn't back you up more, honey," he said gruffly. "All along."

All along? *Now* he was sorry? After her life had been gutted? She pushed the bitterness aside with some effort. Gave him a brusque nod.

"I was wondering if you might have dinner with me sometime," he said tentatively. "If you ever come to the city, that is."

She stood there, hand over her mouth. Throat still locked.

Her father cleared his throat. "Well, then. I'll be on my way."

"Of course we can have dinner," she burst out. "I'll call you."

He gave her a sickly smile, patted her shoulder, and fled. Her father never had been able to handle tears. She didn't blame him.

She was sick to death of them herself, at this point.

She wiped the tears away with the sleeve of her baggy sweater, and examined the envelope. Just her name, on a computer-generated white label. Her insides clutched. She pushed the feeling away, fiercely.

T-Rex was gone, damn it. Food for worms.

She pried open the flap, and pulled out a handful of drawings.

They were pen and ink, ripped out of a spiral sketchbook. A series of female nudes. Simple, minimalistic, and yet charged with eroticism. They had the offhand grace of an ancient Chinese calligraphy master.

She leafed through them with trembling hands, bewildered. The drawings were unsigned. It was only when she saw the woman's back that she recognized the subject. That pattern of moles . . . that was her own back. Those freckles were on her own arm. Her foot, with the mole above the toe that he'd said he wanted to fall to his knees and kiss.

It was like a punch, right to her heart.

She flung the sketches to the ground and burst into furious tears. How dare he come waltzing back, after months, to play incomprehensible games with her head, her heart. How dare he.

That twisted, sadistic *bastard*.

She dropped to her knees, rifled through the sketches to see if he'd dashed off an explanatory note. Of course not. Nothing so polite or normal. He was, after all, a cryptic, pain-in-the-ass wacko McCloud.

She stomped past the curious glances of the craftsmen, onto the street. She clutched the sweater against the biting wind. No way would Sean make his grand gesture and not hang around to see how she took it. She'd wait 'til he slunk out of the woodwork to take his punishment.

And then. Oh, then. God help the man.

*   *   *

Sean dug his shaking hands deeper into his jeans pockets as he stared past the lemon custard, huckleberry conserve and fudge that crowded the shelves of the Endicott Falls Gift Boutique. He was staring out of the shop window and across the street, at Books & Brew. Liv's store.

The salesgirls had to wonder how candy and jam could mesmerize him for over an hour. He was so scary, none of them dared ask. He had that Frankenstein look going on, the hospital pallor, the red, nasty scars. All he needed were bolts coming out of his forehead.

He was so scared, his hands were ice cold. His belly churned.

He'd almost given up when he saw Liv's father sign for the drawings. Old Bart marched out a few minutes later, got into his car and left. All clear.

He'd staked the place out for hours, but he still wasn't prepared when she came out. His stomach clenched, his heart went nuts, a grassfire spread under the surface of his skin. He stared, hungrily.

Her dark hair whipped in the wind. She was so pale. Way too thin. And she wasn't wearing a coat, for the love of God. It was blustery and raw out there, but her slender throat was exposed. Most of a shoulder, too. She had only a loose, knee-length sweater around herself.

Maybe the drawings hadn't worked. He'd hoped to go non-verbal at first, take a detour around arguments. No such luck.

He stumbled out the door to meet his doom. Crossed the street like a sleepwalker. Cars screeched to a halt, beeping indignantly, but he just came blindly on, until he stood before her. As close as he dared.

"What the hell do you think you're doing here, Sean?" Her voice wobbled. "What sick game are you playing with me now?"

He inhaled. The exhale came out in a series of hiccupping, nervous jerks. "No games," he said. "I'm throwing myself at your feet."

She gasped. "Oh, really. Well. You can just pick yourself up and go throw yourself someplace else. Like the Dumpster. Go away, Sean. I don't want to see you. Ever. Again. Got it?"

It was what he expected. Less than he deserved. Still, he couldn't do as she asked. It was not one of the options open to him. He sank down onto his knees. She gasped, and skittered back a few steps.

"What the hell?" She waved her hands at him. "Stop it! Get up!" Mud seeped through the knees of his jeans. He shook his head.

"I don't believe it!" Her voice was thin, breathless. "You think I'm so stupid that you can charm me with your clown act? You think I'll let you stomp on me for the third time? Fuck you, Sean Mc-Cloud!"

His jaw clenched, painfully. He shook his head again. "I never meant to do that to you," he said tightly. "Never. I swear to God."

Liv put her hand over her mouth. Two tears flashed down over her cheeks. He wanted to catch them. Feel their heat. Taste their salt.

She groped for her pocket, but the sweater thing didn't have one. "Oh, shit," she mumbled snappishly. "It never fails."

He reached into the pocket of his shearling coat and pulled out a packet of tissues. He presented them to her with a solemn flourish.

She snatched them out of his hand, pried one out and blew into it. "Get up, you melodramatic jerk. I'm not playing your games."

"I'm not leaving until you let me talk to you," he said quietly.

"You'll be kneeling in the mud for a very long time," she warned.

"You'll have fun explaining that one to the Chamber of Commerce," he pointed out.

Her eyes blazed with fury. "You smart-assed son of a bitch."

"Sorry," he said meekly. Shit. He had to muzzle the flip remarks.

The boutique door tinkled. "Um, Liv?" a nervous girl's voice inquired. "Is everything OK? Should I, like, call somebody?"

"Thanks, Polly. I'm fine," Liv said coolly.

Sean swiveled his head. Polly was regarding him as if he were a slavering wild beast. "Um . . . you're absolutely sure?" she squeaked.

"I'm sure." Liv honked angrily into her tissue. "Get up," she hissed at him. "You might as well come inside. The sooner you say your piece, the sooner it'll be over and done. I have things to do."

He was relieved to get inside, where the wind wasn't whipping at those tender pink ears, that exposed throat. He wanted to wrap his warm coat around her, but she'd never go for that in her current mood.

The odor of sawdust, plasterboard, polyurethane and paint tickled his nose. People gawked as they went by, but he was laser-beam focused on that elegant, upright back. Only Liv could wear a paint-spattered gray flannel frock and waffle stomper boots and still look somehow regal.

She led him through the refurbished and refitted café, and into a small back office. It was just a plasterboarded, taped-up cube, not yet spackled or painted. Liv went to the window and stared out, as if she could somehow see out of the thick plastic that was taped over the hole.

He looked around. A space heater blasted stale warm air over his ankles. A hot plate sat on a desk crowded with invoices. A mug, tea bag dangling out of it. A sleeping bag and pillow lay on a cheap couch.

"What the hell is this?" He looked at her, appalled. "Are you sleeping in here? Don't you have a place of your own?"

"Sure, I have a place," she said. "Sometimes I lose track of the time. I crash here if it's late. Some nights I don't have the nerve to . . ."

"To go out in the dark?" he finished.

She frowned. "Not that it's any of your business."

He swallowed hard. "You shouldn't be here alone, Liv. Not ever."

Her snort was eloquently derisive. "Well. Isn't that just too bad."

He reached to stroke that gleaming mass of hair. She sensed him moving in on her, and jerked away. "So?" she asked. "How are things?"

He was nonplussed. "Huh? What things?"

"You know. With your family. How is Erin? Margot?"

"Oh. Them. Fine," he said, relieved to have a starting place. "Erin's almost there. Few more weeks, and I'll be an uncle. Connor's out of his mind. Won't leave her alone for a second. Drives her nuts."

"Ah," Liv murmured sourly. "Good for her."

He pressed on. "And Margot, she's good too. Starting to show. She felt the baby move last week. She called everybody, she was so excited."

"That's wonderful," Liv whispered. "Are Miles and Cindy OK?"

"Fine. Miles's hand and arm are all healed up. Cindy's good, too. Teaching music in Seattle. Gigging a lot, cutting a new album with her band. She and Miles are a big item these days. Inseparable."

"Oh. That's lovely." Her voice was bitter. "How very nice for them."

Shit. Every damn thing he said underscored how furious she was.

"The last time I talked to your brothers, they mentioned that there was an investigation in progress," she said. "To verify if Kevin was . . ."

"Buried up on the hill?" He said it for her. "No. It was Craig Alden's body in that grave, not Kev's. Dental records have confirmed it."

That startled her so much, she actually turned, wide-eyed. "Oh, my goodness," she whispered. "So you don't know where Kev is buried?"

He shook his head. "Nobody left alive to ask. Craig was reinterred, in Tacoma, with his folks. But we left Kev's headstone up on the hill."

Her throat worked. "Do you think he could still be alive?"

"Fucked if I know." His voice was raw. "I've done everything I can for him. All I can do is try to learn how to live my life . . . not knowing."

"I see." She turned her back. "Well. Good luck with that, Sean."

He took a step closer, reached to touch her shoulder. "Liv—"

"No!" She wrenched away, huddling into the corner. "Don't you dare touch me! Not after three goddamn *months* of shutting me out! Like I didn't matter!"

"Not true," he said. "I thought of nothing but you!"

"Then *why*?" she almost shrieked. "Why did you do that to me?"

He shook his head, groping for words to describe the hell of shrinking fear, the bottomless, airless pit of self-loathing. The words wouldn't come. "I was . . . afraid. For you," he started, lamely.

She gave him a narrow look. "Excuse me?"

"Stress flashbacks," he blurted. "I guess that's what they were. Hallucinations. Real horrific fuckers. They were so real. You would walk into the room, and I would grab you and kiss you, and all of a sudden you were dead, and I was the one that had stabbed you, or shot you, or whatever. I was scared even to see you. Scared that I could still hurt you. I thought maybe Osterman had . . . that he could still . . . oh, shit."

Her hands moved up to cover her mouth. "Oh, God. Sean."

"I tried medicating it," he plodded on. "It just seemed to get worse. I thought maybe I'd snapped, gone nuts, like Dad."

"So you decided to do the hard thing?"

The cool tone in her voice made him wince. He was still in a world of hurt, with no end in sight. He clenched his teeth, and nodded.

"Of course. Expect me to understand," Liv raged. "You had to be alone. You had to leave me alone. Wrong move, Sean!"

"Was it? What did you want me to say?" he broke in savagely. "Hey, babe, I've got this little bitty problem. I keep murdering you whenever I see you. Sounds like a real confidence builder, huh?"

"It's better than being abandoned!" She lashed out at him, flailing.

He blocked her slap, and the flurry of frenzied blows that followed it, then pinned her hands to the wall. "I never stopped loving you," he said roughly. "It's been tearing me to pieces."

She shook her head. "Let go of my damn hands. I need a tissue."

He gave her one. She blew her nose, hid her face. "Just go, Sean."

"No," he said. "I just can't do that."

She dropped her hand, and glared at him. Her curling lashes glittered with tears. He could practically hear her spine stacking up. The look of fury in her beautiful eyes rang all his bells.

"Forget it. You can't bully me into trusting you again," she announced. "Let go of me!"

"No." He scooped her up before she could wiggle away and lifted her, pressing her body against the wall so that she straddled his hips. He dug his fingers into the wind whipped hair, and kissed her, hard.

It was like lightning through a wire, the need that roared through him. The emotion, the sensations. Her soft female heat pressed against his crotch, her shabby skirt twined around his legs. She shivered, fighting him even as her thighs tightened and pulsed around his.

She kissed him back, angrily, hungrily. His heart revved up.

He tilted her face up. "You love me," he said roughly. "I can make you want me. That's enough for now. We'll work on trust later."

"No way, you arrogant jerk," she hissed. "You got it backwards."

"No, I don't. I understand you perfectly." He scooped her up, hands under her ass, and carried her to the couch. He sank down, depositing her on the cushions. "But if it's the only card I have to play, I'm goddamn well going to play it."

She pushed his face away with shaking hands when he tried to kiss her again. "OK," she said. "Granted, you can muscle me around. You're very strong. And yes, you're good at making me come. But that's all. It ends there. When you're done, I'll still tell you to leave. So leave now. Spare us. It'll just hurt that much more."

"No." He put his hand over hers, rubbing his cheek against it. Kissing her palm, her fingers, that delicate knob of bone on her wrist. "If I make you come once, why not again? And again, and again, and damn, before you know it, sixty-five years have gone by." He slid his hands beneath the skirt, over the thick wool socks until they gave way to bare, smooth female skin halfway up her thighs.

She swatted at him. "Stop it, you lust-crazed pig. So that's your plan? Just enslave me sexually for all eternity?"

"Ah, man," he said thickly. "Sounds like heaven."

She wiggled furiously. "Smart-ass dog," she muttered.

"Yeah." The dress was so loose, there was no impediment to sliding his hand still farther, feeling her cotton panties, the humid female warmth between her thighs, the deep, sexy dip of her waist.

Her murmurs sounded like protest, but her breath was jerky, her cheeks hot pink. His hand insinuated itself under a thermal weave undershirt, and found the tender, jiggling heft of her tits, propped in the scaffolding of a cotton bra. Her nipples were tight.

Her heart thudded, quick and fast, against his hand.

Tears flooded his eyes. He hid his face against her chest, let her paint-spattered sweater absorb them. It moved him to tears. How fucking beautiful she was. How fragile. Her body was a treasure box that held the priceless jewel of Liv Endicott's soul.

His princess, his queen, empress. His goddess.

A sharp tug, and the cotton of her panties gave way, leaving her hot nest of curls naked to his caressing fingers. He tossed her skirt up over her waist. Oh, man. That soft skin, torn panties clinging to one white thigh, that lovely, hot pink slit in her dark curls. Beckoning him.

Her eyes were closed, tangled hair spread out across the couch cushions, the smudgy, sooty shadows of her lashes dark against her tear-streaked face. That stain of sunrise pink in her pale cheek, the soft lower lip caught between her white teeth, every detail devastated him.

The contrast between her delicate female body and the thick wool socks, the shabby skirt, the battered boots, was unspeakably erotic.

She moved against him, gripping his shirt, shoving his heavy jacket off his shoulders as if it pissed her off that he was still wearing it.

He let go of her just long enough to wrestle the sleeves off his arms. His hands were starving for contact with her hot skin. His dick felt like a ravening beast lunging at the chain, but he had to redeem himself first, as best he could. Making her come was his favorite way, cheap, short-term solution though it might be.

He didn't care.

He slid his finger reverently into the tight, suckling heat of her pussy, mouth watering. He'd been aching for a taste of her sweet girl juice for months. He sagged down to pay passionate homage to her tender female flesh with his tongue.

Ah, God. Like always. Silken salty sweet. Delicious. Every sobbing breath, every lapping sliding stroke. He loved the way she struggled and writhed, bucking and heaving against his face, though he could feel her anger in the sharp, nervous bite of her nails through his shirt.

She was wound so tight, vibrating with furious excitement, but he was instinctively wary of making her come too soon.

Better to drag it out, make her wait. Keep her in this drawn up state of shivering need, for as long as he possibly could.

God knows, he was content to wallow with his face between her thighs for hours. Forever, even. Seeking heaven with his tongue.

* * *

That manipulative bastard took his own sweet time about it.

He brought her up to an agonized point of shivering desperate need, and kept her there, for an endless, struggling eternity.

When he finally had mercy and shoved her over the crest, the climax was so violent, it wiped her out completely.

She was a sobbing mess. Destroyed. All dignity dissolved.

He didn't gloat, though. He had that much sense. He just pressed his face against her belly, nuzzling her, his breath tickling her mound.

Liv twisted to the side, insofar as she could with her legs wrapped around a huge, gorgeous man's broad shoulders, and hid her face in her hands. She expected him to follow up his advantage, and make love to her. Pleasure shimmered through every nerve. Her heart felt hot, glowing. Squishy soft inside her chest. She was melting down. She ached to be filled up, to feel his heat, his weight. His wonderful steely strength. She was poised for him to mount her, enter her, give her a long, hard, furious ride. She was braced for it, breathless for it.

But all he did was nuzzle her muff. It was driving her nuts.

"Stop that," she muttered. "You're tickling me."

He nipped lazily at her thigh, stroked his faintly scratchy jaw against her. Petting her damp curls, her slick, sensitive folds, as tenderly as if he were caressing a purring kitten. "Never," he whispered.

Sean looked thin, his features cut sharper. He seemed so different with such short hair. Hard and intense.

She turned away and stared, hot-eyed, at the plasterboard. Three months of pent up hurt and confusion was bottlenecked inside her. The grief, the abandonment, the piercing loneliness. She couldn't bear it.

"Why?" she burst out. "Why are you here, after all this time? What changed your mind? Did you have a goddamn vision? Or what?"

He lifted his head, but she didn't dare meet his eyes. She couldn't let him hypnotize her. She had to stay sharp.

"I guess I did," he said quietly. "I went up to the mountains. I realized a couple of things up there. One, if I can't trust my own self, I might as well be dead. Two, I don't want to die. Three, if I'm going to live, I have to have you. Because my life isn't worth a handful of shit without you."

"Oh. Really." A teary giggle shook her. "Such poetic eloquence."

"You inspire me, babe."

She wiped her eyes on her sleeves. He shoved a tissue into her hand. He turned her face 'til she was looking into his somber eyes.

"I haven't had one of those episodes since then," he said quietly. "Which isn't to say that it won't happen again. I got messed up pretty bad. But I think—I hope, anyway—that the worst is behind me. So you decide, Liv. If you want to risk it, that is. I can't wait around until I feel like I'm good enough for you. Because I never will."

"Oh, shut up." She tried to wiggle free, but he was having none of that. His embrace just tightened. She sniffled angrily into the tissue. "That's insulting and ridiculous. I never expected you to be perfect. But I can't be with a man who shuts me out whenever the going gets rough."

His face tightened. "I'm sorry. I promise you I won't do it to you, ever again. Before God, my parents' graves, my sacred honor." He hesitated. "Such as it is."

"There's nothing wrong with your sacred honor," she snapped. "It's your lack of plain common sense that bugs me."

He muffled his laughter against her chest, and peeked up at her, sidewise. "Uh, well. Like I said," he ventured. "I'm not perfect. Not even close. But I do have my strong points. And I promise to do my best."

He waited for her to answer. She couldn't. She shook with conflicting emotions. Anger, doubt . . . and a wild, crazy hope.

Her voice was locked in her throat. She could hardly breathe.

Sean groped behind himself for the thick, fleece lined leather coat, and pulled something from the pocket. He held out a tiny velvet box.

She stared at it stupidly. Sean made an impatient sound, grabbed her hand, closed her fingers around it. "Open it," he urged. "Please."

She flipped it open, and stared at the ring inside. Mouth agape.

The white gold ring seemed to flash and pulse against the black velvet backdrop. A diamond glittered, slightly off center, and around it, a ruby, an emerald and a sapphire were mounted in a sensual, geometrical setting that looked somehow both modern and ancient.

It was a stunning piece.

"I thought I should use the same diamond," he said hesitantly. "But I thought I'd jazz it up, give it some color. Make something fresh and new out of it. I hope that you . . ." His voice trailed off.

She struggled to speak, tried again. "Did Tam make this?"

He nodded. "She said to tell you that if you were foolish enough to give in to my bullshit, that she wanted to be your maid of honor," he said, sounding embarrassed. "It's becoming a sort of a family tradition."

She covered her trembling mouth, still staring at the ring. "She's a little ahead of the game, isn't she?"

He shook his head slowly. "More like about fifteen years behind."

She gulped. He took the hand that held the ring box, and gave it a slow, reverent kiss. "I want to make love to you," he said softly.

"I know," she whispered.

"But I don't want to be kicked out on my ass afterwards," he said. "Can I tell you how I want it to be? My wildest, craziest fantasy?"

She shrugged. "Nobody's stopping you," she muttered.

His eyes gleamed. "I want to slip that ring on your finger," he began. "I want to crawl up on that couch on top of you, and very slowly, push my cock into that tight, red hot pussy. I want to stare deep into your eyes and kiss you while I make sweet, slow love to you. For hours. Make you come til you're just glowing. Beaming. Shining."

She looked away, pink. "That much, I could have guessed."

"Oh, am I too predictable for you? I'm not done yet. When we're exhausted, we'll go home. Your place, since it's closer. I want to take a bath with you. Uncork some wine. Cook some dinner. Snoop around, check out the books on your shelves, your DVDs, your photographs. Get in bed with you. Make love again, if we have the strength."

She couldn't meet his eyes. "You would, I bet. Knowing you."

"Probably," he admitted. "I want to wake up in the morning, and feel how right it is, to have your sweet, warm, naked, silky, womanly body wrapped up in my arms. We'll make love again. Take a long, sexy shower together. I'll lick the drops of water off you with my tongue. Comb your hair. Make you coffee. Cook you some bacon and eggs."

She raised an eyebrow. "You mean, you're not going to make love to me again between coffee and the bacon and eggs?"

His grin turned brilliant. "That part's implied. Then I'll take you to work, and spend the rest of the day bouncing off the walls because I'm so fucking happy, I just don't even know what to do with myself."

She dissolved again. She clapped both hands over her face.

Sean tugged them gently away. "I want to spend all my days and all my nights with you." His voice vibrated with emotion. "I want to protect you, stand by you, honor and comfort you. Have children with you. Grow old with you. As many years we get." He kissed both her hands. "I want your company, Liv. Forever."

His voice broke, but she couldn't tell if he was crying too, because her eyes swam with tears. She reached for him, blindly, grabbing him with arms, legs, everything she had, in a tight, shaking embrace.

She couldn't fight it anymore. She wanted to wrap her hair around him, tie him to herself with it. She never wanted to let him go.

But he pried her arm from his shoulder, and pulled her hand between them. The fire flashing in the diamond, the rich colors of the stones, swirled into a pool of shimmering rainbows in her tear drenched eyes. "May I?" he asked softly.

She squeezed her eyes shut. Nodded. He slid the ring on.

It was a perfect, exquisite fit. It felt so comfortable, so incredibly right on her hand, she could feel it all the way up her arm. He cupped her face and kissed her tears away with passionate gentleness, as if she were a flower. Or some delicate little thing made out of fine china.

She couldn't open her eyes. She pressed trembling lips together. Her body vibrated with feelings. Oh, God. She was going to burst.

She couldn't bear it any longer. She made a sharp little growling noise and shoved his face away. "Enough of this!"

He stiffened with alarm. "Huh? What?"

"I am not some goddamn fragile china doll!" she snarled.

His eyes widened. "Uh, never said you were, babe."

"So?" She held up her ringed hand, brandished it at him. It sparkled and flashed gorgeously in the harsh fluorescent overhead light. "I kept my part of the bargain. Now you keep yours, damn it."

"My part of, uh, which bargain?" he ventured, his face wary. "Not that I'm not willing, I just want to be dead sure I've got the right—"

"All that stuff you said? All that gooey, super-romantic hooey about making love to me for hours? The wine, the shower, the bacon and eggs, the forever? Remember that? Is that just more of your jive talking clown act, or are you actually planning to follow through?"

Sean let out a big, shuddering sigh as his worried look relaxed into a big, goofy smile. "God, yes. You bet, baby. I just thought that the restrained, gentlemanly, refined, sensitive act would be more—"

"The drawings were great. I'm going to have them framed. But don't get too sensitive. And don't think." She wrenched at his belt buckle, pulled it loose, fumbled for the buttons of his jeans. "You've got a job of work to do. So get to it."

He let out a sharp, gasping moan when she shoved his jeans down and seized his hot, thick shaft, stroking it greedily. She slid down sideways, onto the couch, and pulled him down on top of herself.

"Oh, yeah." He rose up between her spread thighs with a groan of need. "I have condoms in the pocket of my coat. I could—"

"Don't you dare make me wait one more goddamn *instant!*"

The whipcrack of her voice made his muscles jerk. His cock twitched and throbbed in her hand. "Yes, ma'am," he muttered.

She wiggled with frantic eagerness until she felt the blunt tip of him nudge inside. Finally entering her. They let out the same keening moan of agonized pleasure at the slow, delicious push of his thick shaft into her body. They stared into each others' eyes. Fused into one taut, throbbing whole. Poised in breathless stillness.

"Do not hold yourself back from me," she said to him.

"Never." His low, shaking voice had the solemn ceremony of a sacred rite. "I swear it."

She jerked his head down, kissed him. "I want all of you," she told him. "Everything you've been, everything you'll be. Everything you are."

"Done," he said.

He gathered her tightly into his arms, and gave it to her.